UNDER FIRE

INTO THE FIRE

KIM VANDEL

Kim Vandel

INTO the FIRE

Book One of the Under Fire Series

Author information: http://kimvandel.com

Cover and interior design by Kim Vandel
Pur flame design by Rodger Archer

ISBN: 978-0-9962069-1-4

—**For Mom and Dad**—

Thanks for always being there when I need you.

CHAPTER ONE

I heaved a sigh as I closed my calculus book. It was hopeless. Within the first two weeks of fall quarter, I was going to destroy my dream of medical school.

I shoved the book into my backpack and joined the rest of the students fleeing the auditorium. On the steps outside, I paused long enough to check my phone. Dad still hadn't returned my calls but no surprise there. I hadn't really thought he would.

Heat flared on my wrist as I returned the phone to my hoodie's pocket, and I fought the temptation to dig in with my fingernails. That spot on the inside of my wrist had been burning and itching all morning, and now it was red because I couldn't stop scratching. Like I needed one more thing to deal with.

I pulled my hood up to provide some cover from the sprinkle of raindrops and headed for one of the University of Washington's many libraries. So far, Suzzallo was my favorite and not just because there was caffeine available in the lobby. With its Gothic arches and stained glass windows, Suzzallo looked like it was part of the Hogwarts campus.

A dozen different conversations echoed against the stone walls of the lobby as I entered, and I navigated traffic to reach the café where the hiss of steaming milk replaced the echo of voices. Thankfully, the line was short this morning. Only one person stood between me and the comfort of caffeine. The guy was a walking stereotype of the university professor—a goatee and a tweed jacket with leather patches on the elbows. He probably had a pipe or pair of wire-rimmed glasses tucked in one of his pockets.

He handed his money to the girl behind the counter, exposing a tattoo on his wrist, and I tilted my head to get a look at the design. Three small, red-orange flames fit together to form a larger one. Maybe not such a stereotype after all.

The professor thanked the girl, dumped his change in the tip jar, and stepped away from the counter. Right onto my toes. I stumbled back, and he swung around to catch me. When his hand touched my arm, heat shot down to my wrist. I tugged my arm loose, and the heat faded.

"Sorry about that. Are you all right?"

"I'm fine." I rubbed at my wrist. He must have hit a nerve or something.

"Are you sure?"

"Yeah, don't worry about it. Happens all the time." It was the truth, sadly enough. I should have invested in a pair of steel-toed All Stars years ago.

Regret washed across his features. "I really am sorry. See you later."

I frowned as he moved off toward the barista. Yeah, he'd stepped on my toes, but it wasn't like he'd ruined my whole day. Then again, at least he'd apologized. That was more than most people did.

As I stepped up to the counter, I reached into the pocket of my jeans for a ten-dollar bill. My last ten dollars. The thought was so depressing that I ordered a venti mocha with extra whip. If I was going down, I was going in a supernova of glory.

While I waited for the mocha, I pulled my hood back and scanned the crowd. The professor sat by the door reading on his phone between sips. The guy at the table closest to me had fallen asleep on top of his textbook despite the energy drink sitting on the table. His friend was plugged in to a laptop with a pair of ear buds, probably trying to shut out the drama coming from the girl at the next table over. Based on her half of the phone conversation, there was an epic breakup in progress.

As she threatened to post incriminating pictures online, I grabbed my mocha. When I lifted the cup to drink, fire pricked my wrist again. I gritted my teeth against the sting, switched the mocha to my left hand, and turned from the counter.

A new group of students entered the lobby, and I promptly choked on my second sip. I did a quick check to make sure I hadn't spilled down the front of my hoodie. It was black, but still. Wet showed up no matter what. The hoodie was clean, but I couldn't do anything about my hair. Between the rain and my hood, it was beyond help. I attempted to smooth it down, but I could feel strands of hair flying up around my head like I'd been playing with a Van de Graaff generator.

Three girls—all of them blondes with fake-n-bake tans— accompanied the one guy. Laughter preceded them into the café, and I stood paralyzed, half afraid they would recognize me and half afraid they wouldn't. Well, that he would or wouldn't, but why—*why*—did he have to show up on a day when it looked like I'd been using a balloon on my hair instead of a brush? I voted for not recognizing today.

Not that it would make any difference if Rob Peterson recognized me. I wasn't his type. My skin was too fair and my hair too dark. But I did enjoy staring at him. You know, admiring God's handiwork.

One of the girls spotted me and came over with a smile that revealed a lot of very white teeth. Jen and I had attended Northshore Christian Church for years, and we'd both graduated from Redmond High School last June. She was one of those people you really wanted to hate but couldn't because she was so nice. She didn't rub in the fact that she was perfect because she really didn't think she was.

"Hey, Kate. How are you?"

I smiled back without revealing quite so many teeth. "I'm good."

"How's school going for you?"

"Okay. Just trying to stay on top of everything."

"I know, right? I only have three classes this quarter, but I have no idea how I'll get everything done."

Rob turned in our direction, and I shrank back.

"Jen, are you going to order something?" he said.

"Yeah, I'm coming. You guys remember Kate, don't you? She goes to Northshore too."

I got a semi-genuine wave from Rob and the other two girls and waved back. Then I wished I hadn't. Hopefully no one noticed I'd discovered a new skin disease.

"Please don't keep them waiting because of me," I said.

"Well, it's good to see you. We should do something together. What about that Chase Thomason concert? It's coming up in a couple of weeks, and a bunch of us are going. You should come with us. It'll be fun."

An image of Rob with his blonde, bronzed groupies filled my head, and I tried to picture myself with them. I stood out and not in a good way. Then again, going in a group with Rob was better than not going with Rob at all, right? And odds were that I would look better for the concert than I did this morning.

"Um, okay. That would be good I guess."

"Great! Get your ticket, and I'll let you know what time we're meeting up. Maybe we'll go get something to eat after the concert." She waved and moved off toward her friends. "See you Sunday."

I waved goodbye then took a moment to envision a better-dressed, non-Van de Graaffed version of myself at the concert. I could find something better than a hoodie in my closet, something Rob would ... wait, she did say Rob was going, didn't she? Or did I just assume he would be part of the group? I liked Jen, but I didn't want to stare at her.

I wandered toward a table in the far corner, torn between

celebrating with an espresso brownie and entering the Witness Protection Program. I was leaning toward witness protection when fire erupted on my wrist again. I gasped and set my cup down on the closest table.

The fire cooled as quickly as it had flared up, but when I pulled back my sleeve, there was a bright red mark on my skin. I rubbed my index finger across it once, twice. I scraped at it with my thumbnail. Neither had any effect. What end-of-the-world plague had I been infected with?

Hold on. There was a shape to it.

I lifted my head in time to see the professor leaving the café. My need for understanding argued with my need to avoid looking stupid. The debate raged for a full thirty seconds before understanding won and I rushed after him. I paused to scan the crowd in the lobby and caught sight of him in the library. Weaving between bodies, I hurried to reach the spot where he'd disappeared between the stacks.

By the time I caught up to him, he'd taken a seat at a table on the far side of the room. I stood in the aisle trying to scrounge up enough courage to follow through. What was I supposed to say? Excuse me, but why does my rash suddenly look like your tattoo? He'd probably answer with a question of his own—one about why I'd stopped taking my antipsychotic medication.

He waved me over like he'd been expecting me. I wandered closer, my brain struggling to piece together what was going on. When I reached the table, he nodded to the chair opposite his.

"Hi, Kate. Have a seat."

"How do you know my name?"

"Why don't you sit down? We have a lot to talk about."

I frowned at the chair then at him. "I think I'm good."

When he smiled, humor warmed his eyes. "The truth is that I know a lot about you. I know you're not going to sit down and you're not going to believe anything I say right now." He nodded toward my hand this time. "I know how you got the mark on your wrist, but you're not ready to hear what I have to say. Not yet."

I glanced around, searching for cameras or for people hiding behind the stacks. This had to be part of someone's psych project or someone's messed up idea of a joke. Punk the freshman because she doesn't have enough stress in her life already.

"This is no joke," he said, "and it's not a coincidence. The only reason I went to the café this morning was because I knew you'd be there. The same way I know you're worried about passing calculus. I know your name is really Katarina, not Kate, but you hate it when people call you Katarina. You hate it when your grandfather calls you Katy Bug, but you don't want to hurt his feelings, so you let him do it anyway. You wish there was a way to make your mom happy again, and you're afraid you're the only one in your family who hasn't given up on your brother. Your dad hasn't returned your calls, and you want to know if it will always hurt this bad."

"Stop it." The words trembled. "Who told you that?"

Sympathy replaced the humor in his eyes as he set a business card on the table and slid it toward me. The card displayed the same three-in-one flame as the one on his wrist. On my wrist.

"Call me when you're ready to listen."

My throat felt tight, but anger pushed the words out. "Leave me alone or I'll call the cops."

I marched off toward the restroom, my eyes stinging this time instead of my wrist. I didn't get it. There were thousands of students at the U. Why pick on me? And how did he know those things about me? Most of that information had never set foot outside my head.

The restroom smelled of antibacterial soap and the cheap paper towels that melted when I used them to scrub at my wrist. I scrubbed until the rest of my skin was as red as the flame, but the mark wouldn't come off. If anything, it looked even brighter. Like a brand new tattoo.

While I daydreamed about getting one, it never went any further than that because my mom considered them equivalent to the mark of the beast. If I couldn't get this thing off, she would absolutely freak, and I couldn't deal with her freaking out. Lying wasn't an option for me either, so the only other—even worse—option would be to tell her what had happened. That would dissolve into a crisis where the police were involved and I never left the house again. What I'd said about calling the cops had been a bluff. Maybe he knew that too.

With a sigh, I tossed the paper towel in the trashcan. I couldn't go home like this. So what now? Did I confront him? Pay a visit to campus security? Ignore the mark and hope it went away? Ignoring it would be my first choice. That was also the least likely to solve my problem, and a visit to campus security would turn the situation into an even bigger headache than it was.

I tugged the bathroom door open and went out to the library.

The professor was gone, but he'd left his card on the table. Below the flame symbol, the card had a phone number and the name "Nathaniel Sorenson" on it. His name sounded familiar, but I couldn't remember where I'd heard it before. I'd have to sort it out later.

Mr. Sorenson answered after the first ring.

"I don't know how you did it or why you did it," I said, "and right now I don't really care. Tell me how to get this mark off my wrist. Acetone? Mineral oil?"

"I didn't do it, and it's not coming off. That mark is part of you. You just can't see it yet."

"I can see it fine. That's the problem."

"It's more than a mark on your skin. It's a sign of who you are—who you will be."

"You already know who I am. Obviously."

"It's a sign for you, not me. It's hard for most of us to see

ourselves clearly. Sometimes we have to pass through the fire
before we can see who we really are."

"What's that supposed to mean? And what does it have to
do with this thing on my wrist?"

"It means you've been chosen. That mark is a sign of
your calling."

"You're not making any sense. What calling? Who chose
me?"

Water crashed on his end of the connection. He must have
made it as far as Drumheller Fountain. I was tempted to race
after him and demand answers in person, but then he spoke
again.

"God chose you, Kate. He's called you to be a Guardian."

Great. The guy was a total nut job. A nut job who knew
way too much about me.

"I'm not crazy," he said.

"How ...?"

"I'll do my best to answer your questions on Saturday."

The connection went dead.

I almost hit redial, but I was afraid to hear what else he
had to say. What else he knew about me.

I sank into the chair he'd offered me earlier. While the
incident was bizarre, I hadn't been hurt. The mark was
probably nothing worse than one of those airbrush tattoos. It
would be easy enough to hide from Mom until I could figure
out how to remove it. And as far as how he knew those things
about me ... well, there had to be a reasonable explanation.
Maybe he was one of those hyper-observant, Sherlock
Holmes types. But that didn't explain how he got the mark on
my wrist. And why did his name sound so familiar?

Finally it clicked. I had an entire shelf of books written by
Nathaniel Sorenson. But it couldn't be the same guy, could
it?

I stuffed his card in my jeans pocket—in case I needed it
for evidence later—then made my way to the east end of the
library. I logged on to one of the computers and pulled up the

Internet browser.

The only images I found were either of book covers or random people who looked nothing like the guy I'd met. I tried newspaper archives instead. Eventually an article from *The Denver Post* popped up. It was almost two decades old, but it gave me the answer I was looking for. The interview with Nathaniel Sorenson included a grainy black-and-white photo of the author. He didn't have a goatee back then, but it was definitely him. I'd met one of my favorite authors this morning, and he turned out to be a nut case.

Why was he at Suzzallo doing an impersonation of *The Mentalist*? Maybe it was research for his next book. Or maybe he'd been writing fantasy for so long he'd started to believe it. The only thing I knew for sure was that I was so not buying his next book.

At least I had one piece of the puzzle in place. Maybe, given a little time, I could fit the other pieces together and make sense of my morning.

CHAPTER
TWO

I logged off the computer and headed for the exit. Halfway to the bus stop I remembered my mocha. My precious mocha was most likely in the trash now. One more item to add to the list of reasons my day had sucked so far.

The rain fell faster as I walked, and I hurried to reach the shelter before getting soaked. When the bus arrived, I shuffled forward with the other passengers. A woman who couldn't be bothered to end her phone conversation cut in front of me, bumping my shoulder, and the strap of my backpack slipped. I tried to catch it, but for the second time that day, my toes took the punishment. It was harder to be understanding this time around, especially with no apology. I wanted to grab her phone and toss it onto the freeway, but I didn't. I swallowed the pain and frustration, shouldered my backpack, and limped to the bus.

I swiped my pass across the scanner then started down the aisle. Before I had a chance to sit, the driver floored it so he could pick up enough speed to merge with traffic. I reached out, grabbed the handrail, and swung into the closest seat with a very ungraceful plop. There were days when I'd swear I had a "kick me" sign stuck to my back.

I glared at the driver—though he probably couldn't see it and wouldn't care even if he did—then slid over to the window and traded the bus pass for my iPod. I picked a song with plenty of screaming and cranked the volume.

Rain pelted the window as we made our way across the bridge from Seattle's University District toward Redmond—

home of Microsoft, Nintendo America, and about five million Starbucks. The raindrops smeared across the glass and turned everything into a big gray blur. Water and sky became indistinguishable from the multi-million-dollar homes edging Lake Washington.

The rain hadn't let up by the time we reached downtown Redmond, so I got off the bus and headed for Mom's office. I didn't mind the mile hike from my usual stop to our house, but I wasn't in the mood to get any wetter today. I'd just hang out at the insurance agency and study until she finished for the day.

When I reached the door, I stopped to stash my iPod, and I pulled the cuff of my hoodie down to cover my wrist before stepping inside. Mom was on the phone, but she pointed to the mat beneath my feet, and I dutifully scraped the soles of my Converse clean.

A glance at the open doorways on the left told me both agents were MIA. As usual. The two chairs reserved for clients in front of Mom's desk were also unoccupied, and I sank into the closest one.

After she set the receiver down, she grabbed a bottle of hand sanitizer from the corner of her desk and held it out to me. "I thought I might be seeing you. How were your classes this morning?"

"Good. Well, mostly good." I accepted the bottle without protest. It was easier to go along with the disinfecting than try to convince her she was creating superbugs.

"Do you have much homework?"

"I have some reading for biology and English lit and some calculus problems I need to work on. But those aren't due until Friday."

"Don't put them off until the last minute."

"I won't."

She frowned like she didn't believe me. You'd think I'd spent my entire high school career in academic lunch, but studying had never been a problem for me. It was the social part of school I struggled with. Good thing GPA didn't depend on how many people in your graduating class actually knew you existed.

The office phone trilled, saving me from her lecture. As she picked up the receiver, I returned the hand sanitizer to her desk and escaped to the lunchroom-slash-storage area in the back.

When Mom locked up the office at five-thirty, we took her Civic to the three-bedroom rambler we called home. I shivered as we walked in the front door and turned up the thermostat before dumping my backpack in my room. Mom was taking chicken enchiladas from the fridge when I came into the kitchen. Usually I arrived home early enough to make dinner for us, but because of my detour to the agency today we were stuck with leftovers.

Mom warmed enchiladas in the microwave while I scrounged up ingredients for a salad. Once everything was ready, we filled our plates and carried them to the table. I pulled out my chair, sighing as Mom walked over to turn down the thermostat.

We both took our seats, and for a couple of minutes, the only sound at the table came from a fork scraping against a plate or stabbing through a piece of lettuce.

"Were you able to finish your homework?"

I chewed, buying time until I could answer without frustration leaking into my voice. "Most of it. I'll work on calculus after dinner." She frowned, so I hurried to change the subject. "I forgot to tell you I ran into Jen Harper this morning. She was with some friends from Northshore, and she invited me to go to the Chase Thomason concert with them."

"That was nice of her. Jen is such a sweet girl. And Chase Thomason is wonderful. Are you planning to go?"

"Yeah, I told her I would."

Mom graced me with a smile. "Wonderful" meant Chase Thomason didn't have multiple tattoos or body piercings, he didn't wear guyliner, and he never screamed any of his lyrics. I didn't mention that my only reason for going was the chance to drool over Rob for a couple of hours because guys were a subject you had to treat with lead-lined gloves. They were too closely related to the *you know what* subject.

After dinner, I cleared the table while Mom went to give the bathroom its daily scrub down. I stuck our plates in the dishwasher then wiped off the table and retreated to my room, closing the door behind me. I planned to work on those calculus problems, but I needed to take care of business first. I sat at my desk, grabbed my phone, and dialed Dad's home number. My stepsister answered.

"Hey, Chloe. It's Kate. Is my dad home from work yet?"

"Oh, didn't you know? He left for Peru this morning. Or maybe it was Paris. I can't remember which one, but it was for some medical convention thingy. He won't be back until next week I think."

When someone let you down so many times you lost count, how was it possible to feel disappointed when they did it again?

I forced lightness into my voice. "I guess he forgot to tell me. Hopefully he'll get the voicemail I left for him. Thanks anyway. I'll talk to you later, okay?"

"'Kay. Bye."

It wouldn't have done any good to ask Chloe for help because she'd go straight to her mom, and Connie had learned a long time ago not to get involved. When it came to me and Ty, our stepmom didn't do anything unless Dad told her to.

I set the phone on my desk and debated my remaining options—ask Mom for the money or call Ty. It was a photo finish in my brother's favor.

He gave me his standard greeting. "What's up, loser?"

"I need a favor. I have to buy a book for chem lab tomorrow, and I'm kind of broke right now."

"I thought Dad was paying for your books."

"He is."

"So call him and stop bugging me."

"I did, but he hasn't returned any of my messages. And he sort of left town this morning."

Ty dropped the F-bomb, making me cringe.

"He never paid you back for tuition, did he?"

"He will," I said, "but right now I don't have enough money for the book. I'll buy it online and pick it up at the bookstore in the morning, but I need a credit card number. I know you have Dad's Visa."

"Yeah, and I'm not giving it back."

"So can I have the number?"

"What's in it for me?"

"I won't tell Chloe you were the reason her bestie Megan stopped talking to her this summer."

"Like I care what Chloe thinks. If she had more than one brain cell, she would've figured it out already."

"You'll have to listen to her whine the next time you go over to Dad's, and she'll stop introducing you to her friends."

"Fine. But only because her friends are hot."

"I need the expiration date and security code too."

"Those will cost you."

"Ty," I said wearily.

"Don't bleach my tighty-whities."

"You don't wear tighty-whities." I groaned. "Fine. Two loads of laundry, but that's it. Can I please have the numbers now?"

"Three loads or no deal."

"Two loads and I let you know what time Mom is leaving to run her errands on Saturday."

"Deal."

He read off the numbers, and I wrote them down with every intention of hanging on to them. I didn't want to go through this process again.

In the lull that followed, I considered telling him what had happened this morning but decided not to. Maybe I was too

tired to try explaining it, or maybe I wasn't in the mood to
hear his take on it. He would probably laugh at me or tell me
I needed therapy—or both—and I wouldn't be able to
contradict him. Why would God choose me for anything
when He had someone perfect like Jen Harper to work with?

"You have to keep calling him," Ty said. "Dad won't give
you the money unless you make him."

"He'll pay me back."

More cringe-inducing words came from his end of the
line. "He lied. He said he'd take care of tuition and books. He
promised you wouldn't have to work during the school year,
but he lied. Just like he always does. Why can't you get that
through your head?"

"Doesn't mean he won't do it."

"Whatever."

I rubbed at the spot in the middle of my forehead that was
beginning to throb. "I gotta go. I have calculus problems to
do."

"Remember our deal. Mom better not be home when I get
there."

I didn't bother with a response. I pressed "end" and put
my head down on the desk.

It amazed me sometimes that we were able to
communicate at all. When Dad walked out, Ty had decided
no one could be trusted. I wanted to believe there were still
one or two people in the world I could trust, but after today
… I couldn't help but wonder if Ty was right.

When I woke up on Saturday morning, the mark was still
there. I'd tried everything I could think of to get rid of it, but
nothing worked. Even while I'd been attempting to remove
it, my fascination with the mark grew. When I moved my
wrist the flames seemed to shift like a miniature fire burned
beneath my skin. I would've loved to keep it, but that wasn't
an option. I'd managed to keep it out of sight so far, but it

was only a matter of time before I messed up and Mom noticed.

With my bedroom door closed, I set Mr. Sorenson's business card on my desk and stared at it, working up the courage to call. As I entered his number, I couldn't decide if it was irony or coincidence that today was Saturday, the day he'd said he would talk to me.

"Hi, Kate."

"The mark is still there."

"I know."

"So are you going to tell me how to get rid of it?"

"It doesn't work that way."

I vented my frustration with a sigh. "I give up, okay? Just tell me what you want."

"It's not about what I want. I'm simply the messenger."

"So what's the message?"

"There's more to the world than what we can see with our eyes, and Guardians are part of that unseen world. You're part of it now. Your life is about to change—it's already started to—and the transition is going to be rough. I really am sorry about that."

"You know you're not making any sense, right?"

"I promise it will make sense eventually, but this is the kind of conversation we should have in person. You've looked me up. You know who I am now."

"Yeah. I know who you are." He'd left his card on purpose. It didn't take a mentalist to know I'd try to find out who he was.

"As a gesture of good faith, I'll let you in on a secret few people know. My name is really Nathan Samuelson. Nathaniel Sorenson is a pseudonym I use to keep my family hidden from the public. I'm very protective of them, but I want to open up my home to you. Come meet my wife and kids. Have dinner with us. After dinner you and I can talk. I'll explain as much as I can."

"Look, Mr. Sorenson. I mean, Mr. Samuelson—"

"Call me Nathan."

"Okay, fine. Nathan. Even if I wanted to, there's no way my mom would let me come to your house."

"Tell her you met me. That'll be enough."

"You don't know my mom. It really won't be." Even a background check from the State Patrol wouldn't be enough.

"My wife will call her. She'll say yes."

My eyes drifted closed as the center of my forehead began to throb. He continued to dangle the information I needed out of my reach, and I had no idea how to get to it.

"If your mom agrees to it, will you come for dinner?"

"If she says no, will you tell me how to get rid of the mark?"

"Are you sure that's how you want to do this?" Humor colored his voice. "It's not really a fair deal."

"I'm sure." I had nothing to lose at this point.

"All right, we have a deal then. Go tell her you met me. I'll see you later."

I set my phone down and tried to ignore the apprehension gathering in my chest as I ventured out to the kitchen.

Mom sat at the table with the sales ads spread out in front of her. I started the grocery list during the week, and she finished it Saturday morning before she did the shopping. She added antibacterial wipes to the list as I shuffled past her to pull a mug from the cupboard.

"So I never told you who else I saw at the U the other day," I said as I poured coffee into the mug. "After I ran into Jen, I met Nathaniel Sorenson. You know, the guy who wrote *Aram's Maze*. I got to talk to him a little bit."

"Really?" Her expression wavered between disapproving and supportive. "I know how you love his books."

"Yeah, he said—"

The phone rang. Mom was closer to it, so she answered. A moment later she looked at me. "Yes, Kate just mentioned it."

Apprehension bubbled over into full-blown dismay. I set

the coffee pot down as she listened, presumably to Nathan's wife.

"You're very kind. I'm sure she'd love to." Mom returned to the table, grabbed a clean sheet of paper, and wrote something on it before she said goodbye. "You'll never guess who that was. Mr. Sorenson's wife. She said he felt bad the two of you didn't have much time to talk the other day, so they've invited you to have dinner with them tonight. She said you could call for directions." Mom handed the piece of paper to me.

I blinked at the number on the paper then at her. "I can go?"

"As long as it doesn't interfere with your schoolwork."

The paper pressed against my fingers, weighted with more than the phone number written on it. I couldn't believe she was letting me go. I also couldn't shake the suspicion that for once I was going to wish she'd said no.

CHAPTER THREE

The road was barely wide enough for two cars. Not that I'd seen another soul since turning off the main road. The narrow lane wound through maple and alder trees draped in moss that flashed bright green when the Civic's headlights swept across it. Mist hovered in the trees and hung across the road in spots, sometimes blocking my view then closing in behind me after I passed through.

Once in a while, I could see a light farther back in the woods indicating a home, and several times the road branched off with one segment disappearing into the trees. I assumed some of them were driveways, but there was no way to tell for sure because none of the roads had street signs. The place was like a maze, and Nathan's directions were the only thing keeping me from turning into a missing persons report.

When the odometer marked four-tenths of a mile since my last turn, I stopped. Nathan's driveway should be right here, but there was nothing more than trees and mist. As I picked up my phone to call him, the mist shifted to reveal a dirt driveway bordered by ferns. I set down my phone and pulled onto the driveway before it could vanish again.

The Civic bumped along the dirt track for a minute or two before light shone ahead. Dirt gave way to gravel, and the trees opened up into a grassy area with a two-story home. The warm glow from the windows welcomed me as I parked in front of the garage.

I followed the stone pathway to the front porch, but before I could ring the doorbell, the door flew open. A blonde girl, missing both front teeth, grinned at me then snatched something from behind the door and held it up for my inspection. The cat gave me a peeved look as it hung there by its armpits.

"This is Spice," she said. "Sugar got eaten by a bobcat."

"Oh."

She released Spice—who made a break for it past my legs—grabbed my hand, and pulled me inside. I had a glimpse of green walls and dark wood trim as she towed me through the entryway and up the stairs. The color scheme changed drastically when she led me into the first room on the right. It was the kind of décor my brother referred to as unicorn vomit—pink and sparkles everywhere.

She made me sit on the end of her bed then she handed me a Barbie doll and a miniature hairbrush. "These are for you."

"Um, okay. Thanks."

I was trying to figure out how to diplomatically make my escape when Nathan appeared in the doorway.

My kidnapper gave him a grin. "Look, Daddy. We're playing Barbie."

"I see that, but you're supposed be setting the table right now."

You could almost hear her heart break, but Nathan pointed toward the stairs.

"We can play after dinner," she assured me before she slid off the bed.

Nathan held back his smile until his daughter had sprinted past him. "That was Anna by the way. We don't have company very often, and she's excited to have another 'girl' visit. She has three older brothers who would rather use Barbie for pellet gun practice."

I shrugged. Anna seemed like an okay kid, and I could totally relate to the toy-wrecking brother part. At least I only had one brother to deal with.

"I thought I could catch her before she sidetracked you,

but I didn't even hear the doorbell. Thanks for humoring her." He stepped out into the hallway. "Come downstairs, and I'll introduce you to the rest of my family."

I couldn't help but wonder if this was the point where everything went wrong—when Nathan turned out to be a sociopath and I ended up in a body bag—but the tutu on the floor argued against that scenario. I had a hard time believing Anna's dad could be a murderer.

I left Barbie on the bedspread with her hairbrush and followed Nathan downstairs. The family room shared a large portion of the lower level with the kitchen, and the smell of roast beef filled the open room along with the sounds of video game warfare. Nathan directed me toward the kitchen side of the room where he introduced his wife.

Hope was an older version of Anna, except with all her teeth. When I saw her, I began to understand why Mom had agreed to let me come. Hope was one of those people you instantly wanted to trust. She had clear blue eyes, the kind that promised she had nothing to hide, and when she smiled it came from the inside, a true reflection of her feelings. That same openness filled her voice as she made her way around the counter to shake my hand.

"Welcome, Kate. I'm so glad you're here."

"Thanks for having me. Can I help with anything?"

"Everything's ready. We just need to carry it to the table."

She handed me a salad bowl as Nathan headed for the other side of the room and threatened his boys with no video games for the rest of the evening if they didn't turn it off *now*. Anna appeared, took a basket of rolls from her mom, and guided me to the dining room. After we set our dishes on the table, she tugged me over to one of the chairs. She'd taken advantage of her table-setting chore to seat us next to each other, and she'd left less than six inches of space between my chair and hers.

The volume picked up as Nathan herded the boys into the dining room, and he gave quick introductions as Hope joined us and everyone took their seats. The only semi-quiet moment occurred when Nathan prayed for the meal. Conversation erupted the second he finished and covered a wide range of topics. Everything from quick-scoping to ballet lessons.

The food was delicious, but I didn't eat much of it. Something about watching Nathan's family be so happy together made my stomach hurt.

After the meal, Nathan sent the boys back to the family room. I offered to help clear the table, but Hope wouldn't let me. She and Anna carried plates to the kitchen, and I was left at the table with Nathan.

His face held a trace of weariness as he stood. "Why don't we go to my office?"

I should have been excited to see the room where some of my favorite novels had been written, but apprehension was the only thing I felt.

A pair of French doors separated Nathan's office from the family room, and light poured through the glass panes to illuminate a cherry wood desk. Framed prints of his book covers rested on the wall behind it, and bookshelves lined the walls between the desk and the family room.

As he closed the doors, I inspected the contents of the closest bookshelf. "So what classes do you teach at the U?" Whichever ones they were, I'd be sure to avoid them.

"I don't. The only reason I was on campus was to talk to you."

I turned from the bookshelf. "How did you know I'd be at the café? How did you know you were supposed to look for me in the first place?"

Nathan sat at his desk and gestured to the armchair in front of it. "I promised you answers, and I'll give as many as I can."

As I sank into the chair, I glanced back through the doors. The boys were once again involved in pseudo-warfare while Hope and Anna worked in the kitchen. It was a very normal, very sane glimpse of the world, and I had a terrible feeling I was about to lose it. What little I had eaten lay heavily in my stomach as I faced Nathan again.

"The mark on your wrist is called a *Pur*."

"Poor?"

"P-U-R. It's from the Greek word for fire."

"How did you get it on my wrist?"

"I didn't. All Guardians receive a *Pur*, but it usually appears on its own. The way yours appeared has something to do with you, and before you can ask what, I don't know. Trust me, I'd love to give you an explanation, but I don't have one. I know that's not very reassuring right now. It's been a few years since I was called, but I remember what it felt like—suddenly being thrust into a new world with a different set of rules. Eventually you learn how to live in that world, but it takes some time to adjust."

"I just … don't get this. Any of it. Or what it has to do with me."

He ran a hand across his face. "It'll make more sense after I explain a few things to you, but we should start at the beginning. You need to understand where we came from before you can understand where we are," he said. "Guardians have been around for almost two thousand years. We can trace our origins back to the events at Pentecost. Do you remember why the disciples were still in Jerusalem?"

My brain rummaged around until it came up with an answer. "Jesus told them to wait for the Holy Spirit."

Nathan nodded. "On the day of Pentecost, there was a loud sound like a violent wind and the Spirit came in tongues of fire. That sound drew a crowd to the house where the disciples were. There a man in the crowd named Mordecai, and the next morning Mordecai found a flame-shaped mark on the inside of his wrist. He'd heard about what happened to the disciples, so he rejoiced at this sign of God's Spirit being poured out on him as well. But when he gathered again with the other believers, Mordecai realized no one else had this mark. No one could explain it to him either, not until that night when a visitor came to his home.

"Mordecai sensed this was no ordinary visitor, so he invited the man in, treating him as an honored guest. After they'd eaten together, the visitor said, 'A time of great persecution is coming, and God has chosen you, Mordecai, to protect His people. To stand between them and those who would harm them, to watch over them and guard them. You will be a Guardian for His people.'"

Humor chased some of the weariness from Nathan's expression. "I think you can imagine how Mordecai felt. He was convinced there'd been a mistake, and he told the visitor as much. 'I am nothing. I am no one. I have no wealth or possessions. I am not a soldier or a man of great understanding. How can I protect anyone?'

"The visitor replied, 'God has chosen you, and He has given you this mark as a sign. He will also bestow upon you a Gift to help you protect His people. As He gave Samson great strength, He will empower you. As He made Elijah swift to run before Ahab's chariot, He will quicken you. As He gave Solomon wisdom and Gideon courage, He will enable you.'"

I shifted in the chair. Part of Nathan's story sounded painfully familiar. God had chosen Mordecai, a nobody. But unlike me, Mordecai must have at least possessed raw materials to work with.

"Before he left," Nathan said, "the visitor told him others would be called. They would also bear a Guardian's mark. Mordecai was to find them and explain their purpose. As the visitor had warned, persecution came, but so did Mordecai's Gift. He'd lived in Jerusalem since the day he was born, and he knew the city well. When his Gift came, he discovered he could find anything or anyone in Jerusalem. He could even find something that was lost or hidden, and because he knew where things could be found, he knew where they would not be found.

"Mordecai knew where to hide those in danger, and he knew where to find others who were called to be Guardians. These new Guardians each received their own Gift, and they worked with Mordecai to help Christians escape the persecution in Jerusalem. Some of them went out with the Christians who fled, taking the knowledge of what it meant to be a Guardian with them and passing it on to others who were called. Since Mordecai's time, Guardians have been helping those who are persecuted, and we still do in places like India, China, and the Middle East."

I could hear the "but" coming, and Nathan smiled as if he knew what I was thinking.

"But Guardians are human," he said. "Along the way, some began to use their Gifts to serve their own purpose. Instead of protecting the innocent, some Guardians began to prey on them."

The sound of gunfire carried to us from the family room as I struggled to make sense of what Nathan was saying. "Why didn't God take away their Gifts if they were abusing them?"

"Because it truly is a gift. It's given to us, and we choose whether we'll use it to serve others or serve ourselves. But there's a cost when Guardians betray their calling. Like Esau, who despised his birthright, they lose God's blessing. Like Cain, who betrayed his brother, they are cursed to wander the earth. Their *Pur* becomes black. The fire is gone, leaving nothing but ash in its place. It's nothing more than a reminder of what they once were. What they could have been."

"What's so great about their Gifts that they're willing to be cursed? I mean, it would be great to be able to find your car keys when you lose them, but it doesn't really sound like it's worth it."

"Not all Gifts are like Mordecai's. Each one is unique, and it's usually some quality you already have, only magnified. I've always loved to read and learn, to pursue knowledge. When my Gift came, I Knew things that should have been impossible for me to know. I Knew you would be at the café, and I Knew physical contact would draw your *Pur* to the surface, but I don't have any idea why it did. I've never seen that happen before. My guess is that it has something to do with your Gift."

"I don't have a Gift."

"Not yet, but the potential is there. It's only a matter of time before your Gift emerges."

I rubbed at my forehead. Apparently Nathan also had the ability to cause headaches like my brother did. "You didn't really answer my question though. These Guardians—ex-Guardians, whatever—use their Gifts for what? I still don't see what the big deal is."

"Let's say your Gift is Empathy. You can sense the feelings of others. It would be a useful tool in comforting people who are persecuted because you could sense when they were afraid. You could also use your ability to discover their greatest fears and use their fears against them. Or what if you could see in the dark? You could guide people to safety in the middle of the night, or you could use the advantage for all sorts of things—committing robberies, ambushing soldiers." He held up a hand. "What if you could drive the fever from a man's body with the touch of your hand? But with the same touch, you could force every last bit of heat from his flesh and watch him freeze to death."

Fear stirred in a dark corner of my gut. "There are people who can do that?"

"That's only the beginning. Fallen Guardians have power, and power is an addiction. The deeper they go, the more they crave it, and they'll do whatever it takes to have it. They will kill and destroy, and they will open up to darkness itself. We have to stop them. We're the only ones who can."

"How? How do you stop them?"

"We use our Gifts, and we use whatever skills and technology are available to us. When we can—when it won't endanger innocent lives—we turn them over to the authorities. More often than not, they're guilty of a crime."

"So what happens when you can't?"

"Our options are limited because there's no way to remove a Gift. Fallen leave us with little choice, and it's part of their twisted thinking to put us in the position where we have to make a choice. They know we can't ignore them. They're too dangerous."

"Then how ...?" I didn't get it. I kept turning the picture in my head, trying to figure out what it was supposed to be. When it finally snapped into place, it did so with a razor-sharp edge. "Hang on, you don't mean ..."

I waited for him to say something—anything—that would contradict the horrible conclusion my brain had come up with, but he didn't. He looked me in the eye so I could see the truth for myself.

I shook my head because I didn't want to see it. The words emerged against my will. "You kill them."

CHAPTER
FOUR

"Only when we're forced to," Nathan said. "When there's no other way."

"But you can't do that! That's murder!"

"They have to be stopped."

"So stop them, but you can't go around killing people."

"We're not as cold-blooded as you think. Remember, you're entering a different world with an entirely different set of rules. Don't judge us until you've seen what we're up against. You have no idea what Fallen are capable of and how far they're willing to go. Turning them over to the authorities could mean more lives being lost—people who don't stand a chance against them. There are Fallen who could walk into a room full of armed police officers and kill every single one without ever laying a hand on them. What if you're the only thing standing between a room full of innocent people and their deaths? Would you let them die?"

My fingers dug into the chair's cushion, longing for something solid to hold on to. "I can't. I won't kill anyone. It's wrong."

"I'm not asking you to, and I pray you never have to, but you deserve to know the truth. You've been dropped into the middle of a conflict that's been going on for over a thousand years. Your eyes have been opened and shutting them won't make it go away."

I glanced over my shoulder at the family room. That was the world I belonged to, the one where the war never went any farther than the TV screen. I couldn't let him drag me into the madness he wanted to call reality.

"Does your wife know what you do?"

"She's known about the Guardians for as long as I have."

"Your kids?"

"The oldest two know. I'll tell the other two when they're ready."

"Will you tell them you murder people?"

"I'll tell them the truth."

I couldn't imagine Anna with her pink sparkles and Barbie collection calmly accepting her dad's side job.

"I know it's a lot to take in." Sympathy filled his face. "But if I could go back and be given the choice of whether or not I was called, I would choose to be called. I would still want to be a Guardian. It's not an easy life, I admit that, but it is a meaningful one."

"So that's it? I don't get a choice?"

"You always have a choice."

It didn't sound like much of a choice to me. As pathetic as my life might be, I imagined it was better than being cursed by God and wandering the earth for the rest of my life. Which would apparently be as long as it took for a Guardian to hunt me down.

"This has to be a mistake. It doesn't make sense to choose me. If you're not asking me to take shots at people, then what's the point of me being a Guardian? What *are* you asking me to do?"

"Our calling is to protect the persecuted, but our focus has shifted here in America. It's had to. Christians aren't persecuted like they are in other parts of the world, but there are still Fallen Guardians. Fallen will take advantage of those who are powerless, whether Christian or not. We have to be prepared for conflict like any police or security force. We'll train you so you're able to protect yourself and any innocents involved. When your Gift emerges, we'll incorporate that

into your training as well. You'll help us track down Fallen
Guardians and keep them from hurting innocent people."

"Who's 'us?'"

"There's a small group of Guardians in the Seattle area.
We're few in number, but we work together. That includes
you now."

I shook my head. This was insane, and nothing he said
would make it okay.

Nathan's eyes lost focus for a couple of seconds, as if his
gaze had turned inward. When he refocused, he said, "Why
don't you go home and give all of this a chance to sink in?
Call me when you're ready to talk about training."

Somehow I managed to get to my feet, and I stepped
across the threshold of his office like I was stumbling away
from a horrific car accident. I wasn't sure whether I had
survived or not.

Despite what he'd said, Nathan didn't send me straight
home. We went to the kitchen for coffee and dessert, and I
was glad for Anna's chatter because it helped drown out the
hysterical screaming in my head.

I only took a few bites of my chocolate cake, and the
coffee might as well have been hydrochloric acid for as well
as it sat on my stomach. When I gave up on dessert, I said
goodbye, telling a very disappointed Anna we'd have to play
Barbie some other time. I thanked Hope for dinner, and
Nathan walked me to the front door.

"Good night, Kate. Talk to you soon."

The drive home barely registered. Mom was waiting up
for me, so I pulled it together long enough to tell her about
my evening, everything except the conversation in Nathan's
office. Then I told her I was worn out and went to bed, but all
night long images of death disturbed my sleep. I saw frozen
corpses, their unblinking eyes condemning me, demanding to
know why I'd just stood there and let them die. I heard
people shrieking in terror, begging me to intervene because

someone had discovered their darkest fears. Their pleas turned to accusations when I did nothing.

Those images replayed themselves as Mom and I drove to church the next morning. When Jen found me before the service to ask if I'd bought my concert ticket, her enthusiasm grated on me. It seemed so unfair that I was the one stuck with this Guardian nightmare while she got to be perfect *and* happy. It wasn't her fault though, so I forced a smile and said I'd buy my ticket that afternoon.

Mom and I found seats in the sanctuary, and I watched as people greeted each other. They sang, and they laughed at the pastor's jokes. They listened to a sermon I didn't hear because I kept thinking of what Nathan had said. I kept hearing screams from the night before. I sat in that sanctuary full of people wondering what I would do if someone wanted to delve into their secret fears. Would I ignore their pleas for help? Would I close my eyes so I didn't have to watch them freeze to death? Or would I try to stop it? What if I was the only one who could stop it?

Visions of death invaded my sleep again that night and followed me to my classes the next day. I wandered among thousands of students, all of them oblivious to the fact that the kind of stuff you read in Ted Dekker novels really existed out there somewhere.

As I waited for my bus home, I pulled Nathan's card from my pocket and ran my thumb across the flame. I'd kept the card with me all day yesterday, and for some reason I'd brought it with me again today.

I shoved the card back in my pocket when the bus arrived. I was the last one to board, and as I started down the aisle, the driver hit the gas. My backpack dropped to the floor, the zipper popped open, and my phone skidded toward the back of the bus.

My brother's favorite word whispered in my ear, begging me to say its name.

I picked up my backpack, zipped it shut, and went in search of my phone. It had come to a stop under the seat of a guy dressed in a business suit, and he sat there and watched as I got down on the floor. I soon discovered why my phone had stopped beneath his seat. It was stuck to a gooey black mass that had probably been someone's gum a long time ago in a galaxy far, far away.

My phone came loose with a tug, and as I dropped into an empty seat, frustration boiled up. I was so tired of being ignored or only being noticed long enough to read the "kick me" sign. I was tired of being pushed around and feeling helpless to do anything about it. I was so tired of *taking* it. Something inside of me wanted to push back.

I scraped the gum off my phone with a sheet of notebook paper and dialed Nathan's number.

"Okay, I'm ready to talk."

"Good. Let's start with training. The first thing you'll learn is how to protect yourself."

"You're going to teach me self-defense?"

"No, not me. We have another Guardian who's much better qualified to teach self-defense and martial arts than I am, and he has part of his house set up as a training facility. That's where you'll go. He also has a couple of Guardians working from his home, so you'll be able to get to know them too. The more often you train, the better, especially when you're first starting out. What's your schedule like? Are all of your classes in the morning?"

"Yeah, but I can't … I don't have a car." And asking to borrow Mom's was out of the question.

"We'll figure something out. I'll call Hassan and arrange for you to come tomorrow. What time is your last class done?"

My initial burst of frustration had fizzled, allowing reality to barge in with a long list of objections, lack of transportation being one of the least problematic. I should have taken the time to think this through before calling Nathan.

"Why did you decide on pre-med?"

I blinked. "What?"

"Why do you want to be a doctor?"

His question drew a shrug from me. "I want to help people. To make things better."

"What specialty are you interested in?"

"Maybe oncology. Why?"

"Why oncology?"

"I guess because cancer scares me. It might not be so scary if I could do something about it. And maybe I could save a life, even if it's just one person."

I glanced around hoping people were ignoring me as usual. It sounded kind of lame when I said it out loud.

"So you'd be willing to face something that frightens you in order to save a life."

"Yeah, but that's not ..." I swallowed. "It's not the same."

"You're right. It's not. Plenty of people have the opportunity to be a doctor. You have the opportunity to be something more. You can save lives in a way very few people can."

It sounded good—all noble and heroic—but the Guardian method of "saving lives" didn't fit with what I'd had in mind. Taking the chance Nathan offered could turn out to be the worst mistake I ever made.

But what if this was my chance to make things better? Then not taking it would be the worst mistake I ever made.

"I'll talk to Hassan and call you back in a few minutes."

The call dropped, and my head came to rest against the window with a soft thump. Rain obscured my view the way unknowns obscured my future. If by some miracle I managed to get into med school and become an oncologist, I'd have to make decisions every day that could mean the difference between life and death. For some reason it felt like those decisions would be much easier to live with than the one I faced now.

The rainclouds moved on, leaving pale blue sky the next day. After my last class I walked to the bus stop showered in sunshine instead of raindrops. Without a bank of clouds to hide it, Mt. Rainier dominated the southern horizon. Sunlight sparkled across the surface of Lake Washington, setting the trees around it on fire with fall color—brilliant red and gold against the emerald abundance of fir and cedar.

While captivating, the view didn't chase away my anxiety. All too soon we reached my new stop, conveniently located on the way home. I didn't have to switch buses or anything.

The Yarrow Point transit center was a wide spot in the middle of the freeway. A covered walkway provided shelter for waiting commuters, and glass enclosed the stairs between the walkway and the "lid" stretching across the freeway. After I got off, I stood beneath the shelter and watched the bus rejoin traffic, asking myself if I really intended to go through with this. It wasn't too late. I could stay right here and wait for the next bus to take me home. My safe, familiar existence waited for me there.

The stairs would most likely lead to things I didn't want to know about and probably wouldn't like, and yet I didn't turn away. Maybe it was curiosity about the other Guardians or that lingering desire to push back. Maybe it was because a tiny spark of hope had ignited in my heart and made me think there could be more to my life than just trying to survive it.

I took a moment to gather my courage then forced myself to climb the stairs.

Hassan Muhanad waited for me in the commuter drop off/pick up loop. Nathan hadn't given me a description, but I had no doubt about Hassan's identity and not because he was the only one there. I knew he was the Guardian in charge of my training because he looked like the kind of guy who could make your life completely miserable if he felt like it.

He leaned against the passenger door of a sleek, black Audi with his arms crossed, watching my approach from behind a pair of sunglasses. He wore a crisp white shirt, a pair of slate-colored slacks, and one of those big, silver watches. The only softness about Hassan Muhanad came from the curl in his hair and the curve of his lips.

He frowned as I drew closer, and once I stopped in front of him, he continued to frown at me. I stood close enough to see the Armani logo on his sunglasses and the way the lenses shrank me to the size of a grasshopper. If part of training was to intimidate me, he was doing a great job.

"So," he finally said. "You're the new Guardian."

"Yeah. I guess. That's what Nathan says."

He didn't smile or introduce himself. He didn't so much as twitch a muscle. He frowned at me a few seconds longer then shook his head as he pushed off from the car with one shoulder. I moved aside as he opened the passenger door for me, and I made sure my backpack didn't bump against anything when I got in. The door shut behind me in a very permanent-sounding way.

The interior smelled expensive, like leather and whatever cologne he used, and when he turned the key, the rich thrum of the engine declared the Audi several light years out of my price range. He didn't speak to me, and no stereo played in the background. Aside from the sound of the engine, we rode in silence. I studied the view out my window so I wouldn't say something stupid out of nervousness.

Quaint refurbished homes blended with newer, bigger ones, and I caught glimpses of water as we passed narrow side streets. Hassan turned down one of those streets and pulled up in front of a gated driveway a moment later. I assumed the number pad on one stone pillar allowed you to open the gates if you knew the code. The camera on the other pillar sat where it would have a view of anyone who used the number pad as well as anyone coming or going through the gates.

The gates split, the two halves sliding behind the emerald greens on either side, and Hassan drove forward. More emerald greens lined the driveway to provide privacy from the neighboring lots. The driveway sloped down toward the water, and I could see Yarrow Bay as the Audi descended to a stone-paved courtyard where a Nissan Leaf was parked on one side of the courtyard next to a Jeep Rubicon and a Volkswagen Squareback. I doubted any of the vehicles belonged to Hassan. They had to belong to the other Guardians who worked for him.

The house—mansion—wasn't the typical Northwest-style home. It looked more like a European villa, complete with grapevine clinging to the stone exterior. Something you'd expect to find on the shores of Lake Como, not Lake Washington. The U-shaped structure appeared to have two stories, but from the way it rested on the hill, I figured a lower level hid below the ones I could see.

As we crossed the courtyard, I spotted two cameras under the eaves and another in the alcove by the front door. Either Mr. Congeniality suffered from paranoia, or he had some really nice stuff he didn't want ripped off.

My hunch about the vehicles in the courtyard proved correct when he pulled into the garage. A black Range Rover and some kind of sports car sat in the other two bays. A silver motorcycle rested on the far side of the garage in front of a spotless workbench and rack of tools.

The contents of his garage cost more than my degree would, and I couldn't help but wonder where all his money came from. Nathan hadn't given me a lot of personal details about my new instructor.

I was still trying to get a good grip on my backpack to make sure I didn't scratch any paint making my exit when Hassan opened the door and held out his hand. His *Pur* looked blood red against his bronze skin.

He continued to hold his hand out while I stared at it. Then realization kicked in, and heat rushed to my cheeks.

"Oh." I placed my hand in his. "Thanks."

"Come. I'll introduce you to my team."

He headed for a door on the side of the garage. I followed, clutching my backpack to me like a security blanket.

The door opened into a short hallway leading to the kitchen. On the other side of the kitchen, a group of black leather chairs surrounded a glass coffee table, and a petite, dark-haired girl occupied one of the chairs. The pink frames of her glasses matched her iPad cover. Across from her, a huge blond male was sprawled in one of the chairs with what looked like a Sony PSP.

As Hassan led me through the kitchen, I could see more of the room that stretched out past the seating area. Windows lined the side of the house facing the water and drew in sunlight to warm the stone floor.

The room had been set up as an office with four separate work areas, and I immediately pegged the espresso-colored desk as Hassan's. It had nothing except a laptop and a single file folder sitting on top of it. The edges of both the file and the computer were perfectly aligned with the edges of the desk.

The desk closest to his had more of a lived-in look while still being organized, but the third desk was the cheap metal kind you find in a college dorm room, and it desperately needed an intervention. Paper of all shapes and sizes, file folders, a laptop, and a printer all competed for space. A Starbucks cup—hopefully empty—sat on top of one of the piles.

The fourth spot wasn't a desk at all. Two rectangular tables had been shoved together against the far wall, and it looked like an electronics store had exploded over the top of them. I could see several computers and flat screen monitors among the wires and circuit boards. The guy sitting in front of the disaster area was in the process of dismantling some piece of equipment, and his appearance fit with his work area. He probably hadn't shaved or had a haircut in more than a year. His skin was actually paler than mine.

The two occupants of the leather chairs got to their feet at the same time as Hassan's cell phone rang.

Hassan took the phone from his pocket, checked the number, and said, "I need to take this. Introduce yourself."

He waved me toward the others, switching to another language as he answered. Whatever he was saying, it sounded more like an argument than a conversation.

"He always sounds like that. You get used to it."

I turned to face the speaker and had to tip my head back. He was well over six feet tall with a build that screamed NFL. His hand devoured mine when we shook.

"I'm Jackson Shea." He nodded at the girl. "This is Lexi Nakamura. Lexi is Hassan's assistant, and the only person I know who can actually be in two places at once."

"Ha. Ha." Lexi rolled her eyes as she reached out to shake my hand.

Jackson pointed at the guy in the middle of the electronics explosion. "That's Mike over there. He takes care of Hassan's security and information systems. He doesn't get out much, but he keeps working as long as you feed him wasabi peas and green Monster."

I suppressed a shudder.

Mike lifted his head long enough to wave hello. I waved back. "So you guys … you're all Guardians?"

"Technically, Mike's not a Guardian," Jackson said. "He doesn't have a *Pur*, but we'd be lost without him. Me and Lexi are Guardians though, which means Hassan gets to kick our butts during training every morning."

Hassan joined us, slipping his phone back into his pocket. "What Jackson means is he sits around all day eating my food and playing video games."

"Hassan. Dude. You need to lighten up. You're the one

who said I should set up office here, and you're the one who
told Lexi to stop filling the fridge with that soybean-curd-
whatever from Whole Foods."

Hassan scowled. "I can't eat that."

"Exactly."

"Fine," Lexi said as she crossed her arms. "Go ahead and
pollute your bodies with trans fats and high-fructose corn
syrup, but don't blame me when you both drop dead before
you hit thirty."

"Nobody's dropping dead," Jackson said. "Not unless
they eat the garbage you buy. It tastes like cardboard."

"Well, that explains a lot. If you eat cardboard, then it's
no wonder—"

"Enough," Hassan snapped. "Do either of you intend to
work today, or must I pay for arguing?" He glared at both of
them for a moment then said, "Lexi, take Katarina
downstairs. We need to get started. I have a meeting at
three."

It took a second to realize he was talking about me.
"Wait, who said my name was Katarina? Did Nathan tell you
guys that? Because I don't—"

"Your name is Katarina, is it not?" Hassan strode over to
his desk—the perfect alignment one—picked up the folder,
and opened it. "Katarina Aileen Brennan. Born to Nancy and
Mitchell Brennan on August twenty-seven—"

"Hey!" I rushed over and snatched the file from him.
"What is this? Where did you get it?"

He brushed my question aside with one hand.
"Information is easy to find on the Internet."

I opened the file and flipped through the contents, my
heart beating harder with each page. There were copies of my
birth certificate, driver's license, high school transcripts, SAT
scores, and current class schedule. He had a copy of my
parents' divorce papers, my medical history, and even my
non-existent bank account balance. My entire lame excuse of
a life contained in one manila folder.

I closed the folder and held it up, my fingers clenched around the evidence. "This is private. As in *none of your business*. Who said you could do this?"

"I like to have information."

"Well, the next time you want to know something about me, try asking, and if I say it's none of your business, then you don't get to know. And my name is Kate, not Katarina. Got it?"

There was a moment of silence before Jackson burst into laughter. "Welcome to the Guardians, Kate. It's gonna be fun having you around."

CHAPTER FIVE

If Hassan's expression was any indication, he didn't agree with Jackson's assessment. He looked like a funnel cloud trying to decide where to touch down. He settled on Lexi.

"Take our new Guardian downstairs. Now."

"Sure, Hassan."

Lexi grabbed my arm and pulled me toward the kitchen. I took my file with me. I'd known the guy less than fifteen minutes, and I'd already had enough of Hassan Muhanad.

"Sorry," I said after we made it to the kitchen. Ticked off or not, I felt bad Lexi was stuck in the middle of it.

Her lips twitched. "Don't worry about it."

She led me back to the hallway where I'd first come in, opened a door, and started down the stairs. We emerged in another hallway on the lower level where she pointed to a heavy-duty door with a number pad set into the wall beside it.

"That's the weapons room."

She said it so casually. Weapons room.

A glass wall ran the length of the corridor on the right, and I could see exercise equipment on the other side— treadmill, weights, punching bag, and an open area with mats. The windows provided a view of Yarrow Bay, so at least I would have something nice to look at while I was dying from phys ed.

"That's the training room obviously," Lexi said. "And these are the locker rooms."

Across from the death-by-phys ed room, two doors stood next to each other, both marked with squiggles.

"Is that Arabic?"

"Yeah. Hassan's idea. His sense of humor is a little … off. Just remember left for ladies." She hooked a thumb at the door on the right. "Hassan never uses the guys' locker room. He uses his own shower upstairs which means Jackson has this one all to himself." Her delicate features wrinkled in disgust. "I don't go in there. Check out his desk sometime, and you'll understand why Jackson has to bring his towels up to the laundry room himself."

Lexi led the way into the girls' room where several cubbies lined the left wall. A long counter with a double sink and mirror lined the wall on the right. A bench sat in the center of the room, and an open door on the far wall revealed a bathroom.

"It's just you and me," she said, "so put your things wherever. I keep the shower supplied, but feel free to bring your own stuff if you want to. Make yourself at home."

I stood there taking it all in for a moment then sank down onto the bench.

"You okay?" Lexi said.

"It's a little overwhelming."

"Sure, I understand. But you'll do fine. You wouldn't be here if you couldn't handle it."

"Right."

"I'll be upstairs if you need anything."

I didn't think she could give me what I needed—an escape hatch.

Lexi left, and I drew my feet up onto the bench, burying my face in my knees. I wanted so badly to run home, stick my head beneath my pillow, and pretend like none of this had ever happened, but I couldn't. That little spark of hope wouldn't let me.

I changed into the sweats and t-shirt I'd brought from home then stored the rest of my stuff in one of the cubbies, cramming the file of personal information into my backpack. When I emerged from the locker room, Hassan stood in the corridor. The storm clouds had cleared from his face, and he was back to what I suspected was his normal expression—one of general irritation with life, the universe, and everything. He wore a gray t-shirt and a pair of black Adidas soccer pants, and they suited him. If Jackson was football, Hassan was definitely soccer. He seemed less intimidating in his casual outfit, younger too somehow.

Without a word, he started toward the training room. I assumed that was my cue to follow.

He pulled the door open, motioning for me to enter. "Jackson will work on strength and cardiovascular training with you. I will train you in martial arts and hand-to-hand combat. We'll move on to weapons in the future."

The thought of handling a weapon—of actually using one—left a sick feeling in my stomach. I had meant what I said to Nathan. There was no way I would be able to take shots at anyone.

Hassan led me to the side of the room covered with mats, which meant people fell there. I predicted the mats and I would be spending some real quality time together in the days ahead.

When he turned to face me, I knew the lesson was about to start, and I wanted to make sure the tension from upstairs didn't work its way into our training session.

"Wait, I need to …" I faltered as his gaze zeroed in on me, but I drew a breath and forced the words out. "The thing is, I can't help thinking there's been some huge mistake. Like the Seahawks signed Russell Wilson, but someone in the legal department screwed up and put my name on the contract, and now I have to go out and play. I was already freaking out about the whole Guardian thing, and when you had that file on me, it felt like I'd totally lost control of my life. Which is pretty much the way it is, but it's not your fault, and I shouldn't have taken it out on you. So I'm sorry.

Even if you were being really rude by digging up my personal information."

I fought the urge to squirm as he stared at me.

"Apology accepted," he said at last. "And I apologize for offending you. That wasn't my intention, and in the future I'll do my best to get information from you directly. However, a situation may arise where you're unavailable or unwilling to provide information, and I will get that information if I feel it's vital to our operation or to our safety. I won't risk the lives of my team for the sake of your privacy."

I took a moment to digest his words. "Okay. Fair enough."

"Good," he said with a nod. "Let us begin."

He was surprisingly patient with me considering my complete ignorance, the way we'd started off, and the fact I was having a hard time concentrating with him so close to me. He kept putting his hands on my waist or shoulders to correct my stance, and I didn't have a lot of experience with good-looking guys giving me so much as a high five let alone spending any significant amount of time in my personal space. My brother didn't count. Besides, if Ty was going to touch me, it would be to put me in a headlock and make me smell his armpit.

I didn't work up a sweat, but I rinsed off anyway after we finished. I went upstairs to confirm a time for the following day with Hassan, and he told Lexi to drive me back to the bus stop. Her pink stiletto heels clicked across the stones of the courtyard as we walked out to her Leaf. I didn't understand how she stayed upright. I would've done a face-plant just getting out the front door.

"Are you sure you don't want me to drive you home?" she asked as she turned up the driveway.

"I'm sure. I don't mind the bus, and I don't want to change my routine too much. I don't want my mom to notice anything different. I need more time to figure out what I'm going to tell her. We don't communicate very well. We talk about stuff, but some subjects are easier to avoid. Actually, there are a lot of subjects I avoid."

"You seemed to do fine letting Hassan know what you were thinking." Her lips twitched again, and this time she gave in to a smile. "I don't think I've ever heard someone talk to him like that before."

"I've never talked to anyone like that before. Well, no one except my brother. Definitely not people I've barely met. I just … he made me mad. He's kind of a jerk. Why do you guys put up with him?"

"I put up with him because he's my boss and because I've been around him long enough to know he has a few redeeming qualities. *We* put up with him because he knows what he's doing, and he's really good at it."

I got the impression she wasn't talking about his day job—whatever that might be—and the image of his outstretched hand flickered through my mind. For some reason, Hassan's *Pur* seemed more like a warning than a sign of his calling.

The gates closed behind us as Lexi turned onto the street. "As much as it pains me to admit it," she said, "Jackson was right. You get used to Hassan. Besides, we need him. We can't exactly ask for donations, and he finances our team. We also need every Guardian we can get. The more bodies we have, the easier it is to get our job done. And safer too." She glanced at me. "This job can be kind of dangerous sometimes."

I so didn't want to talk about that part. Lexi must have sensed it because she moved on to a different topic.

"How'd your training session go anyway?"

"Fine. Except for the part where I totally suck at martial arts."

She laughed. "Don't worry. You'll get the hang of it."

"How long did it take for you to get the hang of it?"

"My situation was different. Both of my parents are

Guardians, so I started training almost as soon as I could walk."

"Is that normal? How old were you when you were called. Or got your *Pur* or whatever?"

"I didn't get my *Pur* until I was sixteen, but it's fairly common for a Guardian's child to be called, so my parents went ahead with training. I think I would've been heartbroken if I hadn't been called, but I would've found some way to be involved. I'd want to be part of the Guardians whether or not I had a *Pur*."

She was so different from me. I was still trying to figure out how my name ended up on the list, and Lexi would have been petitioning to get on it.

We reached the transit center a couple minutes later, and Lexi pulled into the loop.

"About that talk with your mom," she said. "Don't rush into anything, okay? Guardians get a sense of who we can trust with our existence, and we don't tell very many people. It's kind of hard to explain, but things happen. Stuff that can't be coincidence. Pictures disappear, phone calls drop, computers crash. I've even seen someone have memory loss about what happened the night before. It's like the Guardians are supposed to be hidden, and it's better that way anyway. So take it slow and follow your instinct."

Maybe that was why I'd hesitated to tell my brother anything when we talked last week. "Okay, I will. Thanks for the ride."

"See you tomorrow."

The bus heading home was crowded, and I ended up next to a woman who smelled like she'd sampled every single item on the fragrance counter at Macy's. She didn't acknowledge my presence as I sat down, but being ignored worked for me right now. I needed to think.

I didn't have a clue how I was going to manage both school and Guardian training without making Mom suspicious. I doubted I could keep college student Kate and

Guardian recruit Kate apart indefinitely. Sooner or later the two would stumble over each other, so I needed to figure out some kind of explanation.

When nothing presented itself right away, I pulled out my iPod and focused on easier problems like what to fix for dinner. I'd settled on chicken risotto by the time we reached the stop by the library and City Hall where a dozen or so people waited on the sidewalk. Mixed in with the regular business-variety passengers were a couple of guys who'd most likely been visiting municipal court, a few student types who'd probably been at the library, and a trio of kids coming from the skate park.

I didn't pay too much attention as the new passengers got on, not until one of the municipal court guys slithered down the aisle making no attempt whatsoever to hide the fact he was checking out every female he passed. He was one of those guys who made you feel contaminated just by being on the same bus with him. The kind who made you wish you were more like your mom and carried hand sanitizer with you everywhere you went.

He seemed intent on cruising all the way to the back, so I tried to inch over—away from the aisle—without being too obvious, but of course his scuffed work boots stopped next to my seat. I could see the dirt embedded into the seam between the sole and leather upper. I could smell the dirt along with other things I'd rather not smell. Even the sampler from Macy's fragrance counter couldn't completely kill the odor.

I silently pleaded for him to go away, but as the bus started to move again, he sat across the aisle from me. Out of the corner of my eye, I saw him shift in his seat so he faced the aisle—so he faced me—and I wanted to bang my head against the back of the seat. Why? Why me?

"Hey, how's it going?"

Even his voice was creepy, like it wanted to ooze inside my ears, and I lifted my gaze long enough to confirm the awful truth that he was talking to me. Didn't he know being plugged into an iPod was the universal "Do Not Disturb" sign?

"Great," I muttered. "Terrific."

After a full minute of him staring at me while I ignored him, I started scrolling through my playlist hoping he'd take the hint. When a couple more minutes passed without him even pretending to look away, I decided to make my exit. The stalker routine was getting really old really fast, and enough of my mom's paranoia had rubbed off on me that I didn't want him to know where my regular stop was.

I shouldered my backpack, got off at the next stop, and walked toward Redmond Town Center like it had been my plan all along. When the roar of the engine faded into the distance, I turned back to wait for the next bus.

After dinner I headed for my room to tackle calculus, but when I reached for my book, my fingers touched the file I'd taken from Hassan instead. I pulled it from my backpack and looked through the contents again, slower than I had this afternoon. By the time I reached the last page, I felt exposed. Violated. Did he think he was the only one entitled to privacy? Did he really think it was okay to invade someone else's?

It was like he thought he could do whatever he wanted and the rest of us just had to deal with it. He'd treated my feelings as if they didn't matter, but they mattered whether he liked it or not, and right now I felt the urge to drive over to his house and use a baseball bat on his precious security cameras.

I settled for ripping each page into tiny pieces. I even tore up the folder.

I hated the thought of having to face him tomorrow knowing he had seen everything in that file, but I needed to go back. I needed to find the Kate who'd stood up to him, and I needed to learn how to defend myself so I wouldn't be paranoid the next time some creeper on the bus talked to me. Hassan was a jerk, but he could at least teach me that much.

CHAPTER SIX

Jackson waited for me at the transit center on Wednesday. He sat perched on the hood of his neon yellow Jeep and waved when he saw me. As if I could miss him.

I couldn't help thinking that the difference between Hassan and Jackson was like the difference between night and day. Dark and enigmatic, Hassan was all about concealment—the secluded estate, the security system, the Audi with its tinted windows. I got the feeling that even night vision goggles wouldn't reveal everything because there were too many shadows surrounding him. He knew where to find them and how to use them.

Jackson, with his golden hair and blue eyes, was big, bright, and straightforward. From his size to his car, everything about him advertised his presence.

He jumped off the hood and opened the passenger door, giving me a "hang on a second" as he grabbed a pile of mail from the front seat. I took care with my backpack when he helped me climb in but figured I didn't have to worry too much about whether it bumped his car or not. Thanks to the rain we'd had the week before, dirt and fir needles coated the wheel wells, and when he tossed the mail in back, it slid across a pile of clutter on the seat. A couple of hoodies, a Nike shoebox, and several Starbucks cups peeked out from beneath the envelopes and junk mail. I was almost afraid to catch a whiff of the interior, but the only odors to hit my nose were spearmint gum and coffee.

He went around to the driver's side, and once he got in,

there was a whole lot of Jackson taking up space inside the Jeep. When he turned the key in the ignition, the stereo came to life, and my gaze flew to his.

"You like Thousand Foot Krutch?"

"Yeah," he said. "You?"

"Love them."

He smiled. "Well, all right then. We'll get along fine."

I had to bite my lip to keep from breaking into an idiotic grin as he shifted into gear. It felt like I'd been lost in a foreign country and finally found someone who spoke English.

We drove to Hassan's rocking out to *Rawk Fist*, and when we pulled up in front of the gates a few minutes later, I pointed at the stone pillar.

"Why is the keypad on the right side? You have to get out and walk all the way over there."

"That's the point. If someone's pushing the call button or entering the code, Hassan wants to see who it is."

"Oh."

"But you don't have to worry about it as long as Mike or Hassan is here. There's a sensor on this side that lets them know when someone pulls up to the gate, and once they see it's you, they'll open up. Well, Mike will. With Hassan, it all depends on what kind of mood he's in."

To prove his point, the gates split apart. Jackson drove through to the courtyard and parked next to Lexi's car. We entered through the front door, and Yarrow Bay was the first thing I saw when I walked in. The windows on the far side of the office framed the scene outside like a living work of art— a stunning view of glassy water reflecting the pale blue sky.

Immediately to my left, stairs rose to the upper level. To the right, a hallway lead to what I assumed were the living and dining rooms. Steps led from the entry down to the office area of the main room, and I followed Jackson down the steps. Lexi sat at her desk, and she glanced up when we came in, but Mike remained fixed on the circuit board in his hands.

He was wearing a black t-shirt that said *Prepare to be Assimilated*, and I didn't hide my grin this time.

"Resistance is futile."

Mike lifted his head. "What?"

"The Borg," I said, pointing at his shirt.

He blinked. "You know what it means?"

"Yeah. I'm kind of addicted to sci-fi reruns."

Lexi looked between the two of us, her expression caught somewhere between disbelief and resignation. "Okay. Well, the two of you will have to speak geek later. Hassan went upstairs to change, and I highly recommend getting to the training room before he does."

"Later then."

I headed down to the locker room feeling optimistic. Who knew? Maybe things would go smoother with Hassan today.

But my life never cooperated for more than five minutes at a time, and apparently time was up. Hassan was already in the training room when I got there, and he didn't bother with a greeting.

"Show me your stance."

While customs varied, I was pretty sure saying hello was standard operating procedure no matter where you were from, but whatever.

I did my best to stand the way he'd shown me the day before, with my feet straight forward and my knees slightly bent. He gave me one of those "Are you serious?" looks then proceeded to move me around until I was standing the way he wanted me to. I couldn't tell the difference.

"Next."

I had to think about it for a second. I put my heels together and turned my toes to the proper angle, but my second effort produced the same result as the first—another look and more maneuvering.

"Next."

We repeated this pattern a few more times before I got a new result.

"No. Your foot is in the wrong position."

I gazed down at my foot, begging it to help me out, but it refused. "I don't know where it's supposed to be."

"What do you mean you don't know?"

"I can't remember."

"What do you mean you can't remember? We did this yesterday—less than twenty-four hours ago. How can you not remember?"

"We did a lot yesterday, and this is all new to me."

"This is the most basic part of martial arts. How will you ever defend yourself if you can't remember such a simple thing?"

"I don't know, and getting mad at me isn't going to help, okay? I'm trying, so can you try to be nice?"

He scowled. "Fine."

He wasn't exactly nice after that, but at least the not-so-helpful questions stopped. We worked for another hour before he said we were done for the day, and he left the training room shaking his head. I sank down to the mat and buried my face in my knees.

For a few minutes, I'd let myself think I could fit in, that maybe I could make this Guardian thing work, but being a Guardian wasn't about bonding over music or science fiction. It was about much bigger things, and Hassan was right. How would I ever defend myself? It was like expecting me to read when I couldn't even figure out the alphabet.

"That bad, huh?"

I tipped my head back to find Jackson towering over me. "It was okay I guess. I'm sure Hassan is wondering what he did to deserve getting stuck with me."

"Naw. He'd never admit it, but you're actually doing him a favor. He doesn't like to be happy." Jackson offered me a hand. "And I'm glad we're stuck with you."

"You say that now. Just wait."

He chuckled as he pulled me to my feet.

The pleasure of Jackson's company soured when the first

thing he did was put me on the treadmill. To keep my mind off how much I loathed physical activity, I told him he had to distract me.

"You're obviously not from around here," I said. He had a drawl to his words that didn't originate in the Northwest.

"Nope. Texas born and raised."

"Football?"

He grinned as he crossed his arms in front of his chest, and I watched in fascination as his t-shirt strained to keep up with the movement. His biceps were bigger than my head.

"My dad put a football in my hand the day I was born, and I didn't put it down until I graduated from Texas Christian. I could have gone pro—top twenty draft pick—but had to turn it down."

"Because you got called?" I wheezed.

"Nope. I got called the spring of my junior year. I had to turn it down because it was getting too hard to hide my Gift."

I was short on breath, so I raised my eyebrows to get him to elaborate.

"I got supernatural steroids—increased speed, strength, and agility. It's kind of hard to hold back when you know nobody's gonna be able to stop you on your way to the goal line."

I was still trying to wrap my brain around the whole Gift thing. I didn't doubt it. It just seemed so unreal. I studied Jackson, trying to see something different about him—some evidence of his Gift—but nothing said supernatural. He looked so normal. Maybe perfect-physical-specimen normal, but still normal. It also didn't make sense.

"But … you said … Hassan …"

"Kicks my butt every morning? Yeah, he does. We do a lot of training without using our Gifts because we never know what we'll be up against. We have to be able to fight no matter what. There's a chance you'll be in a situation where you're not able to use your Gift, or like Nathan, your Gift won't help in a fight."

"But you …" I gestured to indicate his size. He stood several inches taller than Hassan and had to be at least forty pounds heavier. I was pretty sure it was all solid muscle too.

"You have to think David and Goliath. Goliath had size and brute strength on his side, but it didn't matter because David knew how to take him down. If I could get a hold of Hassan, I'd squash him like road kill, but I can't get a hold of him." He shook his head. "I tell you what, I wouldn't want to go up against him for real, that's for sure. He's way too smart and way too dangerous even without his Gift."

I wasn't ready to know about Hassan's Gift yet. I figured it would scare me the way he did. "Lexi?"

"We call her Gift Shadowing. It's like … you know how you've got solid, liquid, gas? Well, she sort of turns into something between liquid and gas. She can move real fast too. It'll freak you out the first time you see her do it."

I had no doubt about that. I was already experiencing that surreal feeling where you're lightheaded and your eyes have trouble focusing. Then again, it could have been the lack of oxygen reaching my brain.

"She's another example of why we train without Gifts," he said. "Lexi can't fight when she's Shadowing. Solid objects pass through her. She can use it to avoid getting hit, but she has to be flesh and blood to do damage to anyone else."

For a minute only the whir of the treadmill and my ragged breathing filled the air. Was I ready to know about Hassan's Gift? I worried about reaching the point where I asked too many questions and ended up regretting it, but curiosity got the better of me.

"Hassan?"

"Stealth. The dude's a human cloaking device. He can make himself and other stuff disappear. It's only sight and sound, so I guess if he went heavy on the cologne, you'd be able to find him. Or you could try the Blind Man's Bluff method, but good luck with that because, like I said, he'd be almost impossible to catch even without his Gift." He grimaced. "It scares the crap out of me every time he pops up in the dark. Which is probably why he does it."

I had a hard time believing anything startled Jackson. I also couldn't help thinking of what Nathan had said about Fallen Guardians waiting in the dark. If Hassan was one of the good guys, I didn't want to see what the other side was like.

When Jackson took mercy on me, my face glowed bright red. I knew because I could feel the heat pouring off of it.

He said we were moving on to weights, and I groaned.

"Come on, Kate. You've got your heart rate up. Think of all the fat you'll burn."

"Are you saying … I'm fat?"

"Don't be that way. Take your workout like a man."

I glared at him. That was all I could manage.

He gave me a minute to catch my breath and grab a drink of water. He then led me to the back of the room where he lifted a pair of dumbbells from a rack along the wall. The lightest pair. They looked like lollipops in his hands.

In my hands, they looked like dumbbells and felt a lot heavier than a pound. "Am I going to learn anything else? You know, something besides how to … hurt people."

"Like what?"

I shrugged, which proved much harder to do holding dumbbells. "I don't know. Shouldn't I be studying history or philosophy? Maybe learn ancient Greek or Latin?"

He frowned. "Why would you do that?"

"Isn't that what you're supposed to do when you're a secret soldier or whatever we are? Study so you can figure stuff out? So you're prepared for anything?"

"You're studying the only thing that'll help you."

"Yeah, but how does hunting down Fallen Guardians protect anyone?"

"How do the police protect people? They take criminals off the street."

"But you're not just taking them off the street."

"Not all of them, but sometimes there's no other way."

"Have you ever tried another way? Hassan seems to have plenty of money. Can't you guys build some kind of super villain prison?"

"We don't have the manpower to run a prison, and staffing it with civilians would be a bad idea. We need to get Fallen away from people they can hurt, not hand deliver victims. Besides, Guardians tried the prison thing once, and it didn't work. I don't know what happened, but it was bad. Guardians died. A lot of them."

Even so, there had to be an alternative to capital punishment.

"Look, I get what you're going through," he said. "When I first found out what the deal was, I wasn't too thrilled. I can't honestly say I like it any better now, but I do understand it. I've seen what Guardians are like when they go dark. Yeah, our method sucks, but unless someone figures out how to, well, neuter them so to speak, this is the best we've got."

"So once they go to the dark side, they're gone?"

Massive shoulders rose and fell in response. "I've never heard of any Fallen Guardians who wanted to come back. But I like to think it could happen."

So did I. The alternative was too depressing.

"All right, enough stalling. Start lifting."

Lifting weights—or trying to—proved even more humiliating than displaying my sad state of cardiovascular fitness. My arms were quivering by the time I finished. I went to the locker room and sat on the bench to cool off because what was the point of taking a shower? I'd just sweat the whole way through it.

My legs complained when I got up to shower, and they trembled in protest as I climbed the stairs. I reminded them it was the only way to escape the torture chamber.

Lexi and Mike were still upstairs, but Lexi had moved to one of the chairs in the seating area. I didn't see Hassan anywhere, which was fine with me.

Jackson sat at the kitchen bar devouring an enormous sandwich. "You want one?" he asked between bites. "There's stuff in the fridge, and Hassan's got a pantry the size of Safeco Field. Help yourself to whatever."

I hesitated. I was kind of hungry, but it seemed hypocritical to take something belonging to Hassan after being so ticked off at him for taking something from me.

"Seriously. Hassan doesn't mind. He left for some stockholder meeting anyway, so he'll think I ate it."

"It's true," Lexi said without looking up from her iPad. "He'll think Jackson ate it. And he really doesn't mind."

My stomach rumbled, settling the issue, so I dropped my backpack onto one of the stools at the bar and wandered into the main part of the kitchen.

An island with a stovetop and black granite counter took up the center of the room, and an assortment of stainless steel pots and pans hung overhead. More black granite lined the other counters in the room, a striking contrast to the stainless steel appliances and white cabinets. It was the kind of space you expected to be cold and sterile, but somehow it wasn't. It had a clean, simple feel, and of all the things at Hassan's house, the kitchen was the one that made me jealous. Cooking at home felt like cooking in a closet, and our pots and pans were so scratched up I was surprised Mom and I hadn't died of Teflon poisoning by now.

I bypassed the fridge and went to the door at the far end of the kitchen. Safeco Field might have been an exaggeration, but the pantry had more square footage than my room at home. Lexi clearly did the shopping because almost everything had "organic" or "non-GMO" on the package, and for a second I actually felt sorry for Hassan.

After finding a granola bar that at least had chocolate chips in it, I went to the fridge and found real pop, the kind with chemicals you couldn't pronounce. The caffeine and sugar tempted me, but I grabbed a bottled water instead and sat next to Jackson. While he inhaled his sandwich, I nibbled at the granola bar and pulled a schedule from my backpack to figure out what time I could catch another bus.

When he saw the bus schedule, he said, "I'll take you home."

"That's okay. I don't mind the bus."

"Maybe not, but since you're stuck with public transportation, we all need to know where you live. If something comes up and I need to get to you in a hurry, I don't want to be using GPS to find your house."

"What do you mean if something comes up?"

"Guardian business."

"Oh."

I was glad I hadn't opted for the sandwich because my stomach turned at the mention of Guardian business. Every time I thought I'd managed to cram reality out of sight, it popped free.

Jackson stuffed the last bite of his sandwich into his mouth, and as we headed for the door, I did my best to cram reality out sight again.

CHAPTER SEVEN

I explained how to get to my house as we walked out to his Jeep, and once we made it to the freeway, Jackson reached over to turn off the stereo.

"I told you about myself. Now it's your turn."

I took a sip of water in an attempt to delay the inevitable. I hated these kind of conversations because it always became painfully obvious I didn't have a life.

"There's not much to tell," I said. "I was born here, and I've lived in the same house my whole life. My parents divorced when I was thirteen, I live with my mom, and I'm a freshman at the U. That pretty much covers it."

"There has to be more."

"There really isn't. You'll have to do the talking. Is your family still in Texas?"

"Yep. Even my Great-Granny Myrtle."

"I'm assuming you're not married. Girlfriend?"

"I'm keeping my options open."

"Did you and Lexi use to date?"

"What?" He took his attention from the freeway long enough to scowl at me. "No. Definitely not. Why would you even ask that?"

"Because of the way you guys argue."

"We argue because she's annoying and can't mind her own business." He shuddered. "Dating Lexi would be like dating my sister. It wouldn't happen even if we were the last two people on earth. Seriously. The human race would die out. Besides, she's got a boyfriend."

"Is he a Guardian?"

"No, but he knows about us. He's a detective with the Seattle Police Department. That's how they met. The police and the Guardians were after the same guy."

I hadn't really believed Nathan when he said they tried to turn Fallen Guardians over to the police. Then again, Jackson didn't say they'd turned the guy over. He just said they were looking for the same guy. I decided not to ask how that one turned out.

"So how did you end up in Seattle?"

"Nathan showed up the day I graduated from TCU and told me I needed to move up here. I came, and Hassan needed an accountant, so there you go."

"You're an accountant? No offense, but you don't seem like the type."

"I majored in accounting because I didn't want some CPA ripping me off when I turned pro. Now I get to count Hassan's money instead of my own."

"How did Hassan end up here?"

"He picked Seattle. He says with companies like Boeing, Microsoft, and Pacific Bio-Tech, it's one of the most economically diverse regions in the US."

I flinched at the mention of Pacific Bio-Tech. My dad worked there.

"That's his official press release anyway," Jackson said. "I think what he really wanted was someplace that didn't remind him of home."

"Why?"

"He and his dad don't exactly get along."

"Is he here by himself then? No family?"

"Just him."

"Girlfriend?" Hassan seemed like the kind of guy who'd accessorize with a Brazilian supermodel or two.

"Doesn't have one. He's flying solo."

The way Jackson said it made me think "solo" was a state of existence rather than Hassan's current status. While part of me wanted to blame it on his warm, fuzzy personality, there was probably more to it.

"How old is he anyway?"

"Well, if you can believe what his driver's license says—and I'm not entirely sure you can—he's twenty-seven."

"Really?" I analyzed a mental image of Hassan, trying to be objective. "I guess he doesn't look all that old. But he seems older for some reason."

"I think it's all the money. And the fact he doesn't like anyone."

I nodded. It made sense. Hassan definitely had the old man, "get off my lawn" vibe.

"So what about you?" Jackson said. "You seeing anybody?"

"Me? Yeah right. I'm not dating material."

"What makes you say that?"

"Maybe the fact I've never been asked."

He shot me a look full of disbelief. "You've never been asked on a date?"

"Never been asked. Kind of like never been kissed," I said. Then I wanted to kick myself. My cheeks grew warm as he glanced at my face.

"I find that very hard to believe."

"Well, it's the truth."

Leather creaked as I shifted in my seat. Here was the part where I had to confess I didn't have a life. I took a mouthful of water and let it wash across my tongue hoping it would make my confession more palatable.

"I'm doing good if people know I exist. My only real friend is Danika. We used to see each other at school every day and at church on the weekends, but we're going to different colleges. I mostly just see her on Sunday and sometimes not even then because she has new friends now. You know, people she's met at school. We email or text or whatever during the week, and we do stuff together sometimes, but guys have never figured into the schedule too much. Guys are a touchy subject at my house." I picked at the label of my water bottle. "And it's hard to explain without sounding totally dysfunctional, but my mom needs me around. The divorce kind of ... broke her. My dad took off, and my brother moved out the second he turned eighteen. I'm all she has left."

Who was I kidding? It was dysfunctional.

"Going into Seattle for school this year was a huge ordeal. She wanted me to go to community college first. I finally convinced her I needed to go straight to the U, but it stresses her out, so I spend most of my free time at home pretending I never leave. I'm basically under house arrest, my mom is paranoid about guys and germs and everything else under the sun, and I'm an introvert. If you put all of those things together, you get no social life."

"Okay, that does sound dysfunctional."

I sighed. "I know. But I don't plan on being dysfunctional forever. I have to get out of the house eventually. To keep from going insane if nothing else."

We reached the last stretch of 520, and Marymoor Park spread out on our right while the buildings of Redmond Town Center peeked out from behind the trees on our left. I instructed him to stay in the left lane as the freeway made the transition to suburban chaos.

"So when you're not stuck at home, what do you do?"

I shrugged. "Go to the bookstore or to a movie or something."

"Have you ever gone to a movie with a guy?"

"I've gone with a group that included a guy. Does that count?"

"It counts. So you wouldn't object to a guy asking you out to a movie."

"No."

"But no guy has ever asked you out. Just the two of you."

"Isn't that what I said? Never been asked." I didn't bother to disguise the irritation in my voice. There was nothing quite as humiliating as having your complete lack of social life picked apart and analyzed.

"There's your problem then," he said.

"What?"

"You've never been asked."

I glared at him. "Were you tackled one too many times?"

"Hear me out. Guys are competitive. When one is interested, others take notice. We just need to get you on the GPS—get you a first date. You've got someone in mind, right? Someone you want to notice you?"

Heat blossomed in my cheeks, and Jackson grinned.

"That's what I thought. We need to get you on his GPS."

"It's never going to happen. I'm not his type. And did you miss the part where I said guys weren't interested in me?"

"You only think that because no one's ever asked you out."

"It's the same thing."

"No, it's not. You gotta realize something about guys. We're lazy, our egos are delicate, and smart girls scare us. We tend to go for the easy prey, as in girls who make it obvious they're interested. Sometimes we need a little extra motivation. We need the competition."

"I'm not that smart."

"Nice try. You don't get accepted to the University of Washington unless you have a fantastic GPA, so stop making excuses. You can either sit around and feel sorry for yourself, or you can do something about it. What's it gonna be?"

My self-esteem voted for a pity party. It would be much safer, and I wouldn't have to share my chocolate with anyone.

"Come on, Kate. Sometimes you gotta take a chance and go for the first down."

The bruised apricot color of my house loomed ahead as Jackson turned onto my street. This whole scenario had disaster graffitied all over it, and yet I forged ahead.

"Okay, even if I did buy into your GPS theory, there's

still the problem of being asked out in the first place."

"No, that's the easy part. You've got me. I'll make sure he notices. You just have to figure out where."

Jackson pulled into the driveway, and I stared at him as the idea settled in. He was impossible to miss, and I knew exactly where to take him so Rob would see. But it couldn't be that easy. My life was never that easy.

It couldn't possibly turn out the way I wanted, but my stubborn little spark of hope flared up again, begging me to at least try.

"Well ... this girl I know—Jen—invited me to go to a concert next Tuesday with a group of her friends. I'm pretty sure Rob will be there."

"Sounds good. What time should I pick you up?"

I'd have to give Mom a reasonable explanation of how I met Jackson, and Lexi provided the perfect bridge. When she picked me up from the transit center the following day, I filled her in on the plan as we drove to Hassan's.

"You're not a guy, which is a huge bonus in your favor. I can say I met you through Nathan, and once she meets you, it'll be a lot easier to introduce Jackson as Nathan's friend and your co-worker. And the best part? I can tell her it's not a date because it's not."

"Uh-huh. Is that what Jackson told you?"

"It'll work. It has to work. I'll probably never get another chance like this. So will you help me? Please? I need you to meet my mom, and I need you to help me figure out what to wear."

She eyed my jeans and gray "U-DUB" hoodie. "Well, I'm totally on board with that part of the plan."

Lexi agreed to come over on Saturday, and when she arrived, we started out with mugs of coffee in the living room. Mom was guarded at first, but she quickly warmed up to Lexi because Lexi oozed the qualities Mom valued. Calm, sensible, and organized.

When Mom's quilting hobby came up in conversation, Lexi asked to take a look, so we left our mugs on the coffee table and went to the sewing room—which used to be Ty's room. It had taken an entire year for the dirty sock smell to die after he moved out. Eventually Mom had transformed it into an orderly space scented with orange.

She removed a storage bin from the closet and pulled out a mosaic of pink, lilac, and purple.

Lexi gasped when she saw it. "I love it."

"Do you really?" Mom said.

"Yes. Absolutely." Lexi brushed her fingers across the fabric. "It's amazing. The stitching is flawless."

"If you like it, you should have it."

"No, I couldn't possibly take it. You've put so much work into it."

"I enjoy the work, and I insist."

I smiled, my heart swelling with happiness, but my smile faltered when Mom gave Lexi's arm an affectionate squeeze. But right now I needed her to approve of Lexi, not me. Her approval meant I was one step closer to having a real date.

After Lexi accepted the quilt, she and I headed to my room. I gave her the two-second tour then plopped down on my bed while she opened the closet door.

"Thanks," I said. "You made her happy."

Lexi stopped rummaging. "I think I might owe you an apology."

"For what?"

"The first day you came to Hassan's—when I gave you a ride and you were telling me how you didn't want to talk to your mom—I thought you were whining."

"I was whining."

"Yeah, but I assumed it was the typical 'my parents are ruining my life' stuff. I figured you were being selfish."

I picked at a string on the hem of my jeans. "I am selfish. I don't want to deal with her freaking out."

"Maybe. Maybe not."

My gaze briefly met Lexi's before slipping away. I hadn't invited anyone other than Danika to my house for a long time. She and I had been friends since junior high, since before my family fell apart, and she knew what things were like for me at home. I didn't have to explain anything or make excuses with Danika.

I'd thought this morning had gone well, without any hint at a less than harmonious existence, but Lexi had picked up on something. I had no idea what, and it worried me. If she'd noticed something wrong with what I considered a good morning, then how bad was it?

Lexi returned to the contents of the closet, uttering a sound of disgust. "Hardly anything but jeans and hoodies."

"Sorry. Fashion isn't really my thing."

"I can tell."

Lexi searched for another minute or two before giving a cry of delight. She produced a pair of high-heeled boots I'd bought on impulse at Macy's clearance sale last winter. I'd only worn them once because they killed my toes.

"There's hope for you after all." She set the boots on the floor then grabbed a pair of jeans and tossed them to me. "Put those on so I can see how they look with the boots."

"No way. This pair makes my butt look even bigger than it already is."

"You're not fat."

"Well, I'm not thin."

"They're called curves. Guys like them, and girls like me wish we had them, so stop complaining. And stop hiding under hoodies. Modesty is important, but if I had a figure like yours, I'd show it off a little more."

I held the jeans up, frowning at them.

"Do it. Put them on right now, or I'm leaving."

"Okay, fine. Don't look."

She rolled her eyes, but as I stood up, she faced the closet again. I squirmed my way into the jeans, tugged on the boots, and told Lexi she could look.

"Turn," she commanded. I did a three-sixty, and she smiled. "Perfect. Do you have a white cami?"

"Somewhere."

"Let's try it with this." She tossed a navy, wrap sweater to me. "Your black pea coat should work with the outfit, and I'll loan you a handbag. Don't even think about using the canvas messenger bag in your closet."

"Fine."

I sank onto my bed with a sigh. My toes hurt already, my backside felt a mile wide, and a fashion makeover with Lexi was proving to be almost as fun as a training session with Hassan. But a real date would be worth the pain and suffering. Right?

CHAPTER
EIGHT

In theory, Hassan had crushed my windpipe, but it was hard to remember I was dead when his face hovered so close to mine. I could see each individual lash surrounding his eyes. Eyes the rich brown of autumn. Of fudge and chocolate ganache. I loved chocolate.

He stood and scowled at me then walked away shaking his head, leaving me to pick myself up off the mat. I smothered a groan as I sat up. Between Hassan and Jackson, my poor body was begging me to stop the insanity. I'd be stiff and sore for the rest of my life at this rate.

I had only been training a week, but I could tell Hassan was frustrated with my lack of progress. So was I. Our sessions consisted of him saying "again" until my arms and legs trembled with the effort, then he would demand I "focus" or "pay attention."

Sweat prickled along my scalp and ran down my forehead. I wiped it away with my sleeve then reached around to peel my t-shirt away from my back. I hated being sweaty.

We'd gotten a late start today because Hassan had another one of those meetings for people with way too much money. I'd worked out first, which meant less energy than usual for martial arts lessons. One more way for me to irritate Hassan. But we were almost done, and if I could make it through this session, I could stress over the concert tonight instead of my failure as a Guardian.

He grabbed one of the water bottles from the edge of the

mat and tossed it to me, but it slipped through my fingers, landing in my lap with a plunk. He grabbed one for himself then came to sit by me, probably to rub in the fact he wasn't even breathing hard.

I twisted the cap off of my water bottle and took a drink. As I swallowed, I watched him gaze out the windows at the muted color palette of an overcast day. I still couldn't figure him out. When I'd finally gathered enough courage to ask where he was from, he told me he grew up in Cairo, which I noticed didn't really answer my question. He didn't exactly have an accent, but you could tell English wasn't his first language, and sometimes he'd use the wrong word. Or maybe not the wrong word but one that the rest of us wouldn't have used.

I searched for a hint of something different, something that would indicate his Gift. He caught me looking at him, and I blushed, but I was so overheated he probably couldn't tell.

For a few seconds, we inspected each other, and I decided his eyes were the color of milk chocolate. My favorite kind of chocolate.

"What's on your mind, Kate?"

Surprise delayed my answer. The question hadn't been delivered in his usual "you're an idiot" tone of voice. I didn't want to confess I'd been thinking about his eyes or chocolate though, so I picked the preceding thought.

"Gifts. You can't tell by looking at someone whether or not they have a Gift or what their Gift is. I mean, it kind of makes sense after you get to know them. Jackson was an athlete, so it makes sense he got a performance-enhancing Gift. Lexi is always working on something. She's quick and efficient. So it makes sense her Gift allows her to move even faster—even through obstacles. And you're kind of into the privacy thing, so it makes sense you can hide yourself."

Now that I'd already opened my mouth, I wondered if I was supposed to know about Hassan's Gift. I didn't know why not except I was talking to Mr. Obsessed-With-Privacy.

"Jackson kind of filled me in on everyone's Gifts," I explained.

"Did he?"

"Yeah. He said you were a human cloaking device. You can make yourself and other things disappear."

"I suppose you want to see this now."

"What? No. I really don't want to see it. Or not see it. Whatever."

"Why not?"

"Because I'm already having a hard time dealing with the Guardian thing. Right now I can still pretend my life is somewhat normal, but I can't if you … you know, magically disappear."

He frowned, but it was a puzzled kind of frown rather than the irritated sort. "Why do you have to deal with it?"

"Did you want me to *not* deal with it?"

"No, why do you have to 'deal' with it? Why do you want to pretend your life hasn't changed? You were chosen to be a Guardian. Being a Guardian is a privilege."

"It doesn't feel like a privilege. It feels like a huge headache added to an already long list of headaches. It's one more thing I have to figure out how to fit into my schedule."

"There's nothing to figure out. Being a Guardian is your priority."

"According to you."

"Not according to me. That's the way it is."

"Why? Because you say so?"

His frown turned into the irritated sort. "Why must you be so difficult?"

I blinked at him. "I'm difficult? You're kidding, right?"

"You always have to argue. You always take offense at what I say."

"Because what you say is offensive. Do you ever think about how it might make me feel? Or does it not matter to you?"

"What did I say that was offensive? Being a Guardian is a privilege? How is this offensive to you?"

"It's not that, and it's not just what you say. It's how you say it. It's your whole attitude. The way you treat people."

"How do I treat people?"

"Like their feelings don't matter. Like it's perfectly okay to sift through their personal information. Like they're not supposed to feel humiliated that you know about the worst stuff in their lives—every time they failed, every time they messed up, every time they were ignored or rejected."

I'd thought I was over the stupid file, but apparently not. I could feel tears working their way toward the surface, and I pushed them back down. I refused to cry in front of Hassan.

"Is that why your Gift is Stealth?" I said. "So you can spy on people and get whatever information you couldn't steal off the Internet?"

He didn't say anything. He just looked at me, and I focused on a seam in the mat so I wouldn't have to meet his gaze.

"No. That's not why."

When I looked up, he was still watching me. I couldn't decipher the emotion in his eyes.

"Stealth is a useful skill for someone who was supposed to be a terrorist, don't you think?"

"A terrorist?" I echoed numbly.

"Some fathers want their sons to become doctors or lawyers, but my father wanted me to become a terrorist, only he called it a 'Sword for Allah.' He began my training when I was four years old."

"Four?"

"Four is old enough to hold a gun. To kill something."

I was suddenly very sorry I'd questioned Hassan. Teaching a child to kill—wanting such a thing—was a concept I couldn't grasp.

"But he wanted more than a mindless soldier, so he made sure I had the best education, the best schools. In addition to

English I learned to speak Farsi. Some Turkish and Urdu as well. He made sure I learned what the schools couldn't teach me. How to build and use explosives. The best ways to torture a man. How to kill a man very quickly or very slowly using any kind of weapon or my bare hands. Quite an education, don't you think?"

I had no idea how to respond. My dad might have sucked in the parenting department, but at least he was just selfish. He didn't set out to screw me up on purpose.

"So ... how did you end up as a Guardian?"

"My mother died when I was fourteen, and I found a Bible among her things. I have no idea where she got it because my father would have killed her if he ever found it. I knew what he would do if he found it then. He would have defiled her memory, and I couldn't bear the thought of that, so I took her Bible and hid it. I wanted to keep her memory safe, and I wanted to keep something of her with me because she was the only good thing in my life when I was young."

He took a long drink of water, draining what was left in the bottle, and twisted the cap back on.

"I hid her Bible and forgot about it. I continued with my education, learning to hate and to kill. Then one day my father said he had a job for me. It was a massive operation, and it meant many people would die. Not only soldiers or government workers, but hundreds of innocent people who had nothing to do with his war."

His fingers tightened around the cap until his knuckles turned white from the pressure. The tendons of his wrist strained against the band of his watch.

"I was a grown man. I had wealth and power, but my father still controlled me. I realized that if I did what he wanted, I would lose what was left of myself, and I hated him for it. I had hated him for a long time, but I didn't know how to be free of him. The day before I was to leave, I found my mother's Bible again. I finally understood how to be free from him and from everything I had done."

His eyes were dark chocolate now, intense and with an edge of bitterness to them.

"In one night I went from being my father's greatest asset to being his greatest enemy. He declared I should die for my betrayal, but my aunt—my mother's sister—has always been fond of me. She convinced her husband to make a deal with my father. If I stayed out of his way and didn't try to stop him, my father would remove the price from my head. Or at least stop hiring the assassins himself. My father agreed. It was a waste of his money anyway."

Holy crap. Hassan's dad had sent someone to kill him. And Hassan was still alive. Assassins—as in more than one—had come after him and failed. There was a reason Hassan's *Pur* seemed like a warning. It was.

The privacy thing made a lot more sense now. So did the self-imposed isolation.

He tossed the empty water bottle to the edge of the mat with a flick of his wrist. "I was called shortly after I left. Now I use the things I learned to help the Guardians."

I swallowed. His entire life had been spent learning how to end someone else's. "Your dad kind of makes my dad look like a saint."

His eyes became a softer brown again. "What happened with your father?"

Maybe this was Hassan's way of belatedly asking permission to dig into my personal information. He'd seen the paperwork, so he would know my dad forfeited any custody rights in favor of a quick divorce. What the paperwork wouldn't tell him was Dad never wanted any to begin with.

"We had your basic middle-class American family. One day my dad decided he didn't want it anymore. Too complicated. Too much responsibility. So he found someone who's perfectly content to take care of the house and everything else he leaves behind and not bother him until he feels like spending time with her. Connie always drops whatever she's doing and acts like she won the lottery whenever he pays attention to her. My stepsister Chloe doesn't care what he does or whether he's home or not because he pays off her credit card every month. My dad does whatever he feels like, and even though Connie is what he wanted, she's still not enough. Ty says Dad cheats on her all the time." I shrugged. "Not that it's any of my business."

"It is your business. He's your father."

"Yeah, but he doesn't want to be."

When I met Hassan's gaze, I knew he'd felt the same emotion, and I looked away. I didn't like the thought that, of all the Guardians, Hassan was the one who understood what I felt.

Time to move on to a different subject. This one was totally depressing anyway. "So how do you guys find Fallen Guardians?"

"Guardians from different locations share information as much as possible so we can track them down. We're fortunate to have Nathan here with us because many times he Knows when a Fallen Guardian has come into the area. Sometimes he Knows before they come. We also understand what to look for."

"Like what? What do you look for?"

"They live to prey on others. Mike monitors the news for any signs of Fallen Guardian activity."

"Are there any around here?"

"Not that we know of, but it's only a matter of time." His gaze trapped mine. "Sometimes Fallen Guardians come looking for us. You have only started your training, and you're not ready to face them, so if you see a Fallen Guardian, you run. As far and as fast as you can. Do you understand?"

"Yeah. I understand." I had no objection whatsoever to running away.

"Never tell them your name or another Guardian's name. Never give information of any kind to them. They will use it to find Guardians. They will use it to find your family and anyone else who is important to you."

The thought of a psychotic, supernatural killer showing up at my house and finding my mom sent a shot of anxiety through me.

"Nathan is somewhat of an exception to this rule," Hassan said. "His Gift allows him to be in public more than the rest of us, but he still guards his information very closely."

"That's why he uses a pseudonym. And you hardly ever see a picture of him."

He nodded. "Mike also watches to make sure no one takes too much interest in us. He tries to keep us hidden as much as possible."

I felt a little betrayed as it sunk in Mike must've been the one to create the file for Hassan. I didn't hold Mike responsible though. "That's why you had a file on me. You were trying to protect me."

He shrugged. "I like to have information."

You'd think he could at least fake a little remorse.

My gaze fell on his watch, and I grabbed his wrist, twisting to get a better look. "Is that the right time?" What was I thinking? Of course it was the right time. Probably down to the millisecond. I scrambled to my feet.

"What's wrong?"

"I need to get home before my mom does."

"Why?"

I tugged the door to the hallway open. "It's part of pretending my life is still normal."

"I'll take you home if you need to get there quickly."

I didn't even bother to rinse off. I left my water bottle on the locker room bench, grabbed my things, and rushed upstairs. I'd stopped sweating while we talked, so at least I wouldn't contaminate his leather seats.

He already had the car running when I got to the garage and backed out as soon as my door shut. I couldn't read the odometer, but our surroundings blurred like we'd achieved light speed, and I could feel the hum of the Audi as my fingers dug into the seat.

"Okay, beating my mom home is not worth a speeding ticket. Or death."

"Kate," he said, his tone exasperated. "I'm touching the car. No one can see us."

There was a pause while I gaped at him. "Maybe this isn't ... are you sure this is a good idea?

"Do you want to get home before your mother or not?"

"Okay. Right. Well, don't cause a wreck or anything."

He gave me a dark look as he blew through a stop sign.

"Sorry. I wasn't trying to insult your driving skills, but I'd feel really guilty if we killed someone because I'm afraid to explain the Guardians to my mom."

Insulted or not, Hassan made it to my house without getting in a wreck.

I reached for the door handle but stopped. "Am I going to suddenly materialize in my driveway? That probably wouldn't be a good thing."

He didn't answer. He got out and ran his fingers along the car, never letting them leave the surface as he came around to the passenger side to open my door. With his hand still on the frame, he leaned down so we were almost at eye level. A hint of smile touched the corner of his mouth.

"We've been visible since we turned onto your street."

He offered his hand, but I stood and shouldered my way past him.

"Your sense of humor is messed up."

"So I've heard." He shut the passenger door. "See you tomorrow."

"Whatever. Thanks for the ride I guess." Three steps later I swung back around. "Hey, how did you know how to get to my house?"

I'd been too worried about getting in a wreck to give him any directions.

"I like to have information."

I turned and headed for the front door, fighting the impulse to grab a fir cone and throw it at his car. I would've missed anyway.

CHAPTER
NINE

I forced down a small square of lasagna because skipping dinner would've alerted Mom to how nervous I was. She'd suspect more to the evening than a bunch of friends going to a concert, which could mean me missing out on my shot at a real date.

Convincing her to let me go on a date would be an entirely different headache, one I'd deal with later if I had to. No point stressing out now over something that would probably never happen.

After dinner, I brushed and flossed then put on the outfit Lexi had chosen. I followed her advice about my hairstyle too. She'd told me to leave my hair framing my face instead of pulling it into a pony tail or tucking it behind my ears like usual. When I finished, I didn't look too bad. Almost pretty.

I transferred my wallet, keys, and phone to the handbag Lexi had loaned me, pulled my coat from the closet, and went to the living room to wait for Jackson. Mom emerged from the sewing room when he arrived, and worry crept across her features as I made introductions.

The sapphire blue sweater Jackson wore brought out his eyes, but what you really noticed was the way his sweater lovingly embraced every muscle on his upper torso. There was a lot to embrace.

I'd warned him ahead of time to keep it über-platonic in front of Mom and to keep his *Pur* hidden at all costs. As I slipped my coat on, I made sure to leave several inches of space between me and Jackson.

"So Jen was talking about getting something to eat afterwards. You know, everyone all together in a group. I'll let you know if we—all of us—decide to go. I won't go if it's getting too late."

"I suppose it would be all right." Her gaze returned to Jackson, and the corner of her mouth turned down.

"I promise to have her home no later than eleven, Mrs. Brennan."

Her frown deepened, so I hurried us out the door.

The whoosh of tires on wet pavement accompanied the stereo as Jackson drove. The sheen of water on the road reflected oncoming headlights and the passing streetlights, throwing the glare into the cabin. As he pulled up to a stoplight, Jackson turned to inspect me, and the way his eyes lingered made me paranoid. Like maybe I was having a wardrobe malfunction or something.

"What?" I took a quick peek to make sure my jeans were zipped.

"You look good."

His comment coaxed a smile from me. "Thanks."

The concert was being held at one of the mega-churches on the Eastside, so we didn't have to drive into Seattle. The parking lot hadn't filled up yet, but we still had to walk a ways, and my toes were whining about the lack of space by the time we reached the entrance. I told them to suck it up because they looked good crammed into my boots, and with an extra three inches of height, I didn't feel so short next to Jackson.

After a couple of texts, we located Jen and the others, and all eyes went straight to Jackson. Girls who had barely—or never—acknowledged my existence before wore expressions of disbelief, clearly in shock that someone like me had snagged a date with someone like Jackson. It ticked me off and yet gave me an immense amount of satisfaction at the same time. Especially since one of the girls was Olivia, a fake-n-bake I'd once overheard refer to me as "emo girl."

Well, take *that*, Olivia. Score one for emo girl.

There was some definite sizing-up going on with the guys, including Rob, like they were trying to figure out how much Jackson could bench press. I bit my lip to hide a grin and to restrain myself from telling them they didn't have a prayer.

Jen made sure we all knew each other before we went to find seats. When the crowd bottlenecked at the doors to the auditorium, Jackson put an arm around my shoulders and pulled me close enough he wouldn't be overheard by the people around us.

The deep timbre of his voice filled my ear. "Rob's the one, right?"

My cheeks grew warm, and I was too embarrassed to do anything but nod.

"All right then. Let's get the show started."

Somehow Jackson managed to get us seated where every time he turned to talk to me he'd be able to see what Rob was doing, what Rob was looking at, who Rob was looking at.

We spent most of our time talking, which really meant leaning in to yell at each other over the music, and Jackson kept saying things that made me laugh. For a while I forgot why we'd come to the concert, but it didn't bother me when I remembered. I didn't have a shot at Rob anyway, not really, and having fun with Jackson was a nice substitute. It still counted as a social life.

After the concert, Jen got everyone to agree to food at Rocket Burger, and our group took up the back corner of the 50s diner-themed restaurant. I ended up smooshed into a booth beside Jackson, which wasn't all that bad except three girls—Olivia included—slid into the seat on the other side of the table.

"What are you having?" Jackson asked me.

"Onion rings and a chocolate shake."

"Good call."

Jackson ordered two bacon cheeseburgers, fries, onion

rings, a peanut butter milkshake, and a root beer. He managed to keep a conversation going as he devoured all of it, and then he helped me finish off my onion rings. Olivia and the other two girls ogled Jackson while they sipped their diet sodas. They hardly touched the basket of fries they were sharing.

As our party left the restaurant, we funneled through the door, stringing out into the parking lot in smaller groups, and Jackson ended up in the group ahead of me with Olivia. I briefly entertained the idea of shoving Olivia to the ground, but then I realized I was walking next to Rob. Alone.

"So how long have you and your boyfriend been going out?"

I managed to stop my chin before it hit the pavement. "Um, he's not … I mean, this is the first time we've ever done anything together."

"Did you enjoy the concert?"

"Yeah. It was fun." No need for him to know it wasn't the music I enjoyed.

"Switchfoot will be in Seattle next week, and I think they still have some tickets left. We could get another group together if you're interested." His gaze flickered in Jackson's direction as my heart started to race. "You and I could organize it."

"That … that sounds great."

My hands shook as we exchanged phone numbers, and it took a monumental effort to keep them steady enough to add him to my contacts. Rob Peterson. In my contacts. And he even promised to call me. Maybe it didn't qualify as a date, but it was way better than I'd thought possible.

My heart was still racing as Jackson and I got into the Jeep, and I felt short of breath like I'd spent the last five minutes on the treadmill instead of standing in the parking lot.

"Well?" Jackson said.

"He wants to get a group together for the Switchfoot

concert."

He grinned. "I told you it would get his attention."

"Yeah, well, it's not a date."

"Don't worry," Jackson said as he started the Jeep. "He'll get around to it. Guys don't like competition."

"Speaking of competition, how many phone numbers did you get?"

He grimaced. "A couple girls offered," he admitted. "But for the record, I turned them down. I came with you."

"Don't worry about it. That's how they think of me—as nonexistent." He gave me a troubled look, and I shrugged it off. I was used to it. "By the way, watch out for Olivia. She's mean."

"Yeah, I kind of sensed a disturbance in the Force around her."

She'd been the most aggressive of Jackson's followers. When Jackson took his phone from his pocket long enough to locate his wallet, Olivia had pounced on it and added herself to his contacts.

We didn't talk on the way to my house, but it was a good kind of quiet. I took the opportunity to soak up my moment of success because I knew anxiety over having another conversation with Rob would set in soon.

"Thanks for everything," I said when Jackson parked in the driveway a few minutes later. "Even if the date thing doesn't work out, I had fun."

"You'll get that date. You were kinda glowing tonight."

I laughed. "What, like I'm radioactive? Maybe it was the onion rings. They were pretty spicy."

A grin spread across his face. "No, I mean you. Especially when you're laughing. Don't get me wrong, okay? I like gloomy, sarcastic Kate a lot, but fun and clever Kate is great to hang out with too. Maybe the girls didn't pay much attention to you tonight, but I know the guys did."

"Thanks." It was a nice thing to say even if he was completely delusional.

He walked me to the door and said good night from the front step since Mom hovered at the front window. After he left, I sat on the couch and gave her a rundown of the evening as I freed my toes from their imprisonment. I'd paid enough attention at the concert to tell her a couple of the songs played.

"And Jen was great," I said. "She made everyone feel included."

Mom's frown eased a bit. "Well, I'm glad for that."

I supplied her with a few more non-guy-related details, and even though I was vibrating with happiness on the inside, I portrayed a calm, sensible girl on the outside.

Since I was too wired to go right to sleep, I sent an email to Danika. I hadn't told her everything, but she knew Jackson was helping me get Rob's attention. Yawns were growing more frequent by the time I signed out, but I still had a hard time shutting my mind off when I crawled into bed. I was too busy replaying each happy moment and visualizing ones to come.

I wasn't so happy the next day when I got my calculus test back.

"This is the first D I've gotten," I told Lexi when she picked me up. "Ever. I don't know what the problem is. I've never had this much trouble with a class before. Usually if I keep studying, the material eventually makes sense, but not this time. I swear, there's a wire loose in my brain somewhere, and if I can't figure out how to fix it, I might as well forget about med school. I'll never get in."

"Relax. It's one test, and you have plenty of time to pull your grade up. Both Hassan and Jackson are good at math, and I'm sure Jackson would love to help you."

"Really?"

"Really."

Lexi was right. Jackson volunteered to tutor me, which

provided the perfect opportunity to reveal a little more of my new schedule to Mom.

Over dinner that night, I mentioned I'd be stopping by Jackson's workplace after classes because I needed help with calculus. I wouldn't be alone with him because Lexi was there as well as another employee and their boss. Their boss had okayed the arrangement.

"I don't think it's a good idea." Mom frowned as she flaked off a bite of halibut. "We can find someone else to tutor you."

"Yeah, but probably not for free."

She shook her head. "No, Kate. You hardly know these people."

"But at least I know them. I'd have to get tutoring from a total stranger, and I could end up with some nut job." I was rewarded with a crease of worry on her forehead. "You've met both Lexi and Jackson. I thought you liked Lexi."

"I do. Lexi is wonderful. It's just, well, what if she has to leave for some reason? You'd be all alone in that house with three men."

"Lexi's been working there for almost five years now," I said. "She can vouch for them."

I told Mom about my test grade then, but she still didn't give in until I promised to keep my phone close and leave if the situation ever seemed "unsafe." I agreed based on my definition of the word because the situation at Hassan's would always be unsafe according to hers.

On Sunday morning, I went to church thinking that by now Rob was probably wondering who Kate was and why he had her number in his contacts, but he remembered me. He stood in the foyer with some of the people from the concert, and when Mom and I walked in, he broke away from the group to say hi. In front of Olivia too. Score another one for emo girl.

I introduced him to Mom, explaining our connection through Jen, and told her about the possible group outing to the Switchfoot concert.

"Yeah, I wanted to talk to you about it," Rob said. "If you have a minute."

"Sure." I gave Mom what I hoped was a reassuring look. "Do you want to go find seats? I'll be right there."

Her expression cooled. "The service is about to start."

"I'll be quick. I promise."

The temperature dropped a few degrees as she eyed Rob. She refocused the subzero disapproval on me. "Don't take too long."

I faced Rob wanting to apologize for the frigid cloud of negativity she'd left behind but figured it was better to pretend it didn't exist.

"We should probably get a head count today," he said. "To make sure we buy enough tickets. Are you planning to bring a date?"

Fortunately Jackson had prepped me for this question. "I'm not sure yet. I'll get two tickets just in case."

Rob asked if he could sit with me and my mom, and for a second I thought I'd humiliate myself by passing out.

"Um, yeah. Sure."

No way would I turn down this opportunity. I only hoped we didn't end up with frostbite.

CHAPTER TEN

By Monday I felt really good about life, good enough to put off calculus tutoring for one day and work on my English lit paper. Hassan had gone to New York on business, so I texted Jackson between my bio and chem classes to let him know I'd be skipping my workout. I promised to call later if I got stuck on calculus homework.

As if sensing my happiness, the bus driver waited to hit the gas until I was in the process of sitting down. The bus lunged forward, ramming my knee into the framework of the seat. I clenched my teeth against the pain.

The heavens opened up a few minutes later. Not the drizzle of moisture we usually experienced in the Northwest. This was the kind of rainstorm where drops hit the sidewalk so hard they bounce like Ping-Pong balls. Of course, it didn't really start coming down until after we'd passed the Yarrow Point stop—too late to get off and call Jackson or Lexi for a ride. No big deal though. I could work on my paper at Mom's office instead. Not my first choice, but it beat getting drenched walking home from the bus stop with a sore knee.

Both agents were out, so Mom said I could use the computer in Cliff's office. I made good progress on my paper, but after an hour I needed a break. My backside wanted freedom from the chair, and my brain wanted caffeine. Of course Mom worried I'd get drenched, end up in the hospital with pneumonia, and die from the MRSA infection I acquired while I was there. I assured her a little rain wouldn't kill me.

"Are you meeting someone there?" she said.

"What?"

"Why are you going to Starbucks? Is a boy waiting for you?"

"No. I'm not meeting anyone."

Her lips thinned. "Are you sure?"

"Yes, I'm sure." I struggled to keep my tone respectful. "I told you, I was planning to go straight home and work on my paper until it started pouring."

"The rain doesn't seem to be bothering you now. It's not keeping you from going to Starbucks."

I stifled a growl of frustration. Between Jackson taking me to the concert and Rob sitting with us in church, her paranoia had launched into overdrive.

"I wasn't going to Starbucks. I want to go to Book & Brew. It's only a couple blocks away, a lot closer than home is from the bus stop, and I was planning to use your umbrella. I just want to get coffee and look at books for a few minutes."

I didn't point out that if I'd wanted to meet a boy, I could have done it without her knowing. I didn't need to come by the office first then make up an excuse to leave.

For a few heartbeats, she straightened items on her desk, her mouth pressed into a grim line. "My keys are in my purse." She didn't look at me as she said it.

I went to the lunchroom and yanked open the door to the cupboard where Mom stored her purse. After retrieving the umbrella from the Civic, I tossed the keys back in her purse, grabbed my phone, and stuffed a five dollar bill in my pocket. Dad had finally reimbursed me for tuition. He'd called from Peru or Paris or wherever he was and told Connie to put money in my bank account. He'd only done it so I would stop calling.

One parent pushed me away and one refused to let go. Did they have any idea what it did to me? Did they even care?

"I'll be back in a little while," I said as I headed out the door.

I didn't get a response.

By the time I made it to Book & Brew, my Converse squished with every step, the hem of my jeans was soaked, and my injured knee had reduced me to limping.

The barista didn't bother to look up from his phone as I stepped inside. An older guy sat at one of the tables with a cup of coffee, peering at a section of *The Seattle Times* through his bifocals. A girl my age stood at the magazine rack absorbed in the latest issue of *Entertainment Weekly*.

Coffee or browse first? The barista was still focused on his phone, so I set Mom's umbrella in the rack by the door and wandered into the fantasy/sci-fi section. I hadn't taken time to peruse the shelves of a bookstore since school started, and I missed it. For a few peaceful minutes I was alone with the aromas of paper and coffee and the muted rumble of rain against the roof overhead.

Then something in the air changed. A subtle shift wormed its way into my peaceful moment and drew my eyes away from the books. It pulled my attention to the end of the aisle and the window beyond where I could see the creepy guy from the bus. He stood on the sidewalk, staring at me while rain poured down on him.

A quick check behind me confirmed I was the only one in the aisle. He was definitely staring at me, and I clamped down on the urge to panic. He'd done nothing worse than say hi to me last time, and I refused to give in to paranoia. Turning back to the books, I feigned interest hoping he would move on, but I could still see him in my peripheral vision a couple minutes later. I could feel him staring at me, and it sucked all the fun out of browsing. There wasn't much point in trying anymore.

Unfortunately, he'd taken up position a couple feet from the front entrance. I didn't want to get any closer to him, and I didn't want to give him the opportunity to follow me when I left the bookstore, so I worked my way toward the back of the aisle. I could use the south entrance and circle around the building.

Mom's umbrella was the only hitch in my escape plan. I chewed on my lip while I considered my options. I'd have to come back for it later. Mom was already mad at me, so it wouldn't make much difference if I left it behind.

When I reached the end of the aisle, I peeked at the window. He hadn't moved, so I eased around the end of the shelf and made my way to the exit. I slipped out the door, sticking close to the building in an effort to stay dry, and hung a right toward the main courtyard. When I reached the shoe store on the corner, I stopped and peered around the edge of the building toward Book & Brew. He was gone. I checked behind me and didn't see him there either. Maybe I could grab Mom's umbrella before heading back to the agency.

About halfway to the front door of Book & Brew, an alarm went off in my head. What if he was following me for a reason that had nothing to do with me being young and female?

Hassan had said to run as far and as fast as I could. I didn't run, but I picked up the pace and tugged my phone from my pocket. I scrolled through my contacts and pushed "call" praying he would answer. When I heard his voice, relief flooded my system.

"Kate?"

"Yeah."

Somehow he managed to pick up on my fear with just that word. "What is it? What's wrong?"

"I think … I think I saw a Fallen Guardian. And he might know I'm a Guardian. I can't remember for sure, but he might have seen my *Pur* when we were on the bus the other day."

"Where are you?"

"Redmond Town Center."

"Where at Redmond Town Center?"

"Outside Book & Brew," I said as I walked past the front door and abandoned Mom's umbrella to its own fate.

"Where is he?"

"I don't know. He was watching me, so I left the store. Now he's gone, and I don't know where he went."

"Stay outside. Get somewhere open. Somewhere you can see him coming. Do you understand me?"

I nodded then remembered Hassan couldn't see it. "Okay."

"Call Nathan. He will come and ensure you're safe. I'll call him in a few minutes to make sure he's spoken with you, and I'll call Lexi and Jackson to let them know what's happened. If Nathan doesn't answer, call Mike. He'll make sure someone gets to you."

A car honked at me as I hurried into the crosswalk, and I wanted to plow my Converse into the bumper. Too bad if his BMW was getting wet. He could wait two seconds for me to get across the street.

"Do you understand me, Kate? Stay in the open and call Nathan."

"Okay."

"I'll be on the next flight to Seattle. Call Nathan. Now."

The call dropped.

I scrolled through my contacts again as I passed in front of Macy's where the fountain bubbled away cheerfully despite the downpour. Ice cold rain ran into my eyes and over my hands, making it hard to see my phone and even harder to use. The phone grew slick beneath my fingers and slipped away from me, crashing onto the sidewalk next to the parking lot.

Where were my brother and his profanity when I needed them?

I checked to make sure the coast was clear before bending over to pick up the phone. I only stood still long enough to wipe it off on my hoodie then started walking again. When I glanced over my shoulder, I saw my stalker standing by the fountain.

I didn't hesitate. I ran.

I ignored the pain in my knee, urging my legs to move faster, but my lungs couldn't seem to get enough air. I stopped after only a few steps, struggling to catch my breath. Dizziness washed over me, and I swayed, fought to stay on me feet. What was wrong with me?

A man stepped out from behind one of the cars in the parking lot. Maybe his appearance would scare off my stalker. But memory filtered through my hazy thoughts, warning me I'd seen him before. He'd been standing next to my stalker at the bus stop the other day.

There were two of them. I'd let them herd me into their trap.

I gasped another breath. Took a step and stumbled. Someone caught me as I went down. As my vision turned gray, I pushed at the hand gripping my arm. My fingers slid uselessly across cold skin. I commanded them to try again, but they didn't obey. They couldn't. My body had become a dull weight with only enough awareness left to tell me it was being lifted and carried.

I raged at the darkness closing in and at my own body for betraying me, for giving up so easily. I'd just started to think my life might be worth something. I wasn't ready to lose it.

CHAPTER
ELEVEN

I was laying on my side, a hard surface beneath me. A mechanical hum had replaced the sound of rain, and the odor of musty earth filtered through the air.

As awareness returned, so did alarm. I had to get away—had to run—but my body wouldn't respond. I fought to open my eyes.

Confusion replaced my alarm. A woman stood a few steps in front of me. Her pale hair had been twisted into a mass of dreadlocks, and water trickled from the ends, dripping down onto her feet to join the mud covering her boots. Something about her seemed familiar, and yet I'd never seen her before. I didn't have a clue who she was. Had she saved me from the Fallen Guardians?

I searched our surroundings for answers as I climbed to my hands and knees. We were in some kind of maintenance room with assorted pipes, valves, and electrical boxes along the walls. A clipboard dangled next to the metal door behind her.

The door opened, giving me a glimpse of a corridor on the other side before my stalker walked in and handed something to the woman. My phone. Panic shot through me as she slipped it into the pocket of her leather jacket. This wasn't a rescue.

I staggered to my feet, ready to push my way past them to the door, but a pair of arms wrapped around me from behind, preventing my escape. I recognized the plaid shirt covering those arms. It belonged to the other Fallen Guardian. I was trapped in this room with all three of them.

I thrashed like a fish caught on a line. I threw my weight down, hoping to slip free, but his arms tightened around me, pressing my arms into my ribcage. I stomped on his boot as hard as I could. He didn't budge. I stomped on it again and again, but nothing happened. He didn't make a sound. He didn't show any reaction at all.

"It won't do any good," the woman said. "You can't hurt him."

I tipped my head forward then slammed it back into his face, ready for the pain and the sickening smack of bone and flesh colliding, but he absorbed the impact. It was almost as if the bones of his face softened to endure the blow.

I thrashed harder. When I still couldn't free myself, I took a deep breath, filling my lungs with air. The woman held up her hand, and the scream lodged in my throat.

"No screaming. Not yet."

Icy blue eyes watched as my body bucked and writhed in an attempt to breathe. When she let up, I gasped for air, coughing and gagging on it, and tears welled up in my eyes. I didn't want to die. Not like this.

"You certainly don't look like a Guardian." Her gaze traveled from my head down to my toes and back. "I suppose that's fitting though. We're given our treasure in jars of clay. So what treasure do you hold inside? What's your Gift?"

I clenched my teeth together and put as much defiance into my expression as I could.

Her lips curved into a smile. "You've paid attention during training. Good girl."

When she glanced back at my stalker, he shifted on his feet and lowered his eyes. As if I needed more proof she was the alpha of the pack.

"What's your name?" she asked me.

The tension eased from my body. The situation wasn't as bad as I'd thought. She simply wanted to know my name, and what was the big deal anyway? Why did it matter whether she knew my name or not? There had to be a million Kates in the Seattle area. It wasn't like I'd be giving her my address or social security number.

"My name …" I needed to remember something about my name, something Hassan had told me, but the fog drifting through my head made it hard to think.

"Yes, your name. My name is Eden, and this is Benny." She gestured to the guy by the door. "See how easy it is? Nothing to worry about. We're getting to know each other, that's all. I just want to know who you are."

The fog permeated my head, separating one thought from another until I had trouble connecting them. I could sense something else there—something in the fog reaching toward me, trying to touch me—and I shuddered. It had the same slimy feel to it that Benny had given off the day I saw him on the bus.

My eyes went to him. It had to be his Gift. He was using it to make me cooperate.

Anger helped dispel the fog, and I glared at him. I wasn't buying what he was selling. I wasn't even listening to the sales pitch anymore.

Eden looked back at him, and he shook his head.

"Well, we tried to be nice about it." She motioned Benny forward. "We tried to take the lid off and have a peek, but sometimes you have to break the jar to find out what's inside."

When Benny moved toward me, I kicked at him, but the guy hanging onto me squeezed, drawing a yelp as my arms got way too personal with my ribcage. Benny placed his hands on either side of my head, and the fog billowed in, filled with a thousand slimy things worming into my skull. I could feel their eagerness to burrow deep and numb every protest, mute every thought of resistance they came across.

I fought the haze stealing over my mind. I fought it with everything I had in me, and a tingle ran across my scalp a moment before static electricity snapped at his fingers. He jerked his hands away and stared at me, eyes wide.

His eyes grew even wider, and he stumbled back from me, his hands at his throat as he gasped for air.

Eden watched his struggle with the same lack of emotion she'd watched me with. I squirmed to get free even though I had no clue how to help him.

"Stop! Stop it!"

Benny hit the ground and went still, and I squeezed my eyes shut to block it out. I shouldn't be here. I should be at home writing an English lit paper or working on calculus problems. I should be worrying about things normal teenage girls worried about, not witnessing a man be supernaturally strangled to death.

When I opened my eyes, she was watching me, her head tilted to the side. "You wanted me to stop. Why?"

"Why? You were killing him."

"He's a Fallen Guardian. He tried to get inside your head."

"That doesn't mean you should kill him."

She stared at me, her face blank. Then a smile slowly worked its way across her mouth, the kind of smile that said she was laughing at me.

"Where did they find you? A Guardian who doesn't want to kill." She shook her head, chasing her smile away with the motion. "You'll change your mind soon enough. And don't be upset about Benny. He'll be fine in a few minutes. I can't be too angry with him right now. I sent him out on an errand last week, and he found me a Guardian. He even helped me track her down. It's enough to save his life today."

My gaze went to the figure on the floor. I detected a faint rise and fall of his chest. Then Eden stepped closer, bringing the odor of stale earth with her, and I shrank back.

"You, however, have not done enough to save your life. You can either answer my questions, or you can die a very painful death. It's up to you."

You always wanted to think you'd do the right thing

when the moment came, that you'd find the courage to be a hero, but reality was different. Staying alive seemed more noble than standing my ground.

"Your Gift," she demanded. "Tell me what your Gift is."

The sour taste of fear flooded my mouth.

She reached for me, her *Pur* an oily black flame against her wrist. I tried kicking again, but the guy holding me squeezed so hard that I could have sworn I heard a rib crack. I cried out.

Her hand closed around my throat, and I braced myself for the terror of suffocation, but she let me breathe. She let me scream. My shriek split the air as fire ripped through my body, leaving agony in its wake.

The fire burned on and on as I screamed, and when she finally took her hand away, my knees buckled. Only my captor kept me upright. I sagged forward in his arms, my entire body quivering. Such incredible pain. I had never felt anything like it. Every nerve, every cell in my body burned in the aftermath of her fire.

Benny began to stir, and I wanted to beg him to hurry, to wake up and do something. I wanted to believe he would help me. That someone would help me. Hassan should've realized by now I wasn't safe. Why didn't he call? Why didn't Nathan Know what was happening?

"Tell me," Eden said. "And you won't have to hurt anymore."

I dreaded the horrible death that was coming, but I couldn't give her what she wanted. I couldn't let this happen to my mom or anyone else I cared about. If the only thing I could do before I died was refuse to speak, then that was what I had to do.

She must have seen it on my face. She reached for me again.

Ignoring the pain in my ribcage, I squirmed to break free from my captor. He'd been holding on to me for a long time. His arms had to be tired by now. But no matter how much I struggled, he held tight. I whimpered as Eden grabbed my throat.

I didn't think it could get worse than what she'd already done, but it did. I became a living flame. All I wanted was to escape the agony. I wanted it to end. My prayer—for death, for anything that would free me—was a single word. *Please.*

My throat was raw from screaming by the time she stopped. I slumped forward, moaning as aftershocks of fire prickled through my limbs.

Benny had managed to get to his feet, and he leaned against the door. He was in no shape to help me, but I looked at him anyway, pleading with him to do something. His gaze slid to the floor as Eden grabbed a handful of my hair and yanked my head back.

"If you tell me what I want to know, the pain stops. If you don't, it's going to get much worse."

She lifted her other hand, and fear ripped through me the way fire had a moment ago.

"No! I don't know. I don't have one."

"You don't have a Gift yet?"

"No," I sobbed.

"When were you called?"

"A week … two weeks ago."

She let go of my hair and took a step back. I moaned again, but from a different sort of pain. The ache I felt came as disappointment crushed the tiny bit of self-respect I had for myself. My failure as a Guardian was official now.

My phone rang, and hope rose in my chest. If anyone could trace a cell phone, Mike could. They would find me now. They had to find me.

Eden pulled my phone from her pocket and checked the screen. Satisfaction swarmed across her features. She tapped the screen, held the phone to her ear, and listened for a moment.

"No, sorry, it's not Kate. But thanks for giving me her name, Nathan. I don't suppose you want to give me her last name too."

I started to cry for help, but she cut off my air. It came out as nothing more than a guttural choke.

"Of course it's Eden. Didn't you Know I was coming?" Glacial blue eyes fixed on me. "Oh, she's fine. Kate and I have been getting acquainted. Your new Guardian has a lot of promise. She's holding up quite well."

I tried to call out again, but with the same result.

"Don't worry. I won't kill her. I've been wanting to get in touch with you, and she's made that possible. I'm also very curious to see what her Gift will be. She doesn't look like much, but she was able to resist Benny."

I really didn't like the way she looked at me then, as if a frog on the dissecting table had a better chance of keeping its organs intact than I did.

"Well, it's been nice talking to you, Nathan, but I have to go. I have a few things to take care of before we get together. There's something you should take care of too. You really need to tell your new Guardian the truth. I don't think she fully understands the situation yet."

She ended the call. Had it been long enough for Mike to trace my phone? Would they get here before it was too late?

"It looks like you've done something to earn your life after all."

My life had been spared, but it wasn't over. I sobbed as her hand closed around my throat.

CHAPTER
TWELVE

Losing consciousness would've been a mercy. The best my mind could do was detach itself from the pain.

When mind and body reconnected, I was lying on the floor again and my phone was ringing. I thought about not answering, about not getting up ever again. I wanted to roll over, curl into a ball, and stop existing. But I couldn't manage even that much.

The phone continued to ring as I stared at the pipes overhead. Finally the ringing stopped.

A fresh round of tears welled up. They rolled down my temples and dripped into my hair. No one had prepared me for this, for what it felt like to suffocate. What it felt like to have every cell in your body become its own inferno. To be in so much pain your mind had to turn away. To know you were alone and there was nothing you could do to stop it.

Why choose me to be a Guardian? I had nothing to offer, and nothing could possibly make this worthwhile.

My phone rang again, but I stared at the pipes and cried. Eventually the phone quit ringing.

I could give up. I could shut out everything and everyone and find a safe corner in the back of my mind to hide. Or I could cling to the tiny bit of sanity I had left. I could reach for my phone and deal with what had happened. I really wasn't sure which to choose. Insanity seemed like the better option right now.

When my phone rang, I reached for it.

"Yeah," I croaked.

"Kate." Relief saturated Nathan's voice. "Are you okay? Is Eden there?"

"She's gone."

"Where are you?"

"I don't know. Some room … a building."

"You need to get out of there. Can you do that? Can you walk?"

I gave serious consideration to his question. My body felt like it had been used as a speed bump, but I was fairly sure it still worked. "I think so."

"Get moving, Kate. I don't trust her. She may change her mind and come back for you. Figure out where you are and call me. Hurry."

I ended the call and struggled to sit up. Pain stabbed my side. The muscles of my arms and legs were still smoldering, but just the remnants of Eden's fire motivated me to keep trying. I begged my body to get off the floor, and finally, trembling from the effort, I maneuvered into a sitting position.

With one hand pressed against my ribs, I climbed to my feet using the wall for support. It took a couple of wobbly steps before I regained my balance. I pushed the door open and followed the corridor until I emerged in the parking garage that served the office building across from Macy's. We hadn't gone far. Only far enough to avoid any witnesses.

I called Nathan and told him my location.

"You'll be safer on the move," he said. "Can you make it to Vincent's Café?"

"Probably."

"I'll be at Vincent's in five minutes."

The parking garage looked safe enough, but I followed Hassan's instructions from earlier. I left the garage and used the sidewalk so I would have a better chance of seeing anyone coming toward me. The rain pounded against the walkway and made it hard to hear, so my eyes scanned every possible hiding place for movement. It hurt to breathe, and it hurt to walk, but I was prepared to run if I needed to. I only hoped my body would cooperate if I did.

By the time I reached the parking lot of Vincent's Café, my clothes were soaked all the way through, and my teeth were chattering. Nathan paced beneath the eaves, and as soon as he spotted me, he ran to grab a blanket from the back of his car. He wrapped it around me as he helped me into the passenger seat.

Once he got in, he started the car and cranked the heat. He turned toward me to assess the damage, and my gaze dropped to my lap. The grim set to his features told me how bad I looked. I might not have a single mark on me, not one he could see, but that didn't mean the damage was invisible. Thankfully, he didn't ask what had happened.

"Do you want me to drive you home so you can change?"

I thought about it for a moment then shook my head. "Too hard to explain."

But how would I explain the wet clothes? Or why I'd been gone for so long? What time was it anyway?

A glance at the clock on Nathan's dashboard revealed my ordeal had taken a very short time. Not the eternity it had felt like. I had another five minutes or so before Mom would call or text wanting to know when I planned to come back. Not enough time to get dry though.

"What if you throw those clothes in the dryer?"

When I nodded at his suggestion, Nathan shifted the car into reverse.

"Wait," I said. "I don't have a house key."

"We can use my dryer instead."

He called Hope on the way to his house, and she met us at the front door.

"I set out some dry clothes in the bathroom down the hall," she said. "There are towels and washcloths too, and I'll throw your things in the dryer after you've changed. I have coffee ready, or I can make tea. Whatever you want."

I handed her the damp blanket, headed down the hall, and

shut the bathroom door behind me. I turned the lock then rested my forehead against the door. I wanted to delay the moment when I had to turn and face the mirror, when I had to see the damage for myself.

I pulled my phone from my pocket first. Amazingly enough, it still worked despite the fact it had been dropped, gotten wet, and had Eden's grimy fingers all over it. Her touch had left a smear of mud across one corner.

My hand started to tremble, and I set the phone next to the sink.

When the trembling stopped, I lifted my face to the mirror. I looked the same, and yet I didn't. My fair skin was vampire pale, my dark hair a tangled mess, and my mascara gone, washed away from either rain or tears or both. But these were nothing more than variations of how I appeared every day.

The difference was in the expression I wore. It belonged to a girl who had wandered to the edge of madness and barely made it back. Even worse, I couldn't escape the feeling that I'd lost something along the way. It felt like something had been burned away from me while my body burned. A vital part of me had been stolen, and I would never get it back.

I spun, lifting the toilet seat just in time to empty the contents of my stomach. A second wave of nausea crashed over me, and I dropped down, giving a cry as my knee connected with the wood floor. I moaned as muscles contracted, mercilessly squeezing my ribcage in an effort to purge.

The purge continued until I had nothing except bile and tears left to give, but I continued to kneel, taking ragged breaths, until the nausea passed. When it seemed safe, I pressed down the handle and used the cold porcelain to steady myself as I got up.

I ran cold water in the sink, cupping my hand underneath the faucet so I could rinse out my mouth. I washed my face with more cold water. As I stripped down, I did my best to ignore the angry bruises forming across my arms and ribs. The sweats and hoodie Hope had set out must have been Nathan's because they were way too big for me, but I didn't mind. I liked feeling like I had room to hide.

My phone chimed. I didn't have to look to know the text was from Mom.

Once I changed, I gathered up the towel, the washcloth, and my clothes. I grabbed my phone and unlocked the door. Hope waited for me on the other side.

"I'll put your things in the dryer."

She reached for my clothes, but I clung to them.

"That's okay. I'll do it if you tell me where it is."

"Are you sure you don't want me to do it?"

"Yeah." I reshuffled my load so I wouldn't have to look at her.

"Okay. The dryer is in the mudroom by the garage, and I'll get you something hot to drink while you're doing that. Do you want coffee? Tea? Hot cocoa?"

"Coffee's fine."

"I'll bring it to the front room. Nathan's in there, and he has a dry blanket for you."

I headed for the mudroom and tossed the towel and washcloth into the laundry basket I found there. I threw my Converse into the dryer along with the rest of my clothes and listened to them thump around for a minute while I attempted to get a better grip on my sanity. The one I had didn't feel very firm.

The aroma of coffee scented the air of the front room. I also smelled a hint of wood smoke, and my gaze jumped to the fireplace. There was no fire though. Someone had let it die out.

Nathan followed my gaze. "I thought you might prefer a blanket."

Somehow he knew. In a way, I was grateful I wouldn't have to tell him. But I was also humiliated that he knew about my weakness, my failure.

He sat in one of the chairs next to the front window with a mug of coffee in his hand. Gray light filtered in through the glass panes, falling on him and the side table where another mug of coffee rested. A green fleece blanket waited for me in the chair facing his. I picked it up, wrapping it around me before I eased into the chair and worked my phone hand free. I didn't want to call my mom, but I did anyway.

"I ran into Nathan—Mr. Sorenson." I cleared my throat, but it didn't get rid of the hoarseness completely. "We're going to have a cup of coffee together before I head back."

"You went to meet Mr. Sorenson?"

"No. I didn't plan on it. It just worked out that way."

There was silence on the other end, and my fingers tightened around the phone. She always focused on the little problems because she didn't want to see the big ones. She'd rather freak out over the grease spot on top of the stove than deal with the giant asteroid hurtling toward Earth. She had made it so hard for me to share my small problems with her that now, when my problems were big enough to kill me, there was no hope of confiding in her.

"I'll see you in a little while." I swallowed back tears as I set my phone on the side table.

Nathan held out a mug, and I took it from him, keeping my eyes focused on the liquid inside. The ceramic was warm, not hot—probably Nathan's doing again—but I was okay with drinking lukewarm coffee right now.

We sat for a couple of minutes, sipping from our mugs. I wanted nothing more than to forget what had happened, but there were parts of it we needed to talk about.

"She knows who you are."

He nodded as he swallowed a mouthful of coffee. "Eden and I were Guardians together about twenty years ago. When we were first called."

"That obviously didn't work out."

"No," he said, his voice tight. "It didn't."

There was a mother lode of emotion shoved into those three words. Maybe I wasn't the only one she'd played human torch with.

"There were two guys with her, and I've seen them before. One of them on the bus. She called him Benny."

"Benny Rodriguez. His Gift is Compulsion, and he uses it to convince people to hand over their cash or car keys or to get people to tell him things they shouldn't. He also uses it to convince young women they like him when they don't."

I fought off a shudder. He had checked out every woman on the bus that day and zeroed in on me. Later, when I wasn't so frustrated with her, I would have more appreciation for Mom's paranoia.

"He's at the bottom of the hierarchy when it comes to Fallen Guardians," Nathan said. "He's like the bully's wingman. He gets the bully whatever he or she wants—cash, drugs, information—hoping to get something in return. It could be protection from Guardians or other Fallen. Or maybe a chance to feed off the bully's leftovers."

I felt sick to my stomach again. I could've been considered a leftover today. It didn't seem possible, but things could have been worse.

I gulped a mouthful of coffee hoping the liquid would dilute the acid brewing in my stomach. "There was something wrong with the other guy. I don't know what, but he wasn't … right. She said I couldn't hurt him."

"You can't. He doesn't feel any pain."

"None at all?"

"None."

"Why? Is that his Gift?"

"No. He's simply not capable of feeling pain."

I remembered hearing about that condition—congenital analgesia or something like that. It was one of those things that sounded too bizarre to be true. It made me wonder if I'd managed to hurt him, but he hadn't felt it.

"Who is he?"

"He doesn't have a name," Nathan said. "None except the one inscribed by his master."

I wasn't going to ask what he meant, especially when I needed to ask about other things I probably didn't want to know about.

"So what exactly is Eden's Gift?"

"You can think of her Gift as elemental, although it's a single element—carbon—that she manipulates, not the four elements of earth, wind, water, and fire. She can control the air around you. She can feed you carbon dioxide, starving you of oxygen, or draw carbon monoxide from the air and poison you. If she touches you, she can alter your body chemistry all the way down to the cellular level."

Eden's fire had faded to embers that pulsed with faint heat whenever I moved, but I would remember the agony she'd unleashed on my body long after the embers died out. The memory of the pain would never fade. Neither would my shame.

"I told her what she wanted to know," I said, my voice raw. "I told her I didn't have a Gift."

"You can't punish yourself for that. None of us would have done any better."

I shook my head. Hassan would have. He would've found a way to endure it, and I couldn't bear the thought of facing him again. He already considered me hopeless. I couldn't imagine what he'd think after today.

"I Know what she did." Nathan's eyes were as haunted as mine had been in the mirror. "I was trying to find you. To see where she'd taken you, but the path started in the corridor and led to the room, and I'm only an observer. I couldn't stop it. But I could see it."

My hands tightened around the mug. "What do mean you could see it?"

Had he somehow been there, and I didn't notice? Why didn't he help me if he was there?

"It's difficult to explain how my Gift works," he said.

"For now, think of it as a vision. That's the closest thing. The point I'm trying to make is that Eden came here with a plan. She didn't figure a new Guardian into her plan, and she wanted to know how much of a threat you were before she went ahead with it. What kept you alive today was revealing you don't have a Gift yet."

She figured out I was no threat whatsoever. Who would've guessed being a loser would one day save my life?

"She also said you needed to tell me the truth. The truth about what?"

Nathan set his mug aside and took a deep breath like he was preparing to deliver bad news. I almost told him to stop, that I'd changed my mind. I had a feeling it was going to be worse than anything else he'd told me.

"Some Guardians fall away because a life dedicated to self-sacrifice is incredibly hard. They can't handle the pressure, the fear. Others give in to the temptation of using their Gift for their own gratification. For some, especially for those like Eden with very powerful Gifts, it becomes an addiction. The more they use it, the more they want to use it. The more supernatural power they have, the more they crave it. They want more and more, but they can't create it out of thin air, so they find a way to get it. To get more supernatural power."

"How?"

"They have two sources. Do you remember when I told you some were willing to open themselves up to darkness?"

"Yeah," I said, a knot of apprehension forming in my gut.

"There's a source of supernatural power that has nothing to do with light. It's more than willing to give power in exchange for payment, but the price is high. More than most Fallen Guardians are willing to pay. Especially when there's a source that's much easier to get to."

The knot in my gut tightened. Eden had said that sometimes you had to break the jar to get to what was inside.

"Guardians," I said. "They get it from Guardians."

Nathan's features were drawn with weariness as he
nodded. "We're being hunted."

CHAPTER THIRTEEN

"What do you mean hunted?"

"Your Gift is part of who you are," Nathan said. "The only way to separate a Guardian from their supernatural power is to kill them."

For a moment I couldn't breathe. Fear had stolen the air from my lungs. Then fear transformed into anger so swiftly it gave me a head rush.

"That's a pretty big piece of information to leave out. Nobody thought I might need to know?"

"The reason we didn't tell you is because I Knew you weren't ready to hear it yet."

I started to tell him exactly what I thought about that but stopped. As quickly as my anger had come, it dissipated. He was right. If I had known the truth an hour ago, I wouldn't have made it back from the edge. Not if it meant coming back to a lifetime of looking over my shoulder, a lifetime of living in fear. I wouldn't have answered my phone. I would've found that safe corner in the back of my mind and stayed there.

"Did you Know this was going to happen?"

"No. Only that we needed to hold off on the information for a while."

"So you told everyone to keep me in the dark?"

"I had to."

Even if he'd done it for the sake of my sanity, it still hurt. I knew I sucked as a Guardian, and I didn't want to be one anyway, so it shouldn't bother me I'd been left out. It shouldn't, but it did.

"Being a Guardian isn't easy," Nathan said. "It's a big adjustment, and no one expects you to have a handle on it only two weeks into training. None of us did."

"Lexi did."

"She had more time to get used to the idea, that's all. It's different when you have to live it. Everyone who's called— no matter how long they've been aware of the Guardians— has to take a step of faith. We all have to pass through the fire at some point." He winced. "I'm sorry. Poor choice of words."

"Don't worry about it."

I could feel his gaze on me while I traced a flaw in the mug with my thumb, but he took the hint and moved on.

"The truth is most Fallen are like Benny. They prefer to prey on innocents and avoid Guardians. But others come looking for us. Hunters can get power from other Fallen, but they prefer to take it from Guardians because they like the idea of destroying what God intended for good. In Eden's mind, killing a Guardian not only gives her power, it's symbolic. She rejected her calling. She's supposed to lose. By killing a Guardian, she wins, and she craves that psychological edge as much as she craves supernatural power. Maybe even more."

I shook my head. This was all too surreal. It was like a nightmare you have after staying up watching a *Highlander* marathon.

"You said Benny was at the bottom of the hierarchy. A hierarchy implies more than two, so someone has to be at the top. Is it the hunters, or is there someone else?"

"The ones at the top are those willing to pay the price. They're willing to open up to darkness."

Something surfaced in his eyes, some thought or memory that raised goose bumps along my skin just watching him experience it. He recovered quickly, but it was there long enough for me to decide I didn't need any more information about the hierarchy. If that particular brand of Fallen Guardian frightened Nathan, I couldn't even begin to speculate how much they would terrify me. He'd been right to spoon feed me the truth.

I set my mug on the side table and returned to what I hoped was a safer topic. "So what happens now with Eden?"

"We figure out what she has planned. We find her, and we stop her."

As in stop her heart from beating. They wouldn't be sending her to the King County jail. It made me sick to my stomach to think about someone ending her life, but I was beginning to understand why.

"So if she's a hunter," I said, "then she came here to hunt, right? Not that I'm complaining, but why didn't she kill me?"

"Part of it's the psychological edge. She played God. She had your life in her hands and chose whether you lived or died. What worries me is the part about wanting to see what your Gift will be. As much as I'd like to think it was nothing more than curiosity, Eden wouldn't let that get in the way of what she wants. She's driven to the point of obsession. She'll adjust her plan now because of you, but she'll try to do it in a way that increases her chance of success. It's more than curiosity, but I don't know what. I haven't had time to find any answers yet, and I need to talk to Hassan and Kenji and see what they think."

"Kenji? Who's that?"

"Lexi's dad. His Gift is Memory. He's the closest thing we have to a Guardian database, but he's also a very logical and insightful man. I'll have to give him a call and pick his brain for a while. We need answers."

I rubbed my forehead. All these unknowns made my head hurt. How was I supposed to make sense of anything when my world was in constant flux? Kate the college student and Kate the Guardian recruit had stumbled into each other, and neither of them knew how to stay on her feet.

"What am I supposed to do?" My voice cracked. "How

am I supposed to go to school? Or do anything? They know what bus I ride, and they had my phone. What if they figure out where I live? Or where my mom works?"

Nathan did that unfocused thing with his eyes, and weariness cut even deeper into his features when he refocused. "You're safe. She let us know she's here. Now she wants us to find her."

It didn't reassure me. There were too many gaps in Nathan's Knowledge for my comfort. He hadn't Known about Benny finding me or Eden planning to visit. Or had he? Maybe he'd kept that information from me too.

"How are you going to find her?"

"She'll have set up camp somewhere around here. It'll be a location rich in carbon—plenty of plant life and earth available, a building with land around it—so we search places around Redmond that would provide what she wants."

"Marymoor Park is right across from Redmond Town Center. It has a bunch of unoccupied buildings."

He nodded. "It would give her access to the Sammamish River trail too. I doubt we'll find her, but we need to take a look anyway."

My heart stuttered in panic. "Now?"

"Probably tomorrow evening. Eden is still working on whatever she has planned, so we have a little time. Not much, but enough to wait a day or two and prepare ourselves as much as possible. I want to talk to Kenji first, and we need to wait for Hassan. He's the one who takes the lead in these situations in both the planning and the execution. He'll need time to gather information, and nighttime provides the best conditions for him to use his Gift."

My phone rang, and I groaned when I checked the number. I forced myself to answer. "Hey, Mom, I—"

"How much longer are you going to be? I thought you had a paper to write."

"We're just finishing up. I'll be back in a few minutes."

"How many minutes? Five? Ten?"

"Twenty minutes. A half hour at the most, okay? See you then." The problem with cell phones was you couldn't slam down the receiver when you were done. "I gotta go."

I left the blanket in the chair and headed for the mudroom. When I opened the dryer, the smell of wet canvas and hot rubber billowed out. I carried everything back to the bathroom to change. My Converse were still damp, but at least they didn't ooze water anymore.

Hope waited in the hallway again when I emerged, and she took the loaner sweats from me, tucking them under one arm. With her other arm, she reached out and gently pulled me close, as if she knew it wouldn't take much to hurt me. For a few seconds I stood there. Then, without me giving them permission, my arms found their way around her, and I clung to her. I didn't care if it made my side hurt.

The hugs I knew—the real hugs—were confined to memory, something distant and hazy and tied up in the scraps of childhood my brain had managed to hang on to. Those hugs couldn't compare to having one as an adult. When you were a kid, you didn't realize how much you needed them.

"Everything will be okay," she said. "I don't know how, but it will be."

She obviously didn't have Nathan's Gift, but I needed the hug and didn't want to hurt her feelings, so I nodded. She let me go then, and I followed Nathan out to his car.

He pulled into the parking lot behind the agency a few minutes later. I tried to keep my movement smooth as I twisted to unbuckle my seat belt, but Nathan noticed the hesitation.

"I thought you were moving slow because you were in shock, but you're hurt, aren't you? More than what Eden did."

"I think I might have a cracked rib," I admitted.

"If you need a doctor, we can—"

"No. No doctor. I'll be fine."

Even if I had a cracked rib, there wasn't much they could

do about it, and I couldn't imagine how I would explain the bruises.

Nathan frowned but didn't argue. "You'll be sitting out tomorrow night. You need time to heal, and you need more training."

There was a little disappointment mixed in with my relief, although I couldn't understand why. "Okay, but you'll tell me what happens, right?"

"I'll tell you everything you want to know."

I caught the qualifier in his statement. If nothing else, today I'd learned to pay attention to the wording of anything a Guardian said and to pay attention to what they didn't say. I suspected Nathan and Hassan were the worst offenders in the group. Nathan because he was concerned about my sanity. Hassan because he was Hassan.

I maneuvered out of the Subaru and headed for the front of the building, my jaw clenched against the agony each step caused. Before opening the door, I molded my expression into something that resembled normal, or at least I attempted to. Considering Mom's reaction as I strolled into the agency, I wasn't even close.

"What's wrong?" she breathed.

I grasped at the shred of truth that worked in my favor. "My stomach is really bothering me. I was thinking I could borrow the car and come back for you at five-thirty."

I should have done that in the first place, but of course I only thought of it now. After my life had fallen apart.

"You don't feel well?" She slowly rose to her feet. "Should I call the doctor?"

"No, I don't need a doctor. I just need to go home. I'll be fine."

Worry and indecision scurried back and forth across her features. She wanted to believe everything was okay, but fear wouldn't leave her in peace.

She straightened her blazer, tugging it into place then brushing it flat with her hands. "I don't think it's a good idea for you to spend so much time with Mr. Sorenson. He's much older than you, and he's married. Why does he have so much interest in a girl half his age? There's no reason for it. No good reason."

"It's not like that. You don't have to worry about Nathan—Mr. Sorenson. Really. We had coffee, and we talked. His wife was there and everything."

She glanced around as if to make sure we were alone then lowered her voice anyway. "Is it because you need a father figure in your life? Is that why you want to spend time with him?"

I was so not in the mood to drive down that worn out, potholed, completely dead end road. Dad had made it very clear he didn't want to be a part of our family, so why did she always have to drag him back into it?

"No, it doesn't have anything to do with Dad. It was a cup of coffee and conversation. That's it. So can I pick you up later?"

She tugged on her blazer again. "I suppose."

I didn't stay and reassure her. I didn't have it in me. I headed for Cliff's office, picked up my copy of *Pride and Prejudice* from the desk, and stuffed it in my backpack. Mom walked in as I reached for the zipper.

"Katarina! What is that?"

My hand froze, giving her an unobstructed view of the evidence, and I sighed. It was pointless to try to hide my *Pur* now that she'd seen it.

"What have you done to yourself?"

I finished zipping my backpack, stalling as I searched for the part of the truth she could handle. I doubted even Nathan would Know the answer to this one.

"Is this because of your new friends? Did they talk you into it?"

"No," I groaned.

"Are you taking drugs?"

"No!"

"I knew this would happen. I should never have let you—"

"*Mom*. Just stop, okay? I'm eighteen years old. You can't keep making decisions for me. You need to let me do it myself, and you need to deal with whatever I decide. Even if I mess things up. The fact that someone has a tattoo doesn't mean they're taking drugs, and it doesn't mean I'm jumping on the express lane to the underworld with Ty. I'm not Ty. I'm Kate, the child who actually has a set of morals, so could you stop freaking out over everything?"

I immediately wanted to take it all back. For a moment, she verged on tears. Then her expression froze over, and any hope I had of being forgiven perished beneath a layer of ice.

I lifted my backpack from the desk. "I'll be back by five-thirty."

CHAPTER
FOURTEEN

When I got to the house, I dropped my backpack by the front door, kicked off my Converse, and turned up the thermostat. My phone rang, and I wanted to kill whoever was calling because bending to get it out of my backpack sent a fresh spasm of misery through my side.

The screen displayed Jackson's number, and I let it go to voicemail. The house phone rang next, but I didn't answer.

I downed a couple of ibuprofen to dull the throbbing taking place in multiple body parts then headed to my room to grab clean clothes. What I needed was to wash off my total nightmare of a day. At first I only ran cold, but as I watched icy water funnel down the drain, frustration worked its way up to the surface again, and I turned on the hot water too. Eden had taken enough from me already. I refused to let her take any more.

After I dried my hair and put on makeup, I listened to voicemail. Both Jackson and Lexi had left messages. There were no new disasters. They had simply called to check on me. While I appreciated their concern, I couldn't handle talking to anyone right now, so I sent a text to let them know I was okay.

I threw on a hoodie and a dry pair of Converse then grabbed my phone, wallet, and Mom's car keys. I turned down the thermostat on my way out.

The rain had stopped, but black clouds smothered the sky, bringing the day to an early and thoroughly depressing end. It was dark when I pulled in behind the agency where three parking stalls had to share space with a dumpster and the delivery entrance for Torrero's restaurant. Mr. Torrero's Mercedes took up the two far spots beneath the building's floodlight, so I squeezed into the one between his Mercedes and the dumpster. I slid from the driver's seat and reached for the door, jerking my hand away when static electricity snapped me. My gaze traveled from my hand to the car door and back.

I'd been so focused on trying to survive and then processing everything Nathan said that I'd forgotten about what happened with Benny. Compared to rest of my afternoon, a little static shock fell at the bottom of the list, and I didn't feel like talking to Nathan anymore today. I'd mention it to him some other time. Maybe.

Mom didn't acknowledge me when I set the keys on her desk. I wanted to apologize, but I figured the safest thing for me to do was keep my mouth shut. I'd already said too much.

I waited while she turned off lights and locked the door then I followed her out to the car. I turned my face away so she wouldn't see my jaw clench as I bent to get in the passenger seat or when I grabbed for the seat belt.

The gloom outside reflected the gloom inside the car, and we only drove a couple of blocks before I couldn't stand it anymore. I might need some space, but this wasn't the way I wanted to get it.

"I'm sorry for what I said."

She didn't reply. She concentrated on the road in front of us, and I prayed she would hear me, that she would hear the need underneath my words.

"I didn't do it on purpose. I mean I didn't do it because I wanted to upset you. It wasn't a rebellion thing. But I know how you feel about stuff like tattoos. You had every right to be upset, and I shouldn't have yelled at you."

She stared straight ahead, her features rigid, and my heart began to wilt. I blinked away tears as I turned to watch buildings pass by.

She went straight to her room when we got home, closing the door behind her. I poured myself a bowl of sugar-coated corn flakes to go with my guilt and sat in front of the TV. It didn't take long to lose interest in both my cereal and sci-fi reruns.

My body protested as I got up from the couch to take my half-eaten dinner to the kitchen and pour it down the garbage disposal. Putting my bowl and spoon in the dishwasher seemed to require way more effort than usual. I tried to work on my English lit paper, but my brain kept sending those automated "out of office" replies, so I gave up, took more ibuprofen, and went to bed.

I lay in bed aching from the inside out, exhausted but afraid to close my eyes because I knew nightmares would come as soon as I did. But sleep pulled at me stronger than fear, and my eyes had just drifted closed when my phone rang.

I wanted to ignore it, but knowing my luck, whoever was calling would keep at it until I answered. With a sigh, I threw back the covers, sending a sharp twinge across my ribs. I growled in pain and irritation as I climbed to my feet.

I snatched the phone from my desk and checked the number on the screen. Hassan. He'd probably called to yell at me for not running fast enough this afternoon. For some mentally disturbed reason, I answered anyway.

After our initial greeting, he didn't say anything, and I shifted on my feet. He didn't even have to be in the same room to make me squirm.

"So you talked to Nathan?" I said.

"Yes. He told me what happened."

I waited for the yelling to start, but it didn't.

I took the phone and crawled back into bed, giving him time to get around to the lecture, but another minute ticked by with nothing more than a couple of yips from the neighbor's terrier. Maybe he hadn't called to yell at me after all. At least not tonight. But why call if the lecture was on hold?

Maybe ... Hassan was more human than I'd thought. After getting the details from Nathan, it was possible that even someone like Hassan might be able to scrounge up a drop or two of compassion. But having the capacity to be human didn't mean he liked it or that it was easy for him to express his humanity. Maybe he needed a little help.

"The answer is no. I'm not okay."

He still didn't say anything, but I knew he'd heard me.

"I thought I was going to die. There was a point when I wanted to die. I was scared and alone, and it hurt." My voice wavered on the last word. I sucked in a breath hoping to steady it, but pain bit in to my side, making my breath catch. I let it out carefully. "Today was pretty much the worst day of my life. But I'm young, right? There's plenty of time to have one that's worse."

It was a lame attempt at humor, and neither of us laughed. We both knew my life expectancy had taken a plunge the moment I became a Guardian.

"I'm sorry," I said.

"Why are you sorry?"

Wasn't it obvious? "Because I failed. I didn't run fast enough. I told her what she wanted to know."

"You think you failed."

"I know I did. I'm sorry."

"Don't say that again. You are not a failure."

If this was an offer of forgiveness, I accepted. And judging from the tone of his response, he'd maxed out his "human" limit, so I moved on before he could change his mind.

"Is it your turn to pick me up from the bus tomorrow?"

"You're not coming with us," he said.

"I didn't mean to look for Eden. I meant for training."

"You don't have to come tomorrow."

"I want to. I need to. I need for all of this to make sense, and you guys are the only ones who can help me do that. I can't talk to my mom, and my dad won't talk to me. My brother … well, it's not worth it with him, and I can't tell my best friend either. I don't have anyone else." I smoothed a wrinkle from my comforter. "So are you picking me up or what?"

He was quiet, probably trying to figure out how to get rid of the disaster of a Guardian he was stuck with. He'd called to see if I'd survived, not get my emotional issues dumped on him.

"It's okay if you don't want to," I said. "I know you just got back, and you have a lot to do tomorrow."

"I'll be there." He said it like I'd insulted him.

I smoothed another wrinkle from my comforter, reluctant for the conversation to end. There had to be something wrong with my head if talking to Hassan appealed to me more than sleep. "I guess I'll see you tomorrow then."

He told me good night and followed it with something in Arabic.

"What did you say?"

"Sleep in peace."

I swallowed, but my voice still sounded thick when I spoke. "Thanks."

There was a slight hesitation before he said, "Don't be late."

Then he hung up on me.

After Hassan hung up on me, I turned off my phone. I was dead to the world until my alarm went off the next morning. When I got out of bed, moving didn't cause the agony I expected. My side felt sore, but the worst of the pain was gone. The same went for my knee, and faint yellow-green marked my arms and torso rather than angry plum. It was amazing what a good night's rest could do for a body.

When I turned on my phone, I had voicemail from Jackson and Lexi and a text from Mike, but I didn't have time to respond. Not unless I wanted to walk to the bus stop instead of having Mom drop me off on her way to work. I hurried out to the car.

Clouds of gunmetal gray smeared the sky, but they seemed to be in a penitent mood after what they'd done to me yesterday. They kept the rain to themselves while I waited for the bus.

I had a couple minutes to spare, so I called Jackson. The first thing he said was, "Are you okay?"

"Yeah, I'm ... I'll be fine."

"I couldn't believe it when Nathan called yesterday. If I'd known, I would've insisted you come by for a workout."

"Yeah. Me too."

"We'll find her. I promise you that. She won't hurt you or anyone else again."

The horror of yesterday began to trickle into the calm I'd enjoyed so far this morning. "I should go. My bus will be here any second. Tell Lexi I'll call her after chem lab, okay?"

Once the bus arrived, I found a seat and sent a text to Mike. I then read the intro for today's lab, hoping my brain would be too preoccupied with ionic equations to think about yesterday.

When I made it back to the Eastside, Hassan was waiting for me. Usually he stood beside the car, but today he waited at the top of the stairs. His chai-colored complexion looked heavy on the milk, emphasizing the shadows under his eyes, and a couple of curls were less than perfectly aligned with the rest of his hair. For Hassan, he was a mess.

"Are you okay?" I said as I stopped in front of him.

"I'm fine. Why do you ask?"

"Well, you don't look very good. I mean, you look good." Heat rushed to my cheeks. "But you look like you don't feel very good."

"I'm fine," he said in his "you've just insulted me" tone.

"Okay."

As he studied my face, some emotion I'd never seen from him before settled onto his features. It made his eyes even darker against his washed-out skin.

"Are you sure you're okay?" I said.

"I should never have gone to New York. You're my responsibility, and you're not fully trained. I should have stayed here."

A profession of guilt was the last thing I'd expected. For whatever reason, I didn't like guilt coming from Hassan.

"No offense, but I don't think it would've made any difference."

"I should have been here," he insisted.

"And done what? It didn't matter where you were. Even if you'd been home, you wouldn't have gotten to me in time. There was no way you could've stopped what happened. No one could." I had to look away from him then. I couldn't handle the pain or pity or whatever it was that filled his eyes. "And I really don't want to talk about it anymore, so can we go?" I stepped around him and headed for the Audi.

"You said last night you wanted to talk about it."

"I changed my mind."

I got in the passenger seat, thankful it didn't hurt too much to do so, and Hassan came shortly after. He didn't start the car right away though. Out of the corner of my eye, I could see him watching me. I studied traffic on 520 and tried not to squirm.

With a shake of his head, he started the Audi and pulled onto Yarrow Point Road. "We will have to work twice as hard as before."

I muffled a sigh. Maybe I should have let him feel guilty. I could've used it for a day or two of easy training.

"You weren't prepared for what happened. You need to spend more time training, and you need to begin with weapons."

"No."

His head whipped around so fast I thought he'd drive off the road. "No?"

"No. I'm not doing weapons."

"You're a Guardian."

"Show me where it says in the Guardian handbook I have to use a gun."

"There is no Guardian handbook."

"Then I'm not using one."

Dark eyes impaled me for a second. Then he turned his face to the windshield and stepped on the gas. The Audi shot forward. He did a perfect impression of *The Transporter* through the side streets and flew through the gates of the driveway while they were still opening. There couldn't have been more than a micron of space on either side. I scrunched my eyes shut and cringed, waiting for the screech of metal on metal, but it never came. Only the screech of rubber as the Audi skidded to a stop in the garage.

"Get out," he ordered, and I scrambled to obey.

I didn't even have time to close the door before he came around to my side, and I took two steps back as he descended on me. How was it that Hassan, who was several inches shorter than Jackson, could seem so much bigger?

"Do you want to die?" he said.

"Of course not, but—"

"Then you have to be prepared. You have to be able to defend yourself."

"So teach me how to defend myself without a gun."

Color flooded his face, and he grabbed the passenger door with both hands, flinging it shut. The car rocked from the impact. "Why must you argue with everything I say?"

"Because you never listen! Because you always think you're right, but you're not, and I'm not using a gun, Hassan."

My heart jumped as he took a step forward. I took a step back—away from the violence radiating from him—and my hands came up in an attempt to hold him off.

"I can't even step on a spider," I said, my tone shifting from defiance to pleading. "There's no way I'll be able to use a gun on someone. I told you, there's been a mistake. I'm the wrong person for this job."

He grabbed my arm and yanked back the sleeve of my hoodie to reveal my *Pur*. "There is no mistake. You are the one who refuses to accept who you are, who refuses to accept the truth. You might as well leave now and become Fallen." He shoved my arm back at me. "Stop wasting my time and make your choice."

He walked off, and the door to the house slammed shut behind him, reverberating through the garage.

CHAPTER
FIFTEEN

I stood in the garage and tried to decide which urge took priority—the one that said I should huddle into a ball and cry or the one that told me to leave size seven dents all over the Audi. I settled for hiding downstairs in the locker room until I could figure out what to do.

I grabbed my backpack from the car then opened the door to the house far enough to peek inside. The hallway was Hassan-free, so I crept in and slipped downstairs. I sank down onto the locker room bench and pulled back my sleeve expecting to see indentations where Hassan had grabbed my arm. I saw nothing more than fair skin marked by a *Pur*, and I glared at it.

After five minutes of unrestrained self-pity, I got up and changed into my sweats, although I wasn't sure why.

I went to the training room, leaned against the wall, and slid down to the floor. Maybe I would just sit here until I gathered enough courage to go upstairs and ask Lexi or Jackson for a ride back to the bus stop.

The door to the training room opened a couple minutes later, and Hassan strode in, already dressed for the night ahead in a black t-shirt and military-style cargo pants. They made him appear even more dangerous than usual. Like the last bit of his civility had been discarded.

He sat next to me and rested his arms on his knees, a relaxed pose I knew was deceptive. If an intruder somehow made it as far as the training room, he'd be up and have dealt with them before I even realized someone was there.

The only thing he hadn't changed was his watch. The sign of wealth on his wrist contrasted with the scars on his hands and arm. Two smooth spots on the knuckles of his left hand suggested the skin had been scraped off at one point. He had two scars on the side of his right hand, below his thumb, and three more on his forearm. The scars were long and thin, barely the width of a thread. They were the kind you got from a really sharp knife. I had a similar scar on my finger, but I doubted Hassan got his from a kitchen knife.

I glanced over to find him back to his usual irritated expression.

Why couldn't Jackson be my teacher? I'd never seen him get slightly ruffled about anything or anyone except Lexi. He knew how to push me without pushing too hard, and he never took my crappy attitude personally. Hassan could take a compliment like an insult, and with the exception of the very first day, he'd spent every training session pushing me to the point I was ready to poke his eyes out.

But as my gaze ran across his scars again, I understood why I was stuck with Hassan for a teacher instead of Jackson.

"I don't want to be a Fallen Guardian," I said.

"I know you don't. But you have to trust me."

"I do trust you. I know you're my best chance of staying alive. But you grew up with this kind of stuff. I didn't. The only violence I know is either on TV or it's something my brother does, and he only does it to annoy me." I kneaded the line of tension forming across my forehead. "The whole point of spending the next decade in school is so I can help people live longer, not help them check out early. I want to make things better. I want to make a difference in a good way. Not by learning to kill someone."

"It's not always about death."

"Isn't it? That's all I've heard about for the last two weeks. We have to take a life to save one and somehow avoid getting killed while we do it."

"Life is about life and death," he said, scowling at me. "It always has been. It's another truth you have to face."

I tipped my head back against the wall with a groan. "You have got to be the most irritating person I've ever met."

"And you are the most difficult person I have ever met. You argue and complain all the time. You get your feelings hurt over stupid things, and when you should be crying, you don't. You refuse."

Why? Why Hassan? You'd think that if God wanted me to be a Guardian, he could at least give me a teacher who didn't make me want to quit every single day, someone who didn't take shots at my already low self-esteem.

"Defending yourself doesn't always mean killing someone," he said, "but if you don't know what you're doing, you may end up with the same result. If you're so determined not to kill, then stop arguing about it and learn how to use a weapon." He muttered a few words in Arabic that sounded uncomplimentary. "You always have to argue about everything."

"You already said that."

"You ask too many questions, and you question everything we do. You make everything more difficult than it has to be." He exhaled, a hissing sound weighted with frustration, but it served to release some of the anger from his voice when he spoke again. "Perhaps this is why you were sent to us."

"What do you mean?"

"Because you hesitate. Because you don't want to do this. Maybe you were sent to remind us that being a Guardian is not about death. It's about preserving life."

I picked at a hole in the knee of my sweats. The thought that there might be a reason for all of this was enough to bring tears, but I willed them away. I picked at my sweats until I had myself under control.

"I can't do the weapon thing, Hassan. I just ... can't."

I could sense his anger simmering dangerously close to

the surface again, but all he said was, "We will discuss it some other time."

He shifted his weight, extending one leg in front of him, and I waited for the scent of his cologne to drift to me. It didn't. In fact, it had been missing ever since he picked me up. The subtle blend of musk and spice had become familiar, and I would forever associate it with Hassan. It possessed the same restrained intensity he did. He'd worn it every single day I'd come, so why not today?

Because of tonight. He didn't want the scent to give him away.

"Has Nathan been able to figure out what Eden is planning?" I said.

"No. Only that she has learned how to take a Guardian's Gift, not just their power."

"How?"

"The same way she takes their power. She kills them."

"No, I mean how did she learn to do that?"

"That's one of the questions we must answer."

"Does Nathan Know she can take someone's Gift? Did it pop into his head or something?"

I wasn't really sure what happened during those moments when Nathan's eyes lost focus. He'd said it was like a vision, but I didn't know how visions worked either. Did it play like a video clip in his mind? Could he see the past and the future, or was he restricted to the present?

"A Guardian was killed earlier this year," Hassan said. "One who was able to neutralize other Gifts on a temporary basis. It was assumed he drew power away from Fallen Guardians so they were unable to use their Gifts. Now Nathan and Kenji think this Guardian may have acted as a conduit. He would assimilate those Gifts for a time then release them. When Kenji mentioned this Guardian, Nathan Knew Eden had killed him and that when she absorbed his power, it changed her."

"Why would it change her?"

He shrugged. "How she acquired this ability is not our concern at the moment. It simply means she will be more eager to hunt now."

"Does she know what you guys can do? What your Gifts are?"

"That may be why she's here. To find out."

"If I were a hunter, I'd want your Gift. I'd go after Lexi next."

"I would do the same."

It didn't make me feel better that we agreed for once. I hated the idea of Eden hunting either one of them, but Hassan had survived assassins, and Lexi had been training her whole life. That had to count for something. And if you added their Gifts into the equation, they were probably the two most capable of defending themselves.

I did my best to ignore the troublesome thought wringing its hands in the back of my mind, the one reminding me Eden would be interested in my Gift too. Knowing my luck, I'd end up with something spectacular and land at the top of her shopping list.

"It may be Nathan she wants," Hassan said. "Knowledge would make her a better hunter. Or it may simply be his death she wants and taking his Gift would be an additional benefit."

"Something happened between those two. Something personal." When he didn't offer an explanation, I said, "What happened?"

"You will have to ask Nathan."

What kind of answer was that? He never seemed to have a problem exploiting personal information before, and now all of the sudden he decided to be discreet?

Whatever their history, Nathan was a target whether or not Eden wanted his Gift, and he seemed so vulnerable compared to Hassan and Lexi. He was the one with a wife and kids. I knew the pain of having your family ripped apart, and I knew the ache of missing your dad. I couldn't imagine how much worse it would be to lose your dad forever, especially one who'd been such a huge part of your life.

"Don't let anything happen to Nathan. His family needs him. And you have to let me know what happens tonight. Call or send a text, okay?"

He met my gaze, assessing me for a moment. "It could be very late by the time we finish."

"It doesn't matter. I won't be able to sleep unless I know everyone is okay. You don't have to give me all the details. Just let me know everyone's okay."

"Fine." He stood and held a hand out. "Come. There are things we can work on while you're recovering."

I sighed, but it was my own fault. I'd insisted on coming today.

Being injured turned out to be helpful though. A slower pace allowed me to grasp some of the things he'd been trying to teach me, and he seemed more willing to explain the thought process behind what we were doing—how a move countered an opponent's move or threw them off balance.

After training, I went upstairs and said goodbye to Jackson and Lexi praying it wasn't for the last time. It was morbid to think that way, but I couldn't help it. The horror of yesterday was still too fresh.

"Be careful," I told them.

"Don't worry," Jackson said. "We've got this."

"Sure, we'll be fine. As long as Jackson doesn't trip over his shoelaces."

He glared at Lexi. "That only happened once, and it was your fault."

"Well, double knot," I said. "Just in case."

Hopefully they could avoid arguing tonight.

Hassan drove me back to the bus stop at a more reasonable speed than the trip to his house. Once we reached the commuter lot, he came around to open my door for me.

I climbed out and settled my backpack on my shoulder. "You'll call or send me a text, right?"

He frowned at me as he shut the door. "I said I would."

"Just checking."

Maybe it was my imagination, but his frown seemed to soften a tiny bit.

"Go home. I'll talk to you later."

That night I placed my phone beside my pillow and told myself not to worry. It didn't work. My mind came up with horrifying scenarios faster than I could dismiss them.

It was after two when Hassan called, and adrenaline flooded my system as I rolled up onto my elbow and grabbed my phone. "Hello?"

"We didn't find anything."

"And Nathan? He's okay?"

"He's fine. Everyone is fine."

I dropped back onto my pillow with relief. "Thanks for calling. For letting me know."

He didn't say goodbye or hang up right away. I listened to the quiet that stretched between us, drinking in the comfort provided by the connection. The comfort of knowing there was someone on the other end.

Eventually he said, "Good night, Kate."

I didn't want to end the call, to be alone again, but we both needed sleep.

"Good night."

CHAPTER SIXTEEN

It was the fourth shirt I'd tried on, and while the silver fabric complimented my coloring, the way it clung to my curves made me self-conscious. My debate raged a few seconds longer until the squeal of brakes announced my brother's arrival.

"I'm leaving," I called to Mom as I hurried past the sewing room.

Jackson had said it would be better if he didn't come with me to the Switchfoot concert because I didn't want Rob to think I was too hard to get. But I should definitely bring someone with me so it didn't look like I had no social life. He'd also warned me not to bring a girl who would draw Rob's attention away from me.

I'd figured it would be safe to invite my friend Danika since she wasn't Rob's type either. She was a redhead, and her skin was as fair as mine. Danika couldn't make it though, so I'd invited my brother out of desperation.

It was a bad idea to let Ty drive, but I'd been too much of a coward to ask Mom if I could use her car after yelling at her the other day. I gave myself a suck-it-up speech and went to join my brother in his semi-stolen vehicle.

When Dad left on a business trip a couple of years ago, Ty had his girlfriend of the week drop him off so he could "borrow" Dad's Corvette. He never bothered to return it, and Dad never said a word. He just went out and bought another car. Since the Corvette was in his name and Ty was a lawsuit waiting to happen, Dad kept paying for the insurance. He ended up paying for gas too because Ty still had his Visa.

When Ty shifted into reverse, I double-checked my seat belt. "Can you please stick to ten over tonight? That's still enough to qualify for reckless driving if the cops pull you over."

His answer contained a four-letter word.

He sped across the bridge like it was the autobahn, so while I would've liked to enjoy the view of lights reflecting on Lake Washington, I couldn't. I kept picturing taillights disappearing beneath the surface of the water as the Corvette sank to the bottom with both of us still inside.

We survived the trip across the bridge, and Ty found a parking space close to Seattle Center. He spotted it when an SUV turned on its blinker, signaling the intention to park there, but that was like a flashing neon sign to Ty. He floored it—blowing through a red light—and hijacked the parking spot. The driver of the SUV laid on his horn, and as he passed the now-occupied space, he flipped off Ty. Ty returned the gesture, laughing the whole time, and I hid my face in my hands. I should never have invited him.

My sense of impending doom only grew once we got out of the car because it took all of five seconds for Ty to grab my wrist and pull it closer for inspection.

"No way. When did you get a tattoo? How come you didn't tell me?"

I yanked my hand free and crossed my arms, hugging my coat tighter around me. "Tell you what?"

"That you got a tattoo, loser. Where'd you get it done?"

I stepped around a puddle and entered the crosswalk even though the signal warned me to stop. "I sort of got it from a guy I know."

"A guy?" He cackled as he followed me into the crosswalk. "Okay, make sure I'm there when you tell Mom. I want to see the look on her face when she hears what her little girl's been doing."

"Nice try, pervert. It's not what you think."

As we reached the other side of the street, the Space Needle hovered overhead, the lights around the observation deck making it look like the flying saucer it was supposed to represent. The giant logo on Key Arena's peaked roof came into view, and I headed for the east entrance praying Ty would move on from the tattoo conversation. But of course he didn't.

"Know what my tattoo says?"

"Yes. And no, I don't want to see it."

He grinned. "Has Mom seen yours yet?"

"Yeah. She saw it."

"Did she take you straight to deprogramming, or did it require exorcism?"

"She just ... kind of freaked out."

"I bet she did. Man, I wish I'd been there to see it. Kate the perfect child gets in trouble. Did she ground you? Take away your phone?"

"Very funny. Like that ever worked with you." I suffered a fresh pang of guilt. "I sort of told her she had to deal with it."

"Seriously? I'm impressed."

I spotted Rob up ahead and grabbed my brother's arm, jerking him to a stop. "I know these people don't matter to you, but they matter to me, so can you please edit the language for one night? And the girls are off-limits. They don't need you giving them a personal introduction to sin."

"Whatever happened to free will?"

"I mean it, Ty. I'll sit on you, and you won't be able to breathe."

"Calm down. What's your problem tonight anyway? You're freaking out even more than usual, and what's up with the ..." He broke into a grin. "This is about a guy, isn't it? Is he the one who gave you the tattoo?"

"It's not about a guy," I said. "Well, maybe it is. Okay, it is, but he doesn't have anything to do with the tattoo, and if you ruin my chance of getting a date with him, I swear I'll never speak to you again." Not that it would stop him from doing whatever he wanted.

"Well, that's a relief. I was starting to think maybe you were—"

"Ty."

"Okay already. It was a joke. Would you calm down?" He swore at me as we started moving again. "So does this loser have a name?"

When we walked up, Rob eyed my brother, like maybe he recognized him, and panic hit. Did they know each other? Did they have a class together? What if Ty had already ruined my chance of getting a date with Rob? This would all be for nothing, and I'd have to live with the humiliation of Rob knowing I was related to Ty.

I made introductions, trying to stay calm, and the weirdest thing happened. Rob smiled. Like he and Ty were the best of friends.

What the heck? Had he thought ... Ty was my date?

It was possible. And not as disturbing as it sounded. My brother and I didn't look like siblings. We shared Mom's eye color and fair skin, but that was about it. Ty had Dad's golden brown hair and Dad's features too, so you would never think we were related. At least not until you heard us speak to each other.

Maybe I was reading too much into Rob's reaction, but it gave me hope Jackson was on to something. The evening might not be a complete catastrophe.

It helped that Ty behaved himself. During the opening act, there wasn't a single profane word or innuendo to be heard. He only did it to be a pain—I implied he had no self-control, so he had to prove me wrong—but whatever worked. The only temptation he gave in to was mouthing the word "loser" at me when no one else was looking, although I wasn't sure if he was referring to me or Rob. Probably both of us.

He also honored my wishes concerning the girls in our

group, but that didn't keep him from prowling. With thousands of girls gathered in one location that would be asking way too much, and the concert scene exponentially increased his odds of success because Ty looked like he was in a band. He knew it too. It was one of his favorite ways to pick up girls. He loved to tell them his band Pure Fabrication had just signed a deal with Virgin Records. Sadly enough, girls believed him because he was good-looking, shopped at Hot Topic, and had the ego of a rock star.

Under normal circumstances, I might've been mad at him for ditching me, but when he took off after a Scarlett Johansson look-alike during the intermission, Rob helped himself to Ty's seat.

Even without music, the arena was loud, the rumble of a thousand different conversations filling the air. Rob leaned in so I could hear him. Hopefully the noise drowned out the sound of my heart trying to hammer its way free of my chest.

"Thanks for putting this together," he said.

"I didn't really do much."

"You got the tickets."

"But you're the one who made all the phone calls. You got everyone organized." It was a whole lot easier talking to him on the phone than in person too. On the phone, I didn't have to deal with visual distractions like hazel eyes or perfect cheekbones.

"That was the easy part."

"Maybe for you. I'm not very good with conversational stuff."

"I think you do fine. You're easy to talk to."

He smiled, and I felt overheated all of the sudden.

"We never talked about anything other than the concert though. It would be nice to sit down and talk about whatever." He gestured to the crowd around us. "Maybe someplace where it isn't so loud."

"Yeah. That … that would be nice."

"Why don't we do something together this weekend? We

could do dinner and a movie. I'll buy."

My head bobbled up and down. "Okay."

"I'll call you tomorrow when we can hear each other better. We can figure out the details then."

Rob returned to his own seat, and I focused on taking slow, even breaths so my heart rate would settle down. I couldn't believe it. Jackson's plan had actually worked. With trembling fingers, I sent him a text promising Starbucks for a year. I sent another to Danika announcing my success.

My brother came back a couple minutes later wearing a scowl fierce enough to rival one of Hassan's. Evidently his hunting expedition had failed.

"A girl that hot should not be sidelined," he said as he dropped into his seat.

If my brother possessed a redeeming quality, it was that he avoided married women. The one positive side effect of Dad destroying our family with an affair. Boyfriends, however, were a completely different matter. Ty considered those girls a personal challenge. Even an engagement ring didn't slow him down, but once a girl married, he left her alone.

"So did the loser ask you out or what?"

"Not that it's any of your business, but yes. Rob asked me out. Thanks for not ruining it for me."

He responded with profanity.

Not even Ty could spoil the rest of the concert for me, although he tried. He texted the word "loser" to me a dozen times until I jammed my heel into the toe of his sneakers. Fortunately his response was lost in the chorus of *Meant to Live*, and I was then free to lose myself in the experience. The thunder of bass reverberated inside my chest stronger than my own heartbeat, and the raw edge of guitar struck a harmonizing chord in my soul. The combination of words and melody drove the meaning deeper into my being than either could alone. There among thousands of people, surrounded by flashing lights and the haze of smoke machines, I found an hour of pure happiness.

On the ride home, Ty's language was worse than usual, as if he had to make up for all the self-restraint. When he pulled into the driveway to drop me off, he wished me good luck with Rob only he got real creative with his wording. I smacked his arm as hard as I could.

"Ow! What was that for?"

"It was for your mouth, pervert, so pass it along." I unbuckled my seat belt and climbed out of the car. "Don't get arrested on the way home because you'll be sitting there until Connie gets permission from Dad to bail you out. I'm not coming."

I slammed the door shut on his reply, but I could still hear it through the glass. It was toxic enough to warrant a HAZMAT team.

I let myself into the house and sat on the couch while I waited for the indignation to work its way from my system. I then slipped off my shoes, padded down the hall, and knocked softly on Mom's bedroom door. The door was propped open a few inches, and the lights were off, but I knew she hadn't gone to sleep yet. She never went to sleep until I came home.

I stood in the darkened doorway and wondered what she would say if I told her the guy I'd had a crush on for the last year—the guy all the girls wanted, the guy I never thought I could have—had asked me out. I wondered what she would say if I told her Ty drove me insane, but for some reason I still loved him and wanted to be around him. What would she say if I told her my life was changing too much and too fast for me? That even as my heart grew more familiar with hope, I'd never felt so scared and alone and confused.

My answer came in the silence. She didn't acknowledge me when I told her I was home. She wanted me to think she was asleep.

I neatly folded up all of the things I wished I could tell her and hid them away.

"Good night," I whispered.

I sagged down on my bed, kneading the familiar knot of tension on my forehead. Even though Ty gave me a headache, he was the one person in my family I felt a genuine connection to. Whether it was because we'd suffered through our parents' divorce together or because he was the only one I still had some form of honest communication with, I didn't know.

Sometimes the connection strained to the point of breaking, but it always held and drew us back together again. There was something inside of me that refused to let go of him no matter what, and while he'd probably never admit it, I suspected Ty felt the pull between us too.

Whatever the reason for our connection, as I closed my eyes, I prayed we would never lose it.

CHAPTER
SEVENTEEN

When my phone rang, I turned down the volume on the TV so Rob wouldn't be able to tell my big plans for Friday evening consisted of the couch and sci-fi reruns.

A glance confirmed Mom was still in her sewing room. She didn't know about my date yet because I was too much of a coward to tell her. Besides, Rob might come to his senses and change his mind, and I didn't want to bring up either guys or dating unless I had to.

Once we had our greeting out of the way, Rob asked if I still wanted to get together.

"Yeah. I'd like that," I said. I even managed to sound calm.

"So what's playing right now? Have you looked?"

"Marvel has a new movie out."

"That's what you want to see?"

"Well ... maybe. Why? Have you seen it already?"

"No, but I thought ... I don't know."

"I'd vote for a chick flick?"

"Well, yeah. No offense, but it seems like usually, when you give a girl a choice, she goes with either the romantic comedy or a drama. And most of the girls I know have no idea what Marvel is, not even when you say comic book."

"I'm not exactly normal." I winced. Why not confess right now I spent Friday nights alone? I hurried past my self-incriminating remark. "I don't have anything against romantic comedies or dramas. I just think action and special effects are a better use of the big screen." I bit my lip. What if he thought I was being too pushy? "I mean, unless you wanted to—"

"No, I'm good. Action and special effects sound great."

We finalized our plans for the following night, and as soon as we hung up, I called Lexi to beg for her help again. Thankfully, she took pity on me and agreed to come over in the morning. And like the coward I was, I waited until morning to tell Mom about my date.

She had the ads spread out across the kitchen table while she worked on the shopping list. My throat was tight with apprehension when I approached her.

"Lexi's coming over in a little bit."

"She is? I'm so glad. I have a new quilt to show her."

"Yeah. Good. She'll want to see it." My fingers worked the cuff of my hoodie. "And she ... she's going to help me figure out what to wear tonight."

"What's happening tonight?"

"You know Rob Peterson? The guy who sat with us last week in church? He's the one I helped with the concert, and he, uh, asked if I wanted to go to a movie and get something to eat."

She frowned. "I don't think that's a good idea. You were out late the other night, and we have church in the morning."

"We won't let it get too late. He's planning to go to church too."

"It's not a good idea. Maybe some other time."

"Okay, but see, the thing is ... he's a really nice guy, and it sounded kind of fun. So I sort of told him I'd go already." I did my best to appear determined but not defiant. "I've never gone out on a date before, and I figured that since I'm eighteen now, it was maybe time to do that."

My heart cringed as her features tightened in disapproval.

"I suppose I should be thankful you informed me of your decision." She returned to the ads, dismissing me.

Part of me wanted to weep, and part of me wanted to scream. I wanted to say something or do something to make her look at me, to make her see me.

It would have been so much easier if I'd lied to her. I could have told her I was going to the movie alone. I'd done that plenty of times. I could have met Rob at the theater, and she would never have known a guy was involved.

I couldn't do it though. I didn't want to. I had to hide so much of myself from her already, and thanks to the Guardians, it would become even more tempting to cover the truth with lies. I needed to draw a clear line now and never cross it. Hopefully Mom would be ready to hear the truth by the time my toes began to scrape the line.

My steps dragging, I retrieved the dirty clothes basket from the bathroom and lugged it to the garage, fighting off a shiver as I began to sort laundry. The rainclouds had left us, but they'd taken at least ten degrees Fahrenheit with them.

Once the washer was chugging away, I tipped my head back to scrutinize the water stain overhead. It didn't look any bigger despite the downpour on Monday, but it wasn't going away either. Like a lot of other things around our house, the roof needed to be repaired, and like the rest of those projects it lacked funding.

My sigh sent a puff of steam into the air. Sometimes everything around me seemed to be falling apart.

I returned the laundry basket to the bathroom then went to straighten up my bedroom while I waited for Lexi. When she arrived, she took the time to look at the new quilt, but even her admiration couldn't thaw Mom's anger. Lexi and I retreated to my room after that, and I shut the door to give us some privacy.

"Is she still mad about Monday?" Lexi said. "Or did something else happen?"

Lexi was the only one I'd really talked to about Mom discovering my *Pur*.

"She wasn't over it, not completely, and telling her I had a date tonight didn't help."

She gave me a sympathetic look. "Sorry."

I sat on my bed and scooted toward the wall. "Me too."

Lexi found a black turtleneck sweater in my closet that was "acceptable" for a movie and casual dining. She paired it with the jeans and boots she'd put me in last time.

She then put her hands on her hips and eyed me through lavender frames. "I'm not helping you again unless we go shopping first."

"Fine. It probably won't be an issue after tonight anyway."

"Why?"

"If I mess up this date—which I probably will—I won't get another one, so I won't have to worry about choosing another outfit."

She settled at the other end of my bed. "Nervous?"

"Yeah. A little bit. Or maybe a lot. I never thought I'd get to the 'asked out' part, so I never really thought about the actual 'date' part."

"You'll do fine. Just be a good listener. Most guys love to talk about themselves, and while he's telling you how great he is, you can decide whether or not it's true."

Lexi sat with her legs entwined in lotus position, somehow managing to appear both alert and relaxed at the same time, and a little stab of envy pricked me. My brief attempt at yoga had failed because I couldn't twist my legs into lotus position without falling over or causing myself pain. But being jealous of her flexibility was only part of the problem.

"I don't understand how you can be so calm."

"I'm not the one going out with him."

"I'm not talking about Rob. I mean Eden. Aren't you worried?"

"Nope."

"How can you not be worried? She's out there somewhere. Waiting to kill someone."

"Give us a little credit. We've dealt with Fallen Guardians before, and Eden was dumb enough to advertise her presence. She blew her biggest advantage. She's overconfident, and Benny's a coward. As soon as it gets tense, he'll take off so fast even Jackson will have trouble catching him."

"Maybe Benny will run, but not the other guy."

"Don't worry about him. He won't be an issue."

The guy had held me captive while I was tortured, left a good portion of my body bruised, and hadn't registered a single ounce of the pain I tried to inflict on him. But I wasn't supposed to worry. I had a nagging suspicion I'd missed another company email. It was probably floating around in cyberspace along with the one about hunters and sources of supernatural power.

"I'm not trying to downplay the danger," Lexi said. "It is dangerous, but we know what we're doing, and when we're done, Eden won't be hurting anyone ever again." She smoothly unfolded her legs and stood up. "I need to go, and you need to stop worrying. Go have fun tonight. Got it?"

"Got it. Thanks."

Despite her reassurance, doubt hovered. Lexi claimed Eden was overconfident, but the same thing might be said of Lexi. Then again, what did I know? I hadn't seen anyone other than Nathan or Hassan use their Gifts, and I had no doubt Jackson and Lexi would blow Nathan out of the water when it came to visual display. Lexi was probably right. I needed to have a little faith in them and their abilities.

After Lexi left, Mom went to do the shopping. When she came back, I didn't ask if she needed help unloading groceries. I went out to the car, grabbed bags, and carried them to the kitchen. As I started to put things away, she walked into her sewing room and closed the door.

I had the overwhelming desire to take the jar of peanut butter in my hand and hurl it at the window, the light fixture, anything that would provide the satisfying sound of breaking glass.

I didn't do anything more than put the jar of peanut butter

on the shelf, and as the burst of anger fizzled out, discouragement settled in its place. The smartest thing for me to do was cancel my date with Rob because what was the point? Really? It wasn't like it would go anywhere. Before the night was over, Rob would ask himself what he'd been thinking, he'd give me the "friends" speech, and that would be the end of it. One date wasn't worth all the stress.

But somehow, in spite of the fact it should've been snuffed out after the week I'd had, my tiny spark of hope had grown into something more substantial, and it didn't want to give up so easily. Maybe one date was exactly why I needed to go. If one date with Rob was all I got, then I didn't want to miss it. I should do what Lexi said and have fun. Afterward, I could return to my normal, boring, non-social life knowing for once things worked out the way I wanted them to. Once in a while, good things happened. Even to me.

CHAPTER
EIGHTEEN

When a silver sedan pulled into the driveway that evening, I knocked on the door of Mom's sewing room to let her know I was leaving. No response came, so I wrapped my hand around the knob. I didn't turn it though. After a moment, I let go, grabbed my coat, and went to meet Rob.

We planned to eat first then catch a seven o'clock show. When we'd discussed our options the night before, we discovered we both liked Thai food, and Typhoon was located a couple of buildings down from the theater. It catered to people like me and Rob who wanted something above "hole in the wall" but couldn't afford "fine dining." The clean lines, black furniture, and bamboo accents gave the space a modern Asian feel while the pseudo-ancient statue by the front desk honored the traditional Far East. White candles flickered in glass holders, and an open window to the kitchen allowed the sound of sizzling woks to fill the room. The aromas of red curry and lemongrass, coconut milk and jasmine rice scented the air. My mouth started to water as soon as we walked in the door.

I went through the routine of reading the menu even though I knew what I wanted. It gave me something to do besides fidget while we waited for the waitress to return with our drinks.

The waitress came back, set our drinks on the table, and then pulled a pen and notepad from the pocket of her apron.

When I ordered, Rob's eyebrows rose. "All those exotic choices, and you order plain old *phad thai?*"

"Um ... yeah. I guess so."

"Good." He handed his menu to the waitress. "Now I won't feel bad for ordering plain old *phad thai*."

He smiled at me, and I started to smile back but was distracted by the way candlelight played with the flecks of gold in his eyes. The light moved more subtly through the bronze tones of his hair and against his skin, warming them with golden hues. Even the fabric of his brown shirt seemed to have a slight shimmer to it in the flickering light.

"Miss?"

I tore my gaze away from him to see the waitress holding out her hand. I stared at it in confusion.

"Your menu?"

"Oh. Sorry."

I handed her the menu, and she marched off in the direction of the kitchen. When I turned back to Rob, he was watching me with those gold-flecked eyes. Anxiety fluttered through my stomach.

"So according to Jen, you're premed. What specialty are you interested in?"

"Oncology. But only if I get into medical school, and that may not happen. Not if I can't make it through calculus first."

"That was quick. It took less than ten minutes to find your weakness."

"Okay, but I still get dinner, right?"

He laughed. "Yes. And to be fair, I'll tell you my weakness is Art and Music Appreciation."

"Seriously?"

He nodded. "But it's not my fault. Rumor is the professor had a nasty breakup right before fall quarter started. She's been taking it out on her students, especially the guys."

"Guess I should avoid Art and Music Appreciation."

"At least until she's over the breakup."

A waiter passed by with two steaming bowls of *tom yum*, and my stomach rumbled, threatening to take matters into its own hands if I didn't eat soon. I took a sip of my soda in hopes of pacifying it for a few minutes longer.

"So did I hear right?" I said. "You're an engineering student?"

"Bioengineering if you want specifics."

"Really? That's the kind of stuff my dad does. He works for Pacific Bio-Tech."

"Yeah, I think Jen mentioned something about it a while back. Pacific Bio-Tech is a great company. But you know that already. I'm sure you've heard it all from your dad."

I poked at the ice in my drink with the straw. "Not really. My dad doesn't talk about it much. Not to me."

"You should get him to talk. They've always been one of the top companies as far as imaging technology goes, but they've branched out with a new research division looking for ways to apply their technology to the fight against cancer."

"They are?"

My information about Pacific Bio-Tech came from either the snatches of local news I happened to catch or from articles in abandoned newspapers at Starbucks. The last news segment I'd seen had something to do with getting a better look at heart valve function. This was the first I'd heard of them focusing their efforts on cancer research.

Rob leaned forward, and enthusiasm lit up his eyes as effectively as candlelight. "One of their research teams is developing a technique that combines magnetic properties with photo acoustic imaging, so instead of x-ray or MRI, you'll be able to do molecular imaging. You could do cell counts in the body, and in theory you'd be able to determine if a cancer cell broke away from a tumor to colonize a new organ. A single cell. Isn't that incredible?"

"Yeah. Incredible."

Rob didn't even know my dad, but he knew more about Dad's job than I did.

The truth hit home with a physical pang. Dad didn't just

want to stay out of my life. He wanted me to stay out of his life too. Somehow it had never sunk in before tonight.

Rob went on, oblivious to the fact my abandonment issues had crept into the conversation. "They decided to create a couple of student intern positions for next summer. Not only do you get to do hands-on research with the top people in the field, but it basically guarantees admission to grad school. I applied for one of the positions, but I doubt I'll get it." He shook his head as he pulled a pair of chopsticks from their wrapper. "My grades are good, and I have recommendations, but there are hundreds of applicants from all over the US, and I'm at a disadvantage being a sophomore. They want upperclassmen."

"I'd offer to introduce you to my dad, but I don't see him very often. I guess ... maybe I could leave him a message or something."

His head snapped up. "Really? You would do that for me?"

"Sure. I mean, I don't know if he has anything to do with interns or the selection process, but he's pretty high up in the company."

"That would be—I can't even begin to tell you how much it would mean to me. People would literally kill to get one of those internships."

"Okay, but I can't promise anything," I rushed to say. "He's really busy, and he's kind of hard to get a hold of."

He might not get the message at all. For all I knew, Dad deleted my messages without listening to them.

"I'll take whatever help I can get."

He reached over to squeeze my hand, and my heart pounded so hard I felt the vibration in my ribs.

"Thank you," he said. "I owe you. Big time."

He released my hand, giving my heart a chance to calm. The conversation wandered away from Pacific Bio-Tech as the waitress arrived with our *phad thai*. We learned we both liked to get to the theater early to catch the previews, so we didn't stick around after we ate.

The seven o'clock show was crowded, but we managed to find two halfway decent seats as the previews started. One of my least favorite actors popped up on the screen, and I could feel my nose wrinkle up when the trailer tried to sell him as a brilliant scientist and devoted family man.

"Yeah right." I didn't realize I'd said it out loud until I heard Rob laugh. I shrank down in my seat, whispering, "Sorry."

"Don't worry about it," he said quietly. "I was thinking the same thing."

The woman in front of us turned to give us the evil eye, which only made both of us shake with suppressed laughter as soon as she turned back around.

The other previews were more promising, and the main attraction definitely put the big screen to good use. We stayed after the last scene so we could catch the teaser for the next movie. Most of the audience, including the woman with the evil eye, filtered out while we waited. Only a dozen movie-goers remained.

As the credits rolled, Rob shifted toward me, keeping his voice low. "So what did you think?"

"The story and special effects were great. The costumes and dialogue not so much. I give it a B."

"Ooh. Tough grader. I give it an A-. I had to award a few extra points for the accurate portrayal of thermodynamics."

"You know that totally makes you sound like a nerd, right?"

He laughed. "Yeah, I guess it does."

We finished off the evening with ice cream even though the temperature had dipped into the thirties. I restrained myself and got the smallest size because I didn't want to seem like a pig, but I still ordered my favorite flavor— Chocolate Obsession. When I did, Rob smiled at me then turned to order the same thing. You had to love a guy who loved chocolate.

We were both freezing by the time we made it to his car. He cranked the heat, and we sat there shivering while we waited for the car to warm up. The uncontrollable chattering of my teeth brought more laughter, but I didn't mind that we were laughing at me.

"I had fun tonight," he said after the chattering stopped.

"Me too."

In fact, I'd been having so much fun that I'd forgotten to be nervous, but I was starting to feel it now. Even though we'd been close to each other all evening, it was different with just the two of us sitting in the car.

A hint of a smile remained on Rob's face, but a crease of puzzlement joined it, settling between his eyebrows. "You're different than I expected."

Was that a good thing or a bad thing?

I had half a second to think it might be a good thing, and then I couldn't think at all. My pulse jumped wildly beneath the skin at the base of my throat as he leaned toward me. I experienced a brief surge of panic as his lips brushed against mine, and the panic shot through my system, colliding with the euphoria racing to the surface.

Then it was over, and I mourned the unfairness of it. I hadn't been expecting this. I hadn't seen it coming, so I hadn't been prepared to commit it to memory, to shape it into something I could hang onto for months—years—to come. I knew how unlikely this moment was to be repeated, and my brain scrambled to snatch up the details before they escaped.

I felt disoriented when we pulled up in front of my house a few minutes later, as if our kiss had shorted out my internal GPS system. Did kissing throw off everyone's GPS? Or was it just mine? I had no idea, and as Rob moved closer, I decided I didn't care.

His lips moved over mine, bringing the taste of chocolate, and the car felt too hot thanks to the liquid heat spreading through my veins. His fingers were cool against my skin as they slipped beneath my hair to find a resting place. My every breath was infused with him—with the scent of his skin, his cologne, his leather jacket.

I didn't want my GPS back. Ever. I was perfectly fine with being lost.

Fortunately, I didn't have to make it any farther than the front door, and Rob walked me there.

"I'll see you tomorrow morning?"

I nodded. I was too short of breath to talk.

He gazed down at me. I figured he was waiting for me to go inside, but as I reached for my key, he wrapped his fingers around mine.

"Kate …" He studied our hands for a moment before he lifted his gaze again. "When I asked you out …" He frowned, visibly struggling to find the words he wanted. "I thought—"

A snap interrupted him. We both glanced at the front door, at the sound of my evening coming to an end. The knob started to turn, and I swallowed back a groan. Mom had done nothing but shut me out all day, and now, when I wanted her to keep the door closed, she had to open it.

Rob pulled his hands away and took a step back. "I just wanted to say I had fun. Maybe we can do it again some time."

CHAPTER
NINETEEN

My dad bailed on Thanksgiving. He took Connie and Chloe to Arizona and left a voicemail promising to get together for Christmas.

I'd warned myself for days he would find some excuse to cancel on me and Ty, but it didn't stop the disappointment. Listening to Mom tell me he was a horrible dad just made it worse. She told me on Tuesday when I received the message, and she told me again on Wednesday. She told me all the way to Thanksgiving dinner, the entire ninety minutes it took to drive to Olympia. I was thoroughly miserable by the time we parked in front of Grandpa and Grandma Hathaway's house.

The cozy, low-pitched roof hinted at happier times in Mom's life. As we walked up the steps to the front porch with homemade rolls in hand, I tried to envision her at my age walking up these same steps. I tried to imagine her looking forward to life instead of hiding from it.

When Grandma fussed over me, telling me how beautiful I was, I pasted on a smile. I let Grandpa call me "Katy Bug" and forced enthusiasm into my voice when I answered his questions about school.

Ty showed up not too long after Mom and I got there. He barely said hi to Grandpa and Grandma before he walked off, his skinny jeans sagging, and plopped down in front of the TV. As soon as I could, I joined him on the pink floral couch of unhappiness.

The pocket of my hoodie chimed a few minutes later,

causing a smile to tug at my lips. It had been almost a month now, and I still had no idea how it had happened. It was like there'd been another screw up in the cosmic legal department, but instead of getting stuck with the Guardians, I got stuck with Rob this time. It almost made up for the Guardian part.

When Ty leaned over to read the screen, I elbowed him. "Get off me."

"Sexting your loser boyfriend?"

"I'm not sexting, pervert." I stood and slipped my phone back into my pocket.

"I was messing with you. You don't have to get all mad and take off."

"I need to set the table."

"Fine. I'll help you."

"I don't want your help. Every time you help me with something, it takes twice as long."

He came with me anyway.

The wood floors creaked as we stepped into the dining room. Condensation fogged the single-pane windows facing the driveway, reflecting the overhead light back onto us and the oak table. The scents of antique wood and lemon oil mingled with the aroma of turkey and candied yams drifting in from the kitchen.

Since I'd been little, it had been my job to prepare the table at Grandpa and Grandma's. In some of my earliest memories, I had to stretch up on tiptoes to place silverware next to a plate, and sometimes a masculine hand reached out to help me lift a plate or move a goblet. A lot of things had changed since then.

I removed plates and goblets from a cupboard in the oak sideboard and set them on top. I placed the chest of polished silverware next to the plates. A tablecloth and cloth napkins came from one drawer, a pair of candles and candlesticks from another. They joined the plates, goblets, and silverware on top of the sideboard along with the napkin rings.

Every Thanksgiving, Grandma dug out the napkin rings I'd made when I was seven—disfigured lumps of clay that were supposed to be turkeys. Ty never failed to make fun of them at some point. Five malformed birds waited on the sideboard in the same spot Grandma put them every year. There used to be six of them. I picked one up, testing its dry, lifeless weight in my hand, and felt the sting of tears.

"Stop it," Ty said.

"Stop what?"

"Stop crying over him." He snatched the napkin ring from my hand. "He did us a favor by taking off to Arizona. We would've ended up eating Tofurkey because Chloe's been smoking PETA's crap, and she's too stupid to figure out where the leather for her shoes comes from. Connie would've spent all day smiling at us because she overdid it with the Botox, not because she's happy, and Dad wouldn't even be there. He would've found some lame excuse to go into work except he wouldn't go to work. He'd find someone else to spend the day with."

I knew Ty was right. Thanksgiving at Dad's would have been miserable, but that didn't make me want it any less.

"We're better off without him," Ty said.

"Are we?"

Coffee-colored eyes mirrored my own pain and doubt for the briefest of moments. He wasn't as sure about it as he sounded.

"That's the dumbest question I've ever heard," he muttered as he set the napkin ring on the sideboard. "Of course we are."

Most of the time, I wanted to injure my brother because he was so irritating, but somewhere underneath all the sarcasm his heart was hurting just like mine. I wasn't doing either of us any favors today by dwelling on what we couldn't have.

"Yeah, maybe we are better off," I said. "I don't think I could do Tofurkey."

"You got that right. That stuff tastes like—"

"Ty." He said it anyway, and I sighed. "I'll do your laundry this weekend if you can make it through the rest of the day without swearing."

"Sweet. Wanna make a deal for next weekend too?"

"No." I picked up the burnt orange tablecloth. "Either help me set the table or go away. And pull your pants up. I don't want to see your boxers until Saturday."

He helped me set the table. Sort of. He tugged on his end of the tablecloth every time I straightened it until I threatened to stab his hand with a fork. He drew pictures in the window condensation that I had to wipe clean with the sleeve of my hoodie before anyone else saw them, and he ridiculed my napkin rings, likening them to something found in a cow pasture. I didn't really mind that part though. It was kind of a Thanksgiving tradition.

Once the table was set, I helped Grandma and Mom transfer food from the kitchen to the dining room, and we all took our places. Grandpa and Grandma sat on either end of the table, and I sat on the window side next to Ty. Mom sat across from us by herself. My mind strayed toward Dad again, but I forced it back to the present. The rest of my family was here. I had food and clothing and someplace to live. I was almost done with my first quarter of college, and I hadn't flunked out. I had new friends and a boyfriend, and once in a while, I even caught myself feeling optimistic. There was a lot to be thankful for.

After Grandpa blessed the meal, he began to serve the turkey. "Tyler, I can't remember. Is it legs you like?"

A grin spread across my brother's face. I should have gone for the two-weekend deal. But deal or no deal, I refused to let him turn Grandpa's innocent question into a perverted innuendo. I sunk the toe of my Converse into his ankle and growled, "Don't."

He managed to catch himself before an obscenity left his mouth, but the glare he gave me promised retribution. Mom's gaze darted between the two of us. She knew something was up, and she had good reason to be nervous. My brother had a history of saying shocking things at the dinner table.

This time Ty resisted the urge. "That's fine, Grandpa. I'll take whatever."

Mom was still watching us, so I distracted her by asking for the stuffing. As she reached for the bowl, Ty kicked my ankle. I'd have a bruise later, but it was better than having his gutter-mind ruin Thanksgiving dinner.

I took the bowl from Mom and scooped out a serving more suited to Jackson's body weight than mine, but I planned to eat every single bite of it because Grandma didn't believe in store-bought stuffing. She made her own using fresh apples and walnuts, and drizzled with her homemade gravy, it amounted to taste bud heaven. Definitely worth a bruise.

My stomach was ready to pop by the time we finished dinner, so I worked off some of it by clearing the table. While Mom helped Grandma wash dishes, I slipped out to the front porch to call Rob.

Mom had grudgingly accepted the whole boyfriend thing, but only because I made every effort to act like nothing much had changed. I didn't talk about Rob any more than necessary, and I spent most of my Saturdays and Sundays at home. I worked on school stuff and hid the fact I was happier than I'd been in a long time.

I welcomed the cold air against my face as I stepped outside. It felt refreshing after the big meal and stuffiness of the house. The rain had stopped a while ago, but moisture still hung in the air, creating aureoles around the streetlights. The eaves had sheltered the top step from the rain but not from the temperature, a fact my backside confirmed when I sat down. I huddled farther into my hoodie as I pressed the call button.

Rob barely greeted me before he announced, "I'm coming back early. I'm leaving first thing Sunday morning instead of

Sunday evening."

"Why? Did something happen?"

"You did."

"Me? What did I do?"

"You stayed home. This morning I realized how far away you were and how long it would be before I saw you again, and all I could think about was coming back. If I could leave tonight, I would, but I think my family might protest if I try to take off any earlier than Sunday morning."

I wasn't sure what to say. I fished around for something that hopefully wouldn't sound too stupid. "Well, you're supposed to spend time with your family on Thanksgiving."

"Maybe, but I want to spend all of my time with you. I miss you."

"You do?"

He laughed. "Yes. Is that so hard to believe?"

"I don't know. I guess … I don't think anyone's ever missed me before."

He laughed again, but it quickly faded. "You're serious."

I attempted a smile hoping it would spill over into my voice. "Well, I've never really gone anywhere, so how could anyone miss me, right?"

He was quiet. I could hear the whoosh of tires across wet pavement somewhere down the street.

"I've never missed anyone so much in my whole life. I didn't know it was possible, and it doesn't even make sense. You're not that far away, and in a couple of days, I'll see you again, but right now it feels like a million miles, and it seems like forever. I don't understand it. All I know is I want to be with you, and I'm going insane because I can't."

The air felt too thick for me to get a proper breath. My fingers, growing numb from the cold, had a death grip on my phone.

"Are you still there?"

I concentrated on taking a breath. "Yeah. I'm still here."

"I'm sorry. I probably sound like a stalker."

"No, you … it sounded good."

I fought off a shiver. Cold seeped into my skin, but I didn't want to go inside yet. I wanted to stay here on the steps so he could tell me again how much he missed me, how badly he wanted to see me.

"I've been crazy about a girl before," he said, "but not like this. This is different. You're different."

My brother chose that moment to open the front door. "Hey, get in here before Mom calls the Special Victims Unit. She'll think the ex-con down the street abducted you."

I wanted to weep. Or scream. No form of torture would be too painful for him.

I turned long enough to give him a face-melting look. "I'll be there in a minute, Ty. Go away."

"Seriously, Kate. She'll freak if she finds you out here talking to your boyfriend."

I turned back around to stare at him. All traces of attitude had disappeared from his voice. He almost sounded like he cared. Like he wanted to spare me the headache of dealing with Mom's paranoia.

"Is that your brother?"

"Yeah. I gotta go," I said reluctantly.

"Call me later?"

"Okay. Bye."

I gave into a shiver as I stood up. Ty had already stepped back inside, and he closed the door behind me as Mom emerged from the kitchen at the other end of the hall.

"Were you outside?" she said.

I folded my arms tight against my body in an effort to restore warmth. "For a couple of minutes."

"What on earth were you doing out there? It's dark, and you don't have on anything heavier than a sweatshirt."

"Making a phone call, but I'm done now."

She frowned. She knew who I'd been talking to. I clenched my teeth together to keep them from chattering because that would only make things worse.

"Is it time for pie yet?" Ty said. "Because I want both. Pumpkin and pecan."

The distraction worked. Ty didn't say a whole lot to Mom, and when he did, it was rarely something as innocuous as asking for pie.

"Yes. I was coming to see what kind everyone would like."

"Same for me," I said.

Mom gave me another frown before she moved toward the living room to ask Grandpa what he wanted. As she walked away, Ty pointed at me then himself. He then held up two fingers. I ignored him and went to make a pot of coffee. Whether or not his good deed had earned him an additional weekend of laundry service was debatable. He had a lot to make up for.

CHAPTER
TWENTY

Dessert at Grandma's provided another heavenly taste bud experience. No store-bought pie crusts or whipped cream out of a can. I had to admit that, at least when it came to food, we were better off without Dad today. We didn't have to eat Tofurkey or some expensive mousse Connie bought because it was supposed to be the new-and-improved version of pumpkin pie. I had nothing against vegetarians or high-end bakeries, but sometimes you needed to stick with the classics.

After dessert, Ty offered to take me home. As much as I hated riding with him, I dreaded another ninety-minute drive with Mom even more. Slipping outside to call Rob probably hadn't helped as far as conversation topics for the trip back, so I took Ty up on his offer.

As we headed north on I-5, the State Capitol rose up on our left. Floodlights illuminated the pale marble columns of the Legislative Building, briefly cutting through the mist before disappearing behind a hill. Then I was left with nothing more than the blur of headlights and taillights to distract me from Ty's driving.

"We should go to a movie tomorrow," he said.

My fingers curled into the edge of my seat as he cut across two lanes of traffic to pass a semi. "I can't. I have plans."

"What plans? I thought the loser was out of town."

"If you mean Rob, yes. He went home for Thanksgiving. I'm going shopping with my friend Lexi in the morning, and we're going to our friend Jackson's tomorrow night."

"A party? I'll come with you."

"No, you won't. You weren't invited, and even if you were, you wouldn't have any fun. It's not your kind of party. No drinking until you puke or pass out, no hookups in front of the entire guest list, and no cops coming to break up a fight or make a drug bust."

In the light of the dashboard, I could see disappointment register on his face, but I refused to feel sorry for him. He only wanted to hang out with me because he was between girlfriends, and it wasn't my job to entertain him every time he nuked one of his relationships, which was pretty much every time. They rarely ended without some kind of massive meltdown, and the fallout lingered for years afterward.

I tensed as he made another lane change and came within a hairsbreadth of clipping a minivan's bumper.

"We could go on Saturday," I offered.

"Whatever."

I left it at that because I knew how Ty operated. He had to blow me off now so he could call on Saturday and act like it was his idea.

Somehow we made it to Redmond without dying or getting pulled over by the State Patrol, but instead of dropping me off, Ty came inside and parked himself on the couch. We watched TV until Mom came home. He left as soon as she walked in the door.

I headed for bed soon after he left. Once I set my alarm, I turned off the lights and crawled beneath the covers with my phone. Soft green light from the alarm clock's display edged away the darkness as I selected Rob's number from my contacts.

"You called," he said. "I wasn't sure you would."

"Why wouldn't I?"

"You've had time to think. Plenty of time to decide I'm mental and you need a restraining order."

"You're not mental," I said, settling deeper into the covers. "And I don't need a restraining order."

"I haven't scared you away yet?"

"No. Were you trying to?"

"That's the last thing I want. I had time to think too. Long enough to wonder what I would do if you decided you didn't want to call me back."

"You could have called me. I know I said it's better if I make the call, but that doesn't mean you can't."

"I didn't want to come across like even more of a stalker than I had already." His voice took on a desolate tone. "I was miserable waiting for you to call. I was afraid you'd change your mind about being with me."

I wanted to laugh at the absurdity of such a thought. "I don't think that's going to happen. And it definitely wouldn't happen because you said you missed me, so stop worrying. Disaster averted. If I ever find you standing in my room in the middle of the night, I'll consider a restraining order."

"No home invasions. I promise."

A sleepy laugh escaped. "Okay, then we're good."

We didn't talk for much longer. I needed sleep. For some insane reason, I'd let Lexi talk me into getting up to take advantage of Black Friday sales.

The first thing she did the next morning was present me with a venti drip coffee. "Even Starbucks is up and ready for Black Friday," she said cheerfully.

I glared at her as I took the cup. It was way too early to be smiling about anything. Even coffee.

Getting into her microchip-sized car didn't help my mood either, but there was some advantage to its size when we arrived at Bellevue Square. Lexi was able to pull into a space right away while a Hummer continued to cruise the parking garage looking for a spot where it wouldn't play can opener with someone's Lexus.

Holding my coffee close to shelter it from the press of rabid shoppers around me, we funneled through the doors into Nordstrom. I squinted against the brilliance of polished brass and Christmas lights. As we drifted upward on the

escalator, I could see the multitude of bodies swarming
around the cosmetics counter, and I clutched my coffee
tighter to ward off the feel of claustrophobia. When we
reached the next floor I located a spot behind a marble
column where I could sip my coffee while Lexi perused the
racks. Maybe I could close my eyes for a minute or two and
pretend I was still in bed.

"Kate."

I flinched and almost dropped my coffee. "What?"

"You have to try this on. Right now." She held up a dress
of silky midnight blue.

"We're at Nordstrom, Lexi. I can't afford it."

"That's why we're here at five in the morning. So you can
afford it. Duh."

"It's not even my size."

She grabbed my arm and dragged both me and the dress
to the fitting rooms anyway. I would've made more of an
effort to resist, but Rob had been promising a nice dinner for
our one-month anniversary, and I needed something to wear.

A girl—more Bollywood supermodel than sales
associate—met us at the entrance to the fitting rooms and
introduced herself as Ramya. She and Lexi instantly clicked.
As Ramya catwalked us through the labyrinth of doors,
mirrors, and women who looked way too good for five in the
morning, she gave Lexi the insider information on the shoe
sale. I meekly followed, hoping I could find my way out
when they lost me.

Ramya opened a door, hung the dress next to the mirror,
and swept her arm in a graceful gesture inviting me to step
inside. "I'll come back to check on you. Let me know if you
need anything else."

She disappeared into the labyrinth, and with a sigh, I
handed my coffee to Lexi. She rolled her eyes when I made
her wait outside.

Closing the door dulled the chatter of voices and the click
of hangers. It was me and the dress with a huge mirror and a

gold-striped ottoman that looked comfy enough to curl up on. I wondered how much sleep I could squeeze in before Ramya returned.

"Let me see as soon as you have it on," Lexi said.

I almost fell over trying to get my feet out of my jeans, but everything else came off without too much trouble. I wiggled my way into the dress and then turned to face the mirror. All thoughts of sleep fled as I stared at my reflection.

It was as if the dress had been created for the sole purpose of making my body look good. Like it existed to display every God-given curve to hourglass perfection. Nothing risqué or suggestive, just unmistakably feminine. I knew I'd dropped a few pounds thanks to Jackson and Hassan, but I'd had no idea things were shaping up so nicely.

The cut of the dress wasn't the only thing working for me. My hair transformed into a midnight shadow against the deep blue fabric. My skin became moonlight. My eyes stood out—dark, enigmatic—and my lips turned a kiss-blushed pink.

I had scored another cosmic screw up.

Lexi knocked. "Can I see it now?"

I reached out, fumbling for the door handle because I couldn't move my eyes away from the mirror.

Lexi stepped in, and her reflection went still. "Kate …"

"I know."

"I don't care how much it is. You have to buy it."

I could only nod.

Ramya appeared in the doorway and froze beside Lexi. Then she said, "I'll be right back."

She brought a bolero sweater in the same shade as the dress, and when I slipped it on, whisper-soft warmth enfolded my arms and shoulders. I had never felt cashmere against my skin before, and it was instant addiction.

Both Ramya and Lexi approved of the sweater because it added warmth without hiding the dress, but I had serious reservations about the cost. I wasn't sure I could afford the dress, never mind the sweater, but as I stood and took in my reflection, yearning filled me. I wanted to be the girl I saw in the mirror, the one who would turn heads when she went out to dinner, the girl no one would ignore. It might be worth going broke if I could be that girl for one night.

While I changed back into my jeans and hoodie, Ramya repeated her info to Lexi about the shoe sale along with a recommendation for a pair to go with the dress. I prepared to say goodbye to my summer earnings as I laced up my Converse.

By the time I purchased the dress, the sweater, and a new pair of shoes—the most I'd ever spent on an outfit—I'd put a huge dent in my savings. Hopefully Dad would feel guilty enough about ditching us for Thanksgiving he would have Connie add a little extra to the Christmas checks. Otherwise, when spring quarter arrived, I'd have to go without Starbucks. Not a happy thought.

We left Nordstrom and wandered through the center courtyard on our way to Macy's. The yeasty smell of cinnamon rolls from somewhere nearby made my stomach growl, but we hit Macy's before I whined about food and a second cup of coffee.

Lexi gave her credit card a serious workout before we finally left Bellevue Square. Somehow we squeezed everything into her car so she could drive me home, and I couldn't believe it was only ten-thirty when we arrived. I had plenty of time to take a nap, talk to Rob, and get through the shower before she came back to pick me up for Jackson's party. I was surprised to find her alone when I opened the door.

"Where's Daniel? I thought he was coming."

Her mouth twisted in disappointment. "He got called into work."

"Oh. Sorry. But who needs a boyfriend to have fun, right?"

"Not us apparently. Guess it's girls' night out."

I learned we hadn't been too far from Jackson's place that

morning. I could see the lights of Bellevue Square as Lexi turned onto a residential street lined with barren trees. She turned several more times before taking a drive that brought us to a small collection of townhomes. The homes looked pale yellow in the sparse light, and they all appeared to have the same layout—a two-story living space over the garage and a set of broad, concrete steps leading from the ground level to the front door.

Once we reached the parking lot, I had no problem identifying which townhome belonged to Jackson. His Jeep stood out like a giant hazard sign in front of the garage.

Warmth and the tangy scent of hot apple cider enveloped us as we stepped inside. Mike was already there, and he and another guy joined Jackson in the foyer. Judging from his build, the third guy was a football player like Jackson.

Mike found room for our jackets in the closet while Jackson introduced his roommate Riley.

"So you're Kate," Riley said. "You're cute."

Jackson's eyes echoed his grin as he muscled his roomie aside. "You're gonna have to get in line, dude."

A thrill went through me at those words. I had a boyfriend. I was unavailable.

Lexi had been to Jackson's place before, so she went with Mike and Riley while Jackson gave me a tour. He introduced me to other guests as we worked our way through, and I couldn't help but notice that, except for me and Mike, they were either athletic, good-looking guys or perfectly put together girls who made me feel like a hobbit having a bad hair day. I did my best to smile and pretend I belonged.

Jackson and Riley had picked up for the party, but no amount of picking up could disguise the fact that two single, twenty-something guys lived there. A big screen TV dominated the living room, and a bookshelf full of movies with titles like *Captain America* and *The Matrix* stood on one side of it. On the other side, an entertainment center housed three different videogame systems along with their assorted games. Sports memorabilia served as décor throughout the unit, and they obviously ate their meals at the breakfast bar because the only table in the dining room was for playing air hockey.

The party centered around the college bowl game on TV, and in addition to apple cider, Jackson offered us some football-watching refreshments.

Revulsion filled Lexi's face. "Do you know how much artificial flavoring and food coloring goes into that garbage?"

"Nope," Jackson said, stuffing a chip in his mouth. "Don't want to either."

I had to agree with Jackson. Sometimes ignorance was bliss.

I enjoyed my chips then licked the artificial nacho cheese off my fingers so I could play air hockey with Riley. I lost despite his attempts to even things up by playing badly, and Mike took his place after a couple of games. Mike and I were more evenly matched since Mike's game-playing skills didn't extend beyond the TV or computer screen.

Lexi entertained herself by making snarky comments about our abilities, so when Jackson wandered into the room, I demanded she prove her right to criticize us. It took her about five seconds. She and Jackson were NHL compared to the pee-wee performance Mike and I had put on.

They traded insults as often as they traded goals, but it was all in fun, and we needed fun right now. Things had grown tense as days continued to pass without a single clue about where Eden was or what she was doing. Mike couldn't find anything helpful on the news, at least nothing that could be tied directly to a Fallen Guardian. Nathan wasn't picking up any supernatural hints either. Hassan spent half his time talking on the phone to Nathan or Lexi's dad, but they still couldn't come up with anything. Things wouldn't stay that way though, and we all knew it. We needed to enjoy this stress-free evening while we had the chance.

Jackson's cell phone rang as Lexi sent a shot toward his

end of the table. She crowed in triumph when the puck snapped into the goal.

"That doesn't count," Jackson said as he dug his phone out of his pocket.

"It counts. It's not my fault if you get distracted."

Jackson checked the number, and his expression went from annoyed to serious. "It's Nathan."

He listened for a few seconds then gave Lexi a nod.

"We'll get our jackets," she said.

Heart pounding, I followed her to the foyer. Mike tagged along. I took my jacket when she handed it to me, hurrying to put it on even though I didn't know why.

"What's going on?" I said. "Did something happen?"

Jackson joined us and answered the question for her. "Nathan found her. He Knows where Eden is."

CHAPTER
TWENTY~ONE

Jackson grabbed a jacket from the closet and shoved his arms into the sleeves. "Nathan saw an article in the *Times* about some new housing development in Issaquah and Knew that was it. Hassan's on his way home. We'll go gear up first and then meet Nathan."

My hand froze mid-zip. "Wait, we're going right now?"

"We have a better chance of catching up with Eden if we don't wait, and a deserted construction site means no witnesses. No innocent bystanders getting caught in the crossfire."

"And it's better for Hassan if we go tonight," Lexi added.

Nathan had told me something similar before they went to look for Eden at Marymoor last month.

"I don't get it," I said as I finished zipping my jacket. "What difference does it make? He can still hide himself during the day, right?"

"Yeah, but it's not impossible—if you know he's there— to figure out where he is," Lexi said. "He can't hide his footprints unless he's standing right on top of them. It's even more of a challenge when it comes to something like muddy ground, which is what we'll be dealing with tonight. It's a lot harder for someone to spot footprints or other signs of his presence in the dark. Night gives Hassan an edge, and it provides him with some extra protection in case he loses the element of surprise."

Hassan versus Eden. It could all come down to whether or not Hassan remained hidden from her. I was all for going tonight if it helped him stay alive.

When Riley came to the foyer, I figured he knew about the Guardians. He didn't ask where we were going in such a hurry or why we were leaving in the middle of the party. He only told us to be safe as we slipped out the front door.

Once outside, we split up. Mike rode with Jackson, and I went with Lexi. I had no idea what occupied Lexi's thoughts during the drive to Yarrow Point, but my mind took the opportunity to give me reminders so vivid I could have sworn the car smelled of musty earth. My scalp crawled with the memory of Benny's touch, and my flesh burned with the memory of Eden's. The remembrance of agony stirred in my ribs and spread to my arms where the pressure left me trapped and helpless. The air was too thin to breathe, my chest too tight to draw it in. Fear engulfed me until I was drowning in it. I closed my eyes and sent up a desperate prayer for help.

"Hey, are you okay?"

I opened my eyes in time to watch us roll to a stop behind Jackson. We were already at Hassan's.

I gave Lexi an uneven nod as the gates to the driveway slid open. "I'll be fine."

Our arrival triggered the motion sensors, washing the courtyard in light. Mist danced away from the light to reveal the damp stone underneath. Our footsteps echoed across the courtyard as we walked toward the garage. Hassan had left the door to the Audi's bay open when he came home, so we entered the house that way. Mike headed for the main room while Jackson, Lexi, and I took the stairs to the lower level.

The door to the weapons room gaped open, but Lexi turned toward the locker room, so I did too. She traded her pink-framed glasses for a pair of contacts then pulled black clothes and boots from her cubby. It was the same kind of military-style outfit Hassan had worn before. Seeing it forced me to acknowledge the goal of tonight's endeavor, the reason the door to the weapons room was open.

I sank down onto the bench, resting a hand over my stomach. Maybe those chips hadn't been such a good idea. "So we're really doing this? We're …"

I couldn't say it. While my objections weren't as strong as they had been before meeting Eden, the idea still made me sick. Realizing I might have a part in someone's death tonight was even worse.

"I don't know what the exact plan is yet," Lexi said as she laced up her boots, "but the general idea is for us to provide support while Hassan does the dirty work." She stood straight and scanned my clothing—black jacket, dark jeans, black Converse. "We need to get you outfitted real soon, but you'll be okay for tonight."

I didn't want to be okay for tonight or any other night. I wanted the whole thing to go away and never come back, but that wasn't an option.

I followed Lexi to the weapons room and stepped inside for the first time. It had roughly the same dimensions as our garage at home. Metal shelves occupied the back half, and metal cabinets lined the available wall space in the front half. A variety of plastic and metal cases filled the shelves, ranging in size from something as small as a shoebox all the way up to something big enough to cram Lexi into.

I assumed the shooting range or whatever you called it was through the door to the left where it would have the advantage of being buried in the hillside to absorb the noise. People tended to freak out when they heard gunfire, and I could guarantee Hassan's neighbors had no idea they were living next door to an ex-terrorist with an arsenal in his basement. I was willing to bet most of it was illegal too.

A white, rectangular table stood in the front half of the room, and Hassan was in the process of inspecting the guns and ammunition magazines laid across the top of the table. Jackson, now in the standard Guardian outfit, had rifles propped on both hips. He looked like a walking advertisement for an action movie.

Hassan took one glance at me and said, "No."

"What?"

"You're not going."

"But ..."

I turned to Lexi and Jackson for an explanation. All I got was a shrug-headshake combo from Lexi and its twin from Jackson.

I'd been expecting to go. I thought I had to go, and I'd been trying to prepare myself for the nightmare of facing Eden and Benny again, for the nightmare of providing support while Hassan ... did his thing. A minute ago, I would have done anything to stay behind.

"I'm coming with you."

His gaze lifted from the table. "No. You're not. You don't have any field training yet, and you'll only get in the way. I can't protect you and do my job. You will stay here with Mike."

"No way. I'm not staying with Mike."

"You will do what you're told and not argue with me."

"You're the one who keeps telling me I need to accept who I am. So am I a Guardian or not?"

I immediately regretted challenging him. Anger ignited in his gaze, searing into me, and I struggled to keep eye contact.

"So now you want to be a Guardian." His voice was quiet, ominous. He reached out, picked up a gun, and held it toward me. "Take it. Take it, or you don't go."

Only the buzz of fluorescent lights broke the silence as we stood facing each other. Finally, stomach protesting, I took a step forward and held out my hand.

"Are you sure this is what you want?" he said, the words still laced with that deceptive softness.

It wasn't at all what I wanted, and I didn't understand why I was doing it. I only knew I couldn't stay behind. "I'm coming with you."

I had to make myself stand still as he moved around the table radiating power and violence. I almost expected to feel a snap of static electricity.

"Hold it this way. Like *this*." He forced my hands around the gun and lifted my arms. He knocked my feet apart with his boot. "Balance your weight. Squeeze the trigger."

He gave me another glare before he marched back to the table, muttering in Arabic as he went. Jackson set the rifles on the table then came to stand in front of me. His body did a more than adequate job of blocking Hassan's view as he took the gun from my hands.

"I'll put it in the glove compartment," he said quietly. "He's just ticked off because you're right and he didn't get his way."

Relief washed over me when the gun left my hands. Then I wanted to kick myself. How stupid could one person be? Really stupid, apparently, because I'd fought to be a part of tonight's insanity even though Hassan had presented me with an easy, guilt-free way out.

I had brain damage. That was the only logical explanation.

I became convinced of it as I watched them slip on flak jackets, strap on gun holsters, slide spare ammunition into their pockets, and conceal knives in boots and leg straps. Hassan took binoculars from one of the cabinets, handing a pair to Lexi and another to Jackson, and all three of them picked up rifles on their way out.

I trailed behind them to Mike's work area. Mike had cleared off a few inches of space on one of his tables, and five Bluetooth devices lay in the clutter-free spot. As Mike and Hassan discussed the construction site, Jackson picked up one of the devices and handed it to me.

"These are radios Mike adapted for us. Works like a Bluetooth except we're on a conference call. See those two little buttons on the side? Put it on and give those a squeeze."

He helped me by holding my hair out of the way as I settled the Bluetooth in place and squeezed the buttons. The part of the Bluetooth that hooked around my ear gently tugged against the skin of my scalp. I pulled at the device, but it stayed put.

"Push them again," Jackson said, and the device released. "Pretty sweet, huh? That way you don't lose it in the middle of a fight. Now push the button up at the top."

Static scratched in my ear.

"That lets you know it's on, and you can communicate with the rest of us. Even Mike if you need him. He'll monitor everything from here."

I pressed the two smaller buttons on the side again and tugged at the Bluetooth. It held fast to my skin. "Mike's a genius."

"Yeah he is. He might not have a *Pur*, but he's still got a Gift."

"So how hard do you have to pull before it rips your skin off?"

"It won't take any skin off. Well, not much. Mike says it's about the same as a piece of good double-sided tape. The idea is to keep the radio in place, not graft it permanently to your skin. If some Fallen Guardian has a Gift that can mess with electronics, you don't want it stuck on your head."

Jackson picked up the other devices from the table and placed one over his ear. He stuffed one into his chest pocket and tossed another to Lexi. The last Bluetooth arced gracefully through the air to Hassan who caught it without taking his attention from Mike's computer screen.

"Can Hassan still use the radio when he's cloaked?" I said.

"Yeah, for whatever reason the radio still gets through. Mike thinks it has to do with wavelengths or frequencies or something. I can't remember exactly what he said."

I experienced a little surge of happiness because I understood. "They're two different kinds of waves. Sound waves are mechanical. Radio waves are electromagnetic. They seem like they should be the same thing, but they're not."

Jackson's eyebrows rose. "Did you seriously pull that out of your head?"

"It's basic physics."

"Most people don't speak basic physics. Don't get me wrong, okay? I'm impressed. I'm also a little intimidated you're smarter than me."

"I'm not smarter than you."

"Sure you aren't. The same way you aren't shorter than me."

I wanted to ask why I needed his help with calculus if I was smarter than him, but Hassan called us over to one of the huge flat screen monitors mounted on the wall. Mike had pulled up some kind of satellite image for the construction site that made about as much sense to me as calculus did. I found myself in the familiar territory of clueless and hung back when Jackson and Lexi moved in to take a closer look at the screen.

"Eden has chosen her ground well," Hassan said. "The site is isolated, so it will be easier for her to notice our presence. It's in the early stages of development. The land has been cleared, and foundations for these homes have been excavated." He ran his finger along the screen to indicate which homes. "We'll have to watch our footing. The foundations will most likely be filled with rainwater, which will hide both the depth of the foundation and any exposed pipes."

"Good place to hide some surprises," Jackson said.

Hassan nodded. "I would make use of them if it were me, so don't assume anything is safe. We'll have some cover from the buildings and materials, but not much." His expression turned grim. "She will have plenty of earth to work with."

I already knew what Eden could do with air, and I was afraid to think about what she could do with earth. Despite my attempt to block it out, an image crept into my head. An image of a hole suddenly opening up beneath my feet, of falling and trying to climb out as dirt cascaded over me. The crushing weight of soil that left me immobile. I felt a tremor of bone-deep fear at the thought of being buried alive, suffocating in my own grave.

What if we were doing nothing more than driving to the site of someone's death?

Hassan gave Mike a couple of final instructions before the four of us walked out to the garage. I gave the others plenty of room as they loaded weapons into the back of the Range Rover. Once everything had been stowed away, Hassan took the driver's seat. Jackson claimed shotgun, and Lexi and I climbed into the back seat.

As we started down the driveway, Jackson pulled his phone from one of his pockets. I was surprised Hassan let anyone mess with his car, but he didn't object when Jackson tapped the touch screen and activated the wireless audio streaming. Disciple's *Game On* blasted through the speakers a moment later.

CHAPTER TWENTY-TWO

Hassan drove us to a residential area on the east side of Issaquah, and Jackson turned off the stereo as we pulled up next to a Subaru wagon. Nathan, dressed in black like the others, got out of the Subaru. Lexi moved over into the middle to make room for him, but it immediately became obvious the arrangement wouldn't work. Nathan would be eating his knees if he sat behind Jackson.

"Maybe not," Nathan said.

He walked around to the other side of the car while Lexi and I slid to the right. Claustrophobia hit the moment Nathan shut the door, but with a little shifting, we found an arrangement we could live with.

Jackson gave the extra Bluetooth radio to Nathan, and Lexi handed Nathan her iPad so he could view the aerial images Mike had found. Hassan relayed details about the construction site as we continued through the residential area.

We reached a stretch of road bordered by a greenbelt. Light from houses on the opposite side brushed up against the greenbelt but didn't penetrate beyond the tree line. Only the trees along the edge could be seen. Their pale trunks emerged from a wall of black as we drove past.

There was a flash of white in the headlights a few minutes later when the sign for Heron Ridge Estates came into view. Hassan turned at the sign, following a freshly-paved road that wound up the hill through the greenbelt. The Range Rover's engine hummed louder as we climbed, and before long faint light peeked from around the curve ahead.

The road ended about a half mile past the curve, turning to dirt where a section of the greenbelt had been cleared. A single streetlight stood at the end of the road. The gate of a chain link fence blocked the entrance to the development, and the fence trailed off into the trees on either side.

Hassan stopped in front of the gate and cut the engine. He then took the pair of binoculars Jackson handed to him and inspected the site. A portable office stood a few yards away along with a pile of lumber and a backhoe, and I could see two massive homes under construction. One was a two-story wooden shell with gaping holes where doors and windows would be. The second was nothing more than a skeletal structure of frames and trusses. Beyond those two, I could make out the foundation of a third home.

In a way, the pitiful offering of the streetlight made it worse because you realized how much you couldn't see. Deep shadows hovered behind everything the light touched, and darkness smothered everything beyond it. The clouds hung so low you could almost reach up and touch them.

A curtain of fog drifted in front of the Range Rover, obscuring the view for a moment. When the air cleared again, a single raindrop hit the windshield. The fog was the only thing moving outside, but it sure didn't feel like it. It felt like something was out there, waiting just beyond the reach of the light.

"Step softly tonight," Nathan said, as if he sensed it too. "She's grown very powerful since the last time I saw her. With so much exposed earth, I'm afraid she'll be able to sense us. Maybe pick up the vibrations or something. I don't Know that she can. It's just a suspicion."

Hassan handed the binoculars back to Jackson then turned to survey the road and trees behind us before he started the car and backed away from the gate. Still in reverse, he edged the Range Rover over the curb and parked beneath the shelter of an enormous cedar tree. A couple of branches dipped low enough that they would help camouflage the SUV from anyone at the site, but the site could still be seen through the windshield.

Hassan cut the engine again, and this time Lexi handed him some kind of hi-tech binoculars which he used to inspect the greenbelt surrounding the site.

"We'll enter there."

He pointed to a spot somewhere off to the left as he gave the binoculars to Jackson. Jackson examined the trees then passed the binoculars to Lexi as Hassan explained where he wanted each of them to take up positions after they crossed the fence. Once everyone was in position, Hassan would scout ahead and try to locate Eden.

"Eden is the priority," he said. "The one with the Gift of Compulsion is second. We will search for him later if we must."

"Wait," I said as car doors opened. "What am I supposed to do? And what about the other guy—the guy who was with Benny?"

"He's connected to Eden," Nathan said. "Once she's dead, he won't be a problem."

"What do you mean? Connected how?"

"I'll explain later. Right now it doesn't matter. He's not the one we need to worry about."

I knew he wasn't saying that what Eden had done to me didn't matter, but it had the same effect. If I hadn't been such a failure as a Guardian, I wouldn't have been completely helpless against the nobody on her team—the guy who didn't matter.

Hassan was watching me in the rearview mirror, so I tried keep the hurt from showing on my face, but I didn't think I was successful. Another failure to add to my list.

"I need you to stay here," he said. "Come. Sit in the driver's seat."

I accepted my assignment as benchwarmer without comment.

Hassan held the door for me, and I slid into the driver's

seat while the others began to remove equipment from the back of the Range Rover.

"The car will be visible in a moment," he said. "Stay alert. Keep your eyes open and tell us if you see anything." His gaze swept over me, and he frowned. "Where is your weapon?"

"In the glove compartment."

"Place it on the passenger seat where you can reach it. The safety mechanism is in the grip, so you don't have to worry about the gun firing until you pull the trigger." He waited until I had done what he told me. He then leaned in, and his expression became so intense my heart rate picked up speed. "If someone approaches you—unless it's one of us—you shoot them in the head. Do you understand?"

I couldn't form a reply. Fear and protest had tangled in my throat.

"Kate."

My head jerked up and down.

"You will stay in the car. You don't get out—you don't move—unless I tell you to. If I tell you to leave, you leave. No matter what you hear or what you see. You will not question my orders or argue with me. You will do it."

"Okay," I managed.

"Promise me. I can't do what I need to do if I have to argue with you every time I give an order. Promise you will do what I say."

"I promise."

I meant it whole-heartedly. I didn't want to be the reason his attention wandered at a crucial moment, the reason something horrible happened to him, to any of them. Everyone needed to come out of this alive because to lose one of them was unthinkable. Two months ago, I had no idea they existed. Tonight, I didn't know how I would ever exist without them.

"Please be careful," I said. "Benny can get inside your head, and he doesn't even have to touch you. Neither does

Eden."

Some of the intensity eased from his expression. "Don't worry about me. They will have to find me first."

I pressed the automatic lock after he shut the door, and when he looked at me through the window, I gave him a shaky nod. I was as ready as I was going to get.

He lifted his hand from the Range Rover, and the four of them made their way through the trees. I grabbed the hi-tech binoculars from the back seat and watched their progress in green and black night vision. Even knowing what they could do didn't prepare me for what I saw. My brain and my eyes argued over reality.

Jackson gave Nathan a boost up and then, like one of those guys who did parkour, he took a little hop, grabbed the top of the six-foot fence, and swung his body over, landing neatly on his feet. One moment Lexi walked toward the fence, and the next she dissipated into what looked like a shadow but with more substance. She flowed through the chain links and coalesced on the other side exactly as she had been before—clothes, weapons, everything. By the time I finished watching Jackson and Lexi, Hassan was a hazy silhouette beyond the fence.

They spread out into the dark, and I lost sight of them. I gave up on the binoculars and watched the entrance to the site while I waited to hear something. Minutes passed, but I heard nothing more than the patter of raindrops filtering through the branches to land on the car.

I jumped when Jackson's voice came through the earpiece. He was the first to check in. Lexi and Nathan checked in shortly after that.

"Hold your positions," Hassan said. "I'll work my way west."

The minutes stretched on. When the glass fogged up, I turned the key enough to crack the windows, and cold air carried the scent of cedar into the car. My body shivered in protest as the temperature dropped, but being cold was better than sitting blind.

Jackson was the first to speak again. "I've got movement. North side coming out of the trees. I count five."

My breath caught. Five? There were *five* Fallen Guardians?

"They're fanning out," Jackson said. "My guess is they're looking for us."

"I've got five more on the south side," Lexi said. "Way to go, Jackson. An elephant would've made less noise jumping the fence."

"Shut it, Lexi."

"I can see at least three more at the tree line," Nathan added.

"Does anyone see Eden?" Hassan said.

Three negatives came as I strove to stay calm. This whole thing screamed trap, and everything in me screamed we should run. Where did Eden find all of them? And what had she promised them in return for their help? There weren't enough Guardians to go around, and I doubted she would share.

"Well, crap," Jackson said. "Three more just came through the trees. She's not messing around."

Hassan growled something in Arabic. "Fall back."

Hope trickled into my heart, soothing my anxiety. Maybe this was a trap, but that didn't mean someone had to get caught in it. We could leave with everyone still alive and come up with a different plan. One that didn't involve Eden killing someone.

"Hang on," Jackson said. "I think I've got her."

"Do you have a clear shot?" Hassan said.

"No. And she's holed up with about a hundred yards of open space between me and her. I can make a run for it if you want. I can get to her before the dirt bags reach us."

"No, we need to use stealth with her, not speed. Stay where you are and don't lose sight of her. I'm on my way. Nathan. Lexi. Take rear positions and make sure they don't circle behind us."

I grabbed the night vision binoculars again and scanned along the fence, willing my eyes to see what was happening. When nothing turned up, I used the regular binoculars to check the area closer to the streetlight. Adrenaline shot through my veins when I saw movement in the shadows behind the closest house. Or I thought I did. I almost said something to Hassan, but it might have been nothing more than my imagination. It could have been Nathan or Lexi for all I knew, and I didn't want to distract him with my paranoia.

"*Dude*. I hate it when you do that. You need to give me a heads up before you pop out of thin air."

"I told you I was coming," Hassan said irritably. "Where is she?"

"Straight ahead. Left of that foundation and behind those big old concrete pipes."

"I'll use the foundation and come in from the right. Give me five minutes then drive her toward me. Nathan? Lexi?"

"Almost there," Nathan said. "You're clear."

"In position," Lexi said. "Clear."

The binoculars weren't helping, so I set them aside and focused on what I could see with my own eyes. The fog was still the only thing moving, a vaporous apparition drifting through the light.

The five minutes seemed painfully long until Jackson said, "Here we go. Party time."

A gunshot cracked in my earpiece, echoing outside the car. Another followed.

"They're coming, Jackson," Lexi said. "Moving fast."

"Well, stop sitting on that rifle and give me some backup."

Gunfire erupted, and soon the sounds of scuffling filled my earpiece. There was a snap of breaking wood and a grunt as someone took a hit. I heard another grunt I could identify as Jackson this time.

"Hurry it up, Lexi!"

She snarled in frustration. "They're out of range. I'll have to move in closer."

"Watch your back," Nathan warned. "A couple of them broke off from the group. I lost sight of them, but they were headed in your direction."

Why had I promised to stay in the car? I couldn't sit here and do nothing when they had more than a dozen Fallen Guardians closing in on them. But what could I possibly do to help? Hassan was right. I would only get in the way.

Completely useless, I sat in the car and listened to gunfire mix with verbal exchanges and sounds of physical struggle in my earpiece. A slap of water and splashing noises joined the confusion. Then I heard something that caused my chest to tighten in fear. Eden. Someone was close enough for the radio to pick up her voice. I couldn't make out the words, but I knew it was her.

Hassan, breathing hard, spoke through the chaos coming over the radio. "Fall back. Everyone fall back. Kate?"

"Yeah?"

"Back the car up to the gate. Be ready to leave quickly."

"Okay."

This was my chance. This was how I could help. I could follow Hassan's instructions and get them out of here as soon as possible.

Hand shaking, I started the car, turned on the headlights, and gently stepped on the gas. The car rolled forward, bumping over the curb. The Range Rover was heavier than Mom's Civic, and it moved differently. I juggled caution and the need to hurry.

I backed up to the gate and put the car in park but decided not to set the emergency brake. After unlocking the doors, I checked the rearview mirror. I couldn't see much, so I twisted around to look through the back window. Where were they?

The seconds crawled by as I watched, and I tried not to think about Eden getting her hands on one of them or Benny getting inside their heads and convincing them to stick around instead of heading back to the car. I tried not to think about what Gifts the other Fallen Guardians might have. Gifts like causing paralysis or stopping someone's heart from beating.

No one emerged from the shadows, and the sounds of battle went on. My eyes stung as fear threatened to bring tears to the surface. What was taking so long?

I yelped as my door flew open.

Hassan's voice crackled in my earpiece. "Kate?"

My only response was a shriek as I scrambled across the center console to escape. As my fingers touched the handle of the passenger door, a hand closed around my ankle—the same hand that had held me prisoner while Eden tortured me.

I kicked, trying to free my foot, but he pulled me backward. I clawed at the passenger door and dug in with the foot that was still free. It tangled in the steering wheel, and the horn wailed before he grabbed that leg too. I cried out in pain when he wrenched my foot loose.

"Kate, answer me!"

With one brutal heave, my knees slammed over the console. Tears flooded my eyes when the door handle slipped from my grasp.

I grabbed at the passenger seat and felt a nail tear as my fingers sunk in. The odor of moldy earth assaulted my nose as I strained toward the seat with every muscle in my body. Shifting my weight, I anchored myself with one arm and reached underneath me with the other. My fingernails scratched against the leather.

What happened to the gun? Where was it?

My entire body trembled from the effort to hang on. Another fingernail tore. Finally my fingers brushed the gun, but before I could grasp it, his hands tightened around my calves and yanked. The gun skidded off the edge of the seat and landed on the floorboard with a thump.

A sob broke from my lips. Once he had me out of the car it was over. I wouldn't be able to get away from him, and no one would be able to help me. They were all too busy trying to stay alive.

Frantic, I jerked my legs toward my body and lunged for the floor, stretching as far as I could. He retaliated with another vicious heave, but just before my ribs grated across the console, my fingers closed around the gun. I twisted and grabbed onto the steering wheel to slow my exit. The gun was in the wrong hand, but it didn't matter. It was enough.

I pointed the gun at him. "Stop! Let go!"

He didn't show any sign he'd heard me. He continued to drag me from the car. I tried to kick my legs free, but I only slid further. My fingers began to lose their grip on the steering wheel, so I twisted back around and hooked my left arm through. The horn blared as I fought for enough leverage to draw my legs inside the car. His fingers dug into my calves, and he yanked so hard it felt like I'd been ripped in two. A cry of agony escaped.

"Please stop," I begged him.

Another yank, and the pain became too much. My body was halfway out of the car, and I didn't have the strength to hold on any longer. Grief and terror melded together, falling like dead weight on my chest as I twisted toward him again.

I closed my eyes and squeezed the trigger.

CHAPTER
TWENTY~THREE

The noise was deafening—so startling I almost dropped the gun. It took a second for me to realize I'd missed, and then panic spurred me into action. I leaned back on the seat and kicked with both legs, but instead of trying to free myself, I used the momentum to shove him. The car rocked as he collided with the door. I drew my legs back to give him another full-body shove, and he rammed into the door again. When his hand slipped down to my ankle, I jerked my foot away. His fingers tightened in response but too late. All he ended up with was my shoe. My foot was free.

I braced my foot against the doorframe and had just enough time to switch the gun to my right hand before he took hold of my leg again. As he pulled my foot away from the doorframe, I grabbed the seat belt with my left hand and lifted the gun with my right.

He didn't even flinch as the bullet plowed into his shoulder. The second shot sank into his chest, but he didn't stop. He couldn't feel it.

Grief pressed down on me again. I didn't want to do this.

He yanked on my legs, and I slid from the car. My hold on the seatbelt was the only thing that saved me from smacking my head against the bottom of the doorframe.

I aimed higher this time. A crack filled the air.

Sightless eyes stared at me for a moment before his grip relaxed. I scrambled to get my feet under me as he toppled to the ground. I clung to the seatbelt taking huge gulps of air, my entire body trembling. I had shot a man. I had taken someone's life.

Only by sheer force of will did I keep the contents of my stomach where they belonged. I couldn't fall apart now. I needed to be ready when Hassan and the others came. Later, when this was over and everyone was safe, I could have the luxury of falling apart.

I forced myself to turn away from the body lying on the ground and used the seat belt for support as I climbed into the driver's seat and shut the door. Voices reached through the ringing in my ears and began to form coherent words again.

"Now!" Hassan barked. "Find out what happened to Kate!"

"I'm fine," I said, the words detached from the part of me inside that was screaming uncontrollably. "I'm okay. I'm ready to go."

Throbbing drew my attention to my fingers and the fact that they were clenched around the gun. Another wave of nausea crashed over me. I stuck the gun in the glove compartment then squeezed my hands around the steering wheel, letting the pain in my fingers distract me from the nausea, from the knowledge of what I had done.

Mike joined in the radio communication. "King County Sheriff is on the way, Hassan. They don't have an exact location, but two units are headed for Heron Ridge."

I turned toward the back window in time to see Jackson emerge from the dark, a blur of inhuman speed. He vaulted the fence and skidded to a stop next to my door. His eyes scanned my face before moving to the ground beside the Range Rover. When he lifted his head again, I saw a streak of red on his temple.

"Are you okay?" I said.

He wiped at it with one of his sleeves. "I'm all right. Been playing without a helmet, that's all. You?"

I gave him a nod. Technically, I was okay.

More gunfire filled the air, close this time. With his rifle strapped to his back, Jackson ran to the gate where a heavy-duty chain sealed the entrance. He grabbed the chain with both hands and pulled. The chain snapped apart like pop beads. He flung the gates open, barely missing the back end of the Range Rover, and the fence on both sides rattled when the gates collided with it. He swung his rifle around, bracing it against his shoulder as he stepped through the opening.

Nathan was the next to appear, and he ran toward the gate trying to keep his weight off his left leg. As Jackson sprinted out to meet him, a shadow shot out of the dark and solidified a few feet behind Nathan. Lexi began firing the instant she was material, aiming at several figures at the edge of the light. One of the figures hit the ground and didn't get up. She kept the rifle trained on the others while Jackson carried Nathan toward the Range Rover.

There was movement to Lexi's right. I opened my mouth to call out a warning, but Hassan stepped out of the shadows, splattered with mud.

"Help Jackson," he said to her.

Lexi Shadowed and flew toward the car. Hassan backed toward us with his gun pointed at the Fallen Guardians. Still visible. Why didn't he go into Stealth mode? My breath caught as I realized he was offering himself, giving them an easier target than Nathan.

Before I could protest, the Fallen Guardians rushed him. Hassan managed to drop two of them before a guy almost as big as Jackson reached him and swung down with a massive arm. The blow knocked Hassan's gun from his hand. He staggered and dropped to his knees.

"Hassan!" I screamed.

The Fallen Guardian reached for Hassan, but with a flicker of movement and flash of steel, he stopped. He crashed onto his back with Hassan's knife protruding from his forehead.

Jackson had rejoined the fight. He picked off two more Fallen Guardians as Hassan retrieved his gun from the ground. Hassan lifted his arm, and the last two men fell.

Hysteria rose dangerously close to the surface as I watched Hassan step over to the Fallen Guardian who had hit him. He set his boot on the prone figure's face, bent down, and tugged his knife free. He wiped the blade on his pants and secured the knife in its leg strap before jogging toward the fence.

Sirens wailed in the distance as I turned to face the windshield. Someone opened up the back, and equipment went in with much less caution than when we'd started off the evening. The car swayed as the backseat filled up then the passenger door opened and Hassan got in.

"Go," he ordered.

I put the car in drive and stepped on the gas. We hadn't even made it to the first curve before he pointed to a wide spot on the side of the road and told me to pull over. As the sirens drew closer, I wondered what would happen when they got to the site. The man I killed would be the first body they saw.

Another wave of nausea crashed over me, but I rode it out. It wasn't time to fall apart yet.

"You're bleeding."

My eyes went to Hassan then followed his gaze to the steering wheel. I had blood on my hands. Blood had oozed from beneath my torn nails and smeared across my fingers. It was on the steering wheel too.

"Sorry. I'll clean it up."

He frowned at me. "I don't care about the car."

He took my hand and ran his fingers beneath mine, extending them so he could inspect the damage. He had mud on his fingers, and now it was on mine too.

I tugged my fingers free. "It's not that bad."

The truth was that my fingers felt like they were on fire, but it was nothing compared to what had happened to me before or what could have happened to me tonight. It was nothing compared to what I had done.

Hassan continued to watch me, and his gaze was a little

too perceptive for my comfort. He wasn't buying my denial, but he didn't say anything.

Sirens pierced the air as two patrol cars rounded the bend, racing past us with lights flashing.

Panic hit. "Wait, we can't let them walk in there and—"

"Eden left," Nathan said. "She isn't at the construction site anymore. They'll be okay."

Eden had escaped, and everyone else was dead. Somewhere in the back of my mind, I wondered who had fired the shot that killed Benny.

When Hassan asked Mike for an update, Mike confirmed only two units had been dispatched to the scene, so Hassan gave me the go ahead to pull back onto the road. I drove aimlessly. I knew we'd come this way, but I couldn't seem to remember how we got there or how to get back.

"I don't know where I'm going," I told Hassan, my voice thick.

"Take a left at the stop sign."

We reached the main road that ran along the greenbelt, and after a mile or so, Hassan told me to make a right. Everything grew blurry when I turned down the street, and warmth trickled over my cheeks. I was crying.

I slammed on the brakes and threw the car into park. I didn't even have time to shut the door as I stumbled into the street. I barely managed to pull my hair out of the way before everything in my stomach ended up on the pavement.

It was bad enough to throw up where everyone could see it, but then I remembered they could hear it too. Maybe they'd been smart enough to turn off their radios when the retching started, but I tried to lose my dignity quietly in case they hadn't. When the worst of it passed, I turned mine off.

While I was bent over trying to spit the taste of stomach acid out of my mouth, I noticed I only had one shoe on. I'd left my other Converse at the construction site next to the man I killed. A lost shoe was a dumb thing to get upset over, but fresh tears came anyway.

A car door opened and shut, and a pair of boots appeared in the corner of my vision. Based on shoe size, it was either Nathan or Hassan. Somehow I knew it was Hassan.

"You didn't murder anyone."

How did he know? Did Nathan tell him why I was puking my guts out in the middle of the street?

"I shot him three times," I croaked. "One was in the chest, and one was in the head. Even if he was still alive when we left, he'll be dead before an ambulance can get there."

"He wasn't human, Kate. None of them were. They only look human."

I tilted my head up. My brain struggled to translate the words he was stringing together.

"They were golems created from the dust of the earth. They're an abomination, a mockery of God's creation of Adam. When they're made, their creator inscribes his or her name on their forehead, and that's the only way to stop them. You have to pierce the forehead. The only thing you did was destroy a creature intended for evil."

Details began to register. Even if my attacker didn't react—even if he felt no pain—his body should have. A bullet entering the human body would meet resistance as it tore through flesh and shattered bone, but the bullets had passed through effortlessly, cleanly. There should have been blood, but I'd shot him three times, and he hadn't shed a single drop. The only blood at the scene had been mine.

Frustration welled up until I wanted to scream. Every time I thought I was starting to get a grip on this Guardian thing, someone took all the pieces, shook them vigorously, and dumped them upside down, scattering them to who knew where.

"This is what she does with earth? Why didn't anyone tell me?"

It was a stupid question because I knew why I'd never heard it before, and for the first time, I was completely and totally ticked off at someone other than Hassan. I stood straight, zeroing in on Nathan as he started to speak.

"Don't tell me I wasn't ready to know. I'm sick of finding out stuff after it's already happened." Icy water squished through my sock as I took a step toward the car. "Maybe you should tell me I'm ready to die, Nathan. He had me out of the car, and I hesitated because I thought I was killing someone. If you're so concerned about my sanity, then tell me what's going on before I completely *lose it!*"

They all stared at me, obviously thinking it was too late and I'd already lost my sanity. Well, everyone except Hassan. He'd seen me go ballistic before.

"We need to leave," he said.

"No! I'm not going anywhere until I get some answers. Until someone starts telling me the truth." I hated the note of betrayal that crept into my voice. "You knew, Hassan. You knew the whole entire time. You're the one who told me to aim for the head. You could've told me why, but you didn't."

A curtain parted in the house closest to us, and a face peeked at us through the opening. The dog in the house next door was barking its head off. The last thing we needed right now was for someone to report a disturbance, so I limped around to the passenger side, yanked the door open, and plopped down on the seat. Then I really wished I hadn't. Hassan had been sitting there, and now my butt was wet too.

I slammed the door shut.

Silence pervaded the car as Hassan got in and drove off. He scrounged up a bottle of water from his side of the car and handed it to me. I winced when I twisted the cap off, but it was worth the pain to wash the nasty taste from my mouth.

"My Gift doesn't make me infallible," Nathan said after I'd taken a swallow. "Sometimes it makes things worse. Sometimes the Knowledge is just beyond my reach, and I have to make a judgment call. I made the wrong call on this one, and I'm sorry."

I kept my eyes fixed on the road in front of us. I didn't want to hear it.

Hassan's head turned in my direction, so I faced the passenger window. I was mad at him too. He and Nathan expected too much from me. They expected me to blindly trust their judgment and do whatever I was told without arguing or asking questions. They expected me to be happy about the fact my life had been completely derailed and stuck on a track that shouldn't even exist, but they couldn't be bothered to tell me the truth. Jackson and Lexi were on my black list too. They were guilty of the sin of omission.

I'd officially had it with Guardians. It was immature, but I found a great deal of satisfaction in the knowledge Hassan was soaking wet, the leather seats of his car were filthy, and everyone else was crammed in the back like sweaters in a Space Bag.

When Hassan parked behind Nathan's Subaru a few minutes later, Nathan came and stood outside my door. My plan was to ignore him for the rest of my life, but Hassan hit a button and lowered the window. I let my eyes communicate to him how much I didn't appreciate it.

"I'm sorry," Nathan said.

Pain harassed his features, and exhaustion had joined it, exposing the burden of responsibility weighing him down. He hadn't asked for an emotionally unstable recruit anymore than I'd asked to get recruited. Sure, he had messed up my life, but it wasn't really his fault. He was just doing his job, and when it came down to it, he was still one of my favorite authors.

I sighed. "Sorry for freaking out."

"I think it's understandable given the circumstances." He gave me a tired smile. "Good night."

He told Hassan he would call later then said good night to Jackson and Lexi before hobbling toward the Subaru. When Hassan rolled up my window and put the car in drive, I sighed again.

"Hang on. Jackson can have shotgun."

Jackson didn't even attempt to play the gentleman. He

pried himself out of the back seat as quickly as he could. "Thanks, Kate."

He and I switched places, and when Nathan's Subaru pulled away from the curb, Hassan followed. I drank another mouthful of water as I watched houses pass by. Some of them already had Christmas lights up. After a few houses, the lights all seemed to run together then fade away as lifeless eyes filled my vision. Eyes that were much too human. So human they would haunt me when sleep claimed me tonight.

I blinked to refocus on my surroundings. My hand shook as I downed another gulp of water.

In front of me, Hassan hunched his shoulders like he was trying to find a more comfortable position, and I could see his grimace in the rearview mirror. Human or not, those things could cause a lot of pain, and that blow had to have hurt. Jackson's head probably wasn't feeling too great either. His wound had stopped bleeding, but the side of his face was a mess where he'd wiped at the blood with his sleeve. I doubted I looked much better after all the crying I'd done, and my body ached from the struggle with Eden's golem.

I turned to see how Lexi was doing. "Are you okay? Did you get hurt?"

She held up one hand to display a less than perfect manicure. "I broke a nail. Does that count?"

"No, it doesn't count," Jackson said. "Maybe you should do more than break a nail next time. Maybe you should give me some backup so I don't have a dirt bag trying to crack my head open with a two-by-four."

"I'm not the one who jumped the fence and announced my arrival to the entire Eastside."

"Enough," Hassan snapped. "It doesn't matter if Jackson alerted her to our presence or not. Nathan was right. Somehow she knew when I approached her."

"Could she see you?" Worry edged my voice.

"No, I don't believe so. She seemed to have only a general idea of where I was—behind her or to her right—but it was enough. She began to change the air and make it difficult for me to breathe. Then she sent her golems to find me. I had to keep moving, and each move took me farther from her. I never had a clear shot."

It must have been Hassan's radio that picked up her voice, and I hated to think how close he'd been for that to happen.

"What did she say to you?"

His gaze flickered to the mirror and met mine. "She said she would enjoy using my Gift."

CHAPTER
TWENTY-FOUR

Hassan's gaze rested on me for the longest time. If it had been anyone else behind the wheel, I would've worried about the Range Rover drifting off the road, but it was Hassan. The car remained centered in our lane.

His gaze returned to the road as Jackson twisted around to look at me. Pale light from the dashboard gave an eerie glow to the right side of Jackson's face and cast the left side in shadow, turning the blood on his temple into a smear of black.

He studied me for a moment. "You sure you're okay?"

"Yeah."

Despite my assurance, he continued to inspect me, a trace of fear haunting his features. "It didn't sound like it earlier. I didn't think I'd get to you in time."

I slid my injured fingers out of his line of sight. Hassan was watching me again in the mirror, and I could sense Lexi's gaze on me too.

"I'm fine." It was an outright lie, but everyone needed to stop staring at me. When Jackson started to say something else, I cut him off. "So those were all golems? Even Benny?"

He frowned but took the hint. "No, Benny is definitely human. He's got a Gift, and he can talk. Golems are mute, and they can't do much more than pound on you."

"He *is* human? He's still alive?" My gaze moved between the three of them. "You guys didn't get either one of them?" When Lexi shot me an unpleasant look, I rushed to explain myself. "That's not a burn on anyone's skills. It's panic. I thought … I thought it would be over after tonight."

Eden and Benny were still out there somewhere. This whole evening—all the terror and all the pain—had been for nothing. I wanted to weep.

"I never saw anyone matching Benny's description," Jackson said. "Did you guys see him?" Both Hassan and Lexi replied in the negative. "Huh. Well, either he got smart and took off or Eden killed him already."

He said it so easily, not as if he was talking about someone dying—a thinking, feeling individual one moment and a body laying on the ground the next. I had seen too many bodies hit the ground tonight. I doubted I would ever be able to get those images out of my head. The knowledge they weren't human didn't help because they looked so human. It had looked like seven violent deaths.

"What happens when the cops show up and find a bunch of golems at the construction site?" I said. "Aren't they going to notice nobody … that their wounds aren't normal?"

"They will find nothing except the clothing she put them in," Hassan said. "The golems are created from dust, and they return to dust. The one you destroyed was nothing more than a pile of earth by the time we left."

Humor worked its way into Jackson's expression. "They'll just think it was a party gone wrong. We should've left some empty beer cans. Cops can explain almost anything when they think kids have been out in the woods partying."

"I left my shoe there."

The whine in my voice earned a scowl from Hassan in the mirror. "I'll buy you a new pair."

"I don't want a new pair. I want my shoe."

We reached East Lake Sammamish Parkway, and Nathan's Subaru turned right while Hassan hung a left and headed for I-90. The Range Rover bumped over a metal plate on the road—more of the endless Eastside construction—and a few stray bits of gravel crunched beneath the tires before we reached the on-ramp.

"So how did Eden do it? The golems, I mean. It's not just manipulating earth, it's animating it. How is that even possible?" When no one answered, I groaned. "Tell me. Whatever it is, I'd rather hear it now. It's better than getting a crash course later."

Jackson glanced at Hassan like he was waiting for him to answer my question, but Hassan kept driving as if I hadn't said a thing. Lexi seemed very preoccupied with her broken nail all of the sudden.

I growled in frustration. "You guys need to stop treating me like a head case. I know I have a tendency to freak out, but half the time it's because nobody tells me what's going on. I ask a question, and nobody wants to answer it. I almost die because I'm missing information, but everyone thinks I'm overreacting. You heard Nathan. He doesn't Know everything. Sometimes he gets it wrong."

"You know, Nathan didn't specifically tell us not to mention …" Jackson stopped when Hassan glared at him. "Well, he didn't."

Lexi shook her head. "I can't believe I'm saying this, but I agree with Jackson."

"I didn't ask for your opinion," Hassan said. "Or Jackson's. I remember Nathan's words precisely. I don't need anyone to remind me."

I was dying to see if I could kick the back of Hassan's seat hard enough to knock his head into the steering wheel, but I settled for leaning forward so I could complain in his ear.

"Has it occurred to you that my odds of survival are better if I get out right now and walk home? At least I'd know I was on the freeway and I needed to watch for headlights. I might even be able to get out of the way. Unlike being a Guardian. You and Nathan wait until I get run over and *then* tell me to watch for cars."

When he still didn't respond, both Jackson and Lexi tried

to pry an answer loose.

"Hassan—"

"Dude—"

"Silence," he demanded.

My foot twitched, aching to connect with his seat. "Fine. Whatever." I slumped back against the seat to watch beads of rain run across my window.

"It's called a Book of Creation."

I turned from the window in surprise.

"No one knows where they came from or how many of them exist," Hassan said. "Each Book seems to vary from the others, but they all contain the same basic information. What Jackson likes to call recipes. For Eden to create a golem, she either had to get the information from a Book of Creation or she had to get it directly from a demon. We believe she has a Book because most hunters do. It tells them how to take power from a Guardian."

Hassan was displaying a great deal of faith in my ability to handle the truth, and I didn't want to thank him for it by freaking out, especially after I'd yelled at everyone for assuming I would. I took a moment to let the information sink in and tried to process it logically, not emotionally.

The existence of the Books meant Eden's knowledge was finite, a definite plus. She was limited to what she found in her Book or what she could bargain from a demon. On the downside, all the information was conveniently gathered in one spot.

"What else is in there? What else can she do?"

Jackson was more than willing to speak up now that Hassan had lifted the gag order. "Like he said, it tells her how to take power from a Guardian so she can level up. It also tells her how to get in touch with the dark side. And she can cook up all kinds of stuff with the recipes. Golems, zombies—"

"Zombies?"

"Yeah, but my guess is she'll stick with golems because

she already has a Gift that lets her manipulate earth. For her, it's like paying wholesale instead of retail. It doesn't take as much of her power to dredge up a golem as it would other stuff, and Fallen are basically lazy that way. They don't like to work too hard to get results. Minimum effort with maximum output."

The problem with his line of thinking was that Eden's Gift worked on the human body too. A dead body still had carbon. She wouldn't be limited to golems.

"It's the oldest sin there is," Hassan explained. "Fallen want to play God. They want to be God. They take the truth, and they twist it until it's a mockery of what God intended in the first place. That's what a Book of Creation is about."

"We need to find Eden," Jackson said, "but we also need to find her Book and destroy it."

"Doesn't she have it with her?"

He started to shake his head then stopped. He winced and put a hand to his head like it would keep things from spinning. "She won't have it on her unless she's in the middle of cooking something up. She doesn't want to take the chance Guardians will get a hold of it during a fight, and Fallen kill each other for those things. She'd be asking for someone to go after her and try to take her Book if she kept it with her. But the good news is she won't wander too far from wherever she stashed it, so her Book's around here somewhere. We just need to find it."

"Is it at the construction site?"

"If it was, she sent it off with a golem as soon as we showed up."

"It was probably never there at all," Hassan said. "She knew we would find her."

"How could she know that?" I said. "Nathan didn't know until an hour before we got there."

"Perhaps she didn't know we would come tonight, but she is familiar with Nathan and understands how to use his Gift against us. She alerted Nathan to her presence so he would search for her, and she waited for him to find her." He paused then, the kind of pause where you had to stop and think for a second because something just occurred to you. "She chose her ground well and created a large number of golems, but she didn't use the Fallen Guardian with the Gift of Compulsion."

He fell quiet again, and I could tell he was analyzing details the way he did when he studied his laptop's screen or listened to a phone call or conversation. I had come to understand what Jackson meant when he said he never wanted to go up against Hassan for real. I'd figured out the "too dangerous" part right away, but "too smart" was almost as frightening. He was one of those guys you never wanted to play chess with because the game would be over as soon as you made your first move.

"She prepared for a battle she never intended to win."

"That doesn't make sense," Lexi said. "She's a hunter. The whole point of her existence is to kill Guardians."

"I agree. It doesn't make sense—not yet—but she wasn't hunting tonight. She let me get close enough to believe she was vulnerable, but there were too many golems for her to lose. And if she truly wanted one of us, she should have used the other Fallen Guardian. She didn't."

I didn't like the direction the conversation was heading. Not that I wanted Hassan to be a target, but at least if we knew who and what Eden was after, we might be able to come up with some sort of plan to stop her.

In the interest of not freaking out, I scrambled to come up with a reasonable explanation for Benny's absence. "It's probably like Jackson said. Benny either took off, or Eden, you know, lost patience with him."

Hassan shook his head. "Fear and intimidation can be powerful bonds, and she is intelligent enough not to kill without reason. He is exactly where she wants him. The only reason he wasn't there tonight is because she wants to use him for something else."

"Maybe she wants his Gift."

"If she wanted it, then she would take it from him."

I was doing my best to stay calm, but Hassan wasn't helping me out. "Maybe she likes having someone to push around, someone to run her errands. That's what he was doing the day he got on the bus with me. We probably showed up while he was off doing something for her."

"I don't think it was coincidence. It was part of her plan. Otherwise she would have fled when we first arrived and waited for a better opportunity. Using him would have made the difference tonight." Somewhere behind us, a car changed lanes, and its headlights briefly illuminated the Range Rover's interior. In that moment of light, Hassan's gaze found mine again in the mirror. "She could have killed me, but she chose not to."

Eden had done the same thing with me—held my life in her hands and given it back. But I hadn't walked away free. It felt like she'd branded me that day, claiming the right to return for my life whenever she wanted. My fear would only add to her enjoyment of the hunt. She was definitely sick and twisted enough to mess with my head—Hassan's too—but was that the only reason for what she'd done?

"So why did she let you go?"

Hassan didn't answer right away. "Perhaps this was nothing more than a distraction. Perhaps she wants us to believe she is here to hunt when she is searching for something else."

"But she already has a Book," I said, dismay filling my voice. "What else is there?"

"I don't know, but we need to find out."

CHAPTER
TWENTY-FIVE

We made it back to Hassan's a few minutes later, and I helped by carrying binoculars down to the weapons room. As Lexi, Jackson, and Hassan sorted and cleaned equipment, I slipped out to the locker room to wash my hands.

I watched dirt and blood swirl down the drain, clenching my teeth against the sting of water. Then, as if that pain opened the door for others, I felt the ache in my shoulders, the tenderness of bruises forming across my belly. Every single part of me seemed to hurt, and my thoughts and emotions churned inside like floodwaters about to overrun the riverbank.

Maybe I was innocent of murder, but the moment I pulled the trigger would be forever etched in my memory. The moment when I understood what I was capable of doing. Before tonight, it had been so easy to believe I would never take someone's life. I couldn't believe that anymore.

Each time the Guardian world brushed against mine, it pushed my safe, predictable life a little farther away. It pulled me farther away from who I was. I was becoming someone else as pieces of the old Kate fell away, and I wondered if there would be enough of me left in the new Kate that I still recognized myself. What if the parts of me I lost were the good things? What if the new Kate was someone I didn't want to be?

I closed my eyes and pushed back against the flood. If I lost control now, I'd never get it back.

After patting my hands dry with a towel, I changed into my sweats and a dry pair of socks. I then put on the running shoes I'd bought when I realized Jackson was determined to stick me on the treadmill every day. I set my wet clothes and my single Converse on the locker room bench, slipped the Bluetooth radio into the pocket of my jacket, and headed to the weapons room to ask about bandages.

Lexi pointed me to one of the metal cabinets along the wall where I found shelves full of medical supplies. It wasn't just first aid stuff either. As I read labels, I discovered several items that had no business being in Hassan's house unless he had a medical license—which I seriously doubted—and I suspected some of it was illegal no matter who you were. It begged the question of where it had come from and what he did with it, but I probably didn't want to know the answer.

I helped myself to two flex fabric bandages then shut the doors. When I turned, Jackson had his head bent over the table, giving me a clear view of the gash on his head.

"You probably need stitches."

He looked up at me, and I pointed to the wound.

"It's fine. It'll be a week old by tomorrow."

My eyebrows rose. "A week old? How hard did that two-by-four hit you?"

"No, I mean …" He frowned. "Didn't anyone tell you?"

"Tell me what?"

He glanced at Hassan and Lexi, apparently hoping for backup.

Lexi shrugged. "It never came up. I don't remember talking about it anyway."

"I don't believe we spoke about it," Hassan said as he removed a magazine from one of the handguns.

Jackson gave me an apologetic look. "We weren't trying to keep it from you. I guess we all figured you heard it from somebody else. It's one of the perks of being a Guardian. Your body can take more punishment than the average human being, and you heal up quicker too." He indicated his wound. "A week old by tomorrow."

The morning after my encounter with Eden, my injuries had seemed so minor. I'd assumed they weren't that bad to begin with. But maybe they really had been bad, and I'd done a week's worth of healing overnight.

"Well, at least let me clean it up for you," I said. "If it's going to heal up that fast, you should make it pretty. Contrary to rumor, chicks don't dig scars. Not big, ugly ones."

He grimaced. "Better you than Lexi I guess."

"Hey, as long as I don't have to listen to you whine, I'm good," Lexi said. "Kate's premed. I vote we make her our field medic. The official 'listen to the guys whine' team member."

"At least I did more than break a nail."

I figured Lexi was exaggerating about the whining, but you would've thought I was trying to kill Jackson. I didn't understand how a guy who could snap me in half could be such a baby when it came to a little hydrogen peroxide. My capacity for sympathy dwindled each time his head jerked in one direction or another and bumped into my fingers. Hassan and Lexi were long gone by the time I got his wound cleaned up, and I was seriously reconsidering my career plans. Wanting to strangle your patient wasn't a good sign.

Between Dermabond and butterfly bandages, I was able close up the gash, but then Jackson reached for his head.

"Stop. Don't you dare touch it."

He dropped his hand.

"Hold still."

"You sound like Hassan," he grumbled.

I resisted the urge smack him and undo all my hard work. "Well, don't do that unless you want to start over."

Using a gauze pad and bottled water, I washed the blood from the side of his face because I didn't trust him to do it himself without opening up his wound again.

In the absence of chairs, I'd made him sit down on the

table when we started. It brought his head closer to my eye level, but he still had to bend forward so I could get at his wound. I was amazed that even covered with dirt and blood he managed to smell like spearmint gum.

I took one last swipe with the gauze then stepped back and peeled off the surgical gloves. "I think that'll work. Don't touch it, and don't get it wet. Not until tomorrow."

He lifted his head, and eyes the color of a summer sky focused on me. A smile—half apology, half humor—spread across his mouth. "You'll make a good doctor."

"Thanks," I said grudgingly.

"And I'm sorry we didn't tell you about Eden. About what she can do."

I gave him a shrug as I gathered up gauze and stray bits of wrappers from the table. "Nathan was just trying to help."

A large hand reached out and captured mine, garbage and all, and turned it over to display the bandages. "Doesn't look like it helped very much."

Strength and vitality suffused Jackson's touch. Something in me was drawn to it, but I pulled away from him.

"It's no big deal," I said. "It'll be a week old by tomorrow, right?"

"We still should've told you."

"Probably, but I'm too tired to think about it anymore tonight."

He watched me a few seconds longer before he stood up, placing a massive bicep in my field of vision. "Thanks for gluing my head back together."

He left, heading for the guys' locker room I presumed, while I finished picking up. I didn't see a waste basket, so I started for the hallway intending to use the one in the girls' locker room. Then I wondered if I was supposed to turn off the lights and close the door. After a moment, I shrugged, figuring the possibility of anyone getting this far into Hassan's house was nonexistent, and Jackson would be coming back this way anyway. He could lock up the weapons room. If I was supposed to do it, no one had told me about that either.

I disposed of the trash and grabbed my wet clothes before going upstairs to find Lexi, my ride home. I found her in the main room curled up in one of the leather chairs with her iPad. Mike was in his usual spot, entranced by something on one of the monitors, and Hassan sat on the loveseat with his laptop. He was wearing jeans and a white t-shirt, but I was willing to bet they were designer and cost more than my new dress.

Looking at the three of them, I realized I wasn't ready to go home yet. The only thing left on my agenda was to get into bed and have nightmares, and that didn't sound very appealing. I didn't want to be by myself right now, and if I went home, I would be. It wouldn't matter if Mom was right across the hall.

I dropped my clothes by the front door, returned the Bluetooth to Mike, and grabbed a Diet Coke from the fridge. When I flopped down next to Hassan on the loveseat, my abused body protested and so did Hassan. He looked up from the computer and glared at me for making the screen jump. I gave him a "get over it" look.

Jackson appeared a minute later, excavated his PSP from the disaster on top of his desk, and sprawled in one of the chairs. Soon the clang of swords emitted from the PSP.

I sipped my Diet Coke, determined to enjoy the illusion of normality for as long as it lasted. "I can't wait to see what's next. Maybe we should track down Sasquatch or hunt vampires in Forks."

"There have never been any vampires in Forks," Hassan said.

"Yeah, I know."

He didn't take his eyes from the screen, but his forehead bunched into a frown. "Then why would you say that?"

"Really, Hassan? Do you seriously not get it?"

"Get what?"

A snort of laughter came from Lexi's direction.

"For crying out loud," I said. "You live in Washington— three hours from Forks. How can you not get it?"

"It's not his fault," Jackson said. "Hassan is Pop Culture Disabled. We've tried to educate him, but he won't cooperate. We can't even get him to watch *Star Wars*, so he never gets our dark side jokes."

I turned to Hassan in disbelief. "You've never seen *Star Wars*?"

"No. Why should I?"

"Because it's un-American not to see it."

"I'm not American."

"But you live here. That's close enough." I leaned over and put my hand in front of the laptop's screen so he had to look at me. "Would you stop with the world domination for two seconds? We're scheduling a movie night so we can watch *Star Wars* on the huge flat screen in your living room. The one that never gets used."

"I do use it."

"Watching CNBC in Hi-Def is not using your flat screen. Using your flat screen is watching movies with big explosions in them, ones that rattle the bass in your speakers. Honestly, Hassan, you haven't lived until you've heard a light saber in surround sound. Ask Mike."

Mike nodded enthusiastically on the far side of the room while Hassan scowled at me. I scowled back. His gaze traveled to the other mutineers before returning to me.

"Fine." He pushed my hand away from the screen.

Jackson broke into a grin as he set his PSP on the coffee table.

Lexi's grin was almost as big as his. "Movie night! I'll take care of pizza."

Jackson's grin instantly dried up. "No way. I'm not eating that flavorless cardboard-tofu garbage."

"So you know what cardboard tastes like."

"Yeah, and it tastes better than the stuff you buy."

"Has it ever occurred to you there might be a reason those pizzas you eat are called Tombstone?"

Hassan looked up from the computer screen, and the way his gaze fixed on the two of them reminded me of a cobra considering the best angle for a strike.

"Lexi can bring her own," I said in an attempt to spare lives. "The rest of us can order out."

"Fine," Lexi said. "But don't blame me if all four of you drop dead from a heart attack before you hit thirty. Do you have any idea how much saturated fat there is in a single slice of pizza?"

"Hey, hang on a second."

I didn't want to think about saturated fat in the first place, but I especially didn't want to think about it now because the wording of Hassan's statement had just sunk in. I focused on him, prepared to catch every detail. To catch what he didn't say.

"You said there have never been any vampires *in Forks*. Does that mean they've been somewhere else? Is there a recipe for vampires in a Book of Creation?"

His cell phone rang, so he ignored me. He set his laptop on the coffee table and picked up his phone instead. I figured it was Nathan calling like he'd promised, but after checking the number, Hassan answered in Arabic. He listened for a moment, and when his reply came, it was sharp, the words edged with fury. His anger became a palpable thing, infiltrating the air of the room as he began to argue with whoever was on the other end.

He ended the call then got to his feet and walked away from the chairs. I flinched as he hurled his phone at the wall. It ricocheted off the wall then hit the floor, bouncing and skidding across the stone.

He stood with his back to us, his shoulders rigid. After a moment, his shoulders sagged like a giant hand had pressed down on them. My throat felt thick as I watched the change in his posture because I recognized it. I'd felt the shape of it before. It was discouragement. Defeat. It was losing hope when you never really had any to start with.

Without another word, Hassan went upstairs. I looked to the others for some kind of explanation.

Lexi shrugged. "Trouble back home I think."

She and Jackson exchanged a glance, and I knew I was missing information again. Since it didn't have anything to do with Guardians and wasn't any of my business, I didn't push for details. If Hassan wanted me to know what had happened, he would tell me. Which meant I would probably never know.

Hassan's phone call killed the fun for the evening—what little we'd managed to scrape up after the disaster at Heron Ridge—so everyone headed home and left Hassan to deal with his family problems alone.

Except for the porch light, the house sat in darkness when Lexi dropped me off. I let myself in and removed my shoes by the front door. Once my eyes adjusted, the pale glow from the bathroom nightlight guided me down the hall. I dropped my wet clothes into the laundry basket then padded to Mom's open door and knocked softly.

"I'm home," I said, my voice just as soft.

I didn't wait for a response. I knew I wouldn't get one.

After a trip to the kitchen cupboard for ibuprofen and one to the bathroom to brush my teeth, I crawled into bed. I had barely laid my head on my pillow when the urge to cry hit me. It had very little to do with the events at Heron Ridge and a whole lot to do with being alone.

I thought about calling Rob, but how could I explain why I didn't want to be alone with my thoughts? How could he possibly understand? Tonight he and I existed in two separate worlds.

I had no one to talk to and no one to tell me things would be okay. I should have been used to it by now, but tonight it hurt more than ever.

CHAPTER
TWENTY-SIX

Rob headed back to Redmond early Sunday morning like he'd promised. He called while he was still on the ferry, and we agreed to meet in the foyer before the church service.

I didn't have any trouble spotting him when I arrived. He stood next to the windows where sunshine beamed through the glass, catching fire in the bronze tones of his hair. He was so beautiful it made me ache, and it stirred up a nagging fear that this was a temporary thing.

He waited until Mom headed for the sanctuary and then came and wrapped his arms around me. I drank him in, inhaling the metallic scent of wool and the traces of wind and saltwater clinging to his skin.

"Good morning," he said, giving me a squeeze.

"Good morning." I squeezed back, ignoring my fear. It would steal away my happiness if I listened to it.

Skipping our normal Friday and Saturday night dates gave us a good excuse to spend Sunday afternoon together. Hanging out with Rob was so nice, so normal that training was the last thing I wanted to do on Monday, especially with finals coming up. Somehow I convinced myself to get off the bus at Yarrow Point after classes on Monday, but my motivation level dipped even farther when I saw Hassan.

He had something in his hand, but I couldn't figure out what it was until I reached him. As I stood there looking between him and the object he held, an odd feeling stirred inside my chest.

"Is that my shoe?"

"You didn't want a new one."

"You went all the way back there to get it?"

"No, I didn't go back for your shoe." His tone said I was a complete idiot to entertain such a thought. "We had to make sure Eden abandoned the site."

I didn't know whether to be ticked off no one told me they were going or relieved I didn't get invited.

He pressed the shoe into my hand. "It should have been right by the gate, but I had to search for it."

My thumb brushed across metal eyelets and black canvas. I couldn't believe it. Maybe he didn't go back there to get my shoe, but he remembered. He got out of the car and looked for it. He actually picked it up. It was damp and filthy and had been run over at least once, but he'd found it and brought it back to me.

I had cried when I lost it, and now I wanted to cry all over again. "Thanks."

His shook his head as he opened the passenger door. "Get in. You're late."

Hassan seemed determined to compensate for his single act of kindness by pushing me extra hard in training that week. I sort of understood why he did though. Despite all his efforts I still sucked as a Guardian. Then there was the fact Eden had disappeared without a single clue about where she'd gone or what she had planned, which put him at a major disadvantage strategy-wise. But Eden and I weren't responsible for the extra shot of meanness he'd been adding to his coffee every morning. I knew it had something to do with his phone call from home, and I wanted to cause some serious pain to his dad or whoever had ticked him off because I was the one paying for it.

Between Hassan's foul mood and the pressure of upcoming finals, I looked forward to my anniversary date with Rob more than ever. He'd made reservations for us at Alexander's, a classy seafood restaurant on the east side of Lake Washington. It was probably the equivalent of

McDonald's for people like Hassan who had way too much money, but for middle-class wannabes like me and Rob, it was a big deal.

On Saturday, I pulled my dress from the closet afraid the dressing room scene had been nothing more than a sleep-deprived hallucination, but the outfit looked as fabulous in my mirror as it did in Nordstrom's. So fabulous I put on my black wool coat before I went to tell Mom I was leaving. I didn't want to deal with the panic that would surface in Mom's eyes if she got a good look at it. I didn't want her fears to spill over into my happiness and ruin it for me. Not tonight.

The trees along Lake Washington Boulevard were already decorated in anticipation of Christmas with white lights entwining their bare winter limbs. The lights twinkled cheerfully as Rob pulled into Carillon Point. Stylish office buildings mingled with expensive retail shops, a spa, and several restaurants including Alexander's. The Woodmark hotel served as a popular wedding venue, and park-like seating areas provided a view of the water and marina, making it a great place to enjoy an iced coffee during the summer.

Tonight the view was black satin sprinkled with glitter, and the boats in the marina rested peacefully beneath their covers, settled in for a long winter's nap. The cold made our breath fog in the air and discouraged us from lingering outside when we turned over the car to Alexander's valet.

My heels sunk into the burgundy carpet of the lobby as Rob ushered me to the alcove on the far side of the room. A miniature Christmas tree sat on the coat check counter, and it scented the air in the alcove with evergreen. Once Rob helped me out of my coat, I turned to find him looking at me—well, at my dress—but he didn't say anything. He stared for a few seconds before handing my coat to the attendant. After handing over his own coat, he turned toward me again. When he still didn't say anything, I started to smooth down the dress with my hands. Then I stopped. Mom did the same thing when she was nervous or stressed.

"So this is it," I told him. "The dress I found at Nordstrom. Well, Lexi was the one who found it, but we both liked it." I couldn't help myself. I smoothed the fabric. "So do you like it?"

He answered with a kiss that made the dress worth every single penny. "I love this dress."

He gave me another kiss, and my cheeks flushed with happiness. A bit of embarrassment too. The coat check girl was getting way more from us than our coats.

The lobby doors opened, letting in a gust of cold air along with the couple who entered. I stepped back and wiped lip gloss from Rob's mouth despite his assurances he didn't mind it being there. He took my hand, and we climbed the stairs to the upstairs lobby where a Christmas tree with glass ornaments stood next to the reservations desk. It was perfectly framed against the wall of windows overlooking the marina, and I had a brief moment to think how pretty it was before my heel wobbled.

He had his back to us as he gazed out the windows, but I knew it was Hassan. The dark curls, the self-assured posture, the suit straight off the cover of GQ. His presence. I would've sworn I could close my eyes and still be able to tell you where he was in the room no matter where he stood.

Rob's hand tightened around mine. "Are you okay?"

"I'm fine."

Hassan spun around, and his gaze raked me from head to toe before moving to Rob. When his eyes came back to me, I felt like I'd been caught trying to key the Audi's paintjob. I hadn't planned to ignore him, but he moved to cut us off and make sure I couldn't.

"Who is this?" He growled the words at me, but his eyes were fixed on Rob.

"Uh, this … this is Rob. Rob, this is Hassan."

Hassan gave up a couple of inches in height to Rob, but

he was broader across the shoulders and thicker through the chest. He also had that strange ability to appear much bigger than he was. Maybe it had something to do with the fact I knew he could snap Rob's neck before I had a chance to blink. Maybe it was because he looked like he wanted to.

"It's nice to meet you, Hassan."

When Rob held out his hand, Hassan regarded it with the expression of a man who would rather soil his skin with raw sewage. He accepted the gesture, but I was sort of surprised he didn't wipe his hand on his jacket afterward.

"What are you doing here?" The question came out more sharply than I intended, but I wasn't sorry. He'd taken his foul mood out on me all week. He didn't need to take it out on Rob too.

"An investors' meeting."

"On Saturday night?"

"Yes, on Saturday night. Why?"

"It doesn't …"

I'd almost said it didn't sound like very much fun to be working on Saturday night, but since Hassan and fun didn't go together anyway, it was perfectly reasonable.

"Never mind," I said. "We should go. We have reservations."

"Yes, I can see you're very busy." He flicked a hand in Rob's direction. "Is this how you prepare for finals?"

Anger ignited in my chest, spreading heat up to my face. "Not that it's any of your business, but I studied all day, and I'll study again tomorrow. I didn't blow off finals—or anything else—this weekend. I needed a break, and we've had this dinner planned for a while."

"I see."

He was such a liar. He didn't see anything at all.

"We need to go."

Rob picked up on my cue. "It was nice to meet you." The words were pleasant, but Rob's tone had cooled, and his hand found its way around my waist. His fingers dug in, pressing me against his side.

Hassan gave Rob a nod—more dismissal than response—and I could feel his eyes on us as we walked toward the reservations desk. I willed him to go away. I had accepted the reality of Hassan making me miserable when it came to the Guardians, but he needed to leave the rest of my life alone.

"Who is he?"

There was a healthy dose of anger in Rob's voice. I didn't blame him.

"A friend. Sort of. More like a friend of a friend. It's a long story."

"Well, I'd love to hear it. He knows you well enough to ask about finals."

Great. Now I had to find a way to explain why I spent time with a bunch of Guardians and do it without telling Rob anything about the Guardians. I officially hated Hassan.

Rob glanced over his shoulder as we reached the reservations desk, and so did I. I wanted to make sure Hassan was still visible and where we'd left him, not in stealth mode listening to everything we said. But when I looked back, he was gone.

My eyes swept the lobby searching for something out of place—a shadow falling the wrong direction, a reflection bending the wrong way against the glass. Anything that felt out of place. I didn't see anything, so I closed my eyes. Nothing. As the hostess led us to our table, I told myself to stop being so paranoid. Hassan had better things to do than spy on my dinner date.

But if I ever found out he had spied on me, I was going to do a whole lot more than key the Audi.

The hostess brought us to a table with a view of the marina. She handed us menus before she left, but I didn't get a chance to look at mine.

"How do you know him? Is he a 'friend' as in ex-boyfriend?"

A noise caught in my throat—one that sounded like I was

being strangled—and the couple at the next table glanced in our direction.

I leaned toward Rob, attempting to keep my voice down. "Hassan? You think ... are you insane?"

My response knocked the anger out of his expression. "He's not your ex?"

"No way. That would be totally creepy. He's ancient—like almost thirty—and he hates me. I hate him too. I'd rather stab myself with a butter knife than spend time with him."

"But he didn't like you being here with me."

"He doesn't like anything or anyone. He's psychotic."

Confusion replaced his anger. "So why did he ask you about finals?"

I had to be careful here. I didn't want to dig such a deep hole for myself I would never get out of it.

"Okay, you know my friend Lexi? Well, Hassan is her boss, and she works at his house. It's this gigantic mansion with a home gym in the basement, and the one nice thing he's ever done is let me use it." My Converse came to mind, but I shoved the thought aside. "He lives on Yarrow Point, kind of on the way home, so I stop by there after classes. I said I'd be studying this weekend, and obviously he doesn't have a life, so he doesn't get it. He can't understand why some people don't want to work 24/7."

"Why do you go there if you hate him so much?"

"Well, Lexi's there," I hedged. "And it's free. If I don't have to spend money on a gym membership, I can use it to buy other stuff like coffee and books. Or a new dress." When his eyes dropped to the dress, feminine instinct kicked in. "I thought you liked my dress. I bought it because I wanted to look nice for our dinner tonight."

He reached across the table to grasp my hand. "You do look nice. You look incredible."

"So maybe it's worth it then. I'd rather spend money on a dress you'll see instead of paying some trainer to torture me."

His fingers tightened around mine. "I'm sorry. He doesn't

look that old, just like he has a lot more money than I do, and there was so much tension between the two of you. I assumed you'd been together, and the thought of you being with him, with anyone else ..." His fingers gripped mine even tighter.

I shook my head. Not even close with Hassan.

"For future reference, you don't have to worry." I hesitated a moment before confessing my inexperience. "I don't have any exes."

A look full of self-loathing came over his face. "I'm sorry. I totally overreacted."

"It's not your fault."

No, our first fight was all thanks to Hassan and his complete lack of social skills.

I reassured Rob he wasn't to blame, but he apologized again before we took the time to peruse our menus. I'd pretty much lost my appetite, so I picked something vaguely appealing and turned my attention out the window. The dark expanse of water lay beyond the marina, and I could see lights in the distance. Yarrow Point. I could probably figure out which house was Hassan's if I wanted to, but I definitely did not want to. He'd already spoiled enough of my evening—my life—as it was, and that included my entire summer because now I had to find a new spot to enjoy my iced coffee.

The waiter came to take our orders a couple of minutes later. Once we were alone again, Rob reached across the table to reclaim my hand. "I'm sorry."

"It's fine. Really. Let's talk about something else, okay?"

He brushed his thumb back and forth across my knuckles. "We could talk about winter break and how it's a long time to go without seeing you."

Rob planned to go home over the break not just to visit his family but to work. His cousin let him stay in the guest room rent-free while he attended the U, but he still had to pay for his share of food and utilities. He also had to put gas in his car and help pay for tuition. The restaurant in Poulsbo where he'd worked since high school let him pick up shifts when he was home, and he made really good tips. Sitting across from him, looking into his gorgeous hazel eyes, it wasn't too hard to figure out why. He could dump my lunch order in my lap, and I'd still tip twenty-five percent.

"I don't think you realize how addictive you are," he said. "I barely made it through Thanksgiving weekend."

His other hand joined the one already on the table and traced a feather-soft line across the top of my wrist. He watched its progress for a moment before lifting his eyes, and the way his gaze fastened onto mine sent a shiver through me.

"Maybe you could come see me. We'd have to fit it around my work schedule, but that way we'd have some time together. I wouldn't have to wait so long to see you again."

Aside from the major roadblock of Mom's paranoia, I'd been stupid enough to promise Hassan more training time over break. And it was quite possible I'd need to find a way to earn some extra money myself.

I swallowed down the bitter taste in my mouth. "I'll try."

I tried to enjoy the rest of our evening too. I really did, but it had the taint of disappointment.

CHAPTER
TWENTY~SEVEN

Rob and I saw each other at church the next morning and agreed to meet that afternoon to study together. No way was I going to invite Rob to study at my house though. Studying at his place was also out unless I wanted to take up lying or deal with telling Mom I'd be hanging out with my boyfriend, a memory foam mattress, and way too much privacy. We needed a neutral, public location, so I suggested the library.

After lunch, I borrowed Mom's car and drove to downtown Redmond. My pulse skyrocketed when the library—and the bus stop where Benny had found me—came into view. Nathan had said it was safe for me to ride the bus, but I wasn't riding the bus today. And he'd told me that over a month ago. Before Heron Ridge. What if Eden changed her mind? What if she decided to come after me again?

My eyes scanned the sidewalk on both sides of the street as I approached the parking lot. Once I parked, I sat and watched people come and go past the giant bird sculptures in front of the library. It took a text from Rob to get me moving. He was inside waiting for me, and he didn't have a clue golems existed, that there were creatures who could masquerade as human. He had no idea there were humans who could get inside his head or starve him of oxygen and turn his flesh into a living inferno.

I doubted any Fallen Guardians or golems would be wandering around, but my heart raced when I got out of the car. I walked toward the entrance studying faces and checking wrists when they were visible. As I stepped through the doors into the lobby, I waited for a shift in the air indicating Eden's presence. I prepared to fight the numbing fog of Benny's Gift.

Nothing happened. I sank down onto the bench beside the drinking fountain to let my heart slow down. After a minute or two, the fear eased, and then what I felt was anger, a burning resentment my life was being taken away from me one precious piece at a time.

I headed inside to find Rob. He sat at one of the tables in the back corner with nothing more than a textbook to threaten him, and his head snapped up when my backpack thumped onto the table.

"Are you okay?"

"Fine." I dropped into the chair next to him and ripped open the zipper.

"Did your mom say something? Did she not want you to meet me here?"

My biology book landed on the table with a thud. "No. It's not her."

"Is it me? Did I do something to upset you?"

I stopped flipping pages. The worry in his eyes brought a nudge of guilt, and I reached over, threading my fingers through his. "It doesn't have anything to do with you. You're pretty much the only person, place, or thing not causing me stress right now."

"Are you sure?"

"I'm positive."

His fingers tightened around mine hard enough to cause discomfort. "The last thing I ever want to do is hurt you. You know that, right?"

It was kind of a weird thing to say, but I nodded.

He searched my face like he wanted to make sure I meant it. Then his grip eased up, but only so he could pull me toward him for a kiss reminiscent of the one at Alexander's.

Jackson picked me up from the bus stop after my biology final on Monday. As I fastened my seat belt, he said, "How'd it go?"

"Good. There was only one question I wasn't sure about."

"Right on." He offered his fist for a bump.

Once we got to Hassan's, I said a quick hello to Lexi and Mike before going downstairs to throw on my sweats. I intended to continue training during finals week, but I refused to spend one second longer at Hassan's than absolutely necessary. As soon as we were done, I planned to get back on the bus and meet Rob at the library.

Hassan waited for me in the training room. As I walked over to the mat, he studied me like a bug he preferred to slowly dismember rather than swat and get it over with.

"You're late," he announced.

"I told you I'd be here by ten, and I was."

"It's ten minutes after."

"I had to change first."

"You're late."

I waited until the urge to throw something at him passed. "Okay, you win. I'm late. Next time I'll tell you ten fifteen and be five minutes early."

His expression darkened. "You treat this as a joke. As if it doesn't matter."

"You're the one who's freaking out over what time it is. What difference does it make anyway?"

"If you took your responsibility seriously, you would be here on time. You have no understanding of what it means to be a Guardian, and you will get yourself killed because of it."

I failed to see how being on time for training—which I had been—had anything to do with not getting myself killed. "You know, you were a jerk to me all last week—more than usual—and if this week is a repeat, then forget it. I'm not coming. I really don't need you shredding my self-esteem during finals."

"You see? You push training to the side as if it doesn't matter."

"You're not even listening to me. This doesn't have anything to do with training. It has to do with you. All I did was walk in here, and you started yelling at me. The same exact thing you did last week. I'm not the one who called and ticked you off, so stop taking it out on me. Buy yourself a bunch of phones and throw them against the wall."

He went still. Anyone with half a brain would have taken it for the warning it was and left the room, but I stood there like an idiot as fury settled over his features.

"That has nothing to do with you."

"That's the point. I have no idea what your problem is, so keep me out of it."

He stabbed a finger at me. "You are my problem. Every day you come here, and you waste my time."

In that moment two things became very clear to me. Hassan was never going to change, and I'd had enough. I was so over and done with being treated this way. I headed for the door.

"Where are you going?" he demanded.

"Anywhere but here."

"You see? You have no idea what it means to be a Guardian."

I stopped and spun back around. "I. Don't. Care. Is that easy enough for you to understand? I didn't ask to be a Guardian, and I don't want to be a Guardian. I'm sick of being lied to and treated like I don't deserve to exist, so find someone else to kick around. I'm done."

"You understand nothing. You can't even see the lies right in front of you. If you want the truth, I will give you the truth because you're too foolish to see it. You're too foolish to see he doesn't care about you."

"What are you talking about? Who doesn't care?"

"Your boy from the restaurant."

"You mean Rob?"

He waved my question aside. "His name doesn't matter."

I was about ready to go to the locker room, dig out my house key, and take a trip upstairs. The Audi wouldn't be the only victim either. There was a silver sports car flaunting its pristine condition on the far side of the garage.

"And I suppose you were able to figure out he doesn't care in the whole sixty seconds you saw him," I said. "The whole sixty seconds you were totally rude to him by the way."

"He doesn't love you."

"Like you would know anything about that! And so what? We've only been going out for a month."

"It makes no difference. He will only hurt you, and you can't see it because all you do is think about what you don't have. Just as he does."

"Since when are you the relationship expert? As far as I can tell, you can't even walk into the room without making everyone want to rip your head off. Have you ever met someone willing to spend more than five minutes with you?"

Color flooded his face, and with two steps he was so close to me that the rest of the world stopped existing. Fear raced through me—regret for provoking him, disbelief he was actually going to hit me—and I readied myself for the coming violence. But he didn't touch me. He didn't even try.

"You cry and complain about what you have to give up, but you know nothing of sacrifice. Why are you here, Kate?"

A thought nudged its way into my consciousness, one I'd been trying very hard to ignore, and my voice came out as little more than a whisper. "Good question."

Hassan didn't say anything as I left the training room. He let me go. I went to my cubby, grabbed my clothes, and crammed them into my backpack. After I heard the door to the stairwell slam shut, I peeked into the corridor to make sure he was gone.

The wary expressions and lack of conversation upstairs told me Hassan had already passed through. Lexi, Jackson, and Mike all focused on me as I came into the room, but I didn't offer any enlightenment.

"Jackson, can you take me to the bus?"

"Uh, sure. Let me grab my keys." We were down the driveway and out the gates before he spoke again. "Everything okay?"

"No."

He waited for me to explain, but I didn't.

"Want to talk about it?"

"No."

To Jackson's credit, he shut up. He didn't say another word until we stopped at the transit center. "You want me to pick you up tomorrow?"

"I'm not coming tomorrow."

"All right," he said, his voice full of concern. "Call me if you change your mind."

"I won't." I opened the door and took one last look at him, choking off the urge to cry before it could get too close to the surface. "Bye, Jackson."

CHAPTER
TWENTY-EIGHT

A sense of numbness settled over me as the bus made its way toward Redmond. I studied the watery gray light outside my window and tried to comprehend what I had done.

When the bus approached the stop by the library, fear shook me from my daze. A girl my age waited on the sidewalk, and I watched her as I stepped off the bus. She didn't even notice me. I headed for the library wondering if I would ever stop being afraid.

I changed in the restroom, trading my sweats for the jeans I'd stuffed in my backpack. With more than an hour to go before Rob showed up, I found an empty table and attempted to study calculus, but the argument replayed itself in my head. More than once, the urge to cry swam close the surface, but I pushed it back under.

When Rob arrived, he bent to give me a kiss before taking the chair next to mine. "How did your test go?"

"Good. No major problems. How was yours?"

"Piece of cake."

"Only a genius would say that about a thermodynamics final."

I did my best to match his smile but obviously failed because he drew back to get a better look at my face.

"Are you sure everything went okay?"

I nodded. "Yeah. The test was fine. Really."

"Well, if you're worrying about calculus, don't. We have the rest of the day to get you ready."

While Jackson could have helped me prepare for my final, Rob was also an excellent calculus tutor. Good thing too, since I wouldn't be seeing Jackson again.

"What about you?" I said. "You need to study."

"I have Art and Music Appreciation tomorrow, and the professor has a new boyfriend. So unless they breakup tonight, I'm in good shape. I could sleep through it and still get a perfect score." He smiled, leaning over to give me another kiss. "Don't worry about me. We live and breathe calculus today."

We worked through calculus problems all afternoon, and Rob dropped me off before Mom came home from work. After dinner he continued to help me study via email and cell phone until my brain felt like someone had stuck it in a food processor and hit purée.

The final went okay Tuesday morning. I'd most likely end up with a C, which was better than failing, and it wouldn't pull my GPA down too far.

After my English lit final on Wednesday, I hunched down in my seat when the bus passed by the Yarrow Point transit center. As I got off in Redmond, my phone rang. I checked the number in case it was Mom, but the screen displayed Jackson's number. If I'd been a mature, responsible adult, I would've answered, but like the coward I was, I let it go to voicemail.

I silenced my phone after that but still had to check the number every time the front pocket of my backpack vibrated. After the third call I didn't answer, Rob gave me a quizzical look, and I set the phone in my lap so I could check the number without drawing attention to what I was doing. All of the calls came from Jackson.

Once Rob dropped me off at home, I went through the painful process of listening to the message Jackson had left. He sounded genuinely ticked off, not the irritated tone he used with Lexi.

"Hassan's a loser, and everyone knows it. He won't man up and tell us what he said to you, but he's either gonna apologize, or I will find a way to go *Terminator* on his hide. I promise you that."

I deleted the message, turned off my phone, and did my best to study for chemistry.

When I crawled into bed that night, tears finally broke through to the surface, but I didn't even understand why I was crying. Why did it hurt to walk away from something I'd never wanted in the first place?

Two more messages waited for me in the morning.

"I know Hassan is difficult," Lexi said. "Trust me, I know, and I know he regrets whatever he said to you. He's under a lot of pressure, and he's been yelling at everyone, so don't take it personally, okay? And don't give up on him. He'll make things right. Just give him a chance."

The other message was a guilt-inducing voicemail Jackson had left late the night before. "Come on, Kate. Please? Call me."

Somehow I made it through my chemistry final, but I had four text messages from Jackson and another voicemail from Lexi when I was done.

"You have to come back," she said. "Jackson is really upset, and he's threatening to quit. Not just as Hassan's accountant, but our team too. He says he can't respect Hassan as a leader anymore, and he won't listen to anyone, not even Nathan. I know that if you would come back and try to work things out, Jackson would calm down. Everything is falling apart here, and we really need you."

What they needed was for me to stay away. They were falling apart because of me.

Rob and I went to a movie that afternoon to celebrate the end of finals and to say goodbye before winter break, but I had trouble paying attention to anything up on the screen. My phone vibrated twice, but neither call came from Mom.

By the time we left the theater, the sun had already set. The evening was dark, cold, and dismal, and it fit my state of mind perfectly. Rob wrapped his arms around me, lending me the extra heat while we waited for the car to warm up. I snuggled against him and fought the urge to cry.

"Are you okay?" he said. "You've been really quiet the last couple of days."

"It's been a long week. And I miss you already."

"I miss you too. I wish I could come back sooner." He rubbed my arm. "Come visit me."

"I'll try."

After he dropped me off, I shuffled into the house feeling thoroughly depressed. I threw my coat and bag on my bed then went to start dinner. Once chicken fajitas were sizzling in the skillet, I forced myself to listen to voicemail. One from Jackson asking me to call him back and one from Mike.

"Hey, uh, Kate," Mike said. "We were supposed to watch *Star Wars*. So we should do that. Okay. Bye."

When I checked email, it was more of the same. I didn't reply. I deleted them.

Rob called later to say good night, and I turned off my phone afterward, or at least I thought I had. As I was about to get into bed, it buzzed on top of my desk. I had every intention of ignoring it, but then I found myself climbing out of bed to see who'd called. Nathan's message was brief, his voice gentle, but he chased away any peace I had left.

"Do you want an easy life, Kate? Or a meaningful one?"

Sleep abandoned me that night, leaving me to wrestle with a head full of doubt and fear.

My plan for the first day of vacation had been to sleep until noon, but about the time Mom left for work, I gave up and stumbled my way to the shower. As hot water washed across my skin, I inspected my wrist. So far my *Pur* was still red. How much time did I have before it turned black? What would happen when it did?

There were other Guardians out there. Maybe I could find them, work with them instead. But the thought of joining a different group of Guardians brought a feeling of loss, not relief. Maybe because this didn't really have anything to do with the Guardians. It wasn't Hassan I was running from.

After my shower, I watched TV because I didn't know what else to do. For the last two months, my schedule had been so full I could hardly keep up. Now I faced a long stretch of days with nothing to do except worry and no one except myself to provide consolation.

I needed to think and figure everything out, but thinking required brain function and brain function required coffee, so I wandered into the kitchen. As the first hiss of steam rose from the coffeemaker, someone knocked on the front door, and I groaned. Ty had left me alone the last few days, but now that we were both done with finals, he would be looking for entertainment. Most likely in the form of giving me a headache. He'd probably brought his dirty laundry with him too.

"I know you have a key," I said as I yanked the door open. "Why can't you ...?"

Frigid air drifted over my bare feet.

"May I come in?" Hassan said. "I would have called first, but I didn't think you would answer. Especially if it was me."

I searched for something to say but nothing came. My eyes went to the Audi sitting in the driveway, and I wanted to kick myself for not looking out the front window before I opened the door.

"I'll understand if you tell me no."

Something in his voice made the decision for me. I took a step back. "I was just making coffee. You want some?"

"Yes. Thank you."

I shut the door once he came inside and left him on his

own in the living room while I scurried off to the kitchen. Hassan's timing really sucked. In addition to being brain dead, I didn't have any makeup on, my hair was still damp from the shower, and my faded pajama bottoms had "Forks Bites" spread across the butt. I felt about as attractive as the troll under the Fremont Bridge.

I selected two mugs from the cupboard then peeked around the kitchen corner. In contrast to my troll look, Hassan wore jeans with a gray sweater and a black jacket. A pair of Diesel shoes completed the outfit. Even without his GQ suit, he emanated the sense of presence I'd felt at Alexander's.

He turned in a slow circle as he surveyed the room—the tired carpet, the beat up coffee table, and the green plaid couch with its sagging cushions. I couldn't even imagine what he thought as he took it all in.

I tried to dredge up some anger as I waited for the coffee to finish brewing. I had every right to be mad at him, but no matter how hard I tried, I couldn't make myself be angry. I kept thinking about the call he'd received. I kept seeing the way his shoulders sagged afterward. He lived in that gigantic house on the lake all by himself. He'd moved there to get away from home, but home had followed him halfway around the world. It wouldn't leave him in peace.

He knew what it was like when someone who was supposed to love you didn't, and I found myself wondering how different my life would be if my dad didn't just ignore me. What if he wanted me dead?

Hassan understood better than the rest of us what an ugly place the world could be. He also understood how a worthless life could become something worth living for.

I knew the answer to Nathan's question then. I didn't want an easy life. I wanted a meaningful one.

I poured coffee into the mugs and carried them to the kitchen table. "It's black. I hope that's okay."

"It's fine."

He joined me at the table, but neither of us spoke. We watched steam curl up from our mugs while the TV murmured in the other room.

"You know why I'm here," he said eventually.

"No. Not really."

Hostility flared across his features, but it receded when he saw I wasn't trying to be difficult. I really didn't know.

He wrapped his hands around the mug in front of him, examining the contents while the muscle in his jaw clenched and unclenched. Finally he looked up at me again. "I have come to ask for your forgiveness. To ask you to come back. To beg if I must."

How many times had I wished for this? An opportunity to make him grovel? This was my chance to get back at him for all the misery he'd caused me, and yet the prospect of making him suffer wasn't as appealing as it had been a few days ago.

I fingered the handle of my mug. "It wasn't all your fault. I haven't exactly made things easy for you."

"Don't make excuses for me. I know I have not treated you as I should. I have been impatient, and I have pushed you. I have refused to listen."

My gaze dropped to my hand, watching my finger trace the handle. "But you were right. I was resisting."

"It doesn't matter. I had no right to say what I did. And what you said about me was true. I allowed personal matters to interfere with training." His fingers tightened around his mug. "When I left Cairo ..."

He gripped the mug so tightly I thought it would crack under the pressure. I couldn't tell if the strain was from fighting to keep the words in or struggling to get them out.

"I was engaged. I left two weeks before the wedding."

My heart stopped beating. It sat heavy and lifeless in my chest, and an inexplicable sense of grief began to take its place.

"When I left, I begged her to come with me. I was afraid

my father would hurt her, that he would use her against me if she stayed. She refused to come. We argued for hours, but there was nothing I could do to convince her. She thought I had lost my mind. She thought I was taking everything from her, trying to humiliate her. She was so angry with me that as soon as I was gone from the house, she went to my father and told him everything. When I finally came out of hiding and contacted her, she told me what she had done. Then she said she would rather die by my hand than live by my side." The corner of his mouth curved up in the shape of a smile, but the gesture was pure bitterness. "I loved her. I tried to change her mind."

I wanted to crawl under the table. "I'm sorry."

He shrugged it off. "It was over a long time ago. Eventually I accepted her decision, but it never really ended because she wants to punish me. I still had some assets in Cairo when I left, and with my father's help, she started to take them from me one by one. It was difficult to stop her because the agreement with my father kept me away from Egypt.

"She has taken everything except a small piece of property I inherited from my mother. She knows what it means to me, so she won't give up. It would be much easier if I returned to Cairo, but my uncle is afraid my father would use it as an opportunity to have me killed, so he has been negotiating for me. He's the one who called me that night." He shook his head. "The property is worth nothing. I should let go of it, but I can't. My uncle has offered her money to leave it alone—much more than the property is worth—but she doesn't want money. She wants my pain, my suffering. She won't stop until she has taken everything she can, and it's only a matter of time before I lose my mother's property."

"I'm sorry."

I didn't know what else to say, and the further the information sunk in, the more ashamed I felt. If I'd been in

Hassan's place I would've given up a long time ago. Maybe the things that made him a pain to be around were the very things that had helped him survive. Maybe I'd been too busy feeling sorry for myself to see it.

He slid the mug aside, and his gaze fixed on me so intently I worried I'd somehow messed up again by expressing sympathy.

"You are meant to be a Guardian," he said. "You belong with us. You need to come back."

Doubt immediately wiggled its way in, asking if this was what I really wanted. Fear asked if it was really worth it. I pushed the fear and doubt aside and searched for my little spark of hope. What I found was a flame. It was small, but it burned steadily.

"Okay."

For the first time, Hassan regarded me with something besides anger or frustration. It looked suspiciously like approval. "You'll come on Monday?"

"Yeah. I'll be there."

"Then I will leave you in peace."

He stood, and I did the same, my chair scraping across the linoleum. For a few heartbeats he stood in front of me, his presence a tangible thing in the air between us.

"You are the only one I have told this to."

"But … Lexi said it was trouble back home. And Jackson acted like he knew what she was talking about."

"They know some of it. They know I'm fighting to keep property in Cairo. That my father is involved and my uncle is trying to help. They know I was engaged, but I have never explained the connection."

I didn't get it. It was Hassan—Mr. Obsessed-With-Privacy—I was talking to, and I was usually the last one in line for information. "So why did you tell me?"

He shook his head as if it didn't make sense to him either. "Perhaps I just needed to tell someone."

"Oh. Well … I won't say anything."

He responded with a nod.

I followed him to the front door, and he opened it, but only so he could point at the front step while he scowled at me.

"Never again open this door without knowing who stands on the other side. Do you understand me?" His tone then turned as ominous as his expression. "And call Jackson before I have to shoot him."

I bit my cheek to stop the smile that wanted to surface. "Okay."

He waited until the deadbolt had snapped into place before striding toward the Audi, and I watched out the front window as he drove away.

Hassan was still Hassan. But maybe that wasn't such a bad thing.

CHAPTER
TWENTY~NINE

The scent of Hassan's cologne lingered, mingling with the aroma of French roast as I walked to the table and grabbed our mugs. The house somehow felt empty without him, more than it had before he'd come. It was as if his presence had filled every inch of space while he was here and left a void in his absence.

I carried our mugs to the kitchen and poured Hassan's coffee down the sink. Mine went in the microwave to reheat while I gathered the courage to call Jackson.

Stalling for another minute or two, I leaned against the counter to sip my coffee, letting its bitterness scald my tongue. Then, before I could lose my nerve, I set aside the mug, strode down the hallway to my room, and grabbed my phone from on top of my desk. The prehistoric office chair creaked as I sank down onto it.

The obvious relief in Jackson's voice when he answered brought a fresh round of guilt.

"I was about to head out the door," he said. "I've got my keys in my hand and everything."

"Oh. Well, we can talk later if you need to go."

"I was on my way to see you."

"You were?"

"Yeah, I didn't know what else to do. You wouldn't answer your phone."

More guilt bled into my system. "I'm sorry I didn't call you sooner. I needed to sort some things out."

"You don't have to explain yourself. Hassan's the one who needs to do the explaining. And he will apologize to you. I'll make sure of it."

"He already did."

"He did?"

"Yeah, he came by this morning."

"What did he say to you?"

"He said he was sorry and asked me to come back."

"No, I mean what did he say to you the other day?"

I hesitated. It would be so easy to throw Hassan under the bus. Everyone assumed he was the guilty party. I couldn't do it though. Not when so much of it was my fault.

"It doesn't matter."

"It does matter. You walked out of training and wouldn't talk to anyone, and I didn't think you were ever coming back. Whatever Hassan said, it must have been pretty bad. He can't treat you like that and get away with it."

"Look, it's not what you think. Hassan was being a jerk, but I didn't leave because of what he said. I just used it as an excuse to give up. So I could quit and tell myself it was all his fault."

"Wait, you want to quit? Why?"

"Because I'm scared. Terrified. And I don't mean Eden. She scares me, but this is different." I drew my legs up, hugging them to my chest, and the chair groaned as my weight shifted. "I'm afraid there wasn't a mistake. God really did choose me."

"That's a bad thing?"

"It will be. Because I'm going to mess up and not just a little bit. It'll be something epic."

"Kate, c'mon. That's not true."

"You don't have to think it's true—I'm glad you don't— but I need you to believe me when I say it's how I feel. That it's the reason I left—the real reason. Hassan being a jerk is a separate issue."

He exhaled a gust of air that crackled in my ear. "All right. If that's what you want."

"It is. And even though I'm still terrified, I'm officially un-quitting, so it would be great if we could start fresh on Monday. Not have everyone mad at each other over what they might have said."

Another sigh. "All right."

"Thanks." The guilt in my system had diminished, but I wasn't completely free of it yet. Jackson wasn't the only one I'd ignored. "I should go. I need to call Lexi."

"Yeah you do. I'm tired of hearing it from her. If I want advice, I'll call Dr. Phil."

That brought a smile to my lips. Friction between Jackson and Lexi was normal, and I needed normal right now.

"Hey, before you go," he said. "You have any plans this weekend?"

"No. Rob went home already, and my brain is pretty much fried after finals. I also promised Hassan I'd do more training during winter break." Not that extra training would help me. "I probably won't do much more than watch TV and try to catch up on sleep this weekend."

"Well, if you feel like getting out of the house for a while, let me know. We'll go do something fun."

"Fun sounds good."

"Give it some thought, and I'll call you in a little while. You'll answer your phone this time?"

"Yeah. I promise."

We said goodbye, and I called Lexi. She alternated between scolding me and criticizing Hassan, Jackson, and the male species in general.

"You're coming back on Monday, right?" Her tone made it clear there was only one correct answer to her question.

"I'll be there."

I had to reassure her at least a half dozen times before she let me go. When we ended the call, a little more of the guilt eased from my system, leaving room for a drop or two of

peace to squeeze its way in. Hassan was right. I belonged
with them.

Four hours later, the squeal of brakes warned me of my
brother's arrival. A peek out the front window confirmed the
Corvette was parked in the driveway. I hid in my room,
hoping he'd go away, but he pounded on the front door until
I went to unlock it.

"Why do I always have let you in? I know you have a
key. Let yourself in."

"Why should I use a key when I can make you open it for
me?" He strolled over to the couch, flopped down, and sent
magazines spilling onto the carpet as he planted his sneakers
on the coffee table with a thump. "What's up, loser?"

I sighed as I closed the door. "Why are you here? If you
drove all the way from Seattle to annoy me, I'm not in the
mood. If you brought laundry, I have better things to do than
wash your boxers. You can do it yourself."

"I don't know how."

"The only thing you don't know how to do," I said as I
bent to pick up magazines, "is think about someone besides
yourself."

"I know how to do that. I was going to take you to a party
tonight because I feel sorry for you. Because you don't have
a life."

"Hard to believe, I know, but I'm still not into partying.
Even if I was, there's no way I'd go with you. You'd ditch
me the second you found a girl, and I'd end up wandering
through some sketchy neighborhood in the middle of the
night to find a bus stop."

"I promise I won't ditch you. Not unless she's hot. Like
surface-of-the-sun hot."

"Forget it. Not happening." I shoved his shoes off the
table and slapped the magazines down in their place.
"Besides, I have plans."

"I thought your loser boyfriend took off already."

I scowled at him as I sank down on the other end of the couch. "Yes, Rob went home for winter break. I'm doing something with Jackson."

His eyebrows rose. "I didn't think you were the type."

"What type?"

"The loser barely left town and you're already going out with another guy."

"I'm not going out with another guy. I mean, we're not *going out*. It's not a date. It's Jackson. We're just friends."

"Whatever. You need to come up with a better excuse than that—as in not so lame—in case the loser finds out."

"I'm not cheating on Rob, and stop calling him a loser. My plans were perfectly innocent until you showed up. Why do you always have to ruin everything for me?"

"Because you freak out every time. Same thing your loser boyfriend will be doing when he finds out you cheated on him."

"I'm not cheating on him."

"So he's okay with you hanging out with another guy?"

"Well, yeah. I mean no, but it's not like that. It's …"

I tipped my head back against the couch with a groan. As irritating as he was, Ty had a point. Going out with Jackson would look bad even though it was totally platonic.

The thought of cancelling on Jackson after ignoring him all week produced a new round of guilt, but I'd feel guilty if I didn't cancel now. With another groan, I lifted my head and did something I'd probably regret. I asked Ty to come with us.

CHAPTER
THIRTY

"Bowling?" The disdain in Ty's voice matched his expression. "That's your idea of Friday night out? You're so lame."

"Are you coming or not?"

"Fine. I'll babysit, but it'll cost you."

"Why can't you—just once—do something nice for me without expecting anything in return."

"Because I'm allergic to being nice, especially to you."

I resisted the urge to kick him because it would make it that much harder to get his cooperation. "Fine. Two loads of laundry."

"Three loads or no deal."

"If I do three loads, then no swearing in front of Jackson. No perverted innuendoes, no obscene gestures, nothing indecent or offensive. Nothing *I* consider indecent or offensive."

"In other words, don't have fun."

"I mean it, Ty. I'll take Dad's Visa and shred it. You'll have to get a job."

"Whatever."

He picked up the TV remote, signaling the end of the negotiations, and I retreated to my room to call Jackson. Jackson agreed to meet us at the bowling alley, so I sent a text to update Mom on the plan, threw on a hoodie, and laced up my favorite pair of Converse. I turned down the thermostat on the way out the door.

My fingers found the familiar indentations in the

Corvette's passenger seat, and they were a few millimeters deeper when we pulled into the parking lot of the bowling alley. Ty had run at least two stop signs, cut in front of a Sound Transit bus, and used the two-way left turn lane like his own personal expressway.

The moment I climbed out of the car, the air stole the warmth from my hands and face. I huddled down into my hoodie as we walked toward the entrance.

"So where are we meeting him?" Ty said.

I shrugged my already hunched shoulders. "Inside. Don't worry, we won't have any trouble finding him. He's about six-seven, two hundred-eighty pounds, and looks like he could bench press your car."

The thump of bass and the clatter of pins greeted us when we walked through the automatic doors. I welcomed the warmth of the lobby even though it carried the faint perfume of bowling shoes.

Jackson stood by the front counter, arms crossed, talking to two girls. Well, the redhead with the lacy tights and short-shorts was doing all the talking while Jackson frowned at both girls—the same frown he'd worn the night of our fake date when Olivia got too aggressive. The frown said they were wasting their time, but the girls didn't seem to notice or didn't want to notice. I couldn't really blame them though. Boyfriend or no boyfriend, I had to admit Jackson was nice to look at.

Ty swore when he spotted Jackson. "Use steroids much?"

I grabbed the sleeve of Ty's jacket and yanked him to a stop. "The ban on profanity started as soon as we walked in the door, so unless you want to do your own laundry, filter."

Jackson saw us, and his frown transformed into a grin. I couldn't help but grin in return. He made his excuses to the girls, and the next second I found myself wrapped in a bear hug that sent an odd little tingle through me.

"Good to see you," he said.

Once I recovered from the surprise, I hugged back,

inhaling the scent of spearmint gum clinging to him. "You too."

He released me and extended a hand to Ty as I made introductions. With his slight build, my brother looked ten years old standing next to Jackson. Ty's hair, closer to brown than blond, was cut in long layers that seemed even longer compared to Jackson's short ones, and his black, distressed jacket gave off a very different vibe than Jackson's white hoodie. He was the trash-talking juvenile delinquent to Jackson's all-American hero.

As they shook, Ty studied Jackson with wary eyes. Like maybe he was trying to decide how much babe hunting competition he'd have tonight.

We were able to get a lane against the far wall where the music wasn't too loud, and Jackson suggested I go first. Ty laughed when I started off with a gutter ball, and smacking his arm didn't stop the laughter. Fortunately, I avoided complete humiliation by knocking over seven pins on my second roll.

Jackson went next, and the ball hit the pins so hard they ricocheted off the back of the lane. Ty's eyebrows rose but he withheld any comments as he stood to take his turn. He tossed his jacket into my face, grabbed a bowling ball, and approached the lane with his skinny jeans riding low enough to show the waistband of his boxers. The girls in the neighboring lane giggled, but judging by their expressions, they didn't mind the view. As he stepped up to the line, one of the girls snapped a picture of him with her phone.

I didn't get it. I had people run into me with their grocery carts because they didn't notice me standing in the aisle, but my brother had random girls Instagramming his backside.

Ty's roll hit dead center, leaving him with a split, and his single word commentary made me cringe. While he waited for the ball to return, he wandered over to chat with his admirers, and there was another round of giggles before one of the girls stuck out her tongue to reveal a piercing.

"Ty, finish your turn."

He ignored me of course. He was too busy adding his future ex-girlfriend's number to his contacts.

"Sorry about dragging him along," I said to Jackson. "He showed up at the house, and then he made a big deal about me going out with you and how it would look to Rob even though we're not *going out*. But I didn't want to cancel on you."

"No, you made the right call inviting him."

"It wasn't just about Rob though. If I hadn't invited Ty to come with us, he would've gone out and partied, and I always feel like I should help him find something less self-destructive to do." The worry that always accompanied thoughts of Ty brought an acrid taste to my mouth, and I swallowed it down. "Even though I tell him to go away and leave me alone, I don't really want him to. Sometimes I think if he's with me, even if he's driving me crazy the whole time, he'll figure out someone cares enough to put up with him, you know?"

"He's lucky to have you." Jackson's eyes were full of warmth as he smiled at me. "We all need someone like you— someone who'll put up with us—and you're good at it."

"At putting up with people? Um, no. I'm really not."

"Putting up with people doesn't mean they don't tick you off. It means you give them another chance when they do." He grimaced, the warmth in his eyes cooling. "Even when they don't deserve it."

I so didn't want to talk about Hassan. "Some people would call what I do enabling. That's not a good thing."

A rattle of pins broke through the dance remix playing overhead, and a burst of cheers followed. My brother, done adding his future ex to his contacts, moved on to taking pictures of her piercing. Her cleavage came next. I wanted to tug my hood over my head and pull the drawstrings tight. It would conceal my shame while preserving my eyesight.

"I'm sorry. I made him promise not to do this kind of stuff, but it's like making him promise not to breathe. I'll finish his turn if he doesn't come back soon. That should make him mad enough to pay attention."

"Don't worry about it. I'm not in any hurry."

Jackson stood and tugged off his hoodie, providing an impressive glimpse of abs before the hem of his t-shirt dropped back into place. I made myself look away, but Ty's audience didn't feel the same need for modesty. They were openly staring at Jackson.

Ty turned to see what had stolen the girls' attention from him and scowled. He shoved his phone back in his pocket then went to retrieve his bowling ball. Apparently Jackson's abs could make him mad enough to pay attention too.

Oblivious to the drama, Jackson tossed his hoodie on the back of the chair and resumed his seat. When he smoothed down his hair, I caught sight of his wrist and the thick leather band encircling it.

"Thanks for hiding your *Pur*." I pitched my voice low enough that my brother and the still-staring girls wouldn't be able to hear. "Ty is way too observant. It took him about five seconds to notice mine."

"I figured it was easier this way."

"It is. Thanks."

Ty's attempt at a spare ended with a gutter ball. He repeated his earlier comment, marched back to us, and flung himself into the chair next to mine. "Your turn, loser."

I rose from the chair with a sigh.

This time around I managed to keep the ball out of the gutter. Jackson left one pin standing on his turn, but I didn't think anyone else could tell he'd done it on purpose. It had to be frustrating for him to be Gifted with all that strength and ability and yet have to hide it, but I'd never heard him express any frustration over it. He almost seemed happy about being called, like he'd found a better deal than playing in the NFL. Maybe his outlook would rub off on me eventually.

Even toning it down, Jackson won. Ty came in second. I barely broke seventy but no surprise there.

We played another game afterward, relying on pizza, nachos, and a pitcher of root beer to keep us going, and admiration replaced the pout on Ty's face as he watched Jackson devour an entire pizza by himself. It broke the ice enough for them to start a discussion on pizza toppings, and by the time we headed for the exit, their conversation had drifted to the topic of energy drinks. Ty voted for Rock Star, but Jackson was a hardcore Monster fan.

My brother shook his head. "That stuff tastes like gasoline."

"They all taste like gasoline."

Which left me wondering how they could stand to drink it and how either one of them knew what gasoline tasted like. Then again, I probably didn't want to know.

Ty came to a halt. He was so distracted he didn't even complain when I walked into him.

"Dude. They have Tekken Tag."

Jackson's head lifted like he'd heard a gunshot. "Where?"

Ty pointed to a darkened corner where a few antiquated arcade games hid, and just like that they abandoned me. I spent the next forty-five minutes sitting on a chair with a pleather cushion that hissed at me every time I moved. While I wanted to be irritated with Ty, having him play Tekken Tag with Jackson was better than having him party with some girl who'd end up hating him a few days later.

When they finally ran out of cash, Jackson turned, took one look at me, and winced. "Sorry. Guess I got a little carried away. I haven't played Tekken Tag since I was at TCU and supposed to be studying for finals." He offered a hand and pulled me to my feet.

"It's okay. It kept Ty off the streets for a while."

My brother walked past, smacking the side of my head as he went. "Let's go, loser."

Jackson offered me a smile in sympathy. "He's obnoxious, but he's all right."

"Trust me," I said as I rubbed my scalp, "obnoxious gets old really fast."

We walked out to the parking lot where the monotone hum of traffic replaced the dance club soundtrack. Jackson gave me another spearmint-infused hug, sending a weird little tingle through me again. I wasn't used to Jackson hugging me. Or maybe the weirdness had something to do with my brain choosing that moment to pull out an Instagram of Jackson's abs.

"See you Monday," he said.

My teeth started to chatter on the way to the car, and while we waited for the Corvette's windows to clear, I rubbed my arms in an attempt to generate some heat.

"How come you aren't going out with Jackson?"

"Because we're just friends." It came out f-f-friends. "And I already have a boyfriend, remember?"

"Yeah, but that guy's so serious and *boring*. Jackson's way more fun."

"Then maybe you should date him."

Ty responded with his favorite phrase.

"Besides," I said, "Jackson's too old for me."

"Whatever. So why do you guys have matching tattoos if you're just friends?"

My hands froze halfway up my biceps. "What?"

He gave me one of those "don't be so stupid" looks.

I went back to rubbing my arms and prayed for the defrost to hurry up and clear the windshield already. "I have no idea what your perverted little brain came up with, but it's all in your head. There's nothing romantic going on between me and Jackson, so knock it off, okay? Not everything has to do with … that."

"Yeah it does."

I growled—at my brother, at the cold, at my inability to think fast enough. "Can we go now?"

"Fine. If you're not gonna tell me."

We left the parking lot with a shriek of rubber.

Jackson had kept his *Pur* hidden, and there was no way he would have mentioned it, so how had Ty figured it out? Or was he guessing? He had to be guessing. Or maybe he'd seen the band on Jackson's wrist and decided it was a good opportunity to mess with my head and cause me stress. He didn't need to do that though because my attempt to avoid relationship problems with Rob had created an entirely different kind of stress. I had another thread to keep track of now that Ty and Jackson had met, and past experience had proven things didn't go well when Kate the college student crossed paths with Kate the Guardian.

Trying to explain why Jackson and I had matching "tattoos" would be hard enough, but if Ty realized we weren't the only ones who had them, he wouldn't stop until he got some answers. Hopefully he'd never have a chance to find out, but I doubted I'd get off that easy. The sooner I came up with some sort of explanation, the better.

Jackson came to pick me up after Mom left for work on Monday. He wore a royal blue hoodie—a shade so cheerful it was annoying—and when he grinned, I fought the urge to growl at him. If he was one of those wide-awake morning types, he couldn't be my friend anymore. Lexi had already filled that quota.

"Ready?"

"No," I said, but I shouldered my backpack and followed him out to the Jeep anyway, glowering at the too-bright paintjob. It hurt my eyes. "Has anyone ever told you your car is the same color as Pikachu?"

His laughter carried across the cul-de-sac. "It's good to have you back."

We climbed into his Pokémon-colored Rubicon, and when he detoured to the closest Starbucks drive-through, I could've kissed him. Well, maybe hugged him. Yeah, I'd had coffee at home but only to pry my eyes open. Actual brain function required additional caffeine.

Jackson insisted on buying me a "welcome back" coffee, and somehow traffic didn't seem so bad with sixteen ounces of dark roast cradled between my palms. We joined the morning migration on 520, and as we inched our way toward Yarrow Point, Jackson kept glancing over at me until I started to get that wardrobe malfunction feeling again. I did a quick check to make sure I was wearing jeans and not pajama bottoms.

"What?" I said.

"I'm glad you're coming back, that's all. I was ready to pack it up."

"I'm sorry. I should've called you."

"You should've let me pound Hassan. It's not too late you know."

I sighed. "Can we please not have this conversation again?"

His mood instantly shifted from pep assembly to detention hall, and he brooded over on his side of the car for a couple of minutes before he spoke again. "You know, Hassan almost married a girl back in Cairo. He pretty much stood her up at the altar."

"Yeah, I know."

His head swung in my direction. "You do?"

"Yeah. He told me." And why was he bringing up Hassan's ex anyway?

"I can't believe he told you. He never talks about it. I had to find out from Lexi."

"Well, if he ever does talk about it, you'll understand why he doesn't want to."

I regretted the words as soon as they left my mouth. Jackson's head turned toward me again as traffic bunched up and he hit the brake.

"How much did he tell you?"

"Enough for some things to make sense." I focused on the taillights of the UPS truck in front of us, but out of the corner of my eye, I could see Jackson frown.

"Well, he's not over her. I've been up here for two years now, and he's never had a girlfriend in all that time. I doubt that's gonna change anytime soon."

Maybe he was right about Hassan staying single, but I didn't think the issue was Hassan still being in love with his ex. She'd pretty much destroyed any feelings he had for her. I figured it had a lot more to do with their ongoing legal battle. She constantly prodded the wound she'd inflicted. She kept reminding him of how much he *had been* in love with her, how much he'd lost.

I couldn't blame Hassan for wanting to stay single, and aside from being burned in a previous relationship, he had other issues that made getting involved with someone a bad idea. Things like his dad sending hit men after him.

What I couldn't figure out was why Jackson wanted to discuss Hassan's love life—or lack thereof—in the first place, but I didn't ask. Hassan was obviously a touchy subject right now, so I sipped my coffee and gave Jackson the space he needed to think about pounding Hassan. I understood that need. I'd wanted to pound him plenty of times myself.

Jackson stopped at the gated entrance to Hassan's driveway and waved at the video camera. A few seconds later, the gates slid open, and Jackson drove through to the courtyard. Everything about Hassan's house looked the same as the last time I'd been there except for the Range Rover. It rested on the south side of the courtyard next to Lexi's Leaf instead of in the garage.

"Why is the Range Rover out here?"

"You might have noticed how the seating arrangement was a little snug going up to Heron Ridge. Obviously we needed something bigger, so Hassan went out and bought a brand new Suburban last week. And let me tell you, his ride is pimped. When he buys a car, he doesn't mess around." As he pulled in next to the Lexi, he added, "Must be nice to do whatever you want."

I pretended not to hear the last part. I grabbed my backpack and headed for the house.

Lexi met me in the entry, already dressed for training in a Hello Kitty t-shirt and pink shorts. "I'm so glad you're back. I've missed you and the little raincloud that follows you everywhere you go."

"You just missed having someone to boss around."

"It's true. The guys never do what I tell them."

Jackson slammed the front door and muttered something

that included "shut up" as he passed by us. Lexi looked at
me, her eyebrows arched in question, but I waited until
Jackson was out of hearing range to answer.

"I think he's mad that I'm not mad at Hassan anymore."

She rolled her eyes. "We've had some serious male
dominance issues around here lately. Hopefully Jackson will
calm down now that you're back, and Hassan will stop being
so reactive to everything." Concern filtered through her
exasperation. "Hassan hated himself for whatever he said to
you, but Jackson didn't want to see it."

"It's my fault. They were getting along fine until I messed
everything up."

"I think 'tolerating each other' would be more accurate.
They're both stubborn, and neither one of them likes to lose.
Hassan did the right thing and apologized, so Jackson needs
to get over it. Don't blame yourself."

Lexi's take on the situation eased some of my guilt, but a
large portion of the blame still belonged to me.

"We'd better get down to the training room," she said.
"Hassan is in a halfway decent mood today, but if Jackson
isn't, we shouldn't leave them alone for too long."

"Okay. I'll be right there."

Lexi headed for the stairs, and I stepped into the main
room.

"Hey, Mike."

He turned from his monitor, blinking as he made the
transition from cyberspace back to Earth. "Hey, Kate. You're
back." He blinked at me again. "We're still planning to have
a movie night, right?"

"Definitely."

I promised we'd talk about scheduling our movie night
later then made my way downstairs. As I walked toward the
locker room, I glanced through the glass to my right. Hassan
had his back to me, but the sight of his obsidian curls sent
anxiety through my chest. It seemed like an entire lifetime
had passed since the conversation at my house on Friday.

Maybe I didn't remember it right. Maybe I'd read too much into his apology. What if he didn't really want me here? What if we ended up right back where we were before? Maybe we weren't capable of getting along for more than a few minutes at a time.

I forced my gaze away from the training room. I needed to think positive. All things were possible, right? Even so, it was probably better not to test Hassan's patience by loitering in the hallway. I hurried to the locker room to change then headed back across the hall.

My goal was to slip into the training room as unobtrusively as possible, but of course Hassan noticed when I opened the door. Dark eyes found me right away, and I attempted a smile. He didn't smile, but he didn't frown at me either. He simply motioned me to his side. Some of my anxiety settled once I stood next to him, which contradicted the way my heart rate had picked up speed.

Jackson and Lexi were too busy sparring to notice my arrival. With Jackson's superior size and strength, I would've thought Lexi didn't stand a chance, but her lifetime of training showed. There was no hesitation to her movements, no need to stop and think things through. A move to evade a blow to her shoulder flowed into a move to strike. She ducked beneath Jackson's arm and spun toward him, landing a hit to his ribcage. It knocked him off balance enough that he went down when she kicked his leg out from under him. Jackson rolled out of the way just in time to avoid having Lexi's foot land in his solar plexus where—I'd learned the hard way—it would drive the air from his lungs. Still on the ground, Jackson swept an arm behind Lexi's legs and sent her to the mat. They both scrambled to their feet, on equal ground once again.

Hassan gave an instruction once in a while, and a couple of times he had them stop so he could explain something to me. Both Jackson and Lexi were breathing hard by the time Hassan dismissed them.

When Hassan told me to stay for an individual training session, my anxiety came rushing back. It had been easy to act like we were getting along when there was something else to focus on, but now it would be just the two of us. Except it wasn't just the two of us.

Instead of following Lexi out the door, Jackson went to the treadmill, and my eyes narrowed on him as anxiety gave way to suspicion. Sure, he'd picked me up this morning instead of going straight to Hassan's for his workout, but it seemed awfully convenient he needed to do cardio right now.

I wasn't the only one with suspicions. Hassan's gaze burned into the back of Jackson's head for a few seconds before shifting to me, and an unspoken agreement passed between us. If Jackson had decided to appoint himself fire chief, then we would deprive him of even a single spark.

That didn't mean Hassan took it easy on me. I was more than ready to call it a day by the time we finished, but Jackson sent me to the treadmill anyway before he left. I went to the locker room long enough to grab my iPod. The blood pounding through my veins and the energy of the music somehow fit with the serene view out the window. I felt awake and alive.

After the treadmill, I decided to skip weight training since Jackson wasn't downstairs to make me do it. I did shower though, so I knew it wasn't me when I caught a whiff of something funky—like BO on steroids—when I emerged from the stairwell.

Hassan was the only one upstairs. He'd changed into a pair of gray slacks and a black button up shirt, and he was in the process of removing a bowl from the microwave as I walked in. I pegged it as the source of the smell.

"No offense, but that stuff stinks. What is it?"

"*Mjeddrah.*"

"What's that?"

"Lentil stew." Both his tone and his expression said I was beyond ignorant. "Samirah likes to spoil me. She makes food for me to put in my freezer so I don't have to eat American food all the time."

For a moment, speech evaded me. "Who's Samirah?"

"The woman who comes every Saturday to clean."

It shouldn't have surprised me. I mean, Hassan didn't strike me as the kind of guy who scrubbed his own toilet, and Lexi didn't have time to clean eight-thousand-plus square feet on top of everything else she did for him. But he was so secretive. I had a hard time believing he gave any non-Guardian besides Mike access to his house. Then again, Mike had probably screened her so thoroughly that Hassan knew everything about her all the way down to her DNA sequence.

"Come. Try it."

He waved me over to the counter where he had three containers set out. I walked to the counter hesitantly and let him feed me a spoonful of lentils. I was able to identify the spice—cumin—and the stew tasted good, but I couldn't get past the overpowering smell.

"It's okay I guess."

He frowned at me then pulled a fork from the silverware drawer. "Try this."

I struggled to hide my dismay as he stabbed some kind of stuffed pasta from one of the containers. I had lucked out with the first taste test, but if he kept this up for long, I'd end up gagging on something.

"What is it?"

"*Ashak.*"

He shoved the pasta into my mouth. Savory beef and garlic mixed with the brightness of mint.

"I like it," I admitted, but his expression was so self-satisfied I wanted to take it back.

He handed me a plate from the cupboard and told me to help myself to the *ashak* as well as the other two items on the counter. I bypassed the lentils and studied the contents of the third container. It looked harmless enough, like nothing more than roast chicken, and I didn't smell anything objectionable, but the stew could have been masking the odor.

"What kind of chicken is this? Did Samirah make it or did you?"

"Of course I didn't make it. Do I look like a woman to you?"

I stopped my inspection to glare at him. "That's so sexist."

"Why is it sexist? Don't women cook?"

"Well, yeah, but this is America. Land of equal opportunity. Men have just as much right to cook as women do."

"Then American men are weak. They should make their women do it."

I wanted to flatten him, or maybe let Jackson pound on him. Once he was flat on the floor, he could tell me how weak American men were. Then I saw it. The little smile at the corner of his mouth.

"You're such a jerk. Does anything besides torturing people amuse you?"

"No."

He took his bowl of *mjeddrah* to the bar while I dished up chicken and *ashak*. I set my plate on the counter long enough to grab a fork and get a Diet Coke from the fridge.

"Did you want something to drink?"

"Bring me a Coke."

I stuck the Diet Coke in the pocket of my hoodie, grabbed my plate and fork with one hand and Hassan's Coke with the other. I carried everything over to the bar, shook the can of Coke, and placed it in front of him with a smile. "Enjoy."

He scowled at me as I sat down.

I was so hungry I inhaled everything on my plate including the chicken which thankfully turned out to be roast chicken. I finished off my Diet Coke while Hassan worked on the last few bites of his stew.

"So where did everyone go?"

"Lexi is taking care of some things for me," he said.

"Jackson and Mike went somewhere together. I don't know where."

I wiggled the tab on my pop can while I debated whether or not to ask some of the questions floating around in my head. I could end up with answers I didn't like. There was also the possibility Hassan might not be in the mood to give any answers. And sometimes, voicing my questions felt like providing him with a detailed map of my insecurities.

A brief scuffle ensued between my need to know and my need for self-preservation. Need to know won. "So how long does it take for a Gift to show up anyway?"

He shrugged. "It's different for every Guardian."

"That's such a Guardian answer," I complained as I popped the tab loose from the can. "Give me a time frame. What's the average?"

He opened his Coke. Much to my disappointment, it hissed but didn't bubble over. "Usually within the first six months of being called." He took a drink before focusing on me again. "Why are you asking this? Are you worried about your Gift?"

My gaze dropped to the piece of aluminum in my fingers. The metal had grown warm with heat borrowed from my skin. "I'm not doing so great with the self-defense stuff, so what if it's the same thing with my Gift? What if I'm the one Guardian in the entire history of Guardians who doesn't get a Gift? Or what if it's something totally lame that doesn't help me at all? If a Gift is something you already have, just magnified, then I'm doomed. Zero times anything is still zero."

"Kate, look at me."

I met his eyes reluctantly.

"Even if your only Gift is to be here with us and make us better Guardians, you have already done that."

"All I've done is cause problems."

"Sometimes change, even good change, is painful."

"Is that a nice way of saying I'm a pain?"

"Some days more painful than others."

I dropped the tab into the empty can with a sigh. "Thanks."

He slid his Coke aside then turned on the stool so he faced me. The weight of his gaze became a physical thing. When Jackson looked at me that way, I felt self-conscious. With Hassan, my soul felt exposed, like no matter how hard I tried I could never hide myself from him. Like he didn't need a map to find my insecurities.

"Do you want to know what I think?" he said. "Why you were called?"

That was the big question, the one I'd been struggling with since the first day when I met Nathan. Why me? There were so many people better-qualified to be a Guardian.

Even though apprehension knotted my stomach, I nodded.

"I believe something is coming, and someday soon we will find ourselves in a situation that requires a Guardian with a very powerful Gift. A Gift so powerful it must be entrusted to an individual who understands the power does not come from her and it does not belong to her. Someone who will not use it for her own desires."

The knot in my stomach tightened. "I don't want that kind of Gift."

"And this is why you were chosen."

"But you don't know that's why. Not the way Nathan Knows stuff. You could be wrong."

"Perhaps," he said. But there wasn't a hint of doubt in either his expression or his voice, and the first traces of panic seeped into my chest. Hassan was very good at taking pieces of information and finding the thread that connected them—a fact that made it hard for me to dismiss his theory.

"Whatever your Gift might be, it will come at the proper time," he said. "It could be tomorrow or a year from tomorrow, but your Gift will come. The rest we will work on, and we start now. It's time for you to begin weapons training."

CHAPTER
THIRTY-TWO

My gaze slipped back to the pop can. I didn't want to start an argument with Hassan, but I wasn't ready to do this. I didn't know if I would ever be ready.

The logical side of my brain pointed out I had no objection to learning unarmed combat. Sure, it was all in the name of self-defense, but I could hurt someone or even kill them with what I had learned. At least in theory. Reality provided a convenient safety net. My skill level hadn't reached the point of being a threat to anyone.

There was no safety net with a gun. You pulled the trigger, a dangerous projectile emerged, and it put a hole in something. All too often that something had been alive until you put a hole in it, and I didn't want to face the moment when I had to choose between my life and someone else's. The last time I had, I'd been spared the consequences of my decision because I destroyed something that shouldn't have existed to begin with.

Logic jumped in again, reminding me Eden and her golems were only the beginning. There were more Fallen Guardians out there with access to a Book of Creation. If they could create golems—or something worse—then there would be circumstances when I needed to use a gun. Hitting Eden's golem in the forehead had been pure luck, and I couldn't afford to rely on luck next time. As much as I hated the thought of touching a gun, the memory of being dragged from the Range Rover finally convinced me. I never wanted to go through that again.

"Okay, I'll learn," I said. "But it's purely for self-defense. Just so we're clear."

"Agreed."

I had a few seconds to gather my courage while Hassan finished his Coke. I then eased off the stool and carried our dishes to the sink. The empty cans rattled as I tossed them into the recycling bin. After Hassan put the food containers in the fridge, he led me downstairs to the weapons room, and the keypad chirped as he entered a series of numbers. He ran his index finger over the tiny scanner beneath the buttons, and the door unlocked with a click. Inside, he lifted a black case from one of the shelves, brought it to the table, and opened it. The gun looked like the same one he'd given me the night of Heron Ridge.

He demonstrated how to fieldstrip, reassemble, and load it, explaining everything as he went. He pointed out the safety mechanisms, and he talked about muzzle rise and aim recovery. The scary thing was that it made sense to me. It was physics.

He went through the process twice before he unloaded the gun, held it out to me, and told me to fieldstrip it. Fear stirred inside me as my fingers grazed the stippled grip of the handle. The tang of metal filled my nose.

I stared at the object in my hand wondering what I was supposed to do with it. I couldn't remember a thing he'd said.

Hassan reached out, wrapping his fingers around mine long enough to force a tight grip on the handle. "This feels wrong because it feels like everything you are not. You want to bring life. You want to preserve it. That's why it will never feel right—why it will never be easy for you to pull the trigger—and that's as it should be. It's who you are."

Who I was. That was the part that frightened me the most. "But what if I mess up? What if I panic and make the wrong choice? I can't take it back."

"You will make the right choice."

"How do you know?"

"Your desire to bring life is stronger than your fear. You will find the strength to do what's right."

"You can't be sure," I said, even though I desperately wanted him to be sure.

"You were hurt at Heron Ridge because you were reluctant to take another life. You were physically ill because you thought you had killed a man." His eyes grew dark, echoing the tone of his voice. "If you ever make the wrong choice, it will be to sacrifice your own life when you should preserve it."

I shook my head. He made me sound like some kind of martyr, but I was too much of a coward for self-sacrifice. I'd already proven I was.

I focused on the object in my hand. It would never feel right, and it would never be easy, but I had chosen to leave easy behind.

"I don't know what to do."

Instead of getting angry with me for not remembering what he'd said, he coached me through each step. He didn't get irritated when I paused or when my hands shook, and as I repeated the process, my hands grew steadier. I started to see each individual piece. I saw how they fit together and how they worked together, how I could manipulate and control them.

When he said we were done, relief settled over me. As we climbed the stairs, a sense of accomplishment joined my relief. I couldn't help but wonder if Hassan had chosen this particular lesson on purpose, if he understood me well enough to know that teaching me to dismantle the gun was the best way to start dismantling my fear of it.

The others had returned while we were in the weapons room. Lexi and Jackson joined us as Hassan spread a map across the coffee table to display a section of land he owned up in the Cascade foothills. It was where I would do my field training.

"When are we taking her up there?" Jackson asked him.

"Soon. Next week at the latest. She needs to be ready."

Using the map as a visual aid, Hassan talked about cover, terrain, and line of sight. I didn't understand half of it, but that didn't stop him from trying to cram it into my head anyway. After an hour I begged him to stop.

"I can't do any more. My brain is about to spring a leak, and I'll end up losing everything you told me. I need to go home anyway."

"I'll take you home," Jackson volunteered.

"You don't need to take her home." Hassan went to his desk, grabbed a key from the drawer, and tossed it to me. "Take the Range Rover."

"Nuh-uh. No way." I tossed the key back at him.

He managed to catch it despite my pathetic lob, and his fist tightened around the key. "This is a waste of time always having to pick you up or take you to the bus."

"I'm not taking your car. I can't. You don't understand how my mom thinks. All she'll see is a guy almost a decade older than me and a car I don't have to pay for, and the conclusion she comes up with won't be Guardians. I'm trying *not* to draw attention to what I'm doing right now. I'll stick with the bus."

"Fine. I'll drive you home then."

"I don't need you to drive me home. I just need a ride to the bus stop."

"I'll take you to the bus stop." Jackson's offer earned him a black look from Hassan.

"Here's an idea," Lexi said. "Jackson picks up Kate in the morning, Hassan takes her home in the afternoon, and Kate doesn't ride the bus. That way no one gets exactly what they want, and everyone is unhappy."

"That doesn't even make sense," I said.

A feline smile spread across her face. "Oh, it makes perfect sense. Doesn't it, Jackson?"

"Shut up, Lexi."

I waited for understanding to kick in. It didn't. Maybe I'd have one of those delayed comprehension moments in the middle of the night, but right now my brain was too overloaded to decipher hidden meanings. I didn't have time for it anyway.

"Fine. Whatever. Someone take me home."

By the time Mom came home, I had the table set and salad made, and the aroma of pork tenderloin filled the house. I was counting on the illusion of a non-dysfunctional family meal to put her in the right frame of mind when I brought up a trip to Poulsbo.

I'd been too upset over the argument with Hassan to enjoy my time with Rob before he headed home for winter break, and talking on the phone wouldn't be enough. I'd been eighteen before I ever kissed a boy, and now that I knew what kissing was like, I really didn't want to go without it for the next four weeks.

When we sat down to eat, she said things had been quiet at the agency, and I felt a glimmer of hope. Mom having a stress-free day improved my chances of getting a yes from her.

"What did you do with your day off?" she said.

"I went and worked out then hung around with Lexi and everyone for a while. It was kind of nice not to worry about school." I chewed a bite of rosemary-seasoned pork then swallowed. "I was thinking that maybe, since I have some free time over break, I should do something fun. Like go to Poulsbo."

Her forehead wrinkled. "Poulsbo? Why would you go there?"

"Well, I've never been there before." I breathed a quick prayer. "And I figured, you know, it might be kind of nice to see where Rob lives."

Her hands froze over her plate. My courage faltered for a second, but then my lips protested the thought of being denied contact with Rob's, and I forged ahead.

"I would take the ferry over, and Rob could pick me up. We'd hang out for a little bit. Not for very long because he has to work. It would only be for a couple of hours, and I'd be back by five."

She shook her head, her face tight. "It's too far."

"It's not that far."

"It's too far, and it's not a good idea."

"Why is it not a good idea?"

Anger settled across her features, as pale and brittle as frost. "It's not a good idea because it's too easy to get caught up in all the excitement and think that's the way a relationship should be all the time. It's too easy to forget what's really important, and before long you'll start thinking that being with him is more important than anything else."

"I won't think that, and Rob and I hang out together all the time. Why is it suddenly different if it's in Poulsbo?"

"Look at how you're acting already. All you can think about is going to see him."

"I'm just trying to understand why it's such a big deal."

"You're at an age where the decisions you make will shape the rest of your life, and yet you're too young to understand how easy it is to get distracted by what you think is love. Love isn't about getting swept away. It's about respect and commitment." Her knife squealed across the plate as she sawed into her pork. "This separation will be good for you. You've been spending too much time with him anyway. This will help you remember school is what you need to be focusing on."

"I know school's important, but I'm not in school right now. That's the point. I don't have to worry about classes or anything. It won't interfere."

"No, Kate." She abandoned her meat, although she still had a death grip on her utensils. "You have years of school left and you would be walking into a situation that could interfere with the rest of your life. One you're completely unprepared for."

I wanted to bang my head against the table because I knew what was coming—the three-letter reason she didn't want me going to Poulsbo.

She shook her head again. "You haven't even thought about what kind of message it would send."

"That I like him? I want to see him? He already knows."

"It's completely different for a boy than it is for a girl. You don't understand how he'll see your willingness to go that far to visit him. What he'll think you're saying to him."

"Mom," I moaned. "He's not going think it's some sort of invitation. And Poulsbo isn't that far."

"You're not going."

"But it's not—"

"The answer is no." Her silverware clattered onto her plate as she stood. The door to her room slammed shut a moment later.

Anger surged through me, and it kept building until I thought I'd explode from the pressure. She always assumed the worst. Why couldn't she trust me to make decisions for myself? Why couldn't she understand I wasn't going to make the same mistakes she had?

My appetite gone, I stacked our unfinished plates together and took them to the kitchen. As I scraped the contents into the garbage disposal, I considered going to Poulsbo without her permission. I could leave after she went to work and come back before she made it home, and she would never know. But I would. And with my luck, a ferry would break down or a bus would be late, and she'd find out anyway.

I could defy her. I was eighteen now, an adult even though she didn't treat me like one. But if I defied her, she would watch me even closer. It would make it harder to spend time with Rob and harder to train at Hassan's. I didn't want to give up time with Rob, and I couldn't afford to cut back on training.

I rinsed off our plates then stuck them in the dishwasher. Silverware and glasses followed. Pots and pans went in the sink for hand washing, and I scrubbed, seizing the opportunity to vent my frustration.

Once the evidence of dinner had been erased, I parked on the couch with my phone and watched TV while I waited for Rob to call. When my phone rang, I relocated to my room, shut the door, and attempted to delay the inevitable by asking about his day.

"The other waiter was a complete moron," he said. "He kept grabbing my orders from the kitchen, but nobody wants excuses. They want their food. I only made half my usual amount in tips."

I leaned back against the door. "Maybe you should take his tips since you did all the work."

"Maybe I should." He made a sound that was part sigh, part groan. "Thinking about you was the only way I made it through my shift. I can't wait to see you."

"Yeah, the thing is … I can't come." My knees sagged, and I slid down until I hit carpet. "I'm sorry. I tried, but she totally freaked out. She thinks I'll start blowing off school so I can be with you all the time and you'll see it as, well, something it's not."

"An opportunity?"

My cheeks warmed. "Sort of. I mean, not when I came to see you or anything. Just in general."

"But I wouldn't think that. I *don't* think that."

"I know. I told her you didn't. Or I tried to anyway. The problem is you're a guy, and she thinks guys don't have any self-control."

"I thought your mom was okay with me."

"It's not you specifically she has a problem with. It's anyone with a Y chromosome. We have my dad and my brother to thank for that one. Eventually she'll figure out she can trust us, but it's not going to happen this week."

Disappointment sat heavily in my gut. There was a little fear mixed in with it too. "I'm sorry."

"Don't be. It's okay."

It wasn't okay. No guy wanted a girlfriend with an invisible fence. Sooner or later he'd get tired of it and move on.

"I'll see what I can do about my schedule," he said. "I can't make it over there this weekend, but maybe sometime next week. I'll come even if it's only for a couple of hours."

"I didn't want you to have to do that."

"It's not my first choice either, but it's better than not seeing you at all."

For now it was better, but how much longer would he feel that way? How much longer until he decided it was better not to see me at all?

CHAPTER
THIRTY-THREE

Mom didn't emerge from her room until I'd already gone to bed. I heard water running in the bathroom, and her door closed again a few minutes later. In the morning, she ignored my offer to pour coffee for her, so I gave up any further attempts at conversation.

On the way to Hassan's, I failed to produce anything better than single-word responses for Jackson, and he had to repeat himself more than once. When he made a comment about me having a hard time waking up, I let him assume I was tired.

Nathan's Subaru sat in the courtyard when we arrived at Hassan's, but Mike was the only one in the main room. He told us the others had gone downstairs already, so Jackson and I headed that way too. As we emerged from the stairwell, I could hear the sounds of sparring coming from the training room, and we stopped in the corridor to watch Nathan and Hassan. I'd never seen Hassan spar with anyone before. He'd always been in instruction mode when I was around.

Nathan directed a hit at Hassan's head, but Hassan deflected it, answering with a kick to Nathan's torso. Nathan stumbled backward, struggling to stay on his feet. Hassan could have taken advantage of it, but he let Nathan recover. After a couple of similar exchanges, he moved in, and Nathan hit the mat so hard Jackson grunted in sympathy.

If Hassan made Nathan—who'd been doing the Guardian thing for twenty-plus years—look like a beginner, I didn't have a prayer.

I went to change, and by the time I made it to the training room Lexi had taken Hassan's place. Hassan assigned me to the sidelines again to watch as Lexi and Nathan sparred, but I had trouble focusing. When he called an end to the group session, I walked to the edge of the mat, sat down with my back against the wall, and pretended not to see Lexi and Nathan glancing at me on their way out of the training room. Jackson stood there like he wanted to come over and say something but wasn't sure if he should. I did my best to telepathically communicate he shouldn't.

Apparently my efforts failed, but as Jackson started toward me, Nathan opened the door far enough to ask him about taking a few practice rounds on the firing range. Jackson looked at me, frowned, then joined Nathan in the corridor. I had a brief moment of relief before it sunk in Hassan was the only one left.

I braced myself as he grabbed his water bottle and sat down next to me, but he let me squirm for a minute as he sipped his water.

"Where is your mind, Kate? It's not here with us."

My shoulders rose and fell. "Taking a vacation day I guess."

He waited. Took another sip. I traced the label of my water bottle with my index finger.

"I have nowhere else to be right now."

His voice bordered on gentle. If he'd been irritated or impatient with me, I could've kept everything locked up tight, but just a hint of sympathy weakened my resistance. The words, too close to the surface, sensed freedom and broke through.

"It's my mom. She treats me like I'm on the verge of being totally out of control and she's the only thing stopping me. She thinks I don't understand what Dad did to her. She thinks I can't see it, so I'm going to end up miserable and alone like her. But she's already made me miserable, and if she keeps it up, I'll be alone too. Maybe I am a lot like her, but I'm not her. I'm not going to make the same choices she did."

"What choice did she make? I thought your father was the one who left."

"He did. The choice she regrets is him."

I should have stopped there. I'd said too much already, but what difference did it make? It wasn't like Hassan would think any worse of my family, and maybe I'd feel better if I got it out of my system.

"She knew what my dad was like before they got married. But she was in love with him and convinced that if he felt the same way she did he'd change. I think he did change for a while. He was her whole world, and he liked it that way. Things weren't as much fun when he had two kids and his wife wasn't worshipping him anymore because she couldn't do everything on her own. She needed him to be there for her. She needed him, so he walked out."

My hand shook, and plastic crackled as I clenched the bottle in an attempt to stop the shaking. The depth of the anger burning through me in that moment was frightening, like nothing I'd ever felt before. I tried so hard to forgive and forget. I tried to love both of them the way I wanted to be loved, but I was tired of trying. I was tired of being the adult while my parents acted like children.

"It destroyed her when he left, and now she thinks I'm going to fall for someone like she did. That I'll give up everything to be with him, and then I'll have to watch him walk away. She doesn't want the same thing to happen to me."

"A noble desire."

"Is it? I used to think she didn't want me to get hurt, but I don't believe that anymore. I think she's trying to undo what she did. I'm her chance to get it right this time."

I tipped my head back against the wall, grateful for something supportive in my life. For a couple of minutes, the only sounds were the muffled pops coming from the direction of the weapons room.

"I'll have Lexi take you to purchase your field gear," Hassan said.

It sounded like an offer to skip training. Maybe he'd realized how much I was hurting today. Or maybe he'd seen a lost cause and decided to save us both a lot of frustration.

When I gave him a nod, he slipped from the room. I sat for another minute then scraped myself off the floor, changed back into my jeans, and trudged upstairs. Lexi had her coat on and her keys in her hand. We walked out to her car together.

As we merged onto the freeway, frustration simmered in my chest. Maybe that was why I decided to do something I'd considered doing a thousand times before. Something I'd avoided because I'd been too afraid to deal with the truth. But maybe hearing the truth was the only way to stop listening to the lies.

"Can I use your phone for a second?" I said.

"Sure. Help yourself."

I pulled her phone from her purse and dialed Dad's number. My heart pounded at the sound of his voice.

"Hello, this is Mitchell."

"Hey, Dad. It's Kate."

He paused. "Well, hi, sweetie. Did you get a new phone? I didn't recognize the number."

There it was. The truth I didn't want to hear. "No, I'm borrowing a friend's."

"Oh, okay. Listen, I'm stepping into a meeting right now. Can I call you back?"

"It will only take a second. I need to ask—"

"Is this about tuition for winter quarter? I guess it's time, isn't it?"

"No, it's not that. I mean, I need tuition but that's not why—"

"I'll have Connie deposit the money in your account this afternoon."

"Okay, thanks, but—"

"And if you need anything else, let Connie know, okay? She can take care of it for you. I'll talk to you—"

"Dad, *wait*. This isn't about tuition. I just need you to listen for a second."

I thought he'd hung up, but then I heard voices in the background on his end. He was still there but not for long.

"My boyfriend ..." I stumbled to a stop. He didn't even know I had a boyfriend. "He ... his name is Rob Peterson, and he applied for one of the summer internships with Pacific Bio-Tech. It would be good if you helped him out. You know, nothing dishonest because he's totally qualified, but maybe you could make sure he gets a fair shot at it instead of having his application buried in the pile."

"Sure, sweetie. I'll see what I can do."

"Thanks."

"I have to go, but I'll talk to you real soon."

"Okay. Love you, Dad."

He didn't hear me. He was gone. The first time I'd talked to him in six months and it was over.

I felt numb as I slipped Lexi's phone back into her purse, but I welcomed the numbness. Without it, I'd have to feel the pain that came from confirming he avoided my calls. I'd have to feel the ache that came from hearing relief in his voice when I asked a favor for Rob, something that didn't require talking to me or spending time with me. Something he could pretend had nothing to do with me.

"Everything okay?" Lexi said.

"No. It's not." The freeway began to warp as tears filled my eyes. "Everything is messed up, and I don't think it will ever get better."

Mom at least informed me she wouldn't be eating dinner before she disappeared into the sewing room. It was an improvement over completely ignoring me. When she still wouldn't let me pour her coffee the next morning, I promised myself that if I ever had kids, I wouldn't resort to emotional blackmail to control their behavior.

Jackson picked me up, and as we drove to Hassan's, I made more of an effort at conversation than I had the previous morning. We arrived to find Nathan's car parked in the courtyard again, but this time everyone was still upstairs. Nathan, Lexi, and Hassan sat around the coffee table like they'd been waiting for us to arrive, and the way they looked at me made me nervous.

"What's up?" Jackson said.

Hassan waved us over. "Come. Nathan wishes to try something."

Jackson claimed his usual spot at the south end of the coffee table. I intended to take the chair between him and Lexi, but Hassan indicated I should sit on the loveseat with him instead. That would've been fine except it also put me next to Nathan and fed the suspicion I was going to be a bigger part of this meeting than I wanted to be.

Nathan confirmed it when he leaned forward and focused on me. "I need to start by explaining my Gift to you, so you can have a better understanding of how it works. I think you've figured out I don't necessarily get to pick and choose what Knowledge I receive, but there's an added complication in that I don't always receive the Knowledge in the same way. Sometimes it comes to me, and I don't have to seek it out at all. A thought comes to mind, and I just Know. At other times it's triggered by something I see or hear like an article in the newspaper or a news report on TV. But often I have to go looking for the information I need.

"A while back, I told you to think in terms of a vision because that's the best way to describe what happens. It's a representation of the real world that guides me to the Knowledge I'm seeking. I try to direct the search as much as I can, but it's like exploring a maze. There are numerous paths, and they're not always clearly marked. Not all of them lead to answers. Sometimes part of the Knowledge will come to me here in the real world, but I have to search the maze to get details. Sometimes I find information in the maze I wasn't looking for, but it's something I need to Know. Something like a new Guardian who's been called."

His smile was probably meant to reassure me. It didn't.

"That's how I Knew where to find you the day we met. Last night I saw you in the maze again. You told me I needed to bring you with me."

"I did?" It seemed like I should remember having that conversation. "So what does it mean?"

"I'm not sure, but I'd like to try something if you're willing. I'd like to see if it's possible for you to search the maze with me."

I glanced around the coffee table. They were all watching me, and their attentiveness put me on edge. It also made me suspect this wasn't standard operating procedure.

"Have you done this before? Had someone search with you?"

"You would be the first."

Why? Why me? Any of the others would gladly have jumped in with both feet—or however you got into Nathan's maze—but of course it had to be me.

I took a moment to mourn the unfairness of it all then sighed. "What do I have to do?"

"Take my hand."

CHAPTER
THIRTY-FOUR

The world became brilliant white. I closed my eyes against the glare and against the force that grabbed hold of me, propelling me into a current too fast to comprehend, a path impossible to predict. It was like taking corners at light speed.

The motion stopped and the brilliance faded. I opened my eyes to see a living room with pale, golden light spilling through the windows. Dust motes drifted through the light, flickering like miniature fireflies above an Oriental rug that had probably been burgundy and gold at one point. It had faded to the softer tones of rose and ochre. The floral paper on the walls was yellowed with age, and the air smelled as dated as everything else in the room.

Pressure on my hand drew my attention to Nathan. I met his gaze wondering which of us was more in shock.

"Are you really here? It's really you this time?"

How was I supposed to know? This was his thing, not mine. Maybe he'd be telling me about this conversation tomorrow, and I'd be thinking again I should remember it. "I'm pretty sure I'm here."

He gave a short laugh, a sound of both delight and disbelief. "Okay, I'm going to let go and see what happens."

"Wait." I clung to his hand.

"Don't worry, I'm not going to lose you. We didn't really go anywhere, remember? We're still sitting in Hassan's house, and I still have your hand. At the worst, letting go will pull you out of the maze. Ready?"

When I nodded, he let go. Nothing happened.

This time, pure delight echoed through his laughter. He walked to the fireplace and ran a hand along the mantel—one of the hand-carved variety with elaborate scrollwork. Metal frames with black and white photos lined the top of the mantle, and a pair of wingback chairs, their wine-colored fabric muted with age, sat on either side of the fireplace. A set of fireplace tools with brass knobs was tucked behind one of the chairs.

"This is incredible," he said. "I described the maze as a vision because it's always had a dreamy, insubstantial quality to it, but this …" He grabbed the mantle with both hands and tugged to test its sturdiness. "This is so real. I don't know what your Gift is, but I like it."

Good thing one of us did. "Is that why we're here? To figure out what my Gift is?"

"I'm not sure." He lifted one of the pictures from the mantle. "The maze takes different forms, and now it's up to us to discover why we're here. It could be an object in the house, or it could be something outside. It could even be the house itself. We won't know until we do some investigating."

He set down the picture and picked up another as I surveyed the room. Nathan was right. It was unbelievably real. Everything from the scuff of shoes across the carpet to the stale air filling my nostrils. I could taste the dust as I breathed.

"Is this how you Knew what was happening to me? The day Eden … you know, found me."

His expression sobered, and he nodded. "After Hassan called me, I went into the maze. I saw you, but I couldn't do anything to help."

I swallowed, wishing the air didn't feel so thick. "Do you see people in the maze a lot?"

"Not unless they have something to do with the information I need." He gestured to the frames on the mantle.

"Photos are different. They may or may not be related to why we're here. Recognize anyone?"

I moved in closer. "No. Both the frames and the pictures are old though. Nineteen-forties? Fifties?"

"That would be my guess."

"Are we seeing something in the past?"

"I doubt it. It looks like everything has been here for a while." He left the mantel and tried to open the front door. The knob refused to turn even after unlocking it, so he moved to the windows.

There was no landscaping out front, just a field with a single cottonwood tree to break the monotony. Emerald green leaves covered the tree, and vibrant grass surrounded it. Wherever or whenever we might be, the season was closer to summer than winter.

A line of fir trees marked the far edge of the field, and off to the right, a couple seemed to be spaced far enough apart for a driveway to pass between them. I couldn't tell for sure though. The angle from the window was bad and the grass too long to get a good look.

Nathan couldn't get any of the windows open. "Let's see what's in the rest of the house. Let me know if anything seems familiar. Or if it's obviously out of place."

We explored the dining room and both bedrooms. Each of them had a similar view of a grassy field bordered by trees. Nathan tried every window, but they were all closed up as tight as the ones in the living room. We moved on to the kitchen next, and like the rest of the house, its age showed. The checkerboard flooring was cracked, the paint on the cupboards peeling, and the drain of the sink stained with rust.

A rotary style phone hung on the wall, and out of curiosity, I picked up the receiver. No dial tone. As Nathan inspected cupboards, I wandered over to the ancient Coldspot refrigerator and opened the door. The fridge was empty, but ice encrusted the tiny freezer in the upper left corner. Someone still paid the electric bill. Why do that if no one lived here?

We searched every drawer, cupboard, and shelf in both the kitchen and the pantry, but we didn't find anything more exciting than mouse droppings and a tin of desiccated tea leaves.

Nathan peered through the window on the back door before testing the knob. The back was locked like the front. Something caught his attention though, and he leaned his ear against the window. "Can you hear that?"

When I pressed my ear against the glass, I could hear a low rumble in the distance punctuated by metallic clangs and grating noises. Then I heard beeping—the sound a truck makes when it backs up. "Construction?"

"It would make sense if this is where Eden is hiding." When he saw me tense up, he said, "Remember, this is only a representation. Even if Eden were here, it wouldn't really be her. Think of it like the holodeck on *Star Trek*. Everything looks real and you interact with it, but none of it actually exists."

That didn't reassure me. He assumed no one else had access to the holodeck. I had no idea what the maze really was, but I wasn't a hundred percent convinced it existed solely in Nathan's head. Entering the maze felt like traveling to someplace—exactly how I would've described teleportation or entering a wormhole. Nathan could get in whenever he wanted, and I had proven someone else could get in. What was to stop a third person from entering? What if there was more than one way in?

"Let's head down to the basement," Nathan said. "Maybe we're supposed to go down instead of out."

I glanced through the window on the back door before following him. A small detached garage stood a few yards away. A dent in the grass suggested a driveway curved to the left, probably heading for the gap in the trees out front. I could just make out the top of a bright red barn through the trees.

The stairs, lit by a single naked bulb, moaned in protest as we descended. The air in the basement was even more stale than upstairs. A film of dirt covered the windows, but they let in enough light for us to see the concrete floor, the stacks of boxes, and the shelves piled from floor to ceiling with the odds and ends accumulated over a lifetime.

We each took a side and wandered through, peeking into boxes and examining the items on the shelves. Some of it was junk, and some of it was a complete mystery to me. I had no idea what use it might serve. Other things were fascinating pieces of the past. On one shelf, I found cloth-bound books with titles like *The Works of Washington Irving* and *Treasure Island* embossed in gold. I ran my fingers over their spines until I reached the last one. The instant my fingers brushed it, I jerked away, scrubbing my hand against my jeans. It felt like something had tried to crawl into my skin.

When the feeling receded, I gulped in a lungful of dank air, called Nathan, and pointed at the book with a trembling finger. "That one."

By the time I thought to warn him, he'd already reached for the book. He pulled it from the shelf without reacting and flipped through pages covered with what appeared to be Hebrew script. I didn't understand how he could touch it. I almost expected to see something dark seep from the pages onto his fingers.

"Well done. You found Eden's Book." He closed the Book with a snap and slid it back on the shelf.

"You're going to leave it there? Shouldn't we burn it or something?"

"It wouldn't do any good. Her Book would still exist in the real world."

"Have you tried it before?"

He shook his head. "It won't work. Events in the maze don't affect the real world. They only represent it."

Obviously I wasn't the expert, but I still thought it was a

good idea. It would make me feel better if nothing else.

Nathan studied the murky view offered by the windows. "Wherever this house is, it's where she's hiding her Book."

"How are we supposed to figure out where we are if we can't get outside?"

"We give Mike as much information as we can and then put him to work. We have him look for a house fitting the description."

Just to be thorough, Nathan tried the windows. They were shut tight, so we went back to rummaging, hoping to come up with something useful for Mike, but we didn't find anything convenient like old bills or family records to help us. As we searched, I kept scrubbing my hand against my jeans. Every time I thought about what had happened, my insides shuddered. Why hadn't Nathan felt it? Or had he? Maybe he had but, unlike me, he'd known what to expect.

We climbed the stairs and did another sweep of the ground floor. Nathan located a set of pull-down stairs for the attic, but in contrast to the basement, the attic held nothing more than a standing mirror and a rocking chair.

We ended up in the living room where we'd started, and Nathan took the poker from the set of fireplace tools.

"One last thing to try."

I scurried back as he swung at the window. The poker bounced off. The glass didn't so much as sprout a crack. My sanity felt the impact though. A laugh—or maybe a sob—caught in my throat.

"That's it then. We were here to find Eden's Book." He set the poker back in its place and held out his hand. "Ready to go?"

"Definitely."

I tried to keep my eyes open this time, but the light was too intense. When the motion stopped, Nathan and I were back in Hassan's house sitting in the chairs around the coffee table with everyone else. As I freed my hand from Nathan's grip, I glanced at Hassan's watch. Nathan and I had spent hours searching the house, but I'd arrived at Hassan's less than ten minutes ago.

"Well?" Jackson said. "Did it work?"

"It worked," Nathan answered. "I don't know how, but Kate took both of us there."

"I didn't do anything."

Nathan ignored my protest. "She changed the maze. It was fantastic—more solid, more realistic than it's ever been before—and she found Eden's Book. We just need Mike to figure out where the house is located."

Jackson grinned. "Right on, Kate. You scored some serious points for the team. What was the maze like?"

"Like a really old, really smelly house." Complete with the creepy basement where things tried to crawl inside your skin.

Nathan leaned toward me, his eyes full of excitement. "You were able to connect to my Gift instinctively. Effortlessly. I've never seen anything like this before. Not unless the two Guardians are Blood-Bound, which clearly isn't the case."

"Blood-Bound?"

"It's not unusual for the child of a Guardian to be called, but it's rare for siblings to be called. Those siblings have a connection we call a Blood-Bond."

A horrible thought crossed my mind, and Lexi must have read it on my face because she said, "Relax. We only know of five sibling pairs in existence, and they're all twins. You're safe."

My shoulders sagged in relief. It was a stupid thing to be afraid of—because I was pretty sure you had to at least be on speaking terms with God before he called you to be a Guardian—but I couldn't imagine anything worse than being supernaturally bonded to Ty for the rest of my life. I loved my brother, but that was asking too much.

I mumbled something about getting a drink as I rose from the loveseat, but on the way to the kitchen my stomach rumbled. I detoured to the pantry, and another hunger pang hit as I reached for the granola bars. I took two before setting the box back on the shelf.

Somehow I knew Hassan stood behind me before I turned to find him in the doorway.

"What happened?" he said.

"What do you mean what happened?"

"Something upset you. Something in the maze. What did you see?"

I shrugged. "A house."

He crossed his arms and leaned against the doorframe like he had all day to wait for an answer. I considered denial but it would be pointless. Besides, maybe he could make sense of what had happened. His perspective wouldn't be polluted with fear like mine was, and he wouldn't have Nathan's bias about the maze.

"The reason I found Eden's Book is because I touched it. It felt like evil with a capital E, like there was something inside of it—some *thing* that wanted out and wanted to use me as transportation." I fought the urge to scrub my hand against my jeans. "I don't think Nathan felt anything when he picked it up. It was nothing more than a book to him."

"Did you tell him this?"

"No, I—" Hysteria rose up again. I crammed it back down, but my voice wavered from the effort. "We were in some bizarre universe where windows don't break when they're supposed to. How should I know what's normal and what's not? How would Nathan know? He's never taken anyone besides himself into the maze before. Maybe it's different for everyone who goes there."

"Perhaps. Or perhaps it has something to do with you, with your Gift. You touched the Book, did you not? And you took Nathan's hand to enter the maze. Perhaps your Gift requires touch." He pushed off from the doorframe and extended his hand in invitation.

Doubt, along with a heavy dose of fear, kept me from

reaching out. "But I was in the Range Rover the night you cloaked us, and nothing happened. You even touched my hand, remember?"

He took a step closer. "We can only try and see what happens today."

I hesitated as my brain supplied multiple disaster scenarios. But how bad could it be? It wasn't like we'd be traveling to some alternate reality. We'd still be standing here in the pantry. If it even worked.

I weighed my fear against the need for answers. Need won out, so I set aside the granola bars and reached for Hassan's hand. At first I felt nothing more than the warmth of his skin against mine. Then a hum of energy swept up my arm, a low drone that disappeared when I strained to hear it. And yet it didn't. I could hear the hum again in the background as I focused on the energy vibrating across my skin. Or was it in the air around me? I couldn't tell. Every time I thought I'd figured out where it was, it moved. It seemed familiar too. Like I'd felt it before.

I tugged my hand away, and a second later Hassan reappeared in front of me. The sensation wasn't nearly as strong now but definitely still there, and my eyes widened as realization struck.

"It's you. I can feel it—I've been feeling it—without even touching you. All this time I thought I was picking up on your mood or something, but it's you."

"What is?"

I shook my head, at a loss to explain it. "It's not a sound or a feeling, but it has both of those qualities. It's there, but at the same time it isn't."

"Did you feel this when Nathan used his Gift?"

"No, not like this."

"But you felt something?"

"It was different. Like jumping into hyperspace."

"Perhaps you're sensing our Gifts."

I could only stare at him as my mind struggled to fit the

pieces together. Was it possible? Entering the maze wasn't what I would expect Knowledge to feel like, but after hearing Nathan describe how his Gift worked, it kind of made sense. And the elusive energy coming from Hassan fit with his Gift, so maybe he was on to something. His theory had a flaw though.

"What about Eden's Book? That's not a Gift. Why would I feel that?"

"A Gift is supernatural power. The Book represents a source of supernatural power. Perhaps you were detecting the source."

I didn't fight the urge this time. I scrubbed my fingers against my jeans.

"It would be extremely useful to us if you could detect sources of supernatural power. It would be even better if you could do it without requiring touch. Come. Tell me if you can sense anything from the others."

He led me out of the pantry so I had a clear view of the seating area. I focused on Nathan first, searching for the sense of presence I picked up from Hassan but with a light speed quality to it. After a few seconds, I tried Lexi. Then Jackson.

"Nothing. Not from them."

"Perhaps you need to be closer. Or perhaps ..."

As he paused to think, Jackson got up and headed our way. I spun to face Hassan.

"Can we please not say anything about this yet?"

"You should at least tell Nathan. He needs to know about your ability."

"But he doesn't need to know right this second, does he? Just give me a little time to process everything. Please?"

"Soon," he warned, and I nodded my agreement. "Give Mike the information about the house he requires and then come downstairs ready to train. You need to be focused today."

"Okay. I will be."

"What's going on?"

I jumped at the sound of Jackson's voice. Hassan threw a hostile look at him before heading toward the stairs.

Jackson watched Hassan go, a frown clouding his expression. "What were you guys talking about?"

"He had a question about what we saw in the maze."

"He has to corner you in the pantry to ask?"

"He didn't corner me." Well, he had, but not the way Jackson thought.

"It sure looked like he did. It looked like he didn't want anyone to hear what he was saying to you."

"He wasn't yelling at me if that's what you're worried about."

I headed back into the pantry to retrieve my granola bars, and Jackson followed, making the room shrink to half its size. Something jabbed my shoulder blade as I pressed up against the shelves in an effort to put some space between us. He towered over me, clearly debating whether or not he should say what was on his mind. I didn't want to wait around for his decision, so I tried to squeeze past him, but he grabbed my arm, forcing me to stop and look up at him.

Concern filled his eyes. "I've got your back if you need me. You know that, right?"

Heart pounding, I freed my arm. "Yeah. I know."

I fled the pantry then, running from the conversation and from what I'd felt when Jackson touched me.

CHAPTER
THIRTY~FIVE

After lunch I followed Hassan downstairs to the weapons room. He took a gun case from the shelf then led me through the second doorway, deeper into the hillside. He flipped the light switch, and fluorescent bulbs flickered to life. Cement, plastic, and metal gave the room an industrial odor.

There were two stalls on the right, each with the classic body outline at the far end. A rectangular folding table and a black metal cabinet stood against the wall to the left. Directly across from the door we'd come through was another door I assumed led to a storage closet.

First Hassan had me work on standing and holding the gun correctly. Next he had me practice loading and unloading a magazine from the gun. He also demonstrated how to check whether or not the chamber held a bullet. He then handed me earplugs and a pair of safety glasses from the cabinet.

"Aim for the center of the forehead."

Nerves gnawed at my gut as I took the gun from him, and I reminded myself of what he'd told me. My aversion to the gun was part of who I was, so I tried to accept it instead of fighting it. I tried to see the target as black and white lines, not the shape of a body, and as I squeezed the trigger, I tried to think in terms of physics—velocity, momentum, friction, gravity.

He had me practice until my hands and arms ached from absorbing the recoil. After emptying the last magazine, I gladly handed the gun back to him. Holes marred the top half of the target, the majority of them piercing the target's head.

The results should have been encouraging, but I knew things would be very different when I had to face a creature that looked human. I didn't even want to contemplate what might happen if I had to face an opponent who was human.

I returned my safety glasses to the shelf and dropped my earplugs in the trashcan beside the table. While Hassan put the gun back in its case, I grabbed the broom and dustpan from the cabinet and swept up shells. They clattered against the bottom of the trashcan.

Even with my back to him I could feel the weight of Hassan's gaze on me as I set the broom and dustpan back in the cabinet.

"I think weapons practice is not what's troubling you right now. Something else is on your mind."

I stalled, closing the cabinet door with a snap of metal. I might as well tell him. Who else was I going to talk to? At least with Hassan I wouldn't have to explain the situation.

"You know how Jackson came into the kitchen this morning? I didn't get a vibe or whatever from him even though he was standing pretty close to me. But when I went to leave, he touched my arm, and I got something."

"Was it different from what you experienced with my Gift or with Nathan's?"

"Yeah. With Jackson, it's like putting your hand on the hood of a muscle car. The engine's idling and all that speed and power is waiting for someone to step on the gas."

I'd felt the same thing when he hugged me at the bowling alley. What I'd thought was me feeling awkward about a close encounter with Jackson's abs had been me sensing Jackson's Gift. Well, mostly. There had been some awkwardness involved too.

"Would you be able to tell the three of us apart based on the quality of our Gifts?"

"You mean if you blindfolded me or something? Definitely. But you're still the only one I can sense without touching."

"I may have an explanation for that. Mine is the only Gift that must interact with our surroundings."

My lips parted. "You're right." It was so obvious now that he'd said it.

"If this is true, you may be able to detect other Gifts like mine with external qualities."

"You mean Eden."

"It would be very helpful if you could alert us to her presence."

I shuffled through my memory, trying to recall if I'd experienced something that would identify her Gift. The only time I'd been close enough was the day she had me trapped, and what I remembered—

"Benny. It felt like a bunch of slimy things trying to get inside my head. It was even worse when he touched me."

Hassan nodded. "Touch is not required, but physical contact increases the strength of his Compulsion. What about Eden?"

"I don't know. Everything happened so fast. Benny tried to make me cooperate, and right after that she ..." I shook my head. "All I felt was fire."

Maybe that would be the sign she was close—when my flesh began to burn.

"You need to speak with Nathan," Hassan said. "He can find answers we won't find on our own. When we have more information, we can plan how to use your Gift to our advantage."

Planning any kind of strategy based on me or my Gift seemed like a bad idea. It was like relying on a sandcastle to hold back the tide. The sooner Hassan figured that out, the better, but it wouldn't do any good to argue with him until after I'd talked to Nathan.

Why couldn't this be one of those times Nathan Knew what was going on without me having to tell him?

I sighed in resignation. "Okay, I'll tell him. Soon."

My brother sent a text Saturday morning, wanting to do something together, and I let him know Mom and I planned to get a Christmas tree. When I suggested he could come over later and help put up the outdoor lights, he replied with a single word: LAME.

Mom and I drove to the Christmas tree farm tucked in among the wineries and soccer fields in the Sammamish River Valley. Finding a tree we liked was easy enough, but getting the tree into the house when we got home proved more difficult. The guy at the tree farm who'd tied it to the roof of the car had pulled the knots so tight neither one of us could get them loose.

"I'll go grab some scissors," I said.

"Not my fabric scissors."

I had to mute a sigh before it escaped. "I know. I have some in my desk."

While I went to excavate a pair of scissors from the paper clips and Post-it Notes in my desk drawer, Mom went to the garage in search of the tree stand.

My steps slowed as I came back outside. Jackson's Jeep was parked along the curb.

"What are you doing here?" I said as we met up beside the Honda. "Is everything okay? Did Mike find Eden?"

"No. Everything's fine. I just came over because Ty said you could use some help putting up Christmas lights."

"You've been talking to my brother?"

"Yeah, we were both playing online this morning."

Before I had a chance to share my opinion on that subject, the Corvette roared into the cul-de-sac. My stomach knotted up. "Please tell me you have your *Pur* hidden."

"Relax. I've got it covered." He nodded at the Honda. "Where do you want the tree?"

He'd asked a simple enough question, but it took me a moment to come up with an answer. My brain was too busy listing all the ways this get-together could end in disaster. "By the front door I guess."

When I offered the scissors, he shook his head. "I got it." He snapped the string loose then lifted the six-foot Noble like it weighed no more than a twig.

Ty grinned as he shut the Corvette's door. "I knew it was a good idea to invite Jackson. He can do the heavy lifting, and we won't need a ladder to hang the outdoor lights."

Irritation burned through my anxiety. "So really, you're planning to let Jackson do all the work while you take all the credit."

"Not all of it. You can do some of the work too."

I followed them to the house, my fingers clenched around the scissors. All I had to do was cut up Dad's credit card and Ty would be the one working for a change. So tempting.

Mom emerged from the garage and greeted Jackson with a frown. Fortunately Ty claimed responsibility for Jackson's presence. He only did it so he could say he'd contributed, but still. It kept her from thinking I had invited a guy—boyfriend or otherwise—to our house.

Her frown smoothed once she learned Jackson had come to help with the lights. "Oh. Well, that's very kind of you."

"No problem, Mrs. Brennan. But I'll help you set up the tree first. "

With Mom's guidance, Jackson held the tree straight while I wriggled beneath the branches to tighten the screws on the stand. As I twisted the last one into place, Ty gave his completely useless, expert opinion.

"It's crooked."

"It only looks crooked because you're lying on the couch instead of helping." I stood and brushed needles from my hands. "I'll go find the outdoor lights."

Like I'd been hoping, Jackson offered to come with me to the garage. I turned on him the instant the door to the house shut behind us. "What are you doing here?"

His forehead wrinkled. "I told you, I came to help with the

lights."

"That's not what I mean. Since when do you talk to my brother?"

"Since the night we went bowling."

"I only invited him because I panicked. I didn't really think it through. You and Ty hanging out is a bad idea. He already suspects there's more going on than us being friends. Right now he thinks it's something romantic, but if you keep spending time with him he'll get a lot closer to the truth. He won't stop until he gets answers from one of us, and I don't know about you, but I suck at lying. I'll end up saying something wrong—completely on accident."

"You don't think your brother could handle knowing about the Guardians?"

"I couldn't handle him knowing. He wouldn't believe me if I told him, not at first, and between the time I told him and the time he accepted the truth, he'd have drawn so much attention to what I'm doing that Mom will lock me in my room until I'm thirty. Possibly forty. If you care about me at all, you'll break off the bromance before it goes any farther."

"All right. If that's what you want."

The knot in my stomach loosened. "Thanks."

I started to turn back to the garage but he said, "Hang on. There's something I need to say to you first." He pushed at a crack in the cement with the toe of his Nike. "I know I've been kind of a jerk lately, and I'm sorry."

I shrugged. "You were worried about me."

"Yeah, but I didn't handle it very well."

"Maybe not, but I can't really complain about someone freaking out when I do it all the time. Don't worry about it."

"So we're good then?"

"Yeah. We're good."

We skirted Ty's longboard and the bike I hadn't touched since eighth grade before I spotted the correct plastic bin. Jackson lowered it from the rafters. I also asked him to take down the bin of Christmas ornaments next to it.

"We'll have to go back through the house," I said. "The garage door doesn't open. One of the springs is broken."

It had been broken for a couple of years now. It didn't make sense to spend money we didn't have installing a new spring when we only used the garage for storage.

Ty stirred from the couch when we came back into the house and went to help Jackson put up the lights. It probably had something to do with him not being able to hear the TV over the sound of Mom vacuuming. But since he'd actually volunteered to do something, I hated to interfere. I did my best to ignore the way my stomach tightened up again as they headed outside.

I worked on untangling a string of tree lights, and when Mom finished vacuuming, she took over so I could start on dinner. I made a huge pot of spaghetti and put brownies in the oven for dessert.

The sun had set by the time Jackson invited us to take a look. His nose and cheeks were red from the cold, and he must have bumped his head at some point because his beanie was crooked. It also had a leaf stuck to it.

I couldn't help but laugh as I reached up to tug the leaf loose. "Were you saving this for later?"

I held it up for him to see, and he snatched it back.

"It's payment for all the work I did." He gestured at the roof with his hard-earned leaf. "So what do you think? Do we pass inspection?"

Beside me, Mom actually smiled. "It looks wonderful."

I had to agree. Between the lights twinkling in the front window and the multi-colored bulbs running along the edge of the roof, the house almost looked cheerful.

We went inside to have dinner, and I was glad I'd made as much spaghetti as I had. Jackson was on his third plate before he showed any sign of slowing down. Between bites, he entertained us with stories of growing up in Texas. My favorite was the one about his Great-Granny Myrtle breaking her best wooden spoon on his backside after he and his brothers used her nylon stockings to catch frogs in the irrigation ditch.

The comments Ty added were sarcastic but still friendly and, thankfully, appropriate to the dinner table. I hadn't heard him swear even once the entire day.

I dished up brownie sundaes, and after downing his second sundae, Jackson said he had to go. Mom was in the middle of washing dishes, so I figured it would be safe to walk out with him.

"I'll be online after ten," Ty announced as he stretched out on the couch.

"Uh … not sure if I'll be online tonight."

The bite in the air as we left the house made me cringe, and I wrapped my arms around myself in an effort to preserve warmth. Jackson pulled on his beanie then stuffed his fists into his pockets.

We stopped next to the Jeep, and I stood on the curb to make up some of the difference in height.

"Sorry for freaking out earlier. It caught me by surprise." I glanced back toward the house. My biggest motivation for keeping him away from my brother was to avoid stress, which seemed like a really selfish reason. "You know, it might not be such a bad thing for you and Ty to hang out once in a while."

"Are you sure?"

"Yeah. Besides, he tends to burn through friends pretty fast. It'll be a miracle if you guys are still talking to each other by the time winter quarter starts."

Jackson grinned but his expression quickly sobered. "I'll be careful."

"I know you will." I offered him a smile. "Thanks for putting up the lights."

"Anytime. Seriously. I'll work all day if it means you fix dinner for me."

"Well, you have to come back in a couple of weeks and take them down, right?"

"Right."

We said goodbye, and I headed back inside. For once, I didn't dread walking through the front door.

CHAPTER THIRTY-SIX

There were only a few shopping days left, and I hadn't found a Christmas present for Rob yet. This was my first time buying a boyfriend gift, and I needed to get it right. Jackson and Mike had both offered ideas, but Rob wasn't into video games and I wanted to get him something more personal than software. Asking my pervert brother for suggestions wasn't an option, which left only one twenty-something guy I could go to for advice.

I dreaded asking Hassan. He'd made his opinion of my relationship crystal clear, and to make things worse, I'd given a less than stellar performance during field training this past week. But by Saturday afternoon I still hadn't come up with anything on my own. After wandering Bellevue Square for hours, I wasn't any closer to a purchase, so I found a semi-quiet corner where I could make a call. I felt both relief and nausea when he answered.

"Kate? What's wrong?"

"Nothing's wrong. I need to ask you something." I took a deep breath. I could do this. "I was kind of hoping you could help me figure out a gift for Rob. For my boyfriend. You know, maybe give me a suggestion. Something a guy his age would like."

"Yes, I'll help you. I'll tell you not to waste your money on him."

I had to grit my teeth to keep from saying the first thing that came to mind. "Look, I don't need relationship advice, okay? I just need help figuring out a gift. Can you handle that or not?"

"Fine. How much are you planning to spend?" When I told him, the silence on his end was heavy with disapproval.

"You know what? Forget I called. I'll figure it out myself."

"No. If this is what you want, then I'll help you. I'll pick you up in an hour."

"I didn't mean help me shop for it. Give me a suggestion. I'm already at Bellevue Square."

"Your boy wants things you can't afford. I know someone who will give you a good deal, but only if I'm with you."

The last thing I wanted to do was go Christmas shopping with Hassan, but I'd run out of options. "Okay. Fine."

"I'll call you when I get there. And you'll need cash. No checks or credit cards."

Cash only. Sure. That didn't sound sketchy at all.

By the time I tracked down an ATM machine and made a withdrawal, Hassan had arrived, and we met up outside Macy's. Giant snowflakes decorated the streetlights, but their holiday cheer failed to soothe traffic along Bellevue Way. Car horns accented Michael Bublé's rendition of *Blue Christmas* playing over the mall's speakers.

Based on the "cash only" policy, I figured we'd be dealing with a guy who sold stuff out of his trunk, but Hassan led me across the street and stopped outside a store with "Desert Jewel" written in gold letters on the front window.

"You brought cash?" he said.

"Yeah, but why do I have to pay with cash?"

"It's better if there's no record of you being here." He glanced inside. "Mike can take care of the video later if necessary."

My gaze followed the path his had taken and found a camera pointed at the door.

"He believes my name is Hassan Mehmet. Don't correct him if he calls me by that name, and don't give him more information than necessary. About either of us."

"I thought this guy was your friend."

"Ahmed Kalil has his uses. Friendship is not one of them."

I was about to say we should go somewhere else, but Hassan reached out, pulled the door open, and waved me forward. Precious metal and gemstones sparkled inside display cases lined with dark fabric, and a hint of ammonia glass cleaner scented the air. I found myself very glad I'd chosen to wear a sweater instead of a hoodie when I left the house this morning. I made a mental note not to drag my feet so I wouldn't draw attention to my scuffed-up Converse.

A couple had their heads bent over one of the display cases, murmuring to each other. Light reflected off the scalp of the man standing across from them, but his head seemed to be the only thing suffering from a hair shortage. He'd left the top two buttons of his dress shirt undone, and it looked like black shag carpet was trying to escape. Gold winked at me from within the depths of the shag.

He looked up as we entered, and a grin split his beard when he saw Hassan. "*Marhaba!*"

"*Marhaba bik,*" Hassan replied.

The man motioned a female employee to come take over with the couple, and then he hurried over to shake Hassan's hand. They briefly conversed in Arabic before Hassan switched back to English for me.

"This is Ahmed. He owns the shop, and he can help you get what you want."

They exchanged a few more sentences in Arabic before Ahmed ushered us over to a glass case with several watches on display. He pulled out a watch like Hassan's except without the diamond chip on its face. "Perfect, don't you think? Every young man would like to have this watch."

He handed it to me, and the metal of the wristband slid across my fingers like satin. Then I caught a glimpse of the price tag and wanted to hand it right back. "Um, yeah. It's really nice."

Hassan stood close by, and when I shot him a panicked look, he leaned forward, his voice warm against my ear. "Don't worry. Ahmed is willing to do a favor for me. He's agreed to sell the watch for the price you quoted."

"Are you sure?"

"I'm sure." He took the watch from me and handed it to Ahmed. "She'll take it."

Ahmed placed the watch in a box with a silky red lining. The box went in a bag, and I traded my cash for the bag. Hassan said goodbye for both of us, and we reentered the world I belonged to—the one where canvas was acceptable shoe material.

The crowd had multiplied during the few minutes we were in the store, and bodies clogged the sidewalk as people claimed their spots for the nightly Snowflake Lane parade. On my own, it would've taken me forever to burrow through the crowd and reach the crosswalk, but it was a short trip following in Hassan's wake. It was almost as if instinct warned people to take a step forward or shift a little to the left so he could pass.

As we waited for the crosswalk signal, my phone chimed. I read the text from my stepmom then slid the phone back into my pocket praying God would have mercy on me and I wouldn't fall apart in public. Or worse, in front of Hassan.

"What's wrong?"

"Nothing." I poked the button for the signal a few more times to make sure it got the message. "There's been a change of plans, that's all. Dad decided Mexico is the place to be for Christmas."

"So? You don't want to go?"

"I wasn't invited." The worst part was knowing it was my fault. If I hadn't tricked him into answering his phone, he wouldn't have felt the need to leave the country to get away from me.

"I'm sorry," Hassan offered.

I shrugged. "It's not that big of a deal. I mean, it's not like

I'm missing out on anything. Even when he's around, he's not really there, you know?"

The signal changed, and I held Rob's watch against the ache spreading through my chest as we stepped into the street. Hassan placed a hand on my back, creating some space between me and the press of people around us.

"Have you eaten dinner yet?" he said.

"No. But I'm not hungry."

"We'll get coffee then." He didn't wait for me to agree. He guided me south once we reached the sidewalk.

My thoughts tumbled against each other as we walked, and I searched for something—anything—to serve as a distraction. The only thing strong enough to penetrate the despair threatening to overtake me was the corner of the watch's box biting into my chest.

"Why did you take me to that store if you're so worried about someone knowing I was there?"

He inspected the faces around us before he replied. "I knew he would give you a good price, and he will think I'm indebted to him because of it. He's an arrogant man. When he believes he has the advantage, he becomes careless. It will be easier to get information out of him the next time we speak."

Tears swelled close to the surface. "So this wasn't about helping me at all. It was about helping yourself."

He took hold of my arm and pulled me to a stop. "You called and asked for my help, and now you want to complain about it? You have what you wanted. You wasted all of your money on a boy who doesn't deserve it."

"I didn't ask you to come down here."

"No. You didn't. And the next time you ask for my help, I'll know you don't really want it."

He freed my arm, as if he couldn't bear to touch me any longer, and the hum that had been dancing across my skin faded. I wanted it back. I felt numb without it.

All the fight drained out of me. "I'm sorry. I appreciate what you did. Really. I'm just feeling kind of dumped on right now, but it's not your fault. You're not the one who did it."

His scowl softened into a frown. "I never intended to use you. I believed it would benefit both of us. You get the gift you want, and I will get information I need. Ahmed has contacts both here and in Cairo. Contacts that have helped me stay alive."

"I'm sorry."

He sighed then—one of those "you're such a pain" sighs. "Are you going to stop complaining and let me buy you coffee?"

I nodded, and he took my arm again, steering me toward Starbucks.

I had to admit he had the right idea. Just the aroma of my favorite beverage lifted some of the gloom hanging over me. We got our coffee, and I followed Hassan to a table. He took the chair that put his back toward the wall. I set my bag on the table, took the chair across from him, and watched as he scanned the café between sips.

"Do you ever let your guard down?"

His gaze flickered to me before returning to the café. "No. I can't afford to."

"So that guy—Ahmed—he thinks your last name is Mehmet?"

"Yes."

"But it's not."

"No."

"Is it really Muhanad?"

Dark eyes settled on me. "Does it matter?"

"No. I guess not." But for some reason, his answer added to the ache in my chest. It kept me from asking if "Hassan" was real or if that name was another part of the illusion he lived behind.

A feminine voice called my name. When I turned, Danika squealed. She broke away from her friends to run over and give me a hug. For the first time in days, a smile made its way onto my face.

"Oh my gosh! I can't believe I ran in to you here!" she gushed. "You're always with Rob every time I see you. It feels like forever since I've actually talked to you."

"I know. It's been way too long."

She rushed back to the other two girls, grabbed their sleeves, and pulled them forward. "This is Rachel—I told you about Rachel—and this is Keegan. We have sociology together."

We said hi and then the three of them looked to the other side of the table like they were torn between pleading for an introduction and running for their lives.

"Oh. This is … Hassan. He's been helping me find a Christmas present for Rob." I gestured to the Desert Jewel bag for emphasis.

Hassan nodded a greeting, his expression neutral. Danika, on the other hand, went from surprise to rabid curiosity. The tiny bit I'd told her about Hassan hadn't exactly been complimentary. I didn't think she'd bring it up, but she had a tendency to verbalize her thoughts before filtering them, so better safe than sorry.

"Okay, well, text me or something," I said. "We need to get together before winter quarter starts."

"Yeah. Okay, I will. We definitely need to catch up." Her eyes went to Hassan again. "Definitely."

The thought of Danika wanting more information about him was enough to make my forehead start throbbing.

All three of them kept glancing back as they wandered toward the counter—the kind of thing you did when you wanted to check out a really hot guy but were afraid to get caught doing it. They were still sneaking peeks at him when they left. Maybe I should have let them hang around a little longer. Five minutes with Hassan would have killed Danika's curiosity and cured all three of them of the desire to look. Permanently.

"Are you feeling okay? You were almost nice to them."

When he paused his study of our surroundings to focus on me, I wanted to be the one who could turn invisible. It was one thing for him to know I was broken. It was another to know he was witnessing the pieces crack and fall apart.

I shifted in my seat, breaking eye contact. "Sorry." To avoid saying anything else I'd have to apologize for, I filled my mouth with coffee.

When we finished, Hassan insisted on walking me back to the car because apparently, between my helplessness and a bag with the Desert Jewel logo on it, I made a tempting target for any thieves who might be lurking in the parking garage. I wasn't worried about getting mugged, but I was glad I didn't have to wander through row after row of cars by myself.

We finally reached our destination, and Hassan opened the driver's side door for me.

"Thanks for your help with the watch. And for the coffee."

"You're welcome."

I slid into the seat and waited for him to shut the door, but he bent down until we were at eye level. For a moment the walls he kept in place were less formidable.

"When I left Cairo, I wanted to forget everything. Even myself. Muhanad is the name I chose when I came here, and it's who I am now. Do you understand?"

"Yeah. I understand." I did. I knew what it felt like to be so miserable you wanted to stop existing. To be someone else because you couldn't handle being yourself.

He closed the door but stood watch until I'd backed out of the parking space. I drove home wondering if it was possible to forget. If the pain ever stopped.

CHAPTER
THIRTY~SEVEN

Nathan Knew we wouldn't find Eden before Christmas, so he gave Jackson the green light to fly home and spend the holiday with family. Mike caught a train to Portland but took a couple of laptops with him and promised to keep searching for Eden.

When Nathan packed up his family and headed over the mountains to Spokane, I felt like throwing a party. He'd been way too enthusiastic when I called to tell him about my Gift. Somewhere in the midst of his speculation about what I could or couldn't do, I'd asked him not to say anything to the others because I wasn't ready for them to know yet. The concept of having a Gift was still settling in. I'd been so worried about not having one, and now that it was starting to emerge, I wanted to go back to being useless. I didn't feel like *me* anymore. And what if Hassan was right about why I'd been called? The bigger my responsibility, the bigger my potential for failure.

Fortunately I didn't have much time to dwell on potential failure. I helped Mom clean the house and prepare Christmas dinner. My grandparents came up from Olympia, and Ty— who'd already moved on from the girl at the bowling alley— brought his latest victim with him. Adrianna had the mental capacity of a rock, but I knew it wasn't her IQ Ty found attractive. His interest had more to do with her tattoos, which were on full display thanks to the plunging v-neck of her blouse.

Other than having to share dinner with Adrianna's

cleavage, the day went well. The only rough spot came during a TV commercial for the Fiesta Bowl. It had nothing to do with Mexico, but the word "fiesta" reminded me Christmas hadn't turned out the way it should have. Ty changed the channel, so maybe the commercial affected him the same way.

The day after Christmas, Rob came from Poulsbo for his cousin's birthday party. He could only stay one night, but I'd take whatever time with him I could get. When he came to pick me up, I grabbed my coat and slipped my phone into one pocket, his present into the other.

We only made it a couple of blocks before he pulled to the side of the road. One kiss turned into a second and a third.

"I missed you," he said. "You have no idea how much."

"I missed you too."

He reached under his seat for a package wrapped in silver paper. He handed it to me, and I peeled the paper away to reveal a black velvet box. When I opened the box, the diamond pendant inside caught light from the dashboard and sparked to life.

"I wanted you to have something beautiful."

My first diamond. How could it not be beautiful? "Thank you."

He lifted the delicate gold chain from the box and undid the clasp, and I held my hair out of the way so he could secure the necklace for me. The pendant came to rest over my heart. I wished I'd worn a black sweater instead of a silver one, so the diamond would stand out more.

Nerves fluttered through my stomach as I took Rob's present from my pocket. What if he thought it was a dumb gift? Most guys didn't wear a watch anymore. They used their phones to check the time.

"I got you something too, but I don't know if you'll like it."

"I'm sure I'll love it, whatever it is."

He smiled as he tore the paper off, but his smile faded

when he opened the box inside. His thumb brushed across the face of the watch, and I wanted to cry. He didn't like it. He was trying to figure out how to tell me without hurting my feelings. All that stress over finding the perfect gift, and I still hadn't gotten it right.

"It's okay. We can get you something else."

He lifted his gaze then, and the look in his eyes sent a completely different kind of flutter through my stomach.

"It's perfect."

He slid one hand around the back of my neck. The clasp of the gold chain caught beneath his fingers, pinching against my skin as he pressed me toward him, but his kiss turned the discomfort into a vague memory. My lips felt swollen by the time he let me catch my breath.

When he finally pulled away from the curb, I decided the watch was more than worth all the stress involved in its purchase.

Rob drove us to his cousin's house. Icicle lights lined the roof of Brandon Peterson's home, and cars lined both sides of the street in front. Cars packed the driveway too, so Rob ended up parking on the next street over, and we walked back to the party. Bass from the stereo was audible from the front walkway, and it vibrated through my chest when Rob opened the door. A feminine screech of laughter assaulted the other end of my hearing range.

Rob led me down the hallway, opened a door, and reached for the light switch. I worried about what we'd see when the lights came on because this struck me as Ty's kind of party— the kind where people took advantage of dark, empty rooms—but the light revealed nothing more than a pile of coats on the bed. Beneath the pile, the bed was neatly made and the desk beside it free of clutter or personal effects. The only thing indicating Rob used the room was the thermodynamics book on the shelf above the desk.

He hung my coat next to his in the closet then navigated the hallway again. He stopped short at the end, and his hand tightened around mine.

"I'm sorry," he said, leaning close to be heard over the noise. "I swear I didn't know she would be here."

"Who?"

"An ex-girlfriend. And it wasn't a friendly breakup." Hesitation filled his eyes. "Maybe we should go."

As much as I dreaded the thought of running into Rob's ex, I didn't want my insecurity to dictate how we spent our evening. "You came all the way back for Brandon's party, so if you want to stay, I'll be fine."

"Are you sure?"

"I'm sure."

He deliberated a moment longer. "Okay, we'll stay for a few minutes. Then we can go have some time to ourselves. I didn't really come back to see Brandon." He emphasized the last part with another squeeze to my hand.

He pulled me in the opposite direction from his ex. We wandered through the obstacle course of bodies until he found Brandon in the relative quiet of the kitchen. I expected maybe a handshake when Rob introduced me, but Brandon handed his beer bottle to the guy next to him and hugged me hard enough to expel the air from my lungs. The hug he gave Rob looked just as painful.

He delivered one last slap to Rob's shoulder before retrieving his drink. "Stalker alert, bro."

"Yeah, I know," Rob said, his face tight. "Who invited her?"

"I have no idea. I've already kicked her out twice, but she keeps coming back. She heard you'd be here tonight, and she said she wants to meet your new girlfriend. Seriously, dude. A stake in the heart. That's the only way you're gonna get rid of her."

"Thanks for the warning." He wished Brandon a happy birthday then grabbed my hand. "Let's go."

"I thought we were staying for a few minutes."

"If she wants to meet you, it's not to satisfy her curiosity.

It means she wants to tear you apart and mail you home in pieces."

We'd taken too long to make our escape though. I knew the girl who strolled into the kitchen was Rob's ex from the way his fingers crushed my hand. There was also the fact she was blonde and had a fake-n-bake tan, and her expression clearly indicated the desire to use Rob's face as a scratching post.

"Go troll somewhere else, Lacey," Brandon said. "What part of 'leave before I call the cops' don't you get?"

She ignored Brandon. I tried to keep my face neutral as she inspected me, but inside my stomach curled in on itself.

"Nice necklace. I have one just like it." Her gaze moved to Rob then. "Well, I guess I know what desperation looks like now."

"You see it every time you look in the mirror."

Brandon's comment drew a bellow of laughter from his beer-holding buddy, but Lacey replied with my brother's favorite phrase. Somehow it sounded even worse coming from a girl with eyelash extensions and French tip nails.

As Rob pulled me past her, she said, "FYI, he's using you."

Brandon yelled at her to shut up, but Lacey's words followed us. "She'll figure it out eventually, Rob."

Something clicked in the back of my mind as he dragged me down the hallway to the guestroom. Stray bits and pieces suddenly had a lot in common.

"It's true, isn't it?" I hated the way my voice trembled.

Rob hesitated in the process of lifting my coat from the hanger. "Don't listen to her. She'll say whatever it takes to get what she wants. She doesn't care who it hurts."

"Answer the question."

"The only reason she came tonight was to get back at me. I broke up with her months ago, but she won't let it go. She keeps—"

"*Answer the question.* Is it true? Was this all about the

internship?"

Free of my coat, the hanger swung back and forth like the pendulum of a clock, ticking off the seconds until it finally came to rest. When Rob turned to face me, his expression was so pained I almost felt sorry for him. Almost.

"It was at first," he admitted. "But not now."

I was such an idiot. A complete and total fool. I snatched my coat from him and rushed from the room.

He followed me down the hall. "Give me a chance to explain."

"I don't want to hear it."

I yanked the front door open, and a blast of cold air smacked me in the face. I fought to get my arms into the sleeves of my coat as I marched onto the front walkway.

Rob hurried to get in front of me and block my path. "You wanted the truth, and I'm telling you the truth. I know it was a horrible thing to do, but I swear to you, that's not how I feel now."

I jerked my arm back as he reached for me. "Get out of my way."

"You have to believe me. I wanted to come clean the very first night we went out. You were different than I thought you would be, and it changed everything. And the longer we were together, the more afraid I was of losing you. I never expected to fall in—"

"*Don't.*" Pain flared white-hot inside my chest. "Just … don't."

He swallowed the words back.

"Do you have any idea what you've done?" I said, pain shredding my voice. "My dad doesn't like to talk to me. He avoids me as much as possible. I had to borrow someone else's phone so he wouldn't know I was the one calling him. I had to trick him into talking to me so I could ask for his help—help for you—and do you know what happened after that? He decided to go to Mexico so he wouldn't have to spend Christmas with me."

"I'm sorry. I didn't ... this isn't what I wanted."

"My whole life I've listened to my dad's lies because I wanted to be close to him, but listening to your lies pushed him farther away. And saying you love me won't fix it. It's asking me to ignore what you did, to start lying to myself." I shook my head. "I can't. I can't take anymore lies."

I walked around him, edging between two cars to reach the street. The heels of my boots clattered across the asphalt as I made my escape. Pain throbbed in my chest—physical evidence of his betrayal—but underneath it was anger at myself for not seeing the truth.

At the corner, I paused long enough to figure out which way to go. The noise from Brandon's party died away as I walked north. Frost glittered along the sides of the road and on the grass beneath the streetlights, and I struggled to button my coat with fingers already clumsy from the cold. I had no gloves, no money, and no bus pass. All I had was my phone and the desire to get as far away from Rob as possible.

I hunched down in my coat, considering my options, and decided walking home was out of the question. It would take me hours. I'd probably end up with hypothermia, and there was the likelihood I'd slip at some point and break my ankle in these ridiculous, high-heeled boots. I needed a ride.

Jackson would have been my first choice, but since he was in Texas, I called Lexi. It went straight to voicemail. I tried Danika next. I sent a text asking what her plans were for the evening, but she'd committed to babysitting for the neighbors until at least eleven.

Nathan was still out of town, and I couldn't bear the thought of calling Mom and having to explain why I needed a ride. And even if my brother agreed to come get me— which he probably wouldn't—I'd have to work some kind of a deal with him first, and then I'd have to wait for him to drive over from Seattle. The other problem with calling Ty was that he could smell a party from miles away. He'd probably ditch me and go back to the party, leaving me in the same position I was in.

Relief surfaced when my phone rang, but it was Rob. I rejected his call and tried Lexi again with the same result. Voicemail.

The farther I walked, the more my nose and ears stung from the cold. My eyes stung too, but I forced the tears back. I refused to cry over him.

Rob called again, and I rejected his call again.

I reached a four-way stop, studied my choices, and followed the street to the right. When the crackle of studded tires came from the direction of the four-way stop, I hurried toward the nearest driveway and ducked behind an SUV in case it was Rob. I waited until the car had passed by and the sound of snow tires faded into the distance before resuming my trek.

My toes prickled in objection to the cold and their lack of space, and a sense of desperation set in when I got Lexi's voicemail for the third time. I'd just have to call Mom and deal with the consequences.

Or there was one other person I could try.

No way. I'd never hear the end of it.

But if Mom bailed me out she would use it against me for years to come. It came down to a choice between my sanity and my pride. With a groan, I pulled the phone from my pocket and sacrificed my pride.

Of course Hassan answered right away. "Kate?"

"Yeah. Sorry to bug you, but I, uh, kind of need a ride home."

"Where are you?"

"You know the grocery store on Rose Hill?"

"Yes. I'll be there in ten minutes."

"Okay. Thanks."

A couple of minutes later, I reached my destination. I stood inside the entrance pretending to browse the DVD rental selection while my extremities thawed. As I set down one DVD case and reached for another, I glanced out the window, and a tiny flash of light caught my eye. I stared at my reflection for a moment then removed the necklace with trembling hands. It disappeared into the depths of my coat pocket.

When the Audi turned into the parking lot, I went out to meet Hassan. There was a car coming from the other direction as he pulled up, so I waited for it to pass by, but the car didn't drive past me. It stopped, and a thread of disbelief tangled my thoughts when Rob got out of the car. As he rushed over to me, the Audi's door eased open, and Hassan rose to his feet.

"Let me drive you home," Rob said, oblivious to the danger he was in. He couldn't feel the ominous snap of energy coming from Hassan. "You don't have to talk to me if you don't want to. Just let me take you home."

"I ... already have a ride."

"Kate, please." Agony permeated his voice.

Another voice called my name. There was no agony in that voice, only the promise of agony to come. Rob looked at Hassan then back at me, and a new kind of pain filled his eyes.

A driver stuck behind the Audi honked, but one glance from Hassan ended further protest. The guy backed up and went down another aisle. When Hassan focused on Rob again, I knew I only had seconds before the situation became even more of a disaster than it already was.

"I need to go."

Power hummed in the air as I stopped in front of Hassan. He stared at Rob—no indication whatsoever he knew I was there—so I tugged on the lapel of his coat.

"Hassan?"

His gaze dropped to me. "Did he hurt you?"

"Did he ... *no*. I mean, not in a need-to-be-arrested sort of way. It's over, and ..." Warmth flooded my eyes. "You were right. I spent all my money on a boy who doesn't deserve it."

Energy buzzed across my skin as Hassan took my arm and ushered me around to the passenger door. When he walked back to the other side, he headed straight for Rob, and I stretched across the driver's seat so I could see him. I was ready to scramble out of the car, but he stopped a couple of steps away. Even though the door was open, I couldn't hear what he said, but tension lined Rob's face and he responded to Hassan with a stiff nod. Hassan got into the Audi, and I tried to ignore Rob's expression as I drove off with a guy who'd probably just threatened to turn him into an organ donor.

We traveled in silence for several blocks before I gathered the courage to speak. "I think this is the part where you tell me I should have listened to you."

"I'm not going to do that."

"It's okay. I know it's my fault."

My body jerked to the left then forward, catching against the seatbelt, as he flew into a deserted parking lot and skidded to a stop.

"This is not your fault."

The tears I'd been holding back rushed to the surface, spilling down my cheeks. "It is. I should have seen it. It was stupid to think he'd ever want me. I should have known what he really wanted."

"You offered him trust. You gave him the opportunity to prove he was worthy of your trust, but he chose not to accept it. You are not responsible for his choice." He scowled at me. "He doesn't deserve your tears either, so stop crying."

I wiped my cheeks as he turned back to the windshield. He pulled out of the parking lot heading in the direction we'd just come from.

"Where are you going?"

"To my house. I can't take you home like this."

He waved in the general direction of my face, and I didn't bother to protest because he had a point. I couldn't show up at home with raccoon eyes and a splotchy face. Not unless I wanted to explain why the evening had been such an epic failure.

Hassan's house was dark except for the exterior lights when we arrived. We entered through the garage, and he flipped on a couple of kitchen lights, leaving the rest of the ground floor in darkness. The house seemed bigger, emptier than usual, but it also had a comforting feel to it. Like we'd found a refuge from the rest of the world.

Light from the kitchen spread far enough I didn't have any trouble finding my way to the half bath off of the main room, and I cleaned up the mascara disaster as much as I could. When I came out, Hassan was brewing Arabic coffee on the stovetop. He'd made it a few times before and it was strong even for me—the kind of coffee my grandpa liked to say "put hair on your chest."

I'd been too distracted earlier to pay attention to what he had on. He was in casual mode tonight with jeans and a white, long-sleeved t-shirt that hugged his torso. He was no Jackson, but he still had plenty of muscle to admire. He was less bulky than Jackson, more fluid.

I laid my coat on the back of one of the leather chairs, slipped off my boots, and joined him in the kitchen. He lifted the pot from the stove and poured coffee into two small, handleless cups with scrolling gold design around their rims. He handed one to me.

"Thanks." I held the cup beneath my nose, letting the aroma soothe some of the ache in my heart.

He took two plates from the cupboard, set them on the counter, and opened a container with some kind of pastry inside. It looked like lemon cake topped with almonds. He cut two slices then added a fork to one of the plates and slid it over to me.

"What's this?"

"*Sfouf.*"

A smile crept across my lips. "Did you say 'sfoof?'"

"Yes, *sfouf*. Almond cake. Why?"

"Just making sure I heard you right." Still smiling, I forked a piece into my mouth. It had a little bit of a kick to it, but not the tang of lemon I'd been expecting. I took another bite. Maybe turmeric? That would explain the yellow coloring.

We took our cake and coffee to the bar, and about halfway through the slice of cake my fork paused.

"You warned me about Rob." My fork returned to its task, although slower than before. "How did you know? Did you have Mike investigate him?"

When he didn't answer, I looked up, silently pleading for the truth. I was so tired of lies.

Brown eyes studied me for a moment. "I had to make sure he didn't pose a threat to us. We can't take chances, and his timing seemed very convenient. He took interest in you soon after you became a Guardian."

There was no apology in his voice, no regret. I should have been furious with him. Even though he'd warned me on my very first day—even though I understood his reasoning—he'd violated my privacy again. I wasn't furious though. Just humiliated he'd known the whole time I was making a fool of myself.

"So you knew he was using me to get the internship."

"I suspected. After meeting him at the restaurant, I knew he wouldn't make you happy no matter what his intentions were."

"How? You didn't even talk to him."

"I grew up in a world of wealth and privilege. I recognize his kind. They're hungry for what they don't have, and getting what they want is more important than how they get it."

"But what if it only started out that way? What if he figured out there were more important things than the internship?"

"Is that what he told you?" he said, his expression hard.

I scraped at stray crumbs with my fork. "Maybe."

"His nature is to take as much as he can and hold on to as much of it as he can. He wants the internship and he wants you, but if he is forced to choose between you and what he hungers for, his hunger will come first. Always."

"People can change."

"He doesn't want to change. He wants to keep you. There's a difference. When he grows hungry for something or someone else, you're the one who will pay the price."

I didn't want to believe our entire relationship—every word, every touch—had been a lie, but what else could I think? Rob had asked me out because of the internship, and after our run-in with Lacey tonight, I had a strong suspicion he'd dumped her for me. I was a means to an end, and she'd paid the price. Getting what he wanted had been more important to him than either of us.

You'd think a lifetime of being lied to would make me better at recognizing a lie when I heard one.

"Can I ask you something?" I set my fork down and slid the cake away, drawing my coffee close instead. "Do you own stock in Pacific Bio-Tech?"

He took his time answering. He slid his plate next to mine. Sipped his coffee. "Some of my investments are in biotechnology."

I focused on the liquid in my cup hoping he hadn't noticed my lip quiver. "Have you ever …" I drew in a breath, held it for a moment, then exhaled. "Never mind. I don't want to know."

"I have never met your father," he said gently. "I have never had communication of any kind with him."

I nodded because I didn't trust myself to speak. It shouldn't matter whether or not he'd met my dad, but it did. It felt like a weight had been lifted from my chest and I could finally breathe.

We finished our coffee, and I put on my coat and shoes. After Hassan grabbed a set of keys from his desk drawer, we walked out to the garage. He shook his head when I headed for the Audi.

"Not the A5. We'll take the R8." He pointed to the silver speeding ticket on the far side of the garage.

What I had assumed was some kind of Ferrari or Lamborghini was another Audi. Its metallic paintjob and flowing lines gave it a fluid appearance, like liquid mercury on wheels. Leather embraced my body as I slid into the seat, and the engine growled to life.

We shot onto the freeway, and I felt the surge of power as he shifted into Stealth mode. The state trooper we passed was little more than a blur out my window. Hassan was totally breaking the law, but tonight I didn't care. Maybe if we flew fast enough the pain wouldn't be able to keep up.

CHAPTER
THIRTY-NINE

As soon as Jackson pulled into the courtyard Monday morning, I knew my day had been derailed. The sight of Nathan's Subaru brought me about as much pleasure as finding grounds in my coffee would. Maybe he'd come for nothing more than training, but I doubted it. I didn't think he'd found Eden either because if he had Jackson would've been inside gearing up already, not taking the time to jam a stick of gum into his mouth as he strolled toward the front door.

I straggled behind, trying to prepare myself for option number three. Nathan had come up with some answers about my Gift.

He sat at the coffee table with Lexi and Hassan in the same arrangement as the day he'd taken me into the maze. The difference was that today Nathan sagged against the back of his chair like it was the only thing keeping him upright.

The night I'd called to tell him about my Gift, Nathan had said that while only minutes passed in reality the toll on his mind and body when he entered the maze was the same as if he'd spent all those hours there. Apparently he'd been spending a lot of time in the maze.

Reluctance kept me on my feet. I stopped next to Lexi's chair, and Jackson stood beside me, working around the gum to repeat his question from the week before.

"What's up?"

Nathan looked at me when he answered, something close

to desperation in his eyes. "I can't get back to the house. I've been trying for days, but I can't do it. I know the information we need is there, and I'm hoping you can help me find it."

I hadn't counted on option number four, and it took a minute for my brain to shift gears. When it did, the prospect of going into that basement again left nothing but dread in my chest.

My gaze went to Hassan, and for once his expression was easy for me to read. He wouldn't pressure me to help, and he wouldn't let Nathan pressure me into it either. The choice was mine. Somehow that gave me enough courage to do the right thing.

"Okay. I'll help."

I wiped my hands on my jeans and sat next to Hassan. The familiar hum of his presence settled some of my anxiety as Nathan leaned forward and held his hand out.

"Picture the room we first entered. Focus on that room. The way it looked, the way it smelled—everything you remember."

I placed my hand in his, closed my eyes, and imagined the yellowed wallpaper and muted fabrics, the stale air. The pull came instantly. Light flashed, and I waited for the aftereffects to fade before opening my eyes.

We'd made it back to the house, and I could see Nathan's thoughts tripping over one another in their haste to get sorted out. The way he stared at me creeped me out because it reminded me of how Eden had looked at me. Like if he could take me apart to see how I worked, I'd already be in pieces.

"You did it."

I pulled my hand loose. "I didn't do anything."

"It has to be you. Something to do with your Gift. That's the only logical explanation." When I moved toward the windows, he said, "But we can figure it out later."

The hope entwined with his words said he'd love to talk about it right now. I let my lack of response serve as an answer.

Dust motes wandered listlessly through the gloom of an overcast day. The leaves of the cottonwood tree out front had turned gold, and the field grass had lost its vibrant color. A chill pervaded the room, keeping the air from closing in on me like it had before, but the taste of dust still clung to every breath I drew in.

"What does the change in seasons mean?"

Nathan shook his head. "I'm not sure. Sometimes when I return to a location, it's to the same conditions over and over. Sometimes they change with every visit. I've never been able to figure out what causes the difference."

Nathan turned his attention to the house. I trailed after him trying to recall how string theory explained alternate realities and thus might explain a shift in time when traveling between them.

Gray inhabited each room we searched. Dust covered the contents like a fine layer of ash. There were no footprints, no sign we had ever walked through these rooms. The tin of dried tea leaves occupied the same spot in the pantry where we'd found it before, and the mouse droppings were just as plentiful. We heard the sound of construction again and saw the same red barn in the distance.

A thought attempted to take shape as I looked through the window, but it scattered as soon as Nathan suggested we head down to the basement.

I followed Nathan down the stairs thinking *holodeck* over and over, but with each step my anxiety grew. The shadows seemed darker this time, the light failing to chase them away. I stood at the bottom of the stairs struggling to get my fear under control. The evil I'd sensed had been confined to Eden's Book, and I wasn't touching that Book again. Nathan could offer me free Starbucks for life and I still wouldn't touch it.

We explored the basement together, and as we approached the shelf with Eden's Book, I hung back, crossing my arms so my hands were safely buried in the material of my hoodie.

Nathan slid the Book from the shelf and held it for a moment. "Nothing. It doesn't feel like anything except a book."

He glanced at me, probably hoping I'd volunteer to give it another try, but that wasn't happening. I'd gotten him this far. He was on his own now.

He flipped through the pages then returned the Book to the shelf. I kept my distance, giving him plenty of room while he examined other items around the Book. Nothing new presented itself, so we moved on.

Searching the basement turned out to be a complete waste of time. I couldn't believe with so much junk sitting around we couldn't find a single clue to indicate who owned the house, what street it was on, or even which city we were in.

Nathan's frustration grew as we did another sweep of the upstairs. By the time we made it to the front room, he looked like he wanted to take the poker to the windows again, but for a different reason than our last trip.

He frowned. "What are we missing?"

Again that thought tried to take shape. "Maybe it's not the house we need to look for. Maybe it's …" I shook my head. I didn't really have any suggestions to offer.

He scanned the room for the hundredth time. "You could be right. It might explain why I couldn't get back here on my own. The answers aren't here. I thought for sure …" He exhaled a gust of air. "I guess we'll have to go back to searching the traditional way."

I was okay with that. I'd be okay with never visiting the maze again.

He held out his hand. "Ready?"

"More than ready."

When Rob and I broke up, my plans for New Year's Eve went down the toilet, and I didn't have a backup plan.

I hadn't heard from my brother since Christmas, which

meant he and Adrianna were still together. I wouldn't be able to pry him away from her tattoos unless I found an activity that was both illegal and compromised my morals in a big way.

Since I'd been scheduled to spend the evening with Rob, Danika had made plans to attend the laser light show at Seattle Center with Rachel and Keegan. After I told her about the breakup, she insisted I come with them, but by the time I went online to buy a ticket, the show was sold out. She felt bad and invited me to hang out at her house for a couple of hours in the afternoon instead. I tried not to sound too pathetic when I accepted her invitation.

Danika's family lived by Perrigo Park. The acres of natural area gave her neighborhood a rural feel. Sometimes when we had decent weather and nothing better to do, Danika and I walked her dog Izzy along the trails, but we wouldn't be walking today. Even though the sky was clear, frost still covered most of the ground, and none of us, Izzy included, liked to explore the trails when it was so cold.

On the way to Danika's house, I had to adjust the defrost every couple of minutes because the Honda's windshield couldn't make up its mind whether it wanted hot or cold air. I switched to hot again as I turned onto her street, and moisture peeled away from the glass, expanding my view of the road ahead.

The thought that had been fighting to take shape in the maze solidified. I'd seen the barn before. I'd seen it from one of the trails by Danika's house.

Fear argued it couldn't possibly be the same barn, but I wouldn't be able to think about anything else until I checked it out. I drove past Danika's house, took the next right, and stopped a quarter mile later where two horses stood in the pasture, their coats steaming in the sunlight. It wasn't a barn, at least not anymore. It had been converted to a horse stable, but the owners had painted it traditional barn red with white trim.

I followed the road a little farther then turned left, keeping track of the stable's position. When the view started to coincide with what I'd seen in the maze, I slowed down, letting the Honda crawl forward as I inspected the side of the road. It wasn't long before I spotted a driveway smothered in grass—parallel dents in the earth I would never have noticed if I hadn't been looking for them. The dents led toward a line of fir trees, and I didn't have to see past them to know what I'd find.

A ripple of fear washed over me, and I stepped on the gas. I turned down the next street, pulled over to the side of the road, and leaned my forehead against the steering wheel praying I wouldn't puke all over Mom's car. Once my stomach settled enough, I worked my phone free from my pocket and called Nathan.

"We've been looking for the wrong thing," I said. "It wasn't construction we heard in the maze. It was industrial."

"Industrial?"

"Those grating noises make a lot more sense when you know it's gravel and concrete they're moving around." I drew an unsteady breath. "I saw the barn—horse stable—we saw out the back window. Cadman and Olympian Precast are less than a mile away. I know where the house is."

"Where are you right now?"

"Down the road from the house."

"Okay, don't go any closer. If Eden's around, we don't want her to know you're there. She might take her Book and run, and we'd have to start over."

"Trust me, that's not a problem."

"I need to make some calls, but I'll get back to you soon. I hope you didn't have big plans for tonight."

"Tonight?"

"We need to move on this as soon as possible."

He asked me a couple of questions about the house's location then gave me a few instructions that barely registered through a haze of rising fear. After we hung up, I dropped the phone onto the passenger seat and fought against panic as memories of Heron Ridge breached the surface. I squeezed my eyes shut to block out the sight of bodies hitting the ground, but it didn't help. The crack of gunfire echoed in my ears, and the odor of earth filled my nostrils. Jagged pain ripped through my fingers, and the warmth of blood pooled beneath my nails. I tasted the terror in my screams.

My phone rang, making me jump. A few ragged breaths passed before I could focus on the present, on the pale winter sunlight surrounding me.

The ghost of pain brushed my fingers as I picked up my phone. "Hello?"

"Go home," Hassan demanded. "I don't want you anywhere close to Eden."

"I'm not. I mean, I'm not staying here. I was on my way to a friend's house. I was supposed to be there fifteen minutes ago." Although how I'd be calm enough to sit through a movie remained a complete mystery to me.

"Go there now and go straight home afterward. Promise me you won't go any closer to Eden."

"Hassan, it's me. Do you really think I'd get closer to Eden?"

"Promise me."

"Fine. I promise."

"Call me or send a text when you leave your friend's house."

"What? You're joking, right?"

"Why would I joke about this?"

"Because it's ridiculous. It's not like I'll get lost on my way home. And besides, you probably have Mike tracking my phone anyway, so you don't need me to let you know when I leave." I received nothing more than stubborn silence in reply and tipped my head back against the headrest with a sigh. "Fine. I'll send you a text. And that last part was a joke by the way—the part about tracking my phone."

He didn't say anything, and outrage flooded my system as

the truth hit.

"You really are tracking me, aren't you?" I clenched my jaw against a snarl. "You're unbelievable, do you know that? Un-believable. I swear, I will find a way to turn off the GPS. I'll take out the battery and—"

"I needed you to be safe."

Something in his tone cooled my anger.

"I have never done it before today, and I only asked Mike to find you because Nathan called and I wanted to be able to find you if something happened. You had to face Eden alone once before. I won't let it happen again."

"Oh." When he put it that way, it didn't sound like such a bad thing. In fact, it seemed like a really good thing. "Then I guess … thanks."

He didn't respond. I listened to the engine idle while I tried to put a name to the emotion I was feeling.

I cleared my throat. "So what's the plan?"

"Mike is gathering information about the house so I can decide the best approach. Nathan is contacting other Guardians. Perhaps we will find nothing more than Eden's Book tonight, but I don't want to take chances. We will bring every available Guardian with us."

I knew there were other Guardians out there, but they'd been more of an abstract concept up to this point. "Who else is coming?"

"The Nakamuras. Most likely the Atwoods will join us as well."

This was the first time I'd heard the Atwoods mentioned, and I hadn't met Lexi's mom and dad yet. Technically Guardians didn't retire, but they left most of the fighting to the younger generation—understandable in such a dangerous line of work. Nathan was pushing the limit with a forty-three-year-old body and non-combative Gift, and someone like Lexi's dad even more so. The Gift of Memory wouldn't help him in a physical confrontation, and the Guardians didn't want to risk losing their live database, not unless the situation required it.

"We'll contact the Guardians in Vancouver and Portland, but we can't count on their assistance, especially Vancouver. They've had their own problems to deal with lately. We may be limited to nine. If that's the case, we'll have to pray nine is enough."

"Well, if anyone can make it work with nine Guardians, it's you," I said. "Don't take this the wrong way, but you're the only one whose thinking is twisted enough to compete with Eden's. You know how to shut off emotion so you can see what has to be done, and you know how to do what it takes. You won't hesitate either. Normally I'd say that's not a good thing, but right now it's exactly what we need. If nine is all we have, then it'll be enough."

He took so long to respond I started to worry he had taken it the wrong way. When his reply came, it wasn't at all what I'd expected.

"Do you know what I thought the first time I saw you?"

He couldn't see me, but I shook my head. Partly because I didn't understand the shift in topic and partly because I was afraid to hear what he'd thought about me. If the expression on his face that day was anything to judge by, it hadn't been good.

"I couldn't understand why someone so young, so innocent would be called to do a job like this. I thought you would never truly be a Guardian, but I was wrong. I know better now. You are what a Guardian was meant to be. You're more of a Guardian than the rest of us will ever be."

I shook my head again.

"And you're right. Nine will be enough."

CHAPTER
FORTY

My mind kept wandering on the way to Danika's house, and my driving skills suffered for it. Twice the car drifted toward the center line as my thoughts drifted toward the night ahead. My verbal skills when Danika's mom answered the door weren't much better. I floundered my way through a greeting before Danika dragged me into the family room where we settled onto the faux fur beanbag chairs.

She held up two DVD cases. "Chris or Theo?"

It took me a full minute to process her question, assess the options, and formulate an answer. "Theo."

From the look of sympathy Danika sent my way as she put the DVD into the player, she attributed my lack of focus to the breakup, which was fine. It worked to my advantage. She'd been my friend long enough to know I needed a little space when I was in recovery mode. If she thought I needed space, it would keep her from asking questions about why I'd been late or why I'd been at Starbucks last week with Hassan.

She hit the pause button when my phone rang in the middle of the movie. The call was from Lexi, so I needed to answer, but with Danika in hearing range, I hesitated. But leaving to have a private conversation might draw more attention than I wanted. I decided to let Lexi do the talking and excuse myself if needed.

"Do you want to spend the night at my place?" Lexi said. "That way you won't have to worry about what time you get home."

"Yeah, that sounds good."

"I'll pick you up at six then."

"Okay. See you later."

Danika started the movie again, and I paid even less attention than before. Another benefit of spending the night at Lexi's was that I wouldn't have to worry about what condition I came home in. It wouldn't matter if my fingers were bleeding or if I was moving slowly because my flesh felt like it had been burned to a crisp.

After the movie, I said goodbye to Danika and her mom and walked out to the car pretending like I had an uneventful New Year's Eve planned. Guilt pricked at my conscience as I waited for the car to warm up. I'd told Jackson the truth. I sucked at lying. But I was getting really good at letting people assume things that weren't true. I knew keeping the Guardians a secret was the right thing to do, but it didn't always feel right. Sometimes I worried about how all the secrecy and half-truths would change me.

My phone chimed with a text message from Hassan demanding an update on my location. I sent a reply then went home to provide more half-truths.

I hadn't told mom about the breakup yet. I couldn't. Not when the pain was still so raw. I'd wait a couple of weeks and find a moment when I could say it as casually as saying I'd missed a bus—it sucked but you dealt with it and moved on.

I'd told Mom Rob would be in Poulsbo for New Year's Eve, so at least I didn't have to explain why I was cancelling a date with him to go hang out with Lexi. I packed a few essentials in my backpack along with a change of clothes, and right before Lexi came to pick me up, I unzipped my backpack to check the contents. I had a feeling I was forgetting something, but I couldn't figure out what. With a sigh, I zipped up my backpack and went to say goodbye to Mom.

In addition to the usual assortment of cars, Nathan's

Subaru and a Nissan sedan sat in the courtyard at Hassan's. I heard the murmur of Nathan's voice as Lexi and I walked in the door, and Jackson's response carried to us from the seating area.

"Too bad it's not an explosives type of situation. It would feel more like a New Year's celebration if Hassan blew something up."

At the moment, the resident explosives expert stood beside Mike's chair studying the image on a flat screen monitor. Hassan turned his head long enough to nod to us in greeting.

Lexi's parents were in the seating area, and they stood as we entered the main room. Silver wound its way through Kenji Nakamura's hair, and his face held the serenity and thoughtfulness I'd always associated with the culture of the Far East. Reiko was petite like her daughter, and when she smiled at Lexi, so much affection filled her face I felt a pang of jealousy.

At the risk of appearing anti-social, I hung back a few steps so I wouldn't have to shake hands as she introduced us. I planned to avoid touching Guardians tonight.

"Papa. *Haha*. This is Kate."

I smiled and said hi, but based on the way Nathan watched me, he noticed I didn't shake hands. Thankfully I had an excuse to leave the room, and some of my tension faded as Lexi and I headed downstairs. The tension came back as soon as we entered the locker room. I'd worn my green camo outfit during field training, and putting the black one on seemed more official. It drove home the fact that tonight was real.

I rifled through my backpack for the roll of antacids I'd brought and gobbled down two of them before grabbing my coat.

The Atwoods had arrived while we were downstairs. They stood off to the side of the chairs talking to Jackson when we returned to the main room. When I'd been on the phone with

Hassan earlier, I had assumed the Atwoods were a couple like the Nakamuras, but their chestnut-colored hair and heart-shaped faces revealed a different relationship.

"They're siblings."

"Twins," Lexi clarified. "Fraternal obviously, but still twins."

"So they have the Blood-Bond Nathan was talking about?"

She nodded. "Blayne and Aleda have a form of telepathy. They say it's impressions rather than actual words, but they know each other so well that it's pretty much the same thing."

I stopped. "They know what we're thinking?"

Lexi stopped too and turned so I could see her roll her eyes. "Don't be paranoid. The Blood-Bond is between the two of them. They only communicate with each other."

"But ... I don't get it then. Not that telepathy isn't totally amazing, but what's the point if it only works with one other person? You guys made it sound like having a Blood-Bond was better than a regular Gift."

"It's better because it's not the same thing. Telepathy is their Blood-Bond. Their Gift is Shape-Shifting."

"So they have two Gifts?"

"Pretty much. And neither of them involves reading your mind, so let's go."

Lexi reached out like she was going to grab my arm and haul me to the seating area. I hurried forward so she wouldn't touch me.

The Atwoods were somewhere in their twenties. They were the same height and had the same outdoorsy, REI type of build. Blayne had his hair pulled back and secured with an elastic band, but it was probably shoulder-length like Aleda's when he left it down. The only big difference between them other than gender was eye color. Blayne had pine green eyes. Aleda's were sky blue.

I kept my distance again as Lexi performed introductions.

"Jackson's been filling us in, so we feel like we know you already." Blayne exchanged a smile with his sister. The kind of smile that made me wonder what exactly they'd heard from Jackson.

No doubt my smile looked as uncomfortable as it felt. "That's great."

Jackson and I were going to have a discussion later—a discussion in which he repeated word-for-word what he'd told them. If he'd said anything embarrassing about me, he'd better hope his PSP was waterproof because it was going for a swim off Hassan's dock.

Hassan called my name, motioning for me to join him at the monitor, and I gladly slipped away from the group.

"Is this the house you saw?"

I studied the satellite image. "The layout looks right. The garage and the tree are where they should be."

"This is the stable you found." He tapped one edge of the screen and another image appeared. Three rectangles surrounded a building, and a thick stand of trees separated the westernmost rectangle from the field on the other side. The house sat in the center of the field.

"It fits with what we saw in the maze."

"Good. Nathan thought so as well. It means we have the correct location."

He called the others over and briefed everyone on the house. It belonged to a lady whose kids had stuck her in a nursing home a few years ago, and they were pretty much waiting for her to die so they could sell the property. It was a mystery how Eden had found the house. Mike couldn't find any connection between the family and Eden or Benny.

In addition to the aerial images of the house and surrounding area, Mike had managed to find a floor plan. Hassan asked if it corresponded with what Nathan and I had seen in the maze. Nathan confirmed it did, and I agreed.

"The Atwoods will act as our scouts," Hassan said. "If there is no sign of Eden or Benny, we will establish a perimeter around the house as a precaution before extracting the Book." His gaze focused on me. "You and Nathan are the only ones who know the exact location of the Book. Nathan will be more effective on the perimeter, so you will guide me to the Book."

It made sense. Nathan would have a better chance of stopping Eden or Benny if they showed up, and I would have a better chance of warning Hassan if they were in the house. At least in theory. But the thought of going down into that basement for real—in the dark—didn't sit well. I wasn't a fan of horror movies, but I'd seen enough to know that the dark, creepy basement with the evil object was the last place you wanted to be.

"What if she moved it somewhere else?" I asked.

"We search until we're positive it's no longer in the house."

"What if Eden and Benny are there?"

"We deal with them first."

I didn't like plan B. If we had to "deal with them first," there was a chance I'd be standing next to Hassan when he pulled the trigger.

"The house is well-hidden," he said to the group, "but this is a heavily populated area. We want to avoid drawing attention to our presence, so plan to use suppressors for your weapons."

Using the aerial images, Hassan explained where he wanted everyone to take position. He and I would go in once the others were in place. Next he gave instructions about what needed to happen if Eden and Benny were home and we had to resort to plan B. When everyone was clear on the details, we headed to the weapons room.

During field training, Hassan had insisted I wear full gear including a loaded handgun, spare mags, and even a knife. It was a good thing he had because I'd done most of my freaking out already. Having deadly weapons strapped to my body tonight didn't cause the same level of panic it would have otherwise. I still must've had the "going into shock" look though, because Jackson wandered over to ask if I was okay.

"Maybe. Probably. I know we don't want to leave Eden and Benny free to roam the streets, but I'm hoping they aren't around tonight."

"Well, if they are, the safest place for you to be is with Hassan." His gaze went to my bare head, and he frowned. "Where's your beanie?"

I sighed. "I knew I forgot something. It's at home."

He pulled his off and tugged it down over my head, sending a tickle of energy along my scalp. Warmth enveloped my head along with the smell of spearmint.

"What about you?"

"I've got a spare in the locker room." Concern swam through his eyes as he scanned my face. "Stick close to Hassan, okay?"

"I will."

We returned to the main room so Mike could get everyone set up with radios, and then we broke into two groups. Nathan, Lexi, and her parents headed for the Range Rover. Hassan assigned me to the Suburban with him, Jackson, and the Atwoods.

Hassan's latest purchase commanded the center bay of the garage and managed to look fast in spite of its size. Light played across the Suburban's black exterior and silver rims the way it would across the features of a sports car.

Jackson took out his phone and turned on the stereo. As Hassan backed out of the garage, Skillet's *Circus for a Psycho* set the mood for our New Year's celebration.

CHAPTER
FORTY-ONE

Aleda stood in the shadow of a cedar while the rest of us crouched in the ditch. What little water there was in the depression had frozen into puddles, and they crunched every time someone shifted their weight. Brittle stalks of grass poked at any body parts that got too close.

Hassan gave Aleda the go ahead, and between one heartbeat and the next, she transformed. There was a stir of air as an owl flapped its wings, and then the night fell still again. Moonlight illuminated her form as she glided toward the trees on the other side of the road. I watched her go, shaking my head at the impossibility of what I saw. I lost sight of her when she drifted into the trees.

Several minutes passed before Blayne tilted his head to the side like he was straining to make out a sound in the distance. "Clear."

Hassan nodded. "Go."

As quickly as Aleda had made her transformation, Blayne made his. A bobcat sprang out of the ditch, bounded across the road, and disappeared into the grass on the other side. Unreal. There was no other way to describe it.

Time dragged on as we waited. My legs began to burn from squatting in the ditch while my backside grew cold. What was the point of having all that insulation back there if it couldn't keep me warm? I'd decided to give my legs some relief and sacrifice my knees to the grass when Blayne's voice came over the radio.

"There's a light on in the basement, but we're not picking up anything to indicate someone's home."

"Sentries?" Hassan said.

"I made a sweep, and Aleda's made two. No sentries as far as we can tell."

"We'll continue as planned then."

He sent in Lexi and her parents first, and Jackson and Nathan followed a few minutes later. Nathan was the last to report he was in position.

Hassan rose to his feet. I set one hand on the grass to keep my balance as I stood, and I limped out of the ditch. My legs loosened up as I walked across the road to join Hassan, but when he held a black-gloved hand out to me, my muscles froze up again. I wanted to beg him not to make me go.

I reached for him not out of readiness, but out of the need for reassurance, and his hand tightened around mine as if he sensed my need. He waited until I gave him a shaky nod then we started down the driveway together. Power surged through my fingers as he cloaked us.

My tenuous grip on reality was strained even farther when we emerged from the tree line. The cottonwood tree had lost its leaves, but the shape of it was undeniably familiar.

I didn't see any of the other Guardians until we were almost to the back door. Movement on the roof caught my eye. An owl perched on the chimney, and its head swiveled in our direction, probably in response to the shift of grass Hassan couldn't completely hide. Aleda released a soft staccato call before her head turned toward the front of the house again.

We climbed the cement steps to the door, and Hassan tested the knob. Locked.

"I will need both hands," he said. "Rest your leg against mine so I can keep you hidden."

I slid my foot over until our boots touched and my calf pressed against his. He released my hand and extracted an object from the pocket of his cargo pants, and the scrape of metal announced his assault on the lock.

After returning the tools to his pocket, Hassan eased the door open. He took my hand again and pulled me aside to make room for Blayne to slip past us. A few seconds later, Aleda drifted through the doorway.

Hassan led me inside and closed the door. The house smelled as stale as it had in the maze, and once my eyes adjusted, I studied the room in disbelief. I recognized the kitchen all the way down to the cracked floor tiles and the Coldspot refrigerator. I had a feeling I'd find an ancient tea tin on the pantry shelf if I bothered to look. That feeling pointed toward the inevitable waiting for me in the basement, and my grip on Hassan's hand tightened. He must have realized I didn't plan on letting go because, as Aleda returned to the kitchen and Shifted back to human form, he dropped the cloak but didn't try to break free of my grasp.

"She's definitely been here," Aleda said. "We can smell golem, but the scent is old. Do you want us to check the basement?"

"No. I would rather have your eyes and ears on the roof."

She nodded as her brother strolled into the room.

"Where do you want me?" he asked.

"Inside," Hassan said. "Here at the door."

Once Aleda left, Blayne closed the door again. He leaned his shoulder against the doorframe as he peered through the glass.

Hassan led me toward the basement. The light escaping through the cracks around the door burned abnormally bright in the darkness.

"Anything?" he murmured.

After a peek to make sure Blayne still faced the window, I closed my eyes, searching for some hint of Eden's presence or the feel of Benny's Gift. The only thing that stood out besides the taste of dust coating my tongue was the familiar hum of Hassan's presence. That could be the reason I didn't sense anything else. I opened my eyes and reluctantly let go of his hand, waving him back a couple of steps. After a moment, I shook my head.

"I will take the precaution of hiding us." He motioned for me to stand behind him as he removed the gun from his holster. "Rest your hand on my shoulder."

Once he'd cloaked us again, he cracked the door open. A narrow beam of light escaped into the kitchen. He inspected the stairs then opened the door all the way, the hinges whining in response.

Hassan descended a couple of steps before pausing, and he dipped his head to get a better look at the basement. He took another two steps, the wood creaking beneath his boots. I wanted to ask how much of the sound he could hide but now wasn't the time.

When he reached the last step, he stopped to listen and study the room. A minute passed before he said, "I'm going to drop the cloak."

He glanced back to make sure I understood what he wanted me to do, and I gave him a nod. The thrum of power flowing through my fingers quieted. I lifted my hand from his shoulder and waited for a different kind of power to reach me. Nothing came, so I shook my head.

"Where is the Book?"

I pointed off to the right. "It should be on a bookshelf towards the far wall." But what if it wasn't? What if it was the one thing in the house that was different from what we'd seen in the maze?

"Take the lead, but go slowly. I'll provide cover." He took a drawstring bag from his coat pocket and handed it to me. "If I tell you to get the Book and run, you do it. No arguing."

My stomach cramped at the possibility of touching Eden's Book. I took the bag from him praying he'd have nothing better to do than keep my fingers Book-free.

I stuffed the bag in my pocket and stepped forward, alert for the slightest thread of energy hinting at Eden's presence.

Stale air filled my senses, and my steps lagged as memory stirred.

"What's wrong?"

"Nothing. I just …"

My eyes widened as it clicked. The old, moldy house odor was the same thing I'd smelled the day Eden and Benny ambushed me. The same thing I'd smelled when that golem tried to pull me from the car at Heron Ridge. Aleda was right. The smell was everywhere.

I turned to ask Hassan if he could smell it too, but Blayne interrupted before I had the chance.

"We have incoming. Multiple targets, moving fast."

"Take them out as quietly as you can," Hassan said. "Eden?"

"No sign of her yet."

The first tick of suppressor fire came through my earpiece. I couldn't let my fear turn this night into another Heron Ridge. Or worse.

"You need to get up there." I forced myself to hold Hassan's gaze so he would know I meant every word, even though my voice shook. "I'll get Eden's Book and run. It's the one thing I'm capable of doing tonight, so let me do it." He hesitated, so I grabbed his sleeve and pushed him toward the stairs. "I'll be fine. Go."

A look of uncertainty—so out of character for Hassan—flashed across his face before he nodded. "Hurry, Kate." Then he vanished.

I fought to keep my fear from showing while I listened for the stairs to creak beneath his weight, but I couldn't hear anything over the noise on the radio. The loss of Hassan's presence told me I was alone.

I turned to face the tangled pathway in front of me with a pounding heart. Clutter filled the room. So many shadows, so many places to hide. Aleda had said the golem smell was old, but she hadn't checked the basement.

I straightened my shoulders and forced worry aside. With

all the fighting going on upstairs, any golems would have come out of hiding by now. But that didn't mean I'd be careless. I unsnapped my holster and drew my gun. My gaze skipped back and forth, searching for movement, as I stepped forward.

As I eased between a coat rack and a stack of newspapers, a burst of static ripped through my earpiece. I flinched, almost knocking over the coat rack. After a pause to steady myself, I continued forward.

Eden's Book was exactly where I'd seen it in the maze— on a shelf with literary classics. But how would I get the Book into the bag without touching it? I didn't know if it would have the same effect on me as it had in the maze, but I didn't want to find out the hard way, and I wasn't sure if my gloves would provide enough protection.

Blayne's voice cut through the noise on the radio. "Aleda has her! North side of the house."

His announcement shot a bullet of fear straight through my heart. Eden might not be in the basement, but that could change really fast.

As Hassan barked orders, I slid my gun back in its holster and peeled off my gloves. I wadded up one of them to give me a couple inches of material I used to nudge the corner of Eden's Book. It tipped off the shelf, creating a miniature dust cloud as it landed. I laid the bag on the floor and maneuvered the Book inside the bag using my glove as insulation. I stuffed my gloves into my pocket, grabbed the bag's drawstring, and tugged it closed. A peek around the edge of the bookshelf told me I was still alone, so I hurried toward the stairs.

The whine of hinges stopped me. I waited, praying one of the Guardians had come to check on me, but then the smell reached me. Stale, rotting earth. I ducked behind a stack of boxes as the stairs creaked.

"I know you're down here, little Guardian. Kate."

How did she know?

I peered through a gap in the boxes as Eden stopped on the bottom step. She had three ragged grooves on one side of her face, like claws or fingernails had raked her skin. Blood oozed down her cheek, pooling at her jaw line before dripping onto her collar, but it couldn't compare to the wealth of blood covering her hands and the front of her coat. Guardian blood. I suppressed a tremor of fear.

"Have you embraced your calling yet? They've taught you how to kill, but have you learned to enjoy it?" Eden's gaze roamed the clutter of the basement. "That's part of being a Guardian, you know. Enjoying the kill. Guardians enjoy it as much as Fallen do. They condemn us for wanting to play God, but they're as guilty of that blasphemy as we are. They take life and justify it as God's will. They're nothing but arrogant, self-righteous murderers."

Her words stirred up doubts I'd thought safely buried. I pushed them back down, forcing myself to focus on the situation. Eden knew I was in the basement, but she didn't know where, and that could be what saved me. Through the gap in the boxes, I estimated the distance to the stairs.

She stepped down onto the floor and stretched her arms out, spreading her bloodstained fingers. "Go ahead. You can end all of this right now. You can save countless lives by taking just one."

As she paused, a thump sounded overhead.

"No?" A smile smeared Eden's lips as she dropped her arms. "So you still value life then. But how much? Do you value the lives of the other Guardians more than your own? Because you can save them. Surrender yourself to me and your friends can go free. They don't have to die tonight." Her smile faltered, and madness overtook her features. "But you do. Haddai said I can't wait any longer. You'll become too powerful."

I didn't know who Haddai was or what brand of insanity made Eden think I posed any kind of threat to her, but it didn't matter. She'd finished talking. She started in the direction of the bookshelf that no longer held her Book.

After a brief debate, I turned off my radio to eliminate the distraction in my ear. I couldn't call for help without giving myself away, and I wanted to make sure I could hear Eden if I couldn't see her.

I glanced over my shoulder, judging the distance between me and the bookshelf. It was about twenty feet behind me and without a direct line of sight. Hopefully she would stick with the easiest route to the bookshelf—the one with the coat rack I'd almost knocked over.

Through the gap between two boxes, I watched her progress. When she drew close to my hiding spot, I slowed my breathing to a trickle. The odor emanating from her helped me avoid taking too deep of a breath. She passed close enough I could see the blood under her fingernails. Even though my heart hammered inside my chest, I held still. Controlled my breathing. Just a few more steps ...

She moved past the coat rack, and I lost sight of her. I extended one foot, shifted my weight, and edged around the boxes. I wanted nothing more than to sprint for the exit, but I forced myself to move cautiously, weaving my way toward the stairs, every step burdened with the fear of discovery.

I reached a set of shelves, the last bit of cover between me and the stairs. I didn't see Eden, and I couldn't hear her either. What if she'd figured out what I was doing? What if she was waiting for me to make a run for it? I'd be exposed once I left the concealment of the shelves, but the stairs were the only way out. And the longer I waited, the smaller my chances were of getting out undetected. Or alive.

I focused on the stairs. I just had to make it to the stairs.

I bolted from behind the shelves. As I reached the stairs, a cloud of air and dust slammed into my back. I stumbled forward, landing on my hands and knees. I tightened my grip on the bag and scrambled to get on my feet, but a kick between my shoulder blades sent me back to the ground. I rolled, reaching for my gun.

"Too late for that."

Eden stomped down on my hand, and I cried out. I released the bag from my other hand and swung at her. The heel of my hand vibrated with pain as it connected with her knee. Eden snarled and dropped her other knee, along with all of her weight, onto my stomach. The impact drove the air from my lungs. I gasped, sucking in what little air I could before her hands closed around my throat and she squeezed.

I clawed at her hands but couldn't pry them loose. Tiny pinpricks of fire began to crawl from her fingers onto my throat, searing into my flesh. I twisted back and forth but couldn't throw her weight off of me. I pulled her hair, and I swung at her face and arms, landing blow after blow, but her grip tightened. My lungs began to burn as she starved me of oxygen, and I reached for her throat, digging in with my fingernails. She growled in response, and the pinpricks multiplied, spreading to my collarbone, my shoulders, my arms.

I imagined the fire slowing and stopping. Moving back toward Eden. As my vision began to fade, I gave one last push.

There was a faint snap. The fire cooled, and the pressure left my throat. For a moment, my body forgot how to breathe. It remembered with a gasp, and the gasping turned into coughing. Finally the coughing stopped, and I could focus on the world again.

Eden stood over me, her face riddled with fear. "Haddai was right."

Before I could process what she'd said, she tugged the gun from my holster, and a new kind of fire invaded my body, blossoming out from my chest. My mouth flew open to scream, but only a gurgle emerged. Eden crouched over me as I writhed on the floor trying to escape the agony. She pressed her hand against my chest, against the fire, and I choked on my protest. Blood filled my mouth.

She brushed fingers warm with blood across my cheek. "If you're still alive when Nathan gets here, give him my love."

Eden stood, and a scuff of fabric told me she'd picked up the bag containing her Book. The one thing I'd been capable of doing, and I had failed. Warmth spilled from my eyes, echoing the warmth spilling from my chest.

The stairs creaked as Eden left. My body soon gave up its writhing. I lay on the cold concrete staring at the cobweb-covered beams above me as blood soaked my coat. A voice in my head warned that closing my eyes was a bad idea, but I was too tired to listen.

As the world began to fall quiet, a tingle spread through my body, a tiny spark of energy. It grew with each passing second until it burned stronger and brighter than my mind could comprehend. It was glorious in its intensity—the entire universe in a single spark—and I had no choice but to surrender myself to its glory.

My mouth literally tasted like something had crawled in there and died. I moaned at the taste.

A whisper of sound prompted me to open my eyes. Gauzy fabric had replaced cobweb-covered beams. Two posts secured the fabric to a wrought iron headboard, and my eyes traced the fabric to an identical set of posts at the foot of the bed. Camel-colored walls contrasted with the rich brown of the comforter and the damask chair next to the bed. Light filtered through sheer curtains covering a pair of French doors, but I couldn't tell what was on the other side.

Another whisper of movement preceded Jackson's entrance into the room. His t-shirt looked like it had spent the last two weeks stuffed in the bottom of his gym bag, and his golden hair stuck out in several directions. He stopped beside the bed, close enough for me to see how bloodshot his eyes were.

"You don't look so good," I croaked.

A laugh caught in his throat. "I didn't get a whole lot of sleep last night." He smiled, but there was an edge to it. "It's good to have you back."

"Back where? Where am I?"

"Hassan's."

"Why am I at Hassan's?"

"Nathan said … well, he didn't say a whole lot. Just that you needed to sleep it off."

"How long have I been asleep?"

"Going on twelve hours now."

I started to sit up, but a twinge of pain stopped me. My hand went to my chest where I felt a thick bandage beneath my shirt. Sudden comprehension drove a scream toward my throat. I clenched my jaw, reducing it to a whimper before it escaped.

Jackson, his expression bordering on panic, pressed a hand against my shoulder to hold me down. "Don't move, okay?"

"How …?" I took a couple of shaky breaths before I felt calm enough to speak. To change the subject. "Where's my stuff? I have to go soon. My mom will be expecting me home." I had no idea how I would hide this from her. We weren't talking about torn fingernails or cracked ribs this time.

"She's not expecting you until later tonight."

"She's not?"

"No." He ran a hand through his hair, making it even more of a mess. "I kinda forged a text on your phone. She thinks you're hanging out with Lexi, so stay still, okay?"

"I can't. I need to sit up."

"I don't think that's a good idea."

"Yes, it is. It's a really good idea."

Laying down was too similar to the position I'd been in before I lost consciousness. I reached out and wiggled my fingers, drawing a frown from him.

"All right, but you have to let me do all the work."

He took my hand, slid his left arm around my shoulders, and gently levered me forward. The movement pulled at a tender spot on my back. An exit wound. My teeth clenched against another whimper.

Jackson propped a couple of pillows behind me, and Nathan and Hassan entered the room as I settled back. Like Jackson, Nathan looked like he'd been pulling all-nighters for several nights in a row. Hassan had it together as far as appearance went, but his complexion was washed out. He stationed himself against the wall, arms crossed, as Nathan sank down into the chair beside the bed.

"How are you feeling?" Nathan said.

The interest in his expression warned me it was more than a courtesy question. The wariness coming from Jackson echoed the warning. Something was off. My gaze drifted to Hassan, seeking some kind of clue, but his thoughts were hidden behind a mask of detachment.

It had something to do with me, with what had happened, and I replayed the moments before I'd blacked out. Incredible pain, fear, and grief. A trickle of energy spreading through my body, growing stronger. The glimpse of unfathomable power, and the irresistible urge to give in to it.

My hands trembled as they smoothed the comforter across my legs. "This isn't normal, is it? Healing up the way I did."

Nathan shook his head. "Guardians can heal, but not like this. I doubt any of us would survive a wound like yours, and if by some chance we did, it would take us much longer to recover. Days or weeks, not hours." His gaze was sharp despite his fatigue. "Can you tell us what happened?"

There were a thousand hairline fractures in the wall separating my sanity from what had taken place in the basement, and when that wall gave way, I'd be huddled in a ball sobbing hysterically. But they needed information, so I'd have to hope the wall could hold out for a little longer.

"I put her Book in the bag Hassan gave me. I was on my way out when I heard the door open. I hid and waited for my chance to get out, but she caught me when I ran for the stairs. We fought, she grabbed my gun, and ..."

Hassan turned his face toward the French doors. A muscle in his cheek bunched up.

"Then she left. She took her Book with her."

My answer didn't satisfy Nathan. I could see the desire lurking in his eyes, the craving to understand my Gift. He wanted to know what had made it possible for me to survive, but I wasn't ready for a full-blown discussion yet.

Thankfully he chose to pursue a different line of questioning. "Did she say anything that might help us figure out what she has planned?"

Half of what she'd said didn't make any sense, and part of it had been her messing with my head. One remark had been directed at Nathan, but I hesitated, unsure whether Eden had done it to mess with his head too or if she'd wanted to send some kind of message. Maybe it was best to let him figure it out.

"She said that if I was still alive when you got there, to give you her love."

Considering the way Nathan paled, maybe she'd meant to do both. He leaned forward and buried his face in his hands.

My gaze moved to Jackson. "I'm assuming she got away."

"Yeah, and Benny was another no-show. We're thinking that's a bad sign. She's not done with him yet, which means she's not done with us."

I smoothed the bedspread again. I hated to ask the question, but I had to know. "Eden had blood all over her jacket when she came down to the basement. Whose was it?"

Nathan lifted his head and exhaled, a sound heavy with grief. "Kenji's."

"Lexi's dad?" I looked to Jackson for confirmation and received a nod. "I thought it must have been Blayne's or Aleda's. Eden had scratches on her cheek."

"Aleda ended up with a concussion and a broken arm," Nathan said, "but Eden left her alive and went after Kenji. He must have been the one she wanted all along. Hassan thinks she orchestrated Heron Ridge to make sure we brought reinforcements the next time we faced her. So we'd bring Kenji. Now she has both his power and his Gift. With Memory, she won't have to be afraid of losing her Book anymore. She won't need it."

"It wasn't just Kenji she wanted last night."

Hassan turned his gaze from the French doors, and our eyes met. He'd been right about me, about my Gift.

"Somehow she knew I was in the basement. She offered to let everyone else go if I gave myself up. She said Haddai told her I had to die. That I'd become too powerful."

There was a moment of silence before Jackson said, "Maybe that's how she learned to take Gifts. She has insider information."

Nathan nodded, worry etched into his features.

"Who's Haddai?" I said.

"My first guess? A demon," Nathan answered. "It would explain a lot about what she's able to do. But she could be referring to another Fallen Guardian. It's impossible to know at this point."

My stomach interrupted the conversation, growling so loudly I blushed. "Sorry. It feels like I haven't eaten for at least a week."

"I'm sure your body burned up a lot of calories healing."

Jackson offered to bring food. After he left, Nathan studied Hassan for a moment then stood from the chair.

"Eat and get some rest," he told me. "We'll talk later."

Nathan followed after Jackson, and Hassan pushed off from the wall with one shoulder, heading for the door.

"Wait. Don't go."

He paused, his back to me. "You need to rest." The words were strained.

"I need you to stay." I knew I sounded totally pathetic, but I couldn't help it. I didn't want to be alone. "Just until Jackson gets back. Please?"

I thought he would refuse. He stood there for several agonizing seconds before he came back and sat in the chair. He fixed his gaze on the carpet, his thoughts tightly sealed away, but I suspected what was going on under the surface. He would take full responsibility for Kenji's death, for our failure.

"It's not your fault."

He closed his eyes as if it would shut the words out.

My eyes longed to close like his. A few short minutes of conversation had worn me out. A tingle of energy began to flow through me, pushing me to surrender consciousness, and my head slumped back against the pillows. Food would have to wait.

"I'm sorry." I fought to get the words out even as my eyelids drifted shut.

His response came slowly, his voice rough. "Why are you sorry?"

"I told you I could do it."

"Kate ..."

I rode to the graveside service with Jackson and Mike. It was the first time I'd seen either of them in a suit and tie, and I decided Jackson needed to dress up more often because *wow*. His shoulders plus a tailored jacket equaled masterpiece. Poor Mike squirmed the entire way to the cemetery, but he endured his suit without complaint. He'd even trimmed his beard for the occasion, so I could see the pink in his cheeks when I told him he looked nice.

Rain had moved through earlier, and moisture clung to the grass and the headstones in the cemetery. Beads of water wept from the edges of the green awning that sheltered Kenji Nakamura's grave.

Nathan and Hope stood beneath the awning with Lexi and her mom. Aleda, appearing fully recovered, stood by Blayne and Hassan. Hassan stared at the casket, his face void of emotion, but the heaviness I felt coming from him told me what his expression didn't.

The one person I didn't see was Lexi's boyfriend. I assumed Daniel had been called in to work again, but what horrible timing. Lexi needed him now more than ever. It made my heart ache to see her and Reiko hanging on to each other as if neither of them had the strength to do this alone, and standing before Kenji's grave made that ache sharper. Survivor's guilt was a very real thing.

After Nathan led a short service, everyone headed for the parking lot. We still had a large formal service and reception to attend.

I tugged on Jackson's sleeve as we emerged from beneath the awning. "I'm going to ride with Hassan."

He scowled in Hassan's direction. "You sure you want to do that?"

Jackson had good reason to question my plan. Hassan had been even less communicative than usual since New Year's Eve. While it might not be my best idea ever, my motivation for ignoring the "Access Prohibited" sign was sound.

"I'm sure."

"All right. I'll stick around long enough to make sure he doesn't drive off without you."

I hurried to catch up with Hassan, my flats slapping across the damp grass, and my foot slipped when I tried to stop. Hassan caught my arm to keep me vertical.

"Can I ride with you?"

Wariness crossed his features before indifference slipped back into place. "I thought you were riding with Jackson."

"I was. Now I'm riding with you."

He frowned at me for a moment then unlocked the car and opened the passenger door. His frown deepened when I shook my head.

"I'm not getting in until you stop."

"Stop what?"

"Stop beating yourself up for what happened. You did everything you could."

His eyes grew dark as all of the emotion trapped inside strained toward the surface. "It wasn't enough."

"Okay, so Eden outsmarted you. It's called losing, and it sucks, but you need to get over it already." I was rewarded with a flash of anger in his eyes. "You're still way smarter than the rest of us, and we don't have time for you to sit around questioning every single decision you made or blaming yourself for things you had no way of knowing. We need you to figure out what she's up to and how to stop her. We need you to be the Hassan who takes charge and yells at everyone, not the one who's so busy obsessing over what he missed that we lose round two before it ever starts. You need to pull it together because if you don't someone else is going to die, and then it really will be your fault."

His face flushed, in sharp contrast to the way his knuckles turned white as his grip on the car door tightened. While a part of me celebrated the success of getting through to him, the other part questioned the sanity of deliberately ticking him off.

His grip on the door loosened after a few seconds, but his jaw remained tense as he said, "You may have a point."

"You know I do."

He glared at me. "Are you finished now?"

"No. I'm not. There's something else I need to say to you, and you need to hear me say it. What happened to me wasn't your fault."

"It was my fault. I should never have left you."

"I told you to leave and—"

"It doesn't matter."

"It *does* matter because it had to be me down there. Me. That's the only way all of this makes sense. Nathan and I were the only ones who knew where to find Eden's Book. You would have left Nathan down there and not thought twice about it, but if you had, he'd be dead right now. You know that. If you hadn't gone to help the others, someone besides Kenji could have died, and if you'd stayed … if you'd stayed, it could have been you." I swallowed, struggling to steady my voice. "It had to be me down there— just me—because I'm the only one who could survive."

I stepped closer, invading his personal space out of desperation to make him hear me.

"I still don't understand why I was chosen to be a

Guardian, but the reason doesn't matter anymore because *I saved a life*. Maybe more than one. I wasn't trying to, but I did, and if that's the only reason I was called, then it's enough. Stop ruining it with all your guilt."

I watched him fight to hang on to the blame, but eventually the emotion brewing in his eyes calmed.

He gazed down at me for what felt like an eternity before he heaved a sigh. "So you've finally decided you're a Guardian. I suppose this means I will never be rid of you."

I bit my lip to keep my smile under control. "Yeah, I think you're pretty much stuck with me. But I'm not that much of pain, am I?"

"You don't want me to answer that question." He nodded toward the car. "Get in."

This time I obliged.

Not too long ago, I'd gotten into his car feeling out of place and dreading what lay ahead. Now the scents of leather and cologne were familiar and comforting. The quiet filling the interior soothed me.

Coming so close to death had given me a new appreciation of the life I'd been given, no matter how miserable it was at times. Maybe there could be more to my life than broken promises and failed relationships. Maybe I didn't have to survive it alone.

Being chosen as a Guardian had thrown me into the fire, but instead of burning me to ash, the flames had ignited something inside me. While I still carried the fear of being lost to the flames—and fear of the pain those flames would bring—there was also hope the fire would free me. That it would burn away the parts of me I wanted to lose and someday I would emerge as the girl I'd always wanted to be.

So I would stand among the flames willingly. Hoping.

CHAPTER
FORTY-THREE

Hassan dropped me off after the reception, and I'd been home for less than two minutes when Ty showed up. He yelled my name, pounding on the door hard enough to rattle the front window.

I sighed as I unlocked the door. "I'm not doing your laundry. Just FYI."

He pushed past me, telling me in explicit terms what I could do with his laundry, then glared at me like I was the one who'd said something offensive. "You know, I always thought I was the liar, not you."

"What are you talking about?"

He grabbed my wrist and turned it over to reveal my *Pur*. "This isn't a tattoo. What is it?"

"Let go." Heart pounding, I tugged free of his grasp. My elbow thumped into the door, and the momentum shoved the door closed. "If you're trying to get me in trouble, you're too late. Mom's already seen it. I told you that."

"What is it?"

"What does it look like?"

He swore at me. "Answer the question, Kate. What is it?"

My mind raced to come up with a plausible explanation. Why was he so interested in my *Pur*? Why come all the way from Seattle to ask me about it?

"It's … nothing."

"Nothing? Then how do you explain this?"

The world swayed beneath my feet as Ty displayed the red three-in-one flame on his wrist. He had a *Pur*. My brother had been called.

ACKNOWLEDGMENTS

First and foremost, I must express my heartfelt gratitude to the Author of my soul, without Whom there would be no stories to tell. The calling to be a writer is a privilege I never want to take for granted.

Many thanks to Fiction Forensics—the best critique group ever—especially Kathleen Freeman and Karen Higgins. Your tough love and thoughtful insight helped transform a good idea into a readable novel. Your friendship means more to me than you'll ever know.

Mindy Peltier, you're an amazing friend, extrovert, and idea machine. Thanks for being just as excited about my book release as I am (even though it's not a biography or a historical novel).

Thank you, Lynnette Bonner, for blazing an indie publishing trail and being willing to answer all my questions.

Nova McBee, I'm so glad our paths crossed and that you kept asking to read my story. I can't wait for the world to read yours.

Thank you, Tina McKenzie, for reading and loving *Into the Fire*. You made my heart happy. Luv ya, sista.

I'm beyond grateful for the YA awesomeness of Charity Tinnin and Jess Evander. The two of you believed in me and my book before you ever read a word. You made me believe it was possible to go the indie route and rock it like a boss. Erynn Newman, thanks for sharing your friends with me.

Barb Tennis, you did some serious hand-holding when I first ventured into the world of writing, and I can't thank you enough.

Conan Vandel, thanks for answering my gun questions (without laughing at me). I'm totally heading for your place when the zombie apocalypse starts.

Thank you, Rodger Archer, for the butt-kicking *Pur* design. I always have been and always will be in awe of your talent.

A huge thank you to my boys for putting up with a mom who's distracted most of the time and likes to read books written for teen girls.

Last but definitely not least, I need to thank my husband. (I totally scored in that department by the way. Just saying.) You never doubted I could do it, even when I did. A girl couldn't ask for a better friend or fan. I love you to infinity and beyond.

ABOUT THE AUTHOR

Kim Vandel grew up on a steady diet of Saturday morning Justice League cartoons and Sunday morning Bible stories. It was inevitable that the two would someday merge into a concept called the Guardians.

She worked in the field of environmental science before staying home to be a full-time mom and writer, and she now uses her science background to bring the speculative element of her fiction to life.

Kim lives with her family in the often gloomy Seattle suburbs, which suits her and her writing style just fine. When she's not reading or writing YA fiction (or tending to Guardian business), you can find her hanging out on social media:

Facebook: Kim Vandel Author Page
Twitter: @KimVandel
Instagram: kim_vandel
Pinterest, Tumblr, and Google+: Kim Vandel

Learn more about Kim at her website (kimvandel.com), and while you're there, subscribe to Kim's newsletter—Vandelized. It's the best way to stay up-to-date on author news and future books.

RECOMMENDED READS

If you enjoyed *Into the Fire*, you might also enjoy:

Haunted by Charity Tinnin

PUNISH THE GUILTY OR SAVE THE INNOCENT?
HE CAN'T DO BOTH.

As a liquidator, it's Noah State's job to carry out justice for the Elite—which is why they send him to Metro Area Four. There's evidence of a resistance movement and chatter about a dangerous uprising. Noah's orders? Stop it at any cost. Failure means death.

But Noah's haunted by the blood spilled in his past and certain God has condemned him for it. Shedding more isn't an option. Then he meets Maddison James, a hospital apprentice with revolutionary leanings, and glimpses a future he thought was lost. A future within reach if they can survive his brother's interference, a resistance more threatening than anyone imagined, and one unforgivable choice.

Saving Yesterday by Jess Evander

HER BLOOD HOLDS SECRETS SHE NEVER KNEW EXISTED.

Despite the fact that she acts as a parent to her alcoholic father, Gabby Creed feels pretty normal. But her life is turned upside-down on her seventeenth birthday when a bracelet appears on her wrist and sucks her back through time.

Turns out she's not even a little bit normal. She's a Shifter—a protector of humans and of history itself. And she's not alone. The other Shifters believe Gabby is special, even more special than the mysterious Michael Pace. Oh, and the Shades—seriously creepy creatures who feed off of human despair—are determined to capture her.

It's all a lot to absorb. So Gabby's grateful to have Michael as her Trainer—or she would be if she could get her rebellious heart under control. Then again, if the rumors about her blood are true, saving yesterday will be the least of her worries.

COMING IN 2016

UNDER FIRE BOOK TWO

AMONG THE FLAMES